The Glass Room

The Glass Room

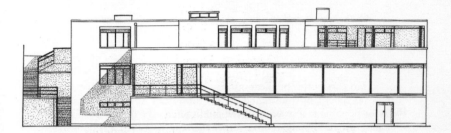

SIMON MAWER

Little, Brown

LITTLE, BROWN

First published in Great Britain in 2009 by Little, Brown
Reprinted 2009 (three times)

Copyright © Simon Mawer 2009

The moral right of the author has been asserted.

A CIP catalogue record for this book
is available from the British Library.

Typeset in Sabon by M Rules
Printed and bound in Great Britain by
Clays Ltd, St Ives plc

Papers used by Little, Brown are natural, renewable and
recyclable products sourced from well-managed forests and certified in
accordance with the rules of the Forest Stewardship Council.

Mixed Sources
Product group from well-managed
forests and other controlled sources
www.fsc.org Cert no. SGS-COC-004081
© 1996 Forest Stewardship Council
FSC

Little, Brown
An imprint of
Little, Brown Book Group
100 Victoria Embankment
London EC4Y 0DY

An Hachette UK Company
www.hachette.co.uk

www.littlebrown.co.uk

Note on Pronunciation

Most of the Czech letters are pronounced more or less as in English. A major exception is the letter c, which is pronounced 'ts'. Thus *inovace*, innovation, is pronounced 'innovatsuh' and *turecká*, Turkish, as in Turkish coffee, is 'turetskah'. Ch is always the 'ch' in the Scottish 'loch'. J is pronounced as the 'y' in 'yes', so *pokoj* is 'pokoy'.

Vowels are lengthened by the diacritical mark ´, a dash above. Thus Landaucrová is 'Landauero-vah', not 'Landauerover'. *Paní*, Mrs, is 'panee'.

The *háček* or 'hook' diacritical mark ˇ peppers the language, modifying a number of vowels and consonants. *Háček* itself contains its own example – it is pronounced 'hah-chek'. Thus *č* is sounded as 'ch' in 'church'. With a *háček*, ě becomes 'ye' (thus *děvka*, whore, is 'd'yev-ka'); ž becomes 'zh', the sound of the 's' in 'pleasure' (thus *Žid*, Jew, is 'Zhid'); and š becomes 'sh', so the Špilas fortress is 'Sh-pilas'. The consonant that gives the most trouble to English speakers is ř. This is the 'rzh' sound in the name of the composer Dvořák, pronounced 'D'vorzh-ahk'. Finally, I have used Město for the name of the city in the book; this is simply the Czech word for town or city, and is pronounced 'Mnyesto', the 'm' and 'n' sounds being elided together.

Author's Note

Although *The Glass Room* is a work of fiction, the house and its setting are not fictional. I have disguised both with name changes, but that will not fool anyone who knows the building on which the Landauer House is modelled or the city that hides behind the name Město. However, penetrating those thin disguises will not lead to any further revelations: Liesel, Viktor, Hana and all the rest are creatures of my own imagination and their story has no basis in fact. A few non-fictional characters do make brief appearances. One such is the talented composer Vítězslava Kaprálová, whose tragically short life seems emblematic of the brilliant but doomed First Republic of Czechoslovakia. I urge the reader to find out more about her, and her country.

Acknowledgements

Iva Hrazdílková gave advice on the Czech used in the novel, as did Jochen Katzer with the German. Their help is very much appreciated. Any language errors that have slipped through the process are, of course, my own.

Besides her assistance with the Czech language, Iva's quick-witted and perceptive advice on many aspects of Czech culture and history – particularly that of her native city – has been unstinting and invaluable. I am greatly indebted to her for all the help she has given.

To Matthew and Julia

Return

Oh yes, we're here.

She knew, even after all these years. Something about the slope of the road, the way the trajectory of the car began to curve upwards, a perception of shape and motion that, despite being unused for thirty years, was still engraved on her mind, to be reawakened by the subtle coincidence of movement and inclination.

'We're here,' she said out loud. She grabbed her daughter's hand and squeezed. Their escort in the back of the car shifted on the shiny plastic seat, perhaps in relief at the prospect of imminent escape. She could smell him. Damp cloth (it was raining) and cheap aftershave and old sweat.

The car – a Tatra, she had been told – drew in to the kerb and stopped. Someone opened the door. She could hear that, and sense the change in the air. Faint flecks of water on the wind and someone opening an umbrella – like the sail of a boat snapping open in the breeze. She recalled Viktor on the Zürichsee, the little dinghy pitching out into the waves, black trees rising from the blacker water beyond their fragile craft. 'Like riding a bike,' he had cried, bringing the dinghy up into the wind, deliberately letting the little craft heel over. 'You get the sense of balance.'

'It's not a bit like riding a bike,' she had replied, feeling sick.

Viktor should be here. Physically here, she meant, for in some way he was here, of course. His taste, his vision enshrined. She slid across the seat towards the blur of light that was the open door of the car. A hand gripped her arm and helped her out onto the pavement. There was a brush of rain across her face and the rattle of drops on the umbrella above her head. She straightened

1

up, feeling the light around her, feeling the space, feeling the low mass of the house just there across the forecourt. Viktor should be here. But Ottilie was, coming to her left side.

'It's all right, darling. I'll manage on my own.'

A strange hand grasped her elbow and she shook it off. 'Do you think I don't know my own house?' She spoke sharply, and immediately regretted the comment for its brusqueness and its pure factual inaccuracy. It wasn't her house, not any longer, not in any legal terms, whatever Martin might say. Stolen, with all the solemnity of legal procedures, at least twice and by two different authorities. But it *was* her house in other, less clearly defined terms. Hers and Viktor's. The vision. And it still bore their name, didn't it? Any amount of juridical theft had not managed to expunge that: *Das Landauer Haus*. The Landauer House. *Vila Landauer*. Say it how you will. And Rainer's too, of course.

Tapping with her cane she walked forward across the space, across the forecourt, while footsteps fell in beside her and tactfully kept pace, like mourners at a funeral walking along with the brave widow. 'The paving is the same,' she said.

'Remarkable how it has survived.'

The answering voice was that of the man from the city architect's office. 'But it is a work of art,' he added, as though works of art of necessity survive, whereas in fact they often don't. A fire here, some damp infiltrating a wall there, the random falling of a bomb, pure neglect. 'See the manner in which von Abt framed the view of the castle,' he said, and then fell silent, embarrassed by his lack of tact.

'I remember exactly,' she reassured him. And it was true, she could recall exactly how it was: the space between the main house and the servants' apartment, Laník's apartment, framing the hill on the far side of the city. 'The future frames the past,' Rainer had said. She could see it in the only eye she possessed now, her mind's eye, so much a cliché but so vividly a fact, all of it projected within the intricate jelly of her brain to give her an image that was almost as real as seeing: the wooded hill – the Špilas fortress – and the cathedral with its hunched shoulders and its black spires exactly, Rainer said, like hypodermic needles.

She walked on. The bulk of the house cut out the light around her as she came nearer. There was a freestanding pillar at that point, supporting the overhanging roof. She remembered the children swinging on it, and Liba calling them to stop. She reached out with her cane and touched the pillar just to make sure, just to locate herself in the open sweep of the forecourt, just to delight in the small intake of breath from the man at her right elbow that told her how amazed he was at the way she could orientate herself. But of course she could. She knew this place like . . . like the inside of her own mind. She knew exactly how to walk around the curve of glassed wall and discover, tucked behind it, the front door.

'A photograph,' a voice called. The small procession halted. There was a shuffling and manoeuvring around her, contact with heavy, male figures. 'Ottilie, where are you?'

'I'm here, Maminko.'

'Smile, please,' said the voice and there came an instant of bright light, as though lightning had flashed briefly behind the even milk of an enveloping cloud. Then the group broke apart and hands guided her back towards the house while someone opened the front door, and invited her forward – 'This way, this way' – into the soft, familiar silence of the entrance hall. A quiet blanket of fog all around her, the opalescent light that was all she would ever see now, that had become her own universal vision. 'The light,' Rainer had said when showing her the milk-white glass panes, 'the soft light of detachment and reason. The future. Pure sensation.' Touching her.

She was aware of others – shapes, presences – crowding in behind her. The door closed. Home. She was home. Thirty years. A generation. She knew the walls around her, the rosewood panels facing her, to her left the stairs turning down into the living room. Sounds, the mere whisper of hearing, gave her the dimensions of the space. She put out her left hand and found the balustrade that guarded the stairwell. People were talking – the architect fellow extolling and exclaiming – but she declined to listen. Unaided she made her way to the top of the stairs and walked down carefully, knowing the moves but having to lift them out of memory, like someone being able to play the piano without looking at the keyboard, recalling a tune that she had last played many years ago. Twelve steps to the curve, and then round and down nine more and the space opened out around her, visible even in the blankness. The lower level of the house. The Glass Space, *der Glasraum*.

'Ah.' A faint sigh, organic, almost sexual, came from somewhere deep within her. She could feel the volume as though it had physical substance, as though her face were immersed in it. Space made manifest. She could feel the light from the expanse of plate glass that made up the south wall, smell the Macassar wood, sense the people standing there between the glass and the onyx wall, between the plain white ceiling and the ivory white floor, people she knew and people she didn't know. The children of course, running across the carpets towards her, Viktor looking up from the chair where he sat reading the newspaper, her brother there, although he had never known the place, her friends, her parents, all of them there.

'Are you feeling all right, Frau Landauer?'

'Quite all right, thank you. Just the . . .' she cast around for the right word '. . . pictures.'

'Pictures, Frau Landauer?' There were no pictures. Never had been, not in this room. She knew that.

'In my mind.'

'Of course, of course. There must be many.'

Many. For example, when it was dark and Viktor left the curtains open so that the windows became mirrors casting the whole room in duplicate, the chairs, the table, the onyx wall, reflected out there in the night. And his mirrored image walking back and forth, back and forth, suspended over the lawn that had itself become ghostly and insubstantial in the reflection. Refraction of the daytime become reflection of the night. That was how Rainer himself put it. He had even used the English words, for the euphony. Euphony was a quality he loved: *der Wohlklang*.

Snow. Why did she think of snow? That peculiar bath of light, the sky's light reflected upwards from the blanched lawn to light the ceiling as brightly as the clouded sun lit the floor. Light become substance, soft, transparent milk. Birds picking hopefully at the ice, and Viktor pressing the button to lower the windows, like fading memories, down into the basement.

'We'll freeze!'

'Don't be silly.'

The slow slide of the pane downwards as though to remove the

4

barrier that exists between reality and fiction, the fabricated world of the living room and the hard fact of snow and vegetation. There is a pause during which the two airs stand fragile and separate, the warmth within shivering like a jelly against the wall of cold outside. And then this temporary equilibrium collapses so that winter with a cold sigh intrudes, and, presumably, their carefully constructed, carefully warmed interior air is dispersed into the outside world.

Someone was coming towards her. She could sense the form as much as see it, perceive the nucleus of shadow against the light. She knew. What was it? A sense of motion, that particular movement, the sway of her hips as she walked? Perhaps even the perception of her scent. Or the sound of her breathing. Somehow, she knew. She said the name before anyone spoke, said it as a statement more than a question:

'Hana.'

'Liesi! God, you recognised me. How the hell did you do that?'

'You don't forget things,' she said. 'You store them up.' She felt arms around her, a smooth cheek against hers. Tears? Perhaps there were tears.

1

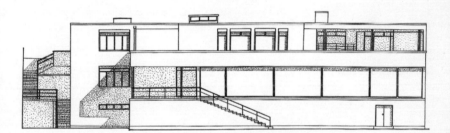

Honeymoon

They left the city immediately after the wedding and drove to Vienna, to the Sacher Hotel, where the manager met them on the steps. Minions scurried round to the back of their car for suitcases. There was much bowing and scraping, much bestowing of compliments. They were *gnädiger Herr, gnädige Frau*, and were to make themselves completely at home. It was the first time that Liesel had heard herself addressed like that, *gnädige Frau Landauer*, tied for life in one way or another to this man at her side, who seemed, for that moment when he was acknowledging the welcome, no longer her beloved Viktor but a stranger, someone she had encountered only a short while before and now saw as calm and detached and somehow admirable. This was how he would be at the factory, she guessed; how he would be with the workers' delegations, with the foremen and the managers. A kind of detached graciousness, as though dealing with a tiresome but respected relative.

The suite they were shown to was elaborate and ornate, the walls silk and the plaster mouldings gilt, the sort of thing Viktor loathed. 'It is exactly the kind of nonsense that we need to throw off, all this romanticism, all this . . . this *clinging to the past*. This is everything our new house will not be!'

Liesel laughed at him. When he got onto the subject of the new house he spoke with exclamation marks – that was how she put it to herself. She could picture them punctuating the air, small pulses of energy. Often talked about, this new house did not yet have shape or form. It merely existed as an abstract, written with capitals and punctuated by exclamation marks: The New House!

9

Liesel's parents had given them a plot of land on which to build, and that was to be Wenzel's wedding present to his daughter and son-in-law: a house of their own. 'Something good and solid,' the old man had said, while his future son-in-law had smiled. '*Good*, yes, but *solid*? No! We don't want a house that looks like a fortress, all turrets and towers and Gothic windows, nor one that looks like a church. Good God, we're living in the twentieth century, not the fourteenth. The world is moving on.'

And once the porters and the maid had left them alone in their suite in the Sacher Hotel the world certainly did move on, for Viktor went up to Liesel and carefully removed her spectacles, and then the silk jacket she was wearing, and then the dress she had on under that. Removal of her spectacles had rendered the world around her a mellow haze of colour, as though she had been plunged into a foggy day. 'What are you doing, Viktor?' she asked, rather nervously. Standing there in her underwear, in the fog, she felt defenceless.

'My darling Eliška, what do you think I am doing?' Viktor replied.

So it was that, rather to her surprise – she had expected to wait until evening – they made love for the first time at four o'clock in the afternoon, on a heavy Biedermeier bed, with the light flooding in through the tall windows and their clothes strewn on the carpet. The experience was curiously dispiriting but it was, she supposed, rather a modern thing to do.

The plan was to spend two days in Vienna, before setting off south. They were to motor through Austria to northern Italy. Alone. Viktor had resisted all pleas that they take a driver, or send a maid or a valet ahead on the train. What happens if you have a breakdown? people had asked. Which only brought laughter. 'We will be driving a Landauer, won't we? Don't they have the greatest reliability of all the cars of Europe? Isn't that the boast on all our advertisements? And' – the final blow this – 'don't *I* make them?'

So they drove alone, in a Landauer 80 cabriolet, the very latest in the range of cars produced by Landauerovy Závody (formerly Landauer Autofabrik), a touring convertible that advertised itself as the Mount of Princes despite the fact that princes and Kaisers had been cast aside with the ending of the Great War. The car was painted cream and powered by a V8 engine that delivered, as Viktor was proud of explaining, the power of eighty horses. They drove through Carinthia and crossed the mountains into Italy near Villach, where he had been stationed during the war. There was much waiting around at the customs house while Viktor argued over whether he should pay an import duty on the car, and much frustration when he had to change to the left-hand side of the road to proceed. And then they were out of the Teutonic world and into the Latin, and the sun was brighter and the breeze softer and there was a quality to the light that Liesel had never seen before – as though it was denser than the same thing north of the Alps. '"*Kennst du das Land wo die Zitronen blühn?*"' Viktor quoted. Do you know the land where the lemon trees bloom? And Liesel continued the poem, and then they completed it together so that they laughed delightedly at their unity of mind and body.

The only small blight on their happiness during this journey was a self-imposed one: after Udine they made a short detour to the war cemetery on the Tagliamento river, and after searching among the graves found a cement tablet with Benno's name on it. His body was not there of course, but muddled up with his comrades in the ossuary nearby. Thinking of her own happiness, a happiness that Benno had not lived to witness, Liesel wept. Viktor, who by one of those coincidences of fate had been the last person from home to see her brother alive, put his arm round her shoulder and hugged her to him. 'He is surely with you in spirit,' he said, which she knew to be a great concession to sentiment on his part, for he believed in nothing like the spirit and certainly not the continuation of the spirit after death. Then he kissed her on the cheek and told her she was the most wonderful woman in the world and she laughed and said, no she wasn't. But still the thought pleased her that he might at least consider that possibility, and by the time they had climbed back into the car and driven on, happiness and light-heartedness had been restored.

In Venice they stayed at the Royal Danieli. For three days they were on their own – visiting churches and palaces, exploring the *calle* and the canals, with Viktor snapping pictures of Liesel with his sleek new Leica – but on the third evening they were invited by

11

an acquaintance of Viktor to a party in an ancient palazzo on the Canal Grande. Beneath faded frescoes by pupils of Tiepolo, ancient Venetian nobility mixed uneasily with young men and women of sleek and dangerous good looks. One of these creatures trapped Liesel in a window seat and, in English as broken as her own, extolled the virtues of Fascism and the merits of modernity. 'One day all this will be swept away.' He sounded like a parody of what Viktor said when he was in one of his political moods. Sweep everything away! Out with the old, in with the new! But Liesel realised with some amazement that this Italian was referring to the whole city, and more than the city: the whole country in fact, this treasure house of art and history. Anything that wasn't a product of the twentieth century, in fact.

'That's absurd.'

He shrugged, as though her opinion meant nothing. 'For example, the Grand Canal drained and turned into a motor road. That is the future.'

'Then the future is peopled with barbarians.'

'Are you suggesting that I am a barbarian, *signora*?'

'I'm suggesting that you sound very like one.'

It was then that someone interrupted them, a voice speaking English with a German accent, but speaking it far better than either she or the Italian. 'Is this person filling your head with nonsense about how wonderful Il Duce is, and how the forces of modernity are being unleashed by Italian Fascism?'

She looked round. He was smoking, holding two glasses of champagne in one hand and his cigarette in the other. He seemed older than the Italian, as old as Viktor maybe, with the look of a boxer in the early part of his career, before he has begun to suffer much damage – a bluntness to his nose, a heaviness to his brow. Putting his cigarette between his lips he held out one of the glasses towards Liesel. 'Have a sip of French tradition. Even the Fascists will not be able to improve on it.'

There was a swift juggling of champagne flutes. Curiously the Italian was no longer there. The newcomer raised Liesel's hand to within a few millimetres of his lips. 'My name is Rainer, I'm afraid. Someone has to be . . .'

'Someone has to be? You mean, someone in your family? It is another tradition?'

The man made a disparaging face. His hair was parted in the middle and rather long; as though, despite the well-cut suit, he wished to convey a certain bohemian look. 'It was a joke. American style.'

'But you are not American.'

'I practise at their humour. One day that is all there will be to laugh at.' He sipped and looked at Liesel thoughtfully. He was shorter than her by two or three inches and his eyes had an unashamed frankness about them. He examined her quite openly: her mouth (red, quaintly curved, she knew), her bosom (rather flat, she feared), her hands (rather long and strong for a woman). Had he been standing a few paces back she imagined he would have examined the line of her hips (broad) and her ankles (she was proud of her ankles). Perhaps he had already done all this before his approach. Somehow – why should she be concerned? – she wished that she was not wearing her spectacles. 'And whose company do I have the pleasure of keeping?' he asked.

'Liesel Landauer's.'

Eyebrows rose. 'Landauer? You are Jewish then?'

'Not exactly.'

'Apostate?'

'My husband's family—'

He drew on his cigarette and blew a thin stream of smoke towards the painted ceiling. 'Ah, I see. You are *Frau* Landauer and you have trapped a Hebrew into renouncing his religion for love's sake.'

She wasn't sure if she quite liked this conversation, the word Hebrew pronounced with just a hint of contempt. 'My husband's family are Jewish, but they are not observant.'

'And the beautiful Frau Liesel Landauer and her fortunate husband are from . . . ?'

'We are Czechish. These are our' – she hesitated, the English word escaping her – 'our *Flitterwochen*?'

'Honeymoon, they say. Czechish? You are not *that* Landauer, are you? Motor cars?'

'Well, yes—'

The man's face lit up. There was something comic about his expression, a sudden childish delight painted over mock seriousness.

'I used to *own* a Landauer. A Model 50 – what they called the Torpedo. Unfortunately I aimed it at a bus and sank it.'

She laughed. 'The bus or the Torpedo?'

'Both, actually.' He raised his glass. 'To all Landauers, and those who ride them.' They drank, although Liesel wasn't quite sure about the toast. Landauer cars or Landauer people? And was there something vaguely suggestive about the word 'ride' which surely meant riding a horse as well as a vehicle? Shouldn't it be ride *in* them? But her English (they were still speaking English) was not good enough to be certain, and thankfully, just when she felt a warmth in her face and the insidious discomfort of perspiration beneath her arms, Viktor appeared beside her and the conversation slipped into German. There were formal introductions, a sharp shaking of hands, a bowing, and the faintest clicking of the stranger's heels. 'Herr Landauer,' he said, smiling in that knowing way he had, 'may I congratulate you on your wonderful motor cars? And your wonderful wife.'

It might have come to nothing, a mere curiosity, a passing acquaintance, like drivers of Landauer cars who meet on the open road and acknowledge each other's passing presence with a comradely wave. But they agreed to meet again. Rainer von Abt had something to show them. He smiled mysteriously when they asked, but declined to explain. 'A special treat for the two honeymooners.' He would meet them at the landing stage outside their hotel at nine o'clock the next morning.

The next day was one of beaten silver, like the plate you could buy in the shops near the Rialto bridge – the shimmering silver of the water turning this way and that to catch the light and fracture it in a thousand different directions. Above that the sleek zinc of a high layer of cloud and between the two, like a layer of decorative enamel, the buildings of the city – pink and gold and ochre and orange. At the appointed time von Abt arrived in the stern of a water taxi. He was dressed in white – white flannels, white linen jacket – and looked as though he might be headed for a tennis game. '*Buon giorno!*' he exclaimed. He handed Liesel and Viktor down into the boat while giving commands to the pilot in what seemed to be expert Italian. The engine bubbled and spluttered and edged the boat – all gleaming wood and brass – out into the stream. '*Avanti*!' their host cried, and they turned and headed out into the basin of St Mark's, the narrow hull sliding past mooring posts and rocking gondolas and evading the stuttering *vaporetti* like a sheep dog running past cows. There was a sensation of floating in light, of being gently buoyed up by the breeze and the luminescence of the water. Liesel felt the wind of their motion flatten her dress against her.

'No wonder the great colourists came from here,' von Abt observed, noticing her expression of delight. 'Imagine spending your whole life bathed in light like this. If you were bathed in ultra-violet all that time, you'd come out black like a nigger. Here you come out white and pure, with colour in your heart.'

Viktor put his arm around her waist, as though defending her against such poetic thoughts. 'Where are we going, von Abt?' he called above the engine noise.

'My secret! But like all secrets in Venice, it cannot be kept for long.'

The boat headed along the great curve of the Riva degli Schiavoni, away from the pink confection of the Doge's Palace and towards the red-brick buildings of the Arsenale. It slowed and finally moored at a public garden beside the mouth of a small canal. Von Abt climbed ashore and led the way into the gardens as though there was no time to be lost, while Viktor and Liesel strolled after him, holding hands and laughing at the absurd adventure and at the urgent enthusiasm of this strange man with the boxer's face and the poet's vision of the city. 'A homosexual,' Viktor whispered in her ear.

She was outraged by the idea. 'Surely not!'

'You can tell. At least *I* can tell.'

'Tell what?' asked von Abt over his shoulder.

Viktor grinned at Liesel. 'That you are a poet.'

'Ah!' The man raised an imperious finger. 'A poet, yes; but not a poet of words. I am a poet of *form*.'

'A dancer then?'

'No.'

'A sculptor?'

'A poet of space and structure. That is what I wish to show you.'

Their footsteps crunched over gravel. There were buildings

among the trees, a strange mixture of styles, not at all ornate and ancient like the rest of the city, but newly built pavilions that might have housed cafés or restaurants, perhaps an orangery or greenhouse. In the furthest corner of the garden was a ponderous neo-classical building. Von Abt strode up the steps and led them into the echoing hallway. There were groups of people walking round and talking in hushed voices as though they were in church. Footsteps clipped beneath the high vault. There were framed designs mounted on display boards, and glass-topped tables with models made of balsa wood and celluloid. People peered and pointed, shifting their viewpoints like billiard players preparing a shot.

'Why are you being so mysterious, Herr von Abt?' Liesel asked.

'You must call me Rainer, for I am certainly not going to call you Frau Landauer. And I am not mysterious. I am showing you everything I do, in the pure and unremitting light of day.' He had stopped before one of the displays. The label was in Italian and English: *Progetto per una Padiglione Austriaca; Project for an Austrian Pavilion, Rainer von Abt, 1929.* 'There!' he said. '*Ecco! Voilà! Siehe da!*'

Viktor made a small noise – 'Ah!' – just as though something had bitten him. 'So!' he exclaimed, crouching down to bring his eyes level with the model. He was looking across a green baize lawn, past miniature trees carved from cork, towards a low-lying box with transparent celluloid sides. There were small chairs inside the box, like the furniture made for dollshouses, and narrow pillars of chrome wire and a reflecting pool made out of the kind of mirror that a woman – that Liesel herself – carries in her handbag. The colours of the model were those that von Abt had extolled in their voyage down from Saint Mark's: ethereal white, glaucous pearl, glistening chrome.

Viktor straightened up with an expansive smile. 'You are an architect!'

'I repeat,' replied Rainer von Abt, 'I am a poet of space and form. Of light' – it seemed to be no difficulty at all to drag another quality into his aesthetic – 'of *light* and space and form. Architects are people who build walls and floors and roofs. I capture and enclose the space within.'

*

16

For lunch – 'You must be our guest,' Viktor insisted – they found a restaurant that boasted a courtyard where they could eat beneath the luminous leaves of a vine. They ordered *moleche*, soft-shelled crabs, and a white wine called Soave. They toasted each other, glasses clinking together across the table and catching the sunlight. They talked, of art and architecture, of painting and sculpture, of the nonsense of the Dadaists and the absurd found objects of Duchamp, of Cubism and Fauvism and a group of little-known Dutch artists whom von Abt admired. 'De Stijl, they call themselves. Do you know them? Van Doesburg, Mondrian? Purity of line, focus on shape and proportion.' The honeymooners did not know this latest group. They knew the word clearly enough – *de stijl*, the style – but the idea of a group of stylish, modern Dutchmen almost seemed a contradiction in terms. Liesel expressed her liking for the *Jugendstil*, the Young Style, and the artists of the Viennese Secession. 'Klimt painted my mother when she was young,' she told von Abt. 'The portrait hangs in the dining room of my parents' house.'

Von Abt smiled at her. 'If the daughter is anything to go by she must be a beautiful woman. I am sure that Klimt did her justice.'

'It is a wonderful painting . . .'

'All gilt and tinsel, no doubt. But . . .' There was always a but. It seemed that von Abt moved round the world butting into obstacles placed in his way by the less intelligent, less gifted, less imaginative. 'But as a *style*, what is the Secession? Wagner? Olbrich? Do you know their building in Vienna? Of course you do.'

'I think it very fine. Bold lines, a statement of intent.'

'But it looks like a mausoleum! Or a railway station! A building should not look like something! It should just *be*, a shape without references, defined only by the material it is built of and the conception of the architect. As abstract as a painting by De Stijl.'

Viktor was nodding in approval but Liesel protested, 'What building is abstract? An abstract building would let the rain in.'

Von Abt's laughter was loud and forthright, so that people at nearby tables looked round to see the source of the noise. 'I am, you see, a disciple of the great Adolf Loos. You know Loos? He hails, I believe, from your home city.'

'I have met the man,' Viktor said. 'I admire his work. It is a shame he felt the need to flee Město. But things are different now. The place is looking to the future.'

This seemed to please von Abt. He praised the virtues of his master, the intelligence, the sense of pure uncluttered form. He drew spaces and constructions before them on the table cloth to illustrate his ideas; he cast towers into the sky and – as Viktor later put it – castles into the air. He extolled the virtues of glass and steel and concrete, and decried the millstones of brick and stone that hung about peoples' necks. 'Ever since Man came out of the cave he has been building caves around him,' he cried. 'Building *caves*! But I wish to take Man out of the cave and float him in the air. I wish to give him a glass space to inhabit.'

Glass Space, *Glasraum*. It was the first time Liesel had heard the expression.

'Perhaps,' said Viktor, glancing thoughtfully at his wife and then back to the architect, 'perhaps you could design a Glass Space for us.'

Commitment

That evening they dined by candlelight on the balcony of their room, watching the glimmering boats, the gondolas and the sandalos, pass below. There was the slap of the water against wooden piles, not the rhythmic sound of the sea but a hurried noise, like cats lapping in the darkness. 'What do you think of our friend?' Viktor asked.

'A curiosity. He's very full of energy.'

'Almost too full. You find him attractive?'

'He would attract a certain type of woman.'

'But not my Liesel?'

She smiled. 'Your Liesel is attracted only by you,' she said comfortingly.

He took her hand across the table. 'When you say things like that, I would happily take you immediately, right here at the table.'

'How outrageous. People would complain and we would both be arrested by handsome *carabinieri* and carried away to that awful gaol that we saw in the Doge's Palace.' They had invented this kind of talk over the few days they had been together. It was something new, something slippery, daring. *Schlüpfrig.* Previously such banter had been about strangers; this was the first time that the subject of their amusement was someone known to them, and whereas previous jokes had appeared harmless enough, this seemed more dangerous.

'What do you think of my suggestion that he might build us our house?'

'Is he to be trusted with something so precious?' she asked. 'We

19

must see his work, mustn't we? Get references, that kind of thing.'
They had already spoken with architects about the new house.
They had discussed proposals, shaken their heads over gables and
towers, questioned ornate and mullioned windows, even
marched round a balsa wood and celluloid model of something
that one studio had suggested. But nothing had seemed right for
Viktor's vision of the future, his desire not to be pinned down by
race or creed, his determination to speak Czech as well as
German, his insistence on reading *Lidové Noviny*, his talk of *ino-
váce* and *pokrok*, innovation and progress. 'Let the world move
on,' he would say. 'We' – he meant those newly created political
beings, the Czechoslovaks – 'have a new direction to take, a new
world to make. We are neither German nor Slav. We can choose
our history, that's the point. It's up to us, don't you see? People
like us.'

And now there was this fortuitous encounter with a young
architect in the amphibious city of Venice, a man whose architectural ideals seemed to be of the future rather than the past.

'I can send a telegram to Adolf Loos. Von Abt claims to have
studied under him.'

'Claims? Do you doubt his word?'

'Do you?'

'I don't know.'

'Well, we will see. We must arrange to meet him again.
Interview him.' He was suddenly businesslike, a disconcerting
manner that he could put on at a moment's notice. One expected
him to gather papers up from the table in front of him and tap
them into some kind of order and slip them away inside a leather
briefcase, then call for a car to whisk him away to another meeting. 'We must find out for ourselves what his ideas might be. He
gave me his card. I will give him a ring.'

'Can't we leave that kind of thing until we're back home?'

'Why wait? Why not strike while the iron is hot?'

The meeting with Rainer von Abt took place the next day. He was
summoned to their suite at six o'clock in the evening, ostensibly
for cocktails but actually to be grilled about the possibility of his
designing their house. It was a fine evening, with the windows
open and the slop and stir of the water outside like the presence of

some large feline animal. Liesel stayed out on the balcony, smoking and sipping her drink and looking out over the basin of St Mark's towards the Isola San Giorgio, while the two men remained inside the room to talk. She was conscious that von Abt glanced towards her from time to time. She told herself that she was unmoved by his attentions. He was short, dark, bouncing in that boxing manner of his, whereas what she admired was tall and angular and almost stooped when standing or sitting, as though making a concession to people of lesser height than he. Viktor. A man of qualities, a man who was altogether admirable.

'It is quite a proposition,' von Abt remarked when Viktor had finished what he had to say. 'Quite a *difficult* proposition.'

'Why difficult? Build a house.' Viktor held his hands open as though to show the simplicity of things. 'Difficult for me, perhaps, but surely straightforward for an architect. If you asked me to build you a motor car . . .'

'Ah, but you build a motor car for a market, don't you? You might wish to build a motor car to your taste, but actually you build a motor car for a market.'

'Precisely,' Viktor agreed. 'The same with a house. Only the market is me alone. And my wife.'

'That is exactly the problem with such a commission. You, your wife.'

'*We* are a problem?'

'The situation creates a problem. You want someone to build a house, four walls—'

'Maybe more, maybe more than four.'

'—and a roof. Doors, windows, upstairs, downstairs, the whole rigmarole. Servants' quarters, I imagine . . .'

'They must go somewhere.'

'Quite so. But it'll be working to order.'

'Rooms for the children,' Liesel called from the balcony.

Von Abt smiled and inclined his head towards her. 'Rooms for the children, indeed. However, *I* wish to do different things than mere construction. I wish to create a work of art. A work that is the very reverse of sculpture: I wish to enclose a space.' And he made a gesture, using both his hands, the space between them as fluid and shifting as the air out of which he modelled it. 'So. It is not like a client making demands and the artisan or the factory worker listening to those demands and doing what he is told. It is me making my vision in concrete and glass.'

Viktor glanced towards Liesel and smiled. She didn't know how to read him in this kind of encounter. She was learning how to read him in matters of love and companionship, but she had never seen him in negotiation with a client or a workers' representative or a supplier. He was smiling, sitting back to consider the matter, with his elbows on the arms of his chair and his hands in front of his face, his long fingers steepled together like the groins of a Gothic vault and his mouth composed in a quiet and confident smile. 'Show me,' he said.

'Show you?'

'Yes. Prepare some drawings. The kind of thing you would wish to do. The kind of' – he paused – '*space* you would wish to enclose. Just sketches.' Almost as an afterthought, he added, 'The site is sloping, quite steeply sloping. Overlooking the whole city. Do you know Město? Perhaps you don't. Below the hill is a park – the Lužánky Park. It used to be known as the Augarten but of course the name has been changed. Where we live, everything has two names. Austrian. Czech. It is the way of our world. So, you must imagine a house at the top of a hill, quite a steep hill, and below it a sloping field, and then laid out before it the whole of the city. A magnificent prospect. Make some drawings.'

Von Abt held out his hands helplessly. 'But how large? I have no information, no idea of what you want.'

'A family home. I have made that clear. A home for my wife and me and our eventual children. Say' – he smiled at Liesel – 'a maximum of three. What area? Say three hundred square metres. Just sketch something out.'

'I will bring you photographs of some of my work. That will suffice.'

'I would like to see some ideas.'

'You *will* see ideas. I work with nothing but ideas.'

Viktor laughed. Liesel had somehow expected that he would be angry, but instead he laughed. 'Show me your ideas, then. Convince me that you are the man for our house.'

Two days later they met again, by appointment, at Café Florian in the Piazza. St Mark's stood like a fantasy of Arabian tents at the end of the great space and the orchestra, camped outside the café like a band of nomads, played selections from Verdi's operas. Rainer von Abt approached their table with all the panache of an opera singer making his entrance. '*Ecco!*' he announced, and placed a portfolio on their table. 'I have laboured day and night, to the disadvantage of my current work. But the demands of true love are more powerful than mere artistic patronage.'

The tapes were untied and the portfolio was opened and Viktor and Liesel put their heads together to look. There were photographs, large glossy prints with studio stamps on the back: an apartment block with white, featureless walls; a square, banded villa set in an anonymous garden; an office block of some kind, all plate glass and white plaster.

'This is all your work?'

'Of course it is.' He leaned forward and pulled out another photograph, one showing a long, low apartment block receding down the perspective lines of a street. 'Weissenhofsiedlung in Stuttgart. Have you seen the place? Le Corbusier, Mies van der Rohe, Behrens, Schneck. Do you know these people?'

'Of course,' said Viktor. 'Le Corbusier, of course. And Behrens.'

Von Abt made a small sound that may have been amusement. '*And* von Abt,' he said, putting the photographs aside. 'Those are some of the things I have done. Now, the things that I have imagined.' He spread out some drawings. These were all architect's sketches, rectilinear, sharp of line, devoid of any kind of embellishment. He pointed with a thick, artisan's finger. 'That one I am working on for people in Berlin. An industrialist and his third wife. They wanted columns and capitals and statues and I told them that if they were looking for ornament, they could look elsewhere. Perhaps you know the essay by Loos, "Ornament and Crime"?'

Viktor smiled. 'Certainly I do.'

'Well then, that is our manifesto. The Communists have theirs and we of the Modern Movement have ours. You ask me to design you a house? I will design you a house. But form without ornament is all I can give you.' He looked round at the long colonnades of the Piazza, at a couple of children immersed in a fluttering cloud of pigeons and being photographed by a commercial photographer with a massive mahogany box camera.

Beyond them were the ornate domes of the Basilica with its mosaics and prancing horses. He gestured towards the scene, as though somehow it had been laid on for his own purposes. 'Here, in the most ornamental city in the whole world, I am offering you the very opposite.'

And at his gesture things began to happen. At least that was the impression Liesel had: the café orchestra set off on a lugubrious traipse round the 'Lament of the Hebrew Slaves'; the photographer bent his head beneath his black cape; and the children, focused through the lens of his machine, shrieked with laughter as though being captured in the box, being inverted and diminished, gave them a physical sensation like being tickled or being frightened. Viktor sipped champagne and considered von Abt's drawings.

'It all seems rather cold.'

'Cold?' For once von Abt appeared lost for words. 'Cold! All my work, all my art is based on this.' He took a pencil from an inner pocket and leaned forward to draw a line as sharp as a razor cut on the nearest sheet of paper. 'This is the first work of art: the woman who lies down.' He looked from Viktor to Liesel, holding her gaze for moment longer than seemed polite. Then he went back to the sheet of paper and drew another line, a vertical cutting at right angles through the horizontal. 'And this. This is the man who penetrates her. The result is the rectangular cross that underpins all my art. What could be warmer than that?'

Liesel took a cigarette and lit it, hoping it would distract her from von Abt's look, hoping she would not blush beneath his gaze. 'Yes, Herr von Abt seems a most uncold person. Don't you agree, Viktor?'

Conception

When the Landauer couple returned home they moved into a furnished villa in the Masaryk quarter of the city. Overlooking the river Svratka and the wooded hills beyond, this was a turreted, crenellated monster of a villa, the very antithesis of their plans for their own house. 'How can I live and breathe in such surroundings?' Viktor had exclaimed when they had first looked round the place. Yet it was in this rented fortress, among the ormolu lamps and velvet drapes, beneath ornate plastered ceilings and chandeliers of Murano glass, that they pursued their ideal of a modern house that would be adapted to the future rather than the past, to the openness of modern living rather than the secretive and stultified life of the previous century.

The Glass Space.

For the moment it was without form or substance, yet it existed, diffuse, diverse, in their minds and in the mind of Rainer von Abt. It existed in the manner that ideas and ideals, shifting and insubstantial, may exist. Space, light, glass; some spare furniture; windows looking out on a garden; a sweep of shining floor, travertine, perhaps; white and ivory and the gleam of chrome. The elements moved, evolved, transformed, metamorphosed in the way that they do in dreams, changing shape and form and yet, to the dreamer, remaining what they always were: *der Glasraum, der Glastraum*, a single letter change metamorphosing one into the other, the Glass Space becoming the Glass Dream, a dream that went with the spirit of the brand new country in which they found themselves, a state in which being Czech or German or Jew would not matter, in which democracy would prevail and art and science would combine to bring happiness to all people.

Towards the end of summer Rainer von Abt came to inspect the site. How, Liesel wondered, would he appear out of the only context she had for him, that fantasy world of Venice in the spring? There he had seemed a character as unreal as the city itself, a creature of imagination and fantasy, capable of conjuring quaint *palazzi* or overwrought churches or melancholy squares out of the mists of the lagoon as though by some kind of innate magic. How would he seem now, coming off the Vienna train into the literal world of Město?

'Just another smug Viennese, I expect,' Viktor suggested as they waited on the platform amongst the milling crowds and the idle porters.

'Why should he be smug?'

'All Viennese are smug. It comes from having lorded it over the Empire for so long.'

She felt indignant on behalf of the man. 'He's not that kind of Viennese at all! How cynical you are, Viktor.'

'I'm realistic.'

Amidst apocalyptic clouds of steam the Vienna train drew in. Doors slammed open and passengers stepped down. She saw von Abt standing at the door of his carriage before he caught sight of them. In a grey homburg hat and black coat he did indeed have the look of a smug businessman. 'There he is!' Liesel waved. Von Abt was peering over the people on the platform with an expression that was almost disdainful, as though he despised both the seething crowd below him and the explosive rattle of the Czech language all around. Then he saw her waving and an expression of relief passed across his face. 'My friends!' he cried, climbing down from the carriage and flinging out his arms. 'My friends!' For a moment he seemed about to hug them, but in the event he merely clasped Viktor's hand in both of his own and raised Liesel's to within breathing distance of his lips. How enchanted he was to see them once more. *Enchanté*, he said. If it were possible, they were looking even happier than they had been in Venice; and Frau Liesel even lovelier.

She laughed at the absurd compliments. He was not a smug

businessman, he was a performer, an artist of verve and flair. She took his arm and led him along the platform, addressing him as *du* rather than *Sie*, the familiar rather than the formal. 'How is Vienna?' she asked. 'Do you miss Venice? Wasn't it wonderful there? Don't you love the place?'

Von Abt made a disparaging face. 'As always Vienna is stimulating and depressing in almost equal measure. Overwrought and undercooked, like its cuisine.'

'And did you have a good journey?'

'Certainly, because of the anticipation of seeing you both again. But passport control at the border was ridiculous. It seems ironical that, though the world is moving forward, it has created a new border control where before none existed.'

'I suppose that's the price of change. It's a small loss of freedom compared with other freedoms we have gained.'

He looked at her with that disturbing smile. 'And are *you* free, Frau Liesel?'

Viktor was striding ahead, past signs saying *Ausgang* and *Vychod*. She tried to read the meaning of von Abt's question. 'Of course I'm free.'

They reached the approximate sunshine of the station forecourt. The scene outside the station seemed the epitome of that freedom – the bustle of people coming and going, the taxi cabs stuttering past, the trams clanging and grinding along the Bahnring, the whole energy and enthusiasm of the new republic. There was a small crowd round a newsstand where the newspapers were announcing the latest technological marvel, the first flight of Germany's new airship, the Graf Zeppelin. Photographs showed the great beast floating like a huge marine animal over the seabed while bottom-dwelling creatures scurried around in its shadow. 'One day soon,' von Abt suggested, 'we'll be able to fly across the Atlantic as easily as taking a train from here to Paris.'

Would it really be possible? Liesel felt all the possibilities of the future. How remarkable this century, which had started so disastrously, might yet prove to be.

Viktor ushered them across the road. 'The Grand Hotel isn't the Sacher,' he said apologetically, 'but it's convenient. Perhaps we can have lunch there before going on to see the site?'

So they ate together in the hotel, in the winter garden, among the palms and the cacti. 'Like old times,' von Abt observed, as though those Venice days were a generation ago and had lasted for years. And Liesel would have been happy to indulge him, to talk about the canals and the churches, about Titian and Tiepolo; but Viktor was impatient with the conversation and eager to talk about the house.

'Ah, the house.' Von Abt nodded. 'Of course, the house. The Landauer House.'

The Landauer House! Waiters cruised among the palm fronds. The room was filled with the sound of diners, the murmur of their conversation and the ringing of cutlery on porcelain, and Rainer von Abt was looking from one to the other of his hosts with that expression of mixed amusement and thoughtfulness, as though to assess the impact of those words: *das Landauer Haus*! It was the first time that Liesel had heard the house, the fictitious house, the fantasy house, the house of dream and imagination, referred to in terms so concrete.

'I wish,' he was telling them, 'not just to design a house but to create a whole world. I want to work from the foundations to the interior, the windows, the doorways, the furnishings, the fabric of the place as well as the structure. I will design you a life. Not a mere house to live in, but a whole way of life.' He opened his hands as though the life were there within his grasp. 'Your abode will be a work of art at which people will wonder.'

He reached into his briefcase and took out a block of cartridge paper and some pencils. 'Look.' His pencil swept lines across the page. 'You said five bedrooms as well as servants' quarters? I have thought that the two should be apart, with room for the motor cars between. Something like this . . .' A shape appeared on his pad, a silver rectangle that, filled with pillars and a triangular pediment, might have become the façade of a classical temple, but cross-hatched with window frames and doorways became, as they watched, a suburban house of geometrical simplicity emerging as though from the white fog of paper.

Viktor frowned. 'A flat roof? Is that suitable for our climate?'

'Modern materials. With modern materials we can fight the elements.' The pencil moved again and mere lines took on substance, solidity. He stroked some shading across the ground and blurred it into shadow with his thumb. With that gesture, that touch of a god-like hand, the sun shone. The pencil moved again and the small, elfin figure of an infant ran along the terrace in front of the house, the future there before them. 'Your child,' he said, looking up. 'Your first child.' He noticed Liesel's blush. 'Have I guessed something?'

She looked from von Abt to her husband and back, wondering whether to disclose this confidence that hadn't yet been conveyed to either of their parents. Viktor nodded faintly. 'Yes, you have,' she confirmed. 'Not many people know yet – just my doctor really – but we're going to have a baby. The news is . . . new. What else can news be? Just a few days old. The baby is due in March.'

Von Abt looked from one to the other. 'I must congratulate you both.'

'The achievement is all Liesel's,' Viktor said with that dry smile. 'I played but a brief role.' There was laughter between the three of them, a moment of shared intimacy such as old friends may have. That was what Liesel felt. Something intense and intimate, as though her pregnancy, the organic fact of it, had created a small, tight circle of special knowledge around these two men. Uncertain exactly how to address him – Herr von Abt? Herr Rainer? – she grabbed the moment. 'Rainer, I wish to choose the interior of the house – the fabrics, the flooring, the furnishings.'

He reached out across the table and laid a comforting hand on hers. 'It will be a collaborative effort. I will build nothing that Frau Liesel will not adore. Nothing!'

After lunch they drove up Černopolní, Blackfield Hill, to see the plot. Viktor drew the car to a halt in a gravel lay-by that overlooked the whole city. It was a wet and blustery day, a foretaste of autumn, and smoke from a thousand chimneys smudged the air. The roofs stretched away like a choppy sea to the distant shore of the Špilas fortress.

'Here we are,' Viktor said. 'This is where you must work. This is your canvas.'

Beyond a gate a meadow sloped down, gently at first, then steeply towards trees at the bottom. Down there the bulk of a large house could be vaguely seen among trees; beyond that was

Parkstrasse and then Lužánky park itself. Raindrops blurred the view through Liesel's spectacles. 'Don't you think the position is fine?' she said.

'Very fine,' von Abt agreed. 'Magnificent.'

She pulled on waterproof overshoes and followed the two men. In the meadow there were apple trees and a single silver birch. Windfalls rotted amongst the grass. Try as she might, she could not picture anything built in this place. There was nothing but this empty hillside and this view of the city. Breathtaking, literally, the wind snatching her breath away.

'I used to come up here with my brother,' she said. 'When we were just children. The birch tree was our god. We'd sit with the sun on our faces and look at the tree and the whole city beyond seemed almost our plaything, a toy town.' Had they heard her? The wind battered her head and snatched her words away. 'Benno used to tell me that there were prisoners in the Špilas castle, chained to the wall so that they had to stand on tiptoe. If they relaxed the chains would cut their hands off. I never knew whether to believe him.' The wind blew a smattering of drizzle in her face. She removed her glasses to wipe them. Von Abt was a blurred figure in the rain, examining every detail of the site from the ground at his feet to the slope of the meadow. 'Here?' he asked, pointing. 'Right here?'

'Wherever you like,' Viktor replied. 'Wherever you think best. I'd say here at the top, wouldn't you? The whole field is ours of course. Down there,' he pointed down the hill, 'is Liesel's family home. The land is all in the family.'

Von Abt had produced a camera from the pocket of his coat, a Leica just like Viktor's. He snapped the lens out and raised the device to his eye, holding himself steady while he shot a series of photographs of the road, the meadow, the slope. 'You have a plan of the place?'

'I've had my surveyors draw one up.'

The architect nodded. He walked down through the wet grass as far as the silver birch and looked back up the hillside.

'Will there be any problem with the slope?' Viktor asked.

'We'll have to excavate. Dig deep and create sure foundations. Gravity is your enemy, but then gravity is always the enemy of the building. If it weren't for gravity we'd build castles in the air.' He looked up to where Liesel stood at the top of the slope, then raised the camera, framing her as she stood there in the long grass with the hem of her coat stained with damp. She felt self-conscious beneath the Cyclops gaze of the little camera, as though it was seeing more than the surface of her, the tall, slightly awkward body, the smooth and expensive clothes, the pale makeup and scarlet arabesque of her mouth, the shining discs of her spectacles. Perhaps, in some mysterious way, it was seeing the occult fact of her pregnancy.

'I like your silver birch,' he called up to her. 'I *love* your silver birch. It will be the axis of your garden, the feature round which the whole design will circle. House and garden as one. Will your brother approve?'

He *had* heard. The fact made her feel absurdly happy, as though Benno himself had just smiled at her. 'I am sure he would have approved. But I'm afraid he's dead. He died in the war.'

'I'm sorry.' He made his way back up to her side.

'Do you know what they did?' she told him as he joined her. 'When he was seventeen and about to go off to join the army, do you know what they did?'

'Who did what?'

'My parents. I was only twelve. I caught *spála*. That's what we call it. Scarlet fever. And when the rash started they banished me to the *chata* down there in the garden.'

'*Chata*? What's a *chata*?'

'A sort of country cottage that people build. I think it must come from the German, don't you? *Hütte*? This one's really just a summerhouse but that's what we call it, the *chata*. It's down there amongst the trees.' She pointed. 'Papi had a bathroom put in – double quick, you can imagine – and I had to live there with the nurse. And why did they do this? All to ensure that Benno didn't catch the disease and maybe develop rheumatic fever and therefore not be able to join the army.' She looked at von Abt. Suddenly the blurring of her sight wasn't caused by rain on her spectacles: suddenly there were tears in her eyes. 'Isn't that stupid? They didn't want Benno to catch scarlet fever in case it would prevent him from joining the army. They should have put us together in the hope that he'd catch it, and then maybe he'd be alive today.'

'I'm sorry.'

She smiled, as though to console him. 'You weren't to know.'

As they climbed back up to the road something shifted in the atmosphere, some coincidence of wind and light and vapour that brought a rupture in the cloud and let the sun break through. She turned and looked back. The grey clouds were grazed with red. The whole orb of the sun was hanging low to the right of the Špilas hill, its light slanting directly across the city to pick them out there on the hillside in a sudden warm amber glow. Beside her, von Abt raised the camera again and captured the moment of illumination with a small, decisive click of the shutter, a measure of milliseconds. 'You know what?' There was something in his expression, a suppressed excitement, the thrill of a secret that, for the moment, he alone possessed. 'You know what?'

His enthusiasm reminded her of Benno, all those plans he used to have. Viktor was standing impatiently by the car. 'What? What should I know?'

'I'll build your house upside down.'

'Upside down? What do you mean, upside down?'

'Just what I say.'

'You must explain.'

But he wouldn't explain, wouldn't tell her. 'Just an idea,' he said as they climbed back into the car. 'Just an idea.'

That evening Liesel's parents held a dinner in honour of the guest. A hopeful from the architectural world of the city had been invited, and the pianist Miroslav Němec. Conversation stumbled occasionally between Czech and German. The architect clearly regarded Rainer von Abt as an interloper and Viktor Landauer as something of a traitor by suggesting that he might employ this Viennese to build his house. Entirely German and quite oblivious to such tensions, Liesel's mother sat at the end of the table with the Klimt portrait looking over her shoulder. Nowadays the face in the painting bore more resemblance to the daughter than it did to the woman who had sat for it two decades earlier: there was the same oval face, the same pursed and thoughtful mouth, the same dark, considerate eyes, the same aquiline nose. But no one, mother or daughter or anyone else, could ever have worn the dress that the artist had created for his subject, a garment that

32

was a vortex of snow and ice, of diamonds and peacock tail feathers.

'Very decorative,' von Abt said as he admired the painting.

'I was the toast of Vienna,' Liesel's mother told him. 'Those were the days, Herr von Abt. When the Monarchy was still alive.'

But Liesel knew the code: 'decorative' was not good. Ornament was Crime. 'Mother, the Monarchy was moribund long before Herr Klimt painted you. It just took a long time dying.'

'It was socialism that killed it,' her mother retorted. 'Had the Socialists not killed it, it would still be there. And now we are left living in a state dreamed up by foreigners.'

There was an awkward pause. At the head of the table, her father smiled enigmatically from behind his moustaches. 'The war is what killed the Monarchy,' Liesel insisted. 'The war killed the Monarchy just as it killed Benno. Stupid old men thinking that they might play around with fighting just as they did throughout the last century. And they found out that they couldn't, that war kills people, ruins lives and destroys countries. But now perhaps we can build a new one, if they'll let us. Socialism *builds* things.'

The silence deepened, became cavernous. Her mother looked appalled. Socialism? The idea seemed outrageous. Not only outrageous but dangerous.

'So how do you find Socialist Vienna, Herr von Abt?' Liesel's father asked. 'My daughter clearly admires it.'

Even von Abt seemed at a loss for words. He who could always discover a retort or a bon mot, needed to scratch around for something to say. 'The Socialists have tried to do something. Their building projects are exceptional . . . The Karl-Marx-Hof . . .'

It was Němec's wife who unwittingly saved the situation. She knew how *she* found Vienna. She found Vienna full of shops and cafés, a positive plethora – she used the word *Überfülle*, her lips enveloping the vowels as they might a strudel – of things that didn't seem socialist at all. Wasn't socialism to do with bringing everything down to the lowest? Well Vienna raised things up to the highest. 'Prague has nothing to compare,' she complained, 'and so I am *forced* to go to Vienna. And then they try and charge me duty at the border.'

The discomfiting moment, the daughter lecturing the mother, the mention of the dead Benno and the cursed socialism, seemed

33

to have passed. But it left its mark on the evening, like an embarrassing blemish that everyone notices but no one remarks on. Except Rainer von Abt. 'If you decide to storm the barricades, I will surely follow,' he murmured to Liesel as they followed her parents to the drawing room to listen to Němec play.

She had to suppress her laughter. 'I'm afraid that you'll leave Viktor behind.'

The guests settled into a semicircle of chairs, with the Bösendorfer at the focus. They talked in hushed tones, as though in church. Němec sat at the keyboard and played something by his mentor Leoš Janáček, a piano suite of mournful tone whose notes meandered through the room, occasionally dying away to silence, occasionally hammering on the startled audience's ears. Liesel's mother listened with a stern concentration that was a rebuke to anyone less attentive than she. In the pause between movements, von Abt leaned over to Liesel and breathed in her ear, 'Why are Czechs always so mournful?'

'They have,' she whispered back, 'a great deal to be mournful about.'

'I'm not surprised, with music like this.'

There was a terrible moment when laughter threatened to bubble up out of control. Viktor caught her eye and frowned. The pianist swayed back and forth, rumbling out deep and sorrowful arpeggios. Von Abt compressed his lips thoughtfully and gazed at the ornate plasterwork of the ceiling, while the giggles rose in Liesel's throat until she feared she might choke.

'I thought you behaved disgracefully this evening,' Viktor said when they were undressing for bed.

'What on earth do you mean?'

'Giggling like a schoolgirl with that fellow von Abt.'

'Don't be absurd, Viktor. We were laughing. We find the same things funny.'

'You were behaving like children.'

'Don't be such a prig!'

The little argument flared and died. In the morning it was forgotten, for there were other, more momentous events to occupy the mind: a meeting with the company lawyers where an agreement was signed between Landauer, Viktor and Landauerová, Liesel on the one hand, and Herr Doktor Architekt Abt, Rainer

('You may leave out the "von"') on the other, for the design of a family home of two storeys and a basement, with a floor area of approximately five hundred square metres, and the addition of a garage for a saloon car and separate quarters for servants of one hundred and twenty square metres, preliminary plans to be completed in two months and final plans by April of the year 1929. Details of construction to be agreed by common consent and the design of furnishings and fittings to be decided over the ensuing months, all designs to be subject to final approval by Landauer, Viktor and Landauerová, Liesel.

Pens scratched in the still atmosphere of the legal office. A banker's draft, drawn on the Živnostenská Banka, was handed across the table. There was a shake of hands, solemn and businesslike with Viktor, warm and two-handed with Liesel, and the commission had been formalised. The Landauer House, a mere figment, would be crystallised into fact.

'He's a strange fellow,' Viktor remarked as they saw von Abt off at the railway station. 'You don't know where you are with him.'

Hana

'How is the baby going?' Hana Hanáková asks.

'It seems fine. The doctor tells me that all is proceeding as normal.'

Hana is the privileged one, Liesel's intimate friend. Although the younger of the two, it is she who mediates on Liesel's behalf between Czech and German, between the world of the arts and business, between the various social circles that interlock and intersect within the bourgeois society of the city. Away from their respective husbands, the two women meet every Wednesday at the café that Fuchs designed for the gardens inside the Schramm-Ring – the Café Zeman – where they sit as always and almost by right in their favourite corner so that they can look out across the tables and see who is there and who might be worth talking about. Hana drinks *turecká*, Turkish coffee, and eats *Sachertorte* and lets people look at her. 'You know *my* latest?' she says. She touches crumbs of cake away from her lips. Her mouth, that feature that seems to fascinate men, is down-turned when in repose. This gives her a look of faint disapproval, to be relieved, suddenly and surprisingly, when she smiles. Her smile, when it strikes you, makes you feel that there is joy and pleasure to be had in life after all.

'No, but you're about to tell.'

'Of course I am.' She leans conspiratorially across the table, her eyes darting sideways in the hope that people at other tables might be lip-reading. 'Miroslav Němec.'

'Oh, Hana, not him, surely not him.'

'Why not? His wife is always going off on shopping expeditions to Vienna leaving him with nothing to do but perform.'

'For you, I suppose.'

'*On* me, my dear. I can tell you, there is nothing, absolutely nothing, like a pianist's fingers.'

'Hana!'

'Have I shocked you? I always thought pregnant women were unshockable. You will be by the time you've given birth. All that gaping and pushing, with half a dozen men peering up your *pochva.*'

'Hana, you really are disgraceful.'

Hana shrugs. 'I'm just truthful. Now tell me about you and Viktor. Is he wildly frustrated?'

'Viktor is not frustrated. He is very content.'

The one looks askance at the other. 'Darling, you're not letting him *in*, are you? You know they say that it can damage the baby.'

Liesel laughs. 'I'm certainly not going to tell you what I am letting him do. Some things are sacred.'

'My darling, these days absolutely *nothing* is sacred. You know that as well as I do.' For Hana that certainly seems to be true. She has posed naked for the photographer Drtikol, and during a year spent in Paris when she was a mere nineteen she was painted nude by the Russian artist Tamara de Lempicka. The painting, all anodised tubes and curves, with hair like strings of liquorice and a mouth like a vampire's, has only recently been exhibited in Prague. There is a rumour – Hana has never denied it, never confirmed it – that she did rather more for de Lempicka than merely pose, that they were in fact lovers.

'For me there are many things sacred,' Liesel insists. 'My marriage, for example. My baby for another.'

'Oh darling, don't be absurd. Your marriage to Viktor is a mere contract.'

'My marriage to Viktor is very much more than a mere contract. It is a marriage of minds.'

Hana laughs. 'You're being sentimental, darling. But your baby is something quite different. Maybe *that* really is the last sacred thing. Really I do rather envy you. However hard I try nothing ever seems to happen with me.'

'You actually want a baby? How wonderful.'

'Sometimes, darling, just sometimes. When I'm feeling lonely.'

Beneath the table Liesel touches her belly. Only the day before she fancied that she felt a movement, and now there it is again, a tiny fluttering certainty in the depths of her being. 'It's there,' she cries. 'I can feel him!'

Hana reaches forward. 'Let me see.'

'Not on the outside. Inside, I can feel him inside. Like a bubble bursting.'

'Perhaps it's wind.'

Their laughter draws the attention of people at nearby tables. 'I think it's true,' Liesel insists. 'I think it really is him.'

'Him?'

'Or her. Perhaps a her.'

'Have you had anyone divine it?'

'Don't be ridiculous.'

'Oh, but it works. If you have the powers.'

'And unscientific.'

'You and your science. Just because Viktor makes motor cars. You need to make a pendulum with your wedding ring, that's all. A cotton thread will do. Everyone knows.' She pauses and looks round as though she might be overheard. '*I* can do it.'

'*You* can do it?'

'Of course. Dear Viktor may loathe me but I am a woman of many talents.'

So they finish their coffees and, giggling, take a taxi to Hana's apartment in the centre of town where the operation is performed, Liesel lying on the chaise longue in the drawing room, in the very place, presumably, where the pianist Němec conducts his private performances. Hana ties Liesel's wedding ring to a length of cotton thread and holds it above her abdomen. 'I think you should pull your dress up, darling. It works much better if there's nothing to absorb the aura of gender.'

'Won't my own aura of gender interfere with the transmission anyway? How can this possibly work?'

'You've become too cynical. You're catching it from Viktor.'

'Viktor is not cynical. He is just realistic.' But still Liesel complies with the suggestion, shifting her hips to hitch her skirt and petticoat up and expose the gleaming dome of her belly. The umbilicus is everted, and there is a median line that has appeared over the weeks, running from her navel to her pubis almost like a line of symmetry. Hana looks down on her with an expression of amazement. 'Darling, you are *gorgeous*.'

'Don't I look like a clumsy whale?'

Her friend's eyes shine. She stands there, sharp and elegant and sterile, looking down on the helplessly exposed Liesel. 'Of course not. You look like a sleek fish. Tamara could have painted you. Goodness, I'm quite . . .'

'Quite what?'

For once Hana seems at a loss for words. 'Overwhelmed . . . I never dreamed . . .'

Liesel feels both vulnerable and proud. 'Never dreamed what?'

'That it could be so beautiful. May I touch? Does it seem rather strange to ask?' The improvised pendulum hangs from her finger. 'May I?'

'Why would you want to do a thing like that?'

'I don't know. I just . . . do.' And she kneels down on the floor beside the chaise longue, and strokes her hands across Liesel's belly like a blind person trying to discover the shape and texture of something that she cannot see. Then something happens that seems so remarkable that they never talk of it afterwards: Hana leans forward and presses her lips against the warm swelling. The contact evokes in Liesel a vague and unnerving sense of sexual desire, focused not on Hana but on her own body, which is so foreign and so strange, so heavy with the future. She rests her hand on Hana's head in something like benediction, or maybe to comfort her, that she is in this blessed gravid state and Hana is not. And then Hana's hand slips inside the elastic of her drawers and cups the warm mound of her pubis.

There is a moment of shock, a few seconds of a strange tableau in which the participants are uncertain of the role each is playing, before Liesel shifts her hips. 'Hana,' she says quietly, 'please.'

The hand slips away. Avoiding Liesel's eyes, Hana gets to her feet. She searches for distraction. 'The pendulum. We've forgotten the pendulum.' She holds it out as though to demonstrate the hard metallic fact of it, something that can be felt and seen, against whatever it is that the two of them have just experienced, which was a slippery, ineffable emotion that was different for each but nonetheless powerful. *Schlüpfrig*. The ring spins round, catching the light in splashes of gold. Hana holds it still and for a moment the band of gold hovers motionless above Liesel's everted navel. Then, hesitantly, it begins to turn. An air current? A shiver from Hana's fingers?

'Look!'

'Shh!'

'It's turning. A circle. It's turning a circle!'

'It's a girl.' The turning is obvious now, incontrovertible, a description of a perfect female circle over the smooth and refulgent dome of Liesel's belly.

'A girl! Oh Hana, we'll call her after you.' And she sits up and hugs her friend as though everything is complete, their love consummated, the gestation over, the child delivered, the matter already decided.

Gestation

'Look at what has just come from von Abt,' Viktor announces one morning, finding Liesel in her room writing letters. Her belly is heavily swollen now. Sometimes the swelling makes her feel big and clumsy; at other times she feels almost translucent, as though the creature inside her can be seen through the wall of her abdomen, a fish swimming there in the ocean of its own amnion, an amphibian climbing out onto a tidal bank, a reptile raising its ugly head, a mammal couched in fur, an animal re-enacting its evolutionary development there in the primeval world of her womb.

'See what he is proposing?' He unfolds the architect's plan on the floor beside her desk, a diazo print showing ghostly lines in dark blue on a pale blue background. Haus Landauer is written across the top left-hand corner. There are two perspective drawings, two floor plans, a front elevation and a street elevation: ruled lines as sharp as razor cuts, a mathematical precision that is beyond the natural. There are no straight lines in nature. Not even light travels in straight lines any longer, so it is said. That man Einstein.

'See what he is suggesting? The house will be sort of hung from the first storey, here. Do you see? Downwards into the garden. The bedrooms and bathrooms on the entrance floor and then the living room below. Huge windows. Plate glass. I mean, the fellow hasn't really bothered with walls. Just glass.' His tone is one of amazement and excitement, as though he has just been the witness of a natural phenomenon that you see only once in a lifetime.

Liesel turns to look, spreading her legs so she can lean forward.

41

The plans show Euclidian perfection, as pure as an idea. There is not a curve in the whole proposal. Her own belly is a curve, something aquatic, oceanic, but not this design for a house. Not a curve in sight. She examines the garden elevation, a long, lean rectangle laid sideways across the page and crossed with vertical lines, a rectilinear universe that might have been designed by that new painter whom Rainer talked about, the Dutchman Mondrian. The perspective drawings show all this as a construction of boxes, a child's game played with wooden blocks. Only a tree, an architect's conceit sketched in beside the building, gives a brief, ephemeral sense of flow. And as Viktor said, the street entrance seems to be on the top floor with the living room below it. She looks up. '"I will build you a house upside down," that's what he said.'

'But is it what we want?'

'Why not? And this room, all glass!' She laughs, shifting her belly, leaning forward again. 'We will be like plants, hothouse plants.'

'Over-hot in summer, perishing cold in winter, I'd say.'

She examines the plan of the main floor – it is a space, just a space. There are no internal walls, merely space. 'What's this line?'

'He proposes some kind of partition to divide the area. Moveable, I think. And there's another partition to separate the dining area. See? Where he has put the table and chairs. The semi-circle.'

'At least there's one curve.' She puts her finger out and touches the slick surface of the print as though by touching it she might understand it better, like a blind person reading Braille. There are small crosses ranked across the plan like graves marked on the map of a cemetery.

✚　✚　✚　✚

'And these?'

'Those are the pillars.'

'Pillars?'

'He wants to build a steel frame. Apparently there will be no load-bearing walls at all, just the whole thing hung on a steel frame. And where the uprights pass through the interior he is proposing to clad them in chrome. *Glänzsend*, he calls it. Shining. Hard steel rendered as translucent as water.' Viktor pulls a letter from his pocket and reads. '"Steel will be as translucent as water. Light will be as solid as walls and walls as transparent as air. I conceive of a house that will be unlike any other, living space that changes functions as the inhabitants wish, a house that merges seamlessly into the garden outside, a place that is at once of nature and quite aside from nature . . ." That's what he says. What is the man going on about?'

'I think it looks wonderful.'

'It certainly looks different. More like that department store that the Baťa people are putting up on Jánská. Do we want to live in a department store? Over here domestic supplies, over there soft furnishings and fabrics, downstairs for cutlery and crockery . . .'

She laughs. 'Viktor, you are losing your nerve. It was you who wanted a house for the future and now you seem to hanker after the solid ideas of the past. Next you will be insisting on a turret with crenellations and ogives. Look.' She points to the top floor, the street level. 'This is a terrace, a great space, with the rooms like a cluster of tents. Our family camped out on the steppe. The inside and the outside are one and the same thing.'

'We're not nomads.'

'You enter here . . .' She traces the curve of stairs – another curve! 'And then descend into this . . . this space.' *Raum*, she says and suddenly she sees the space projected into her inner vision, the purity of line, the thrill of emptiness. 'Can't you see it? It'll be wonderful.'

'I can see it in theory. The fact seems rather remote at the moment. And frightening.'

'But you take risks in your business. You trust to designers. You approve of the building of new factories and offices.'

'But do I want to live in a factory? Or an office?'

She straightens up. Once it was Viktor who was committed to the idea of the modern, and now it is she. 'But this is where *I* want to live.' She touches her belly. 'With my daughter and my husband.'

'How do you know it's a daughter?'

'Hana divined the sex. Didn't I tell you? Astonishing really. With a pendulum.'

'Don't be ridiculous. That woman's a menace.'

'Did you know she's having an affair with Němec? She says he plays her like a piano.'

'How disgusting.' He looks outraged. She has noticed that ever since her pregnancy began he treats her with a kind of remote sterility, as though she were some kind of virginal mother about to give birth to the Messiah or something. 'Don't be so prudish, Viktor.'

'I'm not prudish. You know I'm not prudish. I just don't want my wife descending to Hana Hanáková's kind of vulgarity.'

Winter came with snow, sometimes a blizzard, at other times just faint white moths floating down through the cold air. In the garden at the back of their rented house it gathered in the shadows of the plants and survived there even when the daytime temperature rose above zero. The grass took on a bruised, dead look while the hills on the far side of the river lay like corpses beneath their winding sheets. Nature seemed suspended in this icy season, but still things grew – the child in Liesel's womb, the house in Rainer von Abt's mind. The one convolute, involute, curved and complex – there are no straight lines in nature – the other simple and linear.

In March, when the ground thawed and the whole world turned to mud, the site for the new house was prepared. A mechanical excavator was hired for the task, a machine that gouged and churned the soil until the top of the hillside resembled the scarred and crevassed landscape of the Tagliamento during the war. From the lip of the street the land was cut away, a step down into the lower stratum of soil which was rust-coloured and as hard as rock. The ramp leading down was clad with planks to stabilise it. 'All this for a private house,' muttered the site foreman. 'Anyone'd think we was building a factory.'

Then they sank the foundations – the piles that would support the frame – and laid the concrete base. Excavators chugged and spluttered in the dank air. Cement mixers churned. The site spread like a lesion on the forehead of the hill. Once the foundations had been completed and the concrete piles driven down into the hardpan, the frame of the house had to be erected. The steel pillars came from Germany, from the firm of Gossen in Berlin. The joists were I-beams, but the vertical supports were constructed of four angle-beams riveted back to back to make pillars with a cruciform cross-section. The hammering of the riveters and the clangour of steel cut through the tranquillity of Blackfield Road. Never, probably never in the whole world, had a private house been constructed in this manner.

In April, while the frame grew, the baby was born. They had decided on the modern way, in a clinic run by Doctor Živan Jelínek, a physician who had learned the Twilight Sleep technique under the tutelage of Gustav Gauss in Freiburg. It was Hana who had first mooted the idea. 'Tell me what's wrong with a little touch of morphia, darling?' she had asked. So the pain of delivery was blown away by morphine, and any memory of the whole event excised from her mind by scopolamine, a drug culled from henbane and deadly nightshade that kills, among other things, memory; and into this chemical amnesia Ottilie was born.

Construction

Rainer von Abt at the building site: it is a late April day with a thin and miserable rain falling. Mud is still the chief feature of the place, mud like a curse clinging to your legs and trying to drag you down into the pit. Von Abt stands in muddied brogue shoes on a plank walkway. Dressed as he is in a dark grey suit and a black overcoat, and wearing a pale grey homburg hat, it would be easy to mistake him for the owner. By his side, in rubber boots, stands the site foreman, muddied, dishevelled and harassed. At the moment there is no concrete form to the construction they are looking at. It is no more than a sketch in bold strokes, written into von Abt's mind, transferred onto sheets of paper then revised, reconsidered, discussed for the slightest detail, and now drawn out in the bold horizontals and verticals of reddened steel, a three-dimensional maze raised into the misty air. In the past houses have grown organically, like plants, from the ground upwards. But this house is different: it grows from the frame outwards, like an idea developing into a work of art from the central core of inspiration out into the material fact of realisation. Cement mixers churn and vomit. Men tramp back and forth with hods over their shoulders. Ladders stand as sharp diagonals to the rectilinear skeleton of the frame.

The site foreman unfolds a diazo print and gestures upwards towards the top floor where a workman balances across a girder as easily as a child walking along the kerb of a pavement. 'You want decent load-bearing walls,' he says, 'give the thing some stability.'

'I want nothing of the kind,' von Abt replies with remarkable good humour. 'Stability is the last thing I want. This house must float in light. It must shimmer and shine. It must not be stable!'

The man sniffs. 'It looks more like a machine than a house.'

'That's what it is, a machine for living in.'

The foreman shakes his head at the idea of such a machine. He wants four walls around him, made of stone. None of this steel-girder frame nonsense. If that is for anything it is for office blocks – they are putting up a building like that on Jánská at this very moment, but it is going to be a department store, for God's sake, not a private house.

'Le Corbusier,' von Abt says.

'Eh?'

'What I said is not original. I cannot take the credit. Le Corbusier got there first. *La machine à habiter*.'

'What's that?'

'French.'

'Who needs French? It's bad enough having to deal with German and Czech. You know we had a fight the other day? On the site, right here. Something about politics, a Czech speaker and a German speaker and the stupid thing was, the Czech was called Mlynář and the German was called Müller.'

'Mlynarsch?'

The foreman laughs at von Abt's attempt at the pronunciation. 'It means "miller". The bastards each had the same name. I slung both of them out on their ears, I did. Well, you can't have that sort of thing getting in the way of work, can you? Not when things are looking as bad as they are at the moment.'

There is a call from up above, from the top of the staircase of planks that has been built down from street level. The two men look up. There, against the sky, is the silhouette of a woman.

'Frau Liesel?' von Abt calls. 'Is it Frau Liesel Landauer?' He struggles across the planks and clambers up the uneven staircase to her level. The encounter is a cautious one. When they had first met she was a girl becoming a woman; now she is a woman become a mother. The fulcrum of her life has shifted.

'I must congratulate you on your great achievement,' von Abt says, bowing over her hand.

'You must come and see her,' she tells him.

'I'd love to.'

'She's beautiful, beautiful. Perfect . . .' Perfect what? What feature shall she choose? 'Fingers, hands. You cannot imagine how perfect. Fingerprints, miniature nails, all perfect.' She holds out her own as though they might help explain. 'She sleeps and eats and sometimes looks at you but you don't know what she is seeing quite. She frowns, as though you aren't coming up to her standards, but you don't know what those standards are so you always feel inadequate.' Liesel laughs. She has been warned that some mothers feel depressed after giving birth, but she feels only exultation. 'But I'm here to see the house. How is it going? How long will it be? I want to bring Ottilie here.'

They stand on the edge, looking down on the frame. Somewhere down there, defined within the cage of steel, is her house – the rooms, the space, the furniture, the floors, all conceptually there as a sculpture is somehow there in the mind of the sculptor before he completes it. Men climb ladders and tiptoe across the beams as though searching for this mysterious grail. The site engineer, a small man with glasses and energetic arms, is discussing something with the foreman. 'They all want walls,' Rainer explains, 'and I insist that Frau Liesel does not want walls. She wants space and light for her new child. That's what I tell them.'

He smiles at her and she feels iridescently happy, as though lights have been turned on, multicoloured lights that shimmer and wobble and reflect off moving mirrors. This man has a vision that he is realising for her alone, for her and Viktor and their baby. It seems fantastic. 'Will you come and see her?' she asks. It suddenly seems important that she should show him Ottilie. 'Can I drag you away from your work for a few minutes?'

'Of course you can.'

Her car is waiting, with the chauffeur, Laník, behind the wheel. They drive round to the other house, the turreted and bastioned one in the Masaryk quarter, the one with small windows and weighty walls, the towers and the turrets. The nurse goes and fetches Ottilie while Liesel entertains von Abt in the sitting room. A maid brings coffee and cakes. They talk enthusiastically of furnishings and interiors, of the space in which to create her family, which is not like the space of this room with its heavy drapes, its furniture like coffins and pews, its chandeliers and heavy flock wallpaper. 'A new way of life,' von Abt is saying as the nurse comes in with a bundle of shawls that is Ottilie. 'That's what you will have. Away with all this fustian.'

Liesel takes her child. 'She has been sleeping. In a moment she will awaken and will want to feed. That's it. Sleep and feeding.' She laughs at the absurdity of such a life and holds the baby for von Abt to see. He reaches out and strokes a cheek with the tip of one finger, then looks up at Liesel and touches her hand where it holds Ottilie's shawl aside. 'It is marvellous to see you so happy.'

'I *am* very happy,' she agrees, as though there has been some suggestion that she might not be.

'Viktor is a lucky man.'

'We are both of us very lucky.'

The baby wakes, her eyes suddenly there like jewels amongst the crumpled features. She opens a toothless mouth.

'You see? She is hungry. That is the sum total of her intellectual achievement at the moment. Do you mind if I feed her?'

'Of course not . . .' He makes to go, but she stops him.

'No, please don't bother. If you don't mind . . . And please don't look away. You may watch, Rainer. I would like you to watch.' And there and then, conscious of the immense power she possesses, she unbuttons the front of her dress and releases her breast. Once meagre, her breasts have become functional organs as heavy and full as fruit. As she holds the nipple for the baby, she feels Rainer's eyes on her like a thrilling touch. And then Ottilie takes the nipple in her hard gums and there is the particular ecstasy of her suck. Liesel looks up directly at him. 'There,' she says, and wonders why it is that having Rainer von Abt watch her do this is so important.

'Pure superstition,' Viktor said dismissively when the question of Ottilie's baptism was broached. 'We profess not to believe so why do we have to do this kind of thing for our child?'

'For my mother's sake.'

'First she insisted on a church wedding, and now she demands that her granddaughter be baptised. She is merciless.'

'And I want Hana to be her godmother,' Liesel added.

'That woman!'

'She is not *that woman*. She is my dearest friend. You stopped me naming the baby Hana but you must allow me this.'

'Well she's hardly going to instil fidelity and modesty in our daughter, is she?'

'She'll be very conscious of her responsibilities.'

'As long as she is also conscious of her irresponsibilities.'

The ceremony – a small, private event limited to family members and the godparents – took place in the Church of the Minorites on Jánská, with Ottilie all in white silk and her godmother Hana Hanáková all in black. They made a beautiful pair at the font, the one small and round, innocent and soft, the other tall and sharp, worldly wise and hard. Viktor stood in the background with Hana's husband. 'She's beautiful, isn't she?' Oskar whispered in his ear, but it was unclear whether he was talking about the baby or about his own wife. The priest mumbled Latin words and leaned down towards the baby as though to take a bite from her breast. He was, so Oskar explained, breathing on her to drive the devil out. Hana had explained the whole ceremony to him.

'Is the devil *in* her then? That seems ridiculous. She's just a baby. Barely capable of focusing her eyes on anyone, never mind harbouring the devil.' The absurd ceremony reminded Viktor of his own childhood, of being dragged to synagogue at Passover and Yom Kippur, of the impenetrable ritual and incomprehensible language. His father had always remained aloof from such things, while his mother had been the driving force behind the family's religion. Now, perhaps, Liesel was doing the same with his new family. 'It's pure nonsense,' he whispered to Oskar. 'Surely mankind is intrinsically good, not intrinsically bad.'

Oskar could barely suppress a laugh. 'Mankind intrinsically good? Where were you during the war, Viktor?'

After the ceremony a small reception was held in a hotel nearby. The women crowded round the baby. Cousins and aunts exclaimed at the wonders of babyhood and how the daughter resembled her mother and how good she was, while Viktor and Oskar talked of things that occupied the minds of men, matters of the stock market, questions of economics and business. Hana came over, momentarily relieved of her duties as godmother. 'I must congratulate you on my lovely goddaughter, Viktor,' she said. 'Never was there a more beautiful baby.'

'My contribution was minimal.'

'But vital.'

She put her arm through her husband's and bent and kissed him on his bald head. 'You couldn't go and find my cigarettes could you, darling?' she asked. 'I left my bag somewhere . . .'

He went off obediently, leaving Viktor and Hana together. 'I know you don't like me, Viktor,' she said.

'Don't be absurd. Why should you think something like that?'

She laughed his protest away. Perhaps the champagne had loosened her tongue. 'Don't *you* be absurd. I know you don't like me. You even stopped Liesel naming the baby after me. And truth to tell, I don't much like you. But let me assure you, there are two things that I love above all. One is your wife and the other is your daughter. I will do all in my power to cherish and protect them both.'

Viktor sipped champagne. Ottilie's patience, already strained by oil and water and being breathed on by the priest, had finally snapped at the unwarranted attentions of the photographer. She began to cry. Women gathered round to coo and cluck. 'Cherishing is fine,' Viktor said to Hana. 'I hope that protection won't be necessary.'

Onyx

The house grew, the baby grew. The latter was a strange and rapid metamorphosis, punctuated by events of moment: the grasp of her hands, the focus of her eyes, her first smile, her recognition of Liesel and then Viktor, the first time she raised herself on her hands, the first laugh. The growth of the house was more measured: the laying of steel beams, the pouring of concrete, the encapsulating of space. And then delay, problems with materials and the workforce, argument and frustration stretching over the summer and the autumn before things were resolved.

'It happens,' Viktor said in an unusual display of fatalism. 'These things happen.'

There was no equivalent ceremony to celebrate the moment when the shell of the house was finally completed that winter, no baptism or naming but only a degree of apprehension as they climbed out of the car to look at the building. It appeared like nothing more than a warehouse, a repository for agricultural machinery or building material perched there up on the hillside. They followed von Abt across bare concrete and into the construction. The empty spaces were heavy with the smell of new cement and plaster. The floor was rough and dusty, the walls plain and plastered white. Rooms were lit by single hundred-watt lightbulbs hanging from the ceiling.

'What do you think?'

What did they think? It was impossible to say. It was like contemplating a skeleton and trying to work out how the person would have looked. Viktor helped Liesel over a plank and they went out onto the terrace where there was bright sunshine and a gust of wind. Across the roofs of the city the Špilas fortress rode on the crest of a wave beneath a brisk sky of cumulus. 'I can imagine Ottilie playing here,' she said. The sandpit was already in place, an integral part of the structure. And benches and a paddling pool, all put there at her request.

Viktor noticed a puddle of rainwater against the parapet wall. 'That's the problem of a flat roof, isn't it?' He came back to that point often, niggling at it like a tongue searching out an unfamiliar irregularity in a tooth.

'It's well sealed underneath,' von Abt reassured him. 'Modern materials. We're not living in the nineteenth century. And when we lay the pavement we'll put a slope on it. There's nothing to worry about.'

'But still . . .'

They looked round the other rooms, the bare spaces that would be bathrooms and bedrooms. Their voices echoed down the stairs and into the living room, the wide and empty expanse below. Canvas hung where the glass would go, casting the space in shadow. A plank lay abandoned on the floor. There was a bucket with remains of cement in the bottom, and a sheet of newspaper, the title *Lidové Noviny* plainly visible. The three of them walked round in the twilight, trying to picture the place as it would be, the new life that would be enacted there. Instead there was this concrete space, as large as a garage.

'The partition will be here,' von Abt said, standing in the middle and holding out his arms, 'to divide the sitting area from the library area.'

The partition was a matter of contention. What would the material be? 'It must be onyx,' von Abt had insisted when they had discussed the matter in Vienna some days earlier. Onyx seemed absurd, extravagant. It was a gemstone, a meretricious material, a thing of cameo brooches and decorative boxes. But then von Abt himself seemed absurd at times, with his dramatic flourishes and his talk of space and light, of volume and thrust. 'I have considered alabaster and travertine, but have fallen for onyx. It will be the *pièce de résistance.*'

He stood now in the shadows of the unfinished living space, and extolled the virtues of his idea, described the complex veining of the rock, the lucidity, the delicate colour of honey and gold.

'The colour of a young girl's hair,' he said, glancing at Liesel. 'The colour of your daughter's hair.'

Viktor looked at the two of them, sensing that small current of sexuality that travelled like a spark between them. The evidence was there plain enough, in the widening of her eyes behind her spectacles, in the faint opening of her lips as though to admit something shameful. He wondered about it not with jealousy but with a calm consideration of the possibilities of faithfulness and betrayal.

'How much would it cost, this onyx?'

Von Abt's eloquence stopped. 'Ah. The cost. The cost is, I am afraid, considerable.'

'Tell me.'

'Approximately fifteen thousand dollars. That is about—'

'It is about a small fortune! My God! About half a million crowns. Enough to build an entire house.'

Von Abt nodded. 'But think how remarkable it will be, Herr Viktor.'

'Certainly it will be remarkable. There are many people who possess onyx ashtrays. I don't imagine there's a single one with an onyx wall.'

That was the end of the viewing, really, a sour note of cost intruding on the exercise of fantasy that was required to imagine the house as it would be, not as it was – a thing of light and reflection, not this dull box of grey concrete. They saw von Abt off on the Vienna train and returned to their turreted villa in silence.

'You're angry about Rainer's proposals, aren't you?' Liesel said when they were in the sitting room after dinner.

He shrugged. 'They seem extravagant at times. It's our money he's spending, not his own.'

'The onyx wall, you mean? Viktor, do you know what "onyx" means? It's the Greek for a fingernail. It's Venus's fingernail, isn't that wonderful? The fingernail of the goddess of love.'

'Did von Abt tell you that?'

'As a matter of fact, he did.'

'It's an inordinately expensive fingernail.'

'Oh, don't be so dull, Viktor. If we are going to do something wonderful, then we must make sacrifices.'

Didn't she understand? She lived in her protected world, along

54

with Hana Hanáková and her other friends, and they talked about their painters and their musicians and their actors and actresses, and meanwhile the outside world battled with recession and political unrest. When would the one world impinge on the other? And what kind of shock would they feel then?

He got up and put his book aside. 'I'm going to bed.'

'Darling, have I made you angry?'

'Of course you haven't.'

But she had. She came up to bed later and he lay in the darkness, listening to her as she went to her bathroom to wash, and then crossed the corridor to her room. There was a thin baby's cry and then silence. She would be feeding Ottilie. Although she sometimes did it openly in front of him, the process always seemed alien, something private between mother and child. Her large, milky breasts were quite changed from the small paps he had once stroked and kissed, indeed her whole body seemed different now, a thing designed for mothering rather than sex. The baby made strange grunting noises as she fed, like a pig suckling. And there wasn't much difference, was there? A sow feeding her litter, a woman with a baby. Animals both, with animal needs and compulsions. He lay in the darkness and thought of Liesel and motherhood and the new house. It was in this dark and womblike house – the Castle, he called it – that Liesel had conceived their child. What would be conceived in the new house? Other children, perhaps. And what else?

His mind wandered, in and out of sleep. The onyx wall, he thought of the onyx wall. A fingernail, Venus's fingernail. He thought of fingernails – Liesel's, which were long and painted red, and others which were blunt and uncoloured and bitten down to the quick, holding between them a cigarette.

'Have you got a light?'

Naively he had paused to answer her.

'A light,' she repeated. 'D'you have a light?' There was an air of impatience about her manner, as though she was hurrying to an appointment. All around him was the fairground noise of the Prater, the laughter of children, the calls of stallholders; ahead of him the Nordbahnhof and the train home; and in front of him this woman – smaller than Liesel, with quick, intelligent features and a slight sheen to her complexion – holding an unlit cigarette between her fingers. Her eyes were blue, so pale that they gave the curious illusion of transparency, as though you were looking through them and seeing the sky.

He fumbled for his lighter and watched as she bent towards the flame. She wore a grey cloche hat and her hair was dark and cut short, not cropped as severely as Liesel's and her friends', but short enough to be a statement that she was a modern woman. A Slav, he fancied. There was no more than a smudge of rouge on her cheeks but her lips were a blood-red arabesque. Certainly she was pretty – a neat, precise prettiness – but she wasn't in other respects remarkable. She might have been a maid out for a walk in the park, dressed up for her day off in a narrow knee-length skirt and a white blouse beneath her neat little jacket. There was a brooch pinned on the lapel, a lump of amber like a boiled sweet.

She straightened up and blew smoke away. 'Can I do anything for you then?'

He hesitated. There in the park, with the Riesenrad, the Giant Wheel, looming over them, he considered what she had said, while she looked around at the crowd, as though to see if anything more interesting was in the offing. She drew on the cigarette in short, sharp snatches, as though she wasn't really used to smoking. Maybe she was just about to move away. Maybe she had seen another possibility.

'Yes, perhaps you can.'

'All right, then. Where d'you want to go?'

Why had he not merely dismissed her and gone on to the station to catch the afternoon train back to Město? Curiosity, certainly, and something more, some quality of youth that he saw in her and, incongruously enough, innocence. But many other things. Plain sexuality, of course. The mystery of the unknown. And intangible things: the set of her head, the precise curve of cheek and eyebrow, her gentleness of expression and the quiet amusement that he saw behind her anxious look. 'What about a ride on the wheel?'

She seemed startled. 'That thing? You won't get me up there.'

'Are you afraid? Why are women always afraid of such things?'

It was the mention of her gender that did it. He could see it in her expression. She had been about to shrug her shoulders and move on, but now she paused and regarded him carefully, head on one side. 'That's not true. Women aren't afraid. We just have real fears to deal with, not the silly fears that men dream up.' There was a quality to her answer that startled him, a sharp edge of intelligence that he had not expected.

'Come on then. Prove it.'

The idea seemed to amuse her. 'All right.'

They had to join a short queue. There were some families in front, and a young couple, and then it was their turn. The great wheel, its circumference rising two hundred feet above, wound round and presented a cabin to them, its door held open by the attendant. For a moment it appeared that the group following, two women with half a dozen children between them, might crowd in behind but at the last moment the attendant held them back. Viktor and the young woman stepped alone into the empty cabin.

The box rocked gently, like a boat at the quayside. She tottered against him and there was that moment of unconsidered contact, his arms holding her, her hair against his face. She made a hasty apology and gripped the rail to look out of the window as the gondola shifted forwards and began to climb. 'D'you know the last time I did this I was about ten years old?'

'When was that?'

'Fifteen years ago?'

'You don't look that old.'

She smiled slyly. 'And what about you?'

The park was shrinking below them, the skyline unfolding. A distant view of hills. He thought of the view across Město from the new house; and he thought of Liesel. 'It's none of your business.'

'Please yourself.'

The cabin swayed gently in the breeze. Standing side by side, they looked at the view and seemed to consider their options. 'What's your name?' he asked.

'Kata. And yours?'

'Viktor.'

Should he have given a false name? Was Kata itself false? What was it really? Katarina, something like that? She was, she told him, Hungarian not Slav, although she came from Slovakia; but then there were many Hungarians living across the border in the new country, weren't there? Just another group of people cut off from their origins by politicians drawing lines on maps. 'Like you,' she pointed out.

'Me?'

'Aren't you Czechish?'

'How can you tell?'

Again that knowing smile. 'You learn things.'

The wheel rose to its climax and tipped over into the descent. She gave a little gasp and gripped the rail tightly for a moment, then turned to him and laughed. Her laughter was delightful, a bubble of innocence, as though she had never before picked a man up in the Prater. 'Where do you want to go then?' she asked. 'You got a hotel? I can recommend one if you like.'

'That'd be fine. I'll have to send a telegram first.'

'To your wife?'

He shrugged, watching the world slowly rising to meet them, the Haupt-Allee with its strolling couples, its bicycle riders, its running children and dogs.

'Don't worry, most men are like that,' she said, as though talking about the victims of some debilitating but non-lethal disease. 'It's just the way things are.'

The hotel was old-fashioned and rather run down, a relic from pre-war years when people had more money and a greater need to move around, days when the city was an imperial capital rather than the overfed chief city of a rump state. A porter showed them upstairs to a dingy room that was redolent of many temporary assignations. Once closeted with him in the room, the girl didn't do anything special. There was no artifice, no seduction, no ridiculous striptease. While Viktor sat watching on the bed she just took her clothes off, folded them carefully and put them on a chair. Then, almost so he would not see too much, she turned quickly and slipped beneath the sheets.

'How often have you done this?' he asked.

'Gone with a stranger?' She made a face, a small *moue* of discontent. 'A few times. I'm not a *tart*, you know. I work in the fashion business. This is only when I need a bit of extra.'

'What are you, a mannequin?'

58

She hesitated, on the brink of the lie: 'A seamstress, actually. Hats at the moment, I work with hats.'

'Your own hat?'

'Yeah, I did that.' She laughed. He liked her laugh. 'It's classy, isn't it?'

'Very.'

'And now you need a bit of extra?'

'Of course. The rent, stuff like that. You know what it's like. It's no joke getting by on my wage, not these days. Look, aren't you going to come in? Isn't this what you want?'

He was uncertain of the answer to her question. He who was always sure of himself, was suddenly confused by the mockery he saw in the girl's expression. He reached out and took her hand. There was something innocent about it, something ill-formed and jejune, the fingernails bitten to the quick like a child's. 'I don't know what I want.'

'Oh, yes you do. You want to do this without feeling any guilt. Well I don't feel guilt, so why should you?'

He laughed. 'Are you a philosopher?'

'I'm realistic. If I weren't I'd be picking your pocket or something.'

So he took off his clothes and got into bed with her, and she did what he asked, which would have shamed him with Liesel but which with this girl seemed entirely natural. And afterwards he felt no guilt, only a feeling of sadness. What was that Latin saying? *Post coitum omne animal triste.* After coitus every animal is sad. But sad for what? The passing of that moment of pure, shameless innocence, perhaps.

'Well, I'll be going then,' she said, rolling away from him.

He put out a hand to stop her. 'Wait,' he said. 'Don't just go straight away. I want to talk a bit. I'll give you something extra, if you like.'

'You'll pay me for *talking*?'

'Why not?'

And so they talked. It was a strange conversation. From time to time, usually in the factory, he met women of her class. He would exchange pleasantries with them, but they never talked. And now he did talk with this girl, and she was quick and clever and amusing, lying beside him in the bed smoking a cigarette and telling him what it was like in the world she inhabited, on the planet of the underclass where who you were mattered little and what you did was all, and that not very much. And where you went with a man when you needed a bit extra.

'Look, I've really got to go, eh? I've got things to do.'

'You can't stay the night?'

But she couldn't. If he'd told her at the start, then maybe she could have made arrangements. The next time perhaps, but not now. He watched her climb out of bed and collect up her clothes. Naked, without the accoutrements of fashion, she looked much younger. He watched as she pulled on her clothes and reversed the transformation, turning herself into the woman he had encountered in the Prater: bright, neat and amused, with a thin veneer of sophistication that made him almost laugh with delight.

'How much do I owe you?'

'You don't *owe* me anything. Let's just say it's a present.'

He found his wallet and counted out enough money to make her eyes widen. 'When might I see you again?' The question was unplanned and absurd, a suggestion that came on the spur of the moment as she lifted herself on her toes to kiss him chastely on the cheek.

'Whenever you like.' She found a pencil and scribbled a number on a piece of paper. 'You can contact me here. That is, if you want to. And I pick up letters at the Nordbahnhof post office, if you want to write a note. You can address them to Kata Kalman.'

Then she opened the door and slipped out into the corridor, leaving him alone in the shabby room, with nothing more than her scent on the sheets and her smell on his fingers.

'I have decided,' he told Liesel in the morning, 'you may have your onyx wall.'

She gave a little cry of pleasure. 'What made you change your mind?'

'Fingernails,' he said. 'Venus's fingernails.'

Interior

That summer they went to Marienbad to take the waters. They took a suite at the Palace Hotel Fürstenhof, where Viktor used to spend summers with his parents. The staff greeted him as Herr Viktor and smiled benignly on the *gnädige Frau* and clucked over Ottilie in her bassinet. Their suite overlooked the spa gardens where morning mist drifted among the trees and gave the place a mysterious, oriental air. In the afternoon the band played outside the Kolonada while people strolled back and forth from one spring to another, sipping from their porcelain flasks and believing, with little evidence, that they were being cured of something other than mere ennui. In the evenings there were concerts – a Chopin recital, some Dvořák, the inevitable *mélange* of Strauss.

Posters in the town announced the new Landauer Popular. Landauer Luxury in a Popular Package was the slogan, above pictures of smiling families driving out to the lakes and the mountains for their summer break, with the children waving gaily out of the windows of their new motor car. They had to put up with the attentions of a journalist from a woman's magazine who wanted to ask Liesel about motherhood in the new decade, and a journalist from *Lidové Noviny* who had questions for Viktor about the economic climate and the new car, but for much of the time they were alone with themselves. The nurse took care of Ottilie while Viktor and Liesel went for walks in the woods above the town, Liesel barelegged in shorts and hiking boots and looking as young as she had when they first met. Viktor wore a pair of doeskin breeches that gave him the look of a Bohemian farmer. That was what Liesel told him, laughing. 'A very handsome

Bohemian farmer,' she insisted. The summit of their achievement was to hike over the Podhorn to the monastery at Tepl where Liesel was forbidden entry to the library and museum of the monastery because she was a woman. She had to sit on a bench outside and feel self-conscious about her bare knees while Viktor went inside. They laughed disappointment away and felt superior in the face of such absurd prejudice. Indeed the ridiculous temporary separation served somehow to unite them further – in the woods above the monastery they kissed like lovers and even discussed, laughing at their shamelessness, the possibility of making love there and then, in the open air. Perhaps they would have done it despite Liesel's protests but voices among the trees warned of an approaching group of walkers. They pulled apart and hastily composed themselves as a dozen Sokol hikers clattered past.

When they got back to the hotel they undressed straight away, their bodies rank with the sweat of their walk, and made love beneath the open window of their bedroom, with the sound of carriages in the street below. 'I love you, Viktor,' Liesel whispered when they had finished and were lying side by side in the cool air.

'And I love you,' he replied.

She propped herself up on her elbow and looked down at him thoughtfully. 'Would you ever be unfaithful to me?'

'Whatever makes you think of that possibility?'

'Hana says that all men are capable of infidelity. It's in their genes, she says.'

He laughed scornfully.

Exterior

'Look at this,' Oskar said one day. They were in the reading room of the German House, amid the heavy columns and polished leather. He handed Viktor a copy of the *Frankfurter Zeitung*, folded to a page that discussed the political successes of the Nationalsozialistische Deutsche Arbeiterpartei in the recent elections in Germany. Eighteen per cent of the vote, according to the paper. Over one hundred seats in the Reichstag.

'Pogroms!' he said. 'That's what's coming, Viktor. Pogroms.'

Viktor tossed the paper aside. 'How can there be pogroms in Germany? The only people who hold the German economy together are the Jews.'

'Spoken like a Jew,' Oskar said, laughing. 'But you see if I'm not right. Germany is a chimera of a nation. You don't know if it's lion, serpent or goat. The Germans themselves doesn't know either. Like any monster, you can laugh at it if you keep your distance – but you don't want to get too close.' He drew on his cigar and contemplated Viktor thoughtfully. 'How's the new house going? Hana tells me it's going to be super-modern, like that fellow Fuchs builds.'

'They're laying the flooring tomorrow. You should come and see.'

'Too busy, I'm afraid. She tells me it's going to be a sensation.'

'It's not intended to be a sensation. It's intended to be a home.'

'Of course everyone's doing it these days. Building houses in the new style. Look at the Spiassys and their pile. Very nice if you like that kind of thing, but no artistry. It's all the fault of that fellow Loos, isn't it? Ornament is a crime, isn't that the motto? I wish it were – it'd certainly keep us lawyers in business. But I like a bit of decoration myself. Hana always goes on at me for being old-fashioned, but I do. Artistry as well as good design.'

'Universal, that's the idea behind the project: neither Jewish nor German. Nor Czech come to that. International.'

'All glass, isn't it? I prefer solid brick walls, like this place.' This place, the Deutsches Haus, was a confection of neo-Gothic red-brick from the last century, a hybrid of cathedral and castle, another chimera.

The waiter brought their coffee and brandy. 'You know what the Japanese do with their houses?' Viktor asked.

'No idea, old fellow. What do the Japanese do?'

'They build them out of paper. Then when there's an earth-quake and they collapse no one gets hurt.'

Oskar looked round the massive room, at the fluted pillars and plaster swags and ornate gilded ceiling with its massive chandeliers. 'I suppose people would get hurt all right if this lot collapsed.'

'Crushed to death,' said Viktor, 'all of us.'

The conversation was nothing, a mere jot in the continuum of social intercourse. Nevertheless something stuck, like a speck of dust in the eye. Beneath the calm surface of the new country Viktor felt the tremors of uncertainty.

Tiptoeing as if on eggshells they laid the flooring upstairs – squares of Italian travertine like a mother-of-pearl lining to the shell of the building. Days later they mounted the glass in the living room, the glaziers manoeuvring the wide transparent sheets with all the care of ordnance workers handling nitro-glycerine in the armaments factory on the river Svratka. And as they raised the panes into place, quite suddenly the empty space between two concrete floors metamorphosed into the Glass Room.

Liesel and Viktor stood and marvelled at it. It had become a palace of light, light bouncing off the chrome pillars, light reful-gent on the walls, light glistening on the dew in the garden, light reverberating from the glass. It was as though they stood inside a crystal of salt. 'Isn't it wonderful,' she exclaimed, looking round with an expression of amazement. 'You feel so free, so uncon-strained. The sensation of space, of all things being possible. Don't you think it is wonderful, Viktor? Don't you think that Rainer has created a masterpiece for us?'

In the autumn they travelled to Vienna to finalise decisions about the interior. It was months since Viktor's last visit to the city. As he and Liesel arrived at the Nordbahnhof he wondered whether he might see Kata there, perhaps picking up her mail at the post office; and if he did, what would happen? Would she recognise him and smile secretively as she passed by? And what would he feel at the sight of her? Embarrassment and guilt? Or maybe disgust, that he could succumb to the attractions of such a woman? But the concern was misplaced. Vienna was a city of two million people and his presence in the Leopoldstadt quarter was merely transitory; yet as the taxi cab drove away from the station, there, ineluctably, was the great wheel, the Riesenrad, turning slowly in the cool autumnal air above their heads.

The architect's studio was in the Landstrasse district, in the attic of an old apartment block. The space was decorated in the modern manner, with white walls and spare furnishings, a hint of the way their house would look. Together with von Abt and his assistant they discussed issues of wall coverings and flooring, the minutiae of interior design. They talked about furniture – the 'Venice' chair, which had been intended for the Biennale pavilion, and the new one, the 'Landauer' chair, which would be specially for this gem of a house that was nearing completion in Město. And then there was something extra, a special creation that he was proposing to call the 'Liesel' chair in honour of Frau Liesel Landauer if she would be so gracious as to accept the homage.

'How wonderful,' she said, blushing, as she sat in the eponymous chair – all cantilevered chromed steel and black leather. Viktor sat in the prototype Landauer chair and watched.

'This is the disposition of the chairs in the living room,' von Abt explained, showing the drawings that he had prepared. He indicated the sitting area in front of the onyx wall and the dining area enclosed by its semicircle partition of Macassar wood. 'The dining table will be circular and able to seat six. However, it may be extended to seat a maximum of twenty-four.'

Liesel laughed at the idea – 'When on earth will we have that number?' – while Viktor imagined a horde of relatives descending on the place, with views and ideas about how he should be running the factory and the house and his life. The meeting moved on to other matters, questions of textiles and soft furnishings, the curtains and carpets. Von Abt's assistant already had ideas, already had samples, already knew. She displayed them like a market stallholder showing her wares, her patter fluid and convincing. 'It'll be a revolution,' she said, 'a casting off of the past. A new way of living.'

Liesel's eye shone with delight.

It was when they were just finishing the meeting – mid-afternoon, with the prospect of taking the evening train back to Město – that a telephone call came for Herr Landauer from the Vienna office of the Landauer Motor Company. A problem had arisen that needed discussion. Was Herr Landauer available for a meeting the next morning? It was imperative, something to do with import quotas, a matter of a malleable government official, the possibility of financial persuasion achieving wonders.

He turned helplessly to Liesel. It was understandable that she was reluctant to stay overnight when they had only intended a single day's visit. It was natural that she wished to get back to Ottilie who was even now taking her first tottering steps. It was inevitable that the plan should be changed: Liesel would return home as arranged – Laník the chauffeur would be there to meet her at the station – while Viktor would find a room at the Bristol or the Sacher and attend this nuisance of a meeting the next morning.

'But you've nothing with you.'

'I'll buy what I need. And the hotel can launder my shirt overnight.' There was no difficulty, absolutely no difficulty whatsoever. This was the modern life, the way things worked in industry and commerce. If you weren't able to adapt you would die, like Darwin said. Adapt or die. So he accompanied Liesel to the station and saw her off on the evening train to Město and then walked back down the platform by himself.

Crowds pushed past him, workers hurrying to catch local trains home to the workers' quarters in the north of the city. Steam blasted upwards towards the iron and glass roof. Doors slammed and whistles blew and trains drew out of the station in

66

that deliberate way they have, arms moving out as though to grasp the steel rails and drag them backwards. Only Viktor Landauer stood still. He possessed a telephone number, scribbled on a piece of paper and folded in his pocket diary. He was conscious of it inside his jacket, had been aware of it throughout the summer as his diary lay on his dressing table during the night, felt it whenever he opened the booklet to note something down or look something up. Just a number. Four digits, scribbled with a pencil. He could just as well have erased it. So why hadn't he done so?

He approached the end of the platform where the gates were, and beyond them concourse with the ticket offices and waiting rooms. There was a quickening of anticipation as he pushed through the doors and took a booth to make the telephone call. For an instant, as he waited for an answer, he hoped that there would be no reply. And then the ringing was interrupted and a man's voice was speaking to him.

'*Die Goldene Kugel*,' the voice said.

Viktor hadn't really expected her to answer. The way she had said it – 'You can contact me here' – had seemed to preclude the possibility of it being her own line. 'That is, if you want to,' she had added.

'I want to speak to Fräulein Kata. Kata Kalman.'

'Hold on.' There was noise, the receiver being laid down, the sound of voices, and then the receiver picked up once more and a different voice, still male, asking, 'Who is this?'

'I want to speak to Fräulein Kata.'

'Who is it? Does she know you?'

'I'm a friend.'

'What's your name?'

His heart stumbled. 'Viktor,' he said. Herr Viktor.'

'Hang on.'

There was more noise off. The wooden kiosk was closer by far than the cabin of the Riesenrad, a close, sweltering box, dulled to the sounds from outside, insulated from the reality of the station concourse. It held within it the stale smell of other people, those itinerants who hung around railway stations, the indigent and homeless. There was something scored into the woodwork at eye level: *My little crocodile, I love you*, the scratching said. Viktor's excitement died, to be replaced by a sweat of shame and embarrassment.

'Hello?'

'Yes?'

'She's not here. You can leave a message if you like.'

'I wanted to see her this evening.'

'I don't know if she'll be around. You come round and she might get a look at you. To see whether she likes what she sees.'

'This evening. Tell her I'll come this evening. Where are you?'

'Praterstrasse 47.' And then the phone went down and he walked out into the cooler air of the post office and the racket of the railway station and the crush of people coming in through the entrance archways from the street.

Outside the station he contemplated the city. Trams clanged on the rails, heading towards the Praterstern. Cars hooted, swirling past the horse-drawn cabs, the future overtaking the past. Crowds pushed past him, sure of where they were going. He could still choose not to do this. He faced a wealth of possibilities and he could still choose.

Die Goldene Kugel, the Golden Globe, was a restaurant and café halfway down the Praterstrasse. Viktor stepped off the tram and went past the outside tables into the warm plush of the interior. He took a seat at a banquette just inside the door and called for the menu. There was the usual bustle of the early evening, waiters cruising between the tables, early diners ordering, the talk heavy-laden with the Viennese accent. He ordered a quarter of white wine and something to eat and then he waited, not knowing how to make his presence known, not knowing whether he should even be here, not knowing why he was, in fact. In the event it was she who found him.

'It's Herr Viktor, isn't it?' The voice came from behind him. Unmistakeably, even after the passage of months, it was *her* voice. There was something hoarse about it, laughter lurking in the shadows. He looked round. She had just come in through the main door and stood beside the coatstand on which he had hung his coat and hat. 'Kata,' he said. He rose from his seat, suddenly confused, suddenly no longer in control of anything. They shook hands, absurdly they shook hands like two acquaintances meeting

68

by chance. 'How are you? Sit down. How are you?' He pulled out a chair. She sat opposite him, a small – smaller than he'd remembered – woman with a kind of prettiness about her features. He was content just to see her, that was the ridiculous thing, almost overwhelmed with happiness in fact. He didn't understand that either: why should the mere presence of this almost unknown woman make him happy? But he was happy. Like a child.

She accepted his offer of a cigarette and as she leaned towards him to light it he remembered the taste of tobacco on her mouth. Not unpleasant. Dry as her voice. 'They told me you were around. Fancy that. How are you keeping?'

'Fine, I'm fine. You're looking very well.'

She laughed. 'Me? Oh, I get along.' One of the waiters came over and she asked for a glass. 'I've already eaten,' she said. 'I'll just keep you company 'til you're ready.'

Why did he like that idea so much? Why did the fact of this girl merely keeping him company make him so content? He poured her some wine, and she sipped and looked at him with that smile, as though she knew something that he didn't. Maybe that was true, maybe in the way of such women, she did have secret knowledge. 'Well, well. I'd quite given you up for lost. And here you are.'

He nodded. Here he was. The fact was evident. Here he was, in a café on the Praterstrasse with a woman who was not his wife but with whom he was going to make love. Was that the expression? Have sex. Fornicate. The words stumbled through his mind and were all chased away by the sight of her sitting there, the particular shape of her face, the curve of cheek and brow that he had recalled so vividly. Heart-shaped. Her eyes were so blue. He hadn't remembered that accurately. A blue that made them seem transparent, as though you were gazing through them to the horizon. And the childish hands with their bitten fingernails. He pushed his plate aside – 'Look, I don't really feel hungry' – and she smiled as though she understood such matters, the connections between physiology and emotion.

They went to the same hotel as before. Maybe she was known there, although no one seemed to recognise her. There was the same man on the reception desk, the same porter who, with the same expressionless indifference, showed them to what may have

69

been the same room. But this time they kissed almost like ordinary lovers, her lips just pressing against his, soft and fragile.

'You're married, aren't you? Have you got kids?' Her sharp talk, that Viennese accent moderated by other tones – the sounds of Slovakia, the hints of Magyar. He'd forgotten that, and the rediscovery delighted him.

'A daughter.'

'Lovely little thing, is she?'

'Lovely,' he agreed. 'She's called Ottilie.'

She unbuttoned her blouse and hung it on the back of a chair. He sat on the bed and watched her step out of her skirt, suddenly transformed from the public figure to the private: the clumsy underclothes, the tapes and clips, the hips that seemed that bit wider than when she was clothed, the curve of her thighs and the narrowness of her knees, as vulnerable as a child's. Her skin was white, almost luminous in the shadows of the room. 'How old is she then?'

'She's just a baby. Seventeen months.'

'I love babies.'

It seemed an absurd conversation, the kind casual acquaintances might have had anywhere, in any public place. Yet he was having it here, in this narrow room, between the windows with their view, obscured by muslin curtains, of an anonymous Viennese street and the bed in which he was about to have illicit sex, sex that would have shamed him had it been with Liesel. 'And how's the work?' he asked.

She paused, looking at him, her hands at the buttons of her brassiere. 'It's okay.'

'Hats.'

'Yeah, hats. I've changed job, actually. Get a bit less but I can come and go as I please, more or less.'

'Sounds ideal.'

She tossed the brassiere aside. Her breasts were full and loose, fuller than Liesel's. 'Actually it's working for myself. I've started taking work in, dressmaking stuff. Contacts, you know what I mean? It's always like that in business, isn't it?'

'Contacts? Exactly.'

He reached out and took her hands and pulled her towards him so that she stood directly in front of him. He could feel the

70

warmth of her body. It carried with it her smell, a flowery perfume with, beneath it, something else that was dark and intimate and animal. 'My little dressmaker,' he called her. 'You're very lovely, aren't you?'

But she shook her head. 'I'm just what you see. Nothing special. A bit of a bitch, at times.'

'Not with me.'

'But you're paying me to be nice to you, aren't you?'

'Would you be horrid if I weren't? Are you horrid to your boyfriend?'

'I don't have a boyfriend. Not at the moment. I'm off men, really.'

He cupped one soft breast in his hand, surprised by its mass. 'What about me?'

She looked down on him with an expression that he thought might be regret. 'You're different. I can't get someone like you, can I? Except like this. You want me to stay the whole night this time? Because I can, if that's what you'd like. I've made arrangements, see?'

Of course he did. He wanted to wake in the morning and find her there with him. If not love itself, he wanted the simulacrum of love.

Completion

Work continued throughout the autumn – the fittings, the furnishings, those things that transform a shell into a house and a house into a home. Lorries drew up on Blackfield Road and men in grey overalls humped packages into the building while neighbours watched from nearby gardens. Word went round. The doors were hung, the bathrooms were fitted and tiled, in white up to the ceiling so that they took on the plain sterility of a laboratory or clinic, the floors were laid. In the Glass Room they mounted the onyx wall. The slabs had veins of amber and honey, like the contours of some distant, prehistoric landscape. They were polished to a mirror-like gloss, and once in place, the stone seemed to take hold of the light, blocking it, reflecting it, warming it with a soft, feminine hand and then, when the sun set over the Špilas fortress and shone straight in at the stone, glowing fiery red.

'Who would have imagined,' Hana said when she first saw the phenomenon, 'that such passion could lie inside inert rock?'

Finally they laid the linoleum, linoleum the colour of ivory, as lucid as spilled milk. During the day the light from the windows flooded over it and rendered it almost translucent, as though a shallow pool lay between the entrance and the glass; during the evening the ceiling lights – petalled blooms of frosted glass – threw reflections down into the depths. On the upper floor there were rooms, *zimmer*, boxes with walls and doors; but down here there was room, *raum*, space.

Von Abt moved around the place like a sculptor working with a team of assistants, but the novelty was this: the house was both the work of art and the atelier in which it was being created, the means and the end rolled into one. 'It is like a mother and its child,' he told Liesel, 'both at the same time.'

Curtains of black and natural Shantung silk and beige velvet slid on their runners, closing off areas of the Glass Room as quietly and discreetly as a whispered aside. Carpets – hand-woven woollen rugs – were laid down in their precise geometrical place. And then finally the furniture arrived, the fitted items first: shelves and cupboards for the bedroom, sideboards for the dining area, shelving for the library. Men in white coats moved back and forth like attendants in a medical clinic. Carpenters assembled the circular table. And then came the chairs, the Landauer chairs for the dining table, the Liesel chairs in the sitting area, their steel frames reflecting the light and their upholstery mirroring the carpets, and every piece fitting into the whole, which was like a puzzle in which pieces slotted together in a pattern that it was both intricate and logical.

Liesel's mother examined the house with the disapproving eye of the nineteenth century. 'It's like an office,' she said. 'Like a laboratory, like a hospital. Not like a home at all.'

'Mother, it's the future.'

'The future!' the older woman retorted, as though giving vent to a curse. But Viktor and Liesel watched their future world growing around them and they thought that it was a kind of perfection, the finest instrument for living.

The building was formally signed over and they moved in at the beginning of December, when the weather was cold and sleet dashed itself against the windows and air from the boiler in the basement breathed upwards through the vents at the base of the windows and moved gently through the volume of the Glass Room to bring a warm, dry, gentle atmosphere vaguely reminiscent of a spring day. Liesel stood in a light silk dress and watched the first snowflakes settle, more quietly than feathers, on the garden. The garden itself and the view beyond seemed to be assumed into the interior, the distant Špilas fortress as much a part of the room as a painting hanging on the wall. But inside the room there was no decoration – ornament is crime – except for a single item, a life-size female torso sculpted by the French artist Maillol, the belly faintly swollen as though in early pregnancy, the breasts full, the hips wide, the face with something of the fecund composure of a Renoir nude.

'That is what you need,' Hana had said of the sculpture after she had seen it in the gallery of a Prague art dealer. 'Some touch of the female.'

To Liesel's surprise, von Abt had agreed. So she and Viktor travelled up to Prague to make the purchase and the sculpture now stood on a plinth beside the onyx wall and looked over her left shoulder at whoever might be in the chairs in the sitting area.

'It is beautiful,' Liesel said to Viktor, speaking of the sculpture, and the room itself, and of the whole house. 'Perfect.'

That was it: perfection. Perfection of proportion, of illumination, of mood and manner. Beauty made manifest.

Housewarming

Viktor and Liesel hold a house-warming party. What started out as an informal gathering becomes like the opening of an art exhibition, made worse because the man himself is there – Rainer von Abt. He flies in from Berlin and is fetched from the airfield by the driver. The guests are delighted by this manifestation of the modern age, this architect who descends from the sky for something as ephemeral as a party. Liesel greets him as he steps out of the car. 'Everyone,' she warns him as she leads him inside and down the stairs, 'everyone has been dying to meet you.'

And there they all are, as hostess and architect enter the Glass Room: the intelligentsia of Město, the musicians and composers, the artists and the architects, the critics and the writers, the businessmen and the industrialists, all of them waiting for the great man's appearance, along with journalists and a photographer from the society page of one of the local newspapers. The architects Fuchs and Wiesener are there, each full of grudging praise for von Abt's work; and Filla the cubist who finds echoes of van Doesburg in the plain geometry of the house; and the composer Václav Kaprál with his pretty daughter Vítězslava. Von Abt bows his head over female hands, and shakes manly ones, and pronounces himself delighted with everything but especially delighted with this wonderful house that he has brought to fruition. 'A work of art like this,' he tells one of the journalists, 'demands that the life lived in it be a work of art as well. I am certain that Viktor Landauer and his beautiful wife will do the place justice.'

Viktor makes a little speech. He welcomes the guests, first in

Czech and then in German, and calls for applause for the architect, and when the clapping has died away he talks about André Breton's new novel, *Nadja*, which one of the guests – he nods at Hana Hanáková – has lent him. 'In this novel the author wrote something like this,' he tells them, and cleverly, although he claims to have prepared nothing, he has the whole passage by heart: '"I shall live in my glass house where you can always see who comes to call, where everything hanging from the ceiling and on the walls stays where it is as if by magic, where I sleep nights in a glass bed, under glass sheets, where the words *who I am* will sooner or later appear etched by a diamond."' People laugh at this wittily appropriate quotation. Have they read Breton? If not, they pretend they have. 'Well, this glass house says who Liesel and I are,' Viktor tells them, taking her hand. 'In our wonderful glass house you can see everything. And in this spirit of openness, with no advance notice and no rehearsal, Maestro Němec has agreed to play for us.'

An expectant hush falls as Němec takes his seat at the piano. 'I believe,' he says, 'that this instrument has never yet been played before an audience.' There is a call for him to speak up, those at the back cannot hear. He raises his voice a fraction. 'It gives me much pleasure to caress' – he touches the Bösendorfer with expert fingers – 'such an untried maiden in the midst of this beautiful and, until today, virginal glass house.'

There is more laughter, more applause and then the maestro begins to play – hesitantly at first as though he is unsure of the instrument and is listening for its voice, but then with growing assurance and a faint nod of approval – a piece by Leoš Janáček, mentor of both Kaprál and Němec himself, the man in whose shadow all of the assembled musicians of Město move. When he finishes there are calls for an encore, but he stands and bows and holds out his hand towards Kaprál's daughter. 'Let me pass the responsibility on to the next generation,' Němec says, and a small shiver of delight runs through the guests. Vítězslava Kaprálová is something of a prodigy. Already, at the tender age of fifteen, she is enrolled at the Conservatory and studying composition. She blushes under their collective gaze but still seems remarkably assured as she takes her place at the keyboard. No Janáček for her, but something by Ravel that she is preparing at the

Conservatory for her finals, one of the movements from the piano suite *Gaspard de la Nuit*, entitled 'Ondine'. It is a delicate, wavering piece that somehow seems appropriate to this space, this room, the winter light flooding the plate-glass windows, the people milling about, their forms reflected vaguely in the flooring and precisely but laterally compressed in the slender chrome-plated pillars. When the notes – subtle, apparently repeated but never repetitive – die away into the death of the nymph Ondine, the pianist holds herself quite still for a moment, hands poised over the keys, before looking round at her listeners with a quick, nymph-like smile.

There is more applause, even more than Němec received, and laughter and the clinking of glasses. 'Bravo,' they cry, and, '*výborně*!' How wonderful that a girl so pretty and so young can play with such assurance. And Němec bows towards her and takes her hand – a fragile thing, as light as a bird – and raises it to his lips.

'This is the artistic future of our country,' he announces. 'Vitulka and people like her. A young country with so much energy and so much talent.'

While all this is going on Hana has walked round the other side of the onyx wall and is looking out on the cold garden and the winter trees. 'What do you think?' Liesel asks, coming to stand beside her.

'I think she's only fifteen, so what the hell's he doing flirting with her?'

'I meant the house.'

Hana turns. 'You know what I think about the house, darling. I think it's mesmerising.'

'I don't know what I've done to deserve it,' Liesel tells her.

'Married a wealthy man, my dear. Enjoy it while you can.'

'What do you mean by that?'

Hana shrugs, looking at the view once more, the cold outside. Behind them there is more applause, and laughter as Němec takes the place of the girl at the keyboard and breaks into something different, something fashionable and American and Negro. Honky-tonk, he calls it. Some even clap along to the music. It seems so modern, so hopeful and careless.

'Well, it's too good to last, isn't it?' says Hana.

'What is?'

'Everything.'

'What do you mean, everything?'

'The good times. All this. The world we live in.'

She is right, of course. They crowd into the space of the Glass Room like passengers on the observation deck of a luxury liner. Some of them maybe peering out through the windows onto the pitching surface of the city but, in their muddle of Czech and German, almost all are ignorant of the cold outside and the gathering storm clouds, the first sign of the tempest that is coming. They will argue and debate about trivial things, and until it is too late they will largely ignore the storm on the horizon. Of all the people at the party, of all the people applauding the pianists, drinking the champagne, eating the smoked salmon and the chicken legs, it is only Hana Hanáková who feels that breath of cold air as she looks out on the peaceful city and the setting sun.

Happy Families

Is the Landauer House habitable? one of the journalists present at the party asks in an article in the next edition of *Die Form*, the architectural review of the *Deutscher Werkbund*. A debate ensues in the columns of the journal. Some correspondents claim that the whole building is a lapse of political taste, an exercise in bourgeois excess, and that the duty of modern architecture is to house the working class in decent, well-built dwellings like the Weissenhofsiedlung development in Stuttgart or the Karl-Marx-Hof in Vienna or the Baťa development in Zlin, not to create palaces for plutocrats. Others decry the mean-mindedness of such a critique and extol the purity of line, the austerity of design, the perfection of taste, the sensation they felt (those of them lucky enough to have been invited) of actually being *inside* a work of art. Still others debate the principle of combining dining area with sitting area, study and library. One correspondent even worries about the intrusion of food smells into the sitting area. 'What if the lady of the house wishes to rearrange the furniture?' another asks. 'Will she be able to upset the perfect symmetry of the interior, the careful balance, the proportions? How can one live from day to day in such a place?'

'Have you seen this?' Liesel asks Viktor, showing him a copy of the journal.

He glances through it with a disparaging expression and tosses it aside. 'Absurd,' he says.

'But they deserve a response.'

'Why on earth? Let them argue. It's like children fighting over

79

something they've seen in a shop window. None of them can have it, so what good does fighting do?'

So it is she who, sitting diligently at the desk in the library behind the onyx wall, writes a letter to the editor of *Die Form*. She upbraids their correspondent for speaking without personal knowledge and for introducing political theory into the question of what is simply a home. She and her husband are not victims of Rainer von Abt's taste but collaborators with him in this inspiring project. In the living area, the curtains, employed to divide off different sections as desired, work wonderfully well in creating spaces with as much privacy as one might wish and she can assure readers of the journal that no cooking smells have intruded on the sitting area from the dining area! Living inside a work of art is an experience of sublime delight – the tranquillity of the large living room and the intimacy of the smaller rooms on the upper floor combined together give her family the most remarkable experience of modern living.

She hands the finished letter to Viktor for his approval. He puts down his copy of *Lidové Noviny* and reads it through, smiling up at her with something other than mere agreement. 'Come,' he says, holding out his hand, 'prove it.'

'Prove what?'

'Prove what you say, about creating spaces with as much privacy as one might wish.'

She looks shocked. 'Not here. Someone might come.'

'Then your thesis is disproved.' He still holds her hand, drawing her towards the sofa where he is sitting. His other hand is on her leg, running up the back of her thigh beneath her dress.

'Viktor!'

And so, with the curtains resolutely drawn to ensure that an intruder improbably clambering down through the dense growth of trees on the slope immediately outside the Winter Garden should not be able to spy on them and the door from upstairs resolutely locked in case the nanny (who was always in her bed by this time) should happen, just happen to come in, and the door to the kitchens also locked in case Laníková, the chauffeur's sister who does the cooking, should make her presence felt; thus barricaded and shuttered into a space that seems to deny the very possibility of barricading and shuttering, Liesel consents to have her skirt lifted round her waist and her knickers – silk French knickers with disgracefully wide legs (a present from Hana, of course) – pulled down to her ankles.

'You haven't got a mackintosh,' she whispers in Viktor's ear. Mackintosh, raincoat, *Regenmantel*, is their code word for condom.

'Does it matter? It's only a day or two, isn't it?'

They giggle together and then, suddenly stirred by the moment and perhaps by the laughter, cling tightly to each other for a while, Liesel thinking how much she loves this solemn and successful man who is yet bold enough to construct such a house for her, and loving enough to want her like this, uncomfortably and daringly on the sofa, and paternal enough to adore their daughter as the second most precious thing in his world, the first being, because he tells her this, whispering it in her ear, herself.

Afterwards they settle down to a quiet evening listening to the radio and reading, and as she sits there Liesel fancies that she can feel Viktor's seed inside her, flooding through her womb, searching for that elusive egg, and perhaps finding it.

Birth

At the Landauerovka test circuit the Landauer Popular, that curved beetle of a motor car, chutters round and round the track. Trade delegations from Austria, from Poland, from Germany look on approvingly. The new advertising poster shows the same families as in the summer one, except that now they are heading for snow-capped mountains, their smiles equally cheery as in summer because the Popular car boasts an air-cooled engine originally designed by Oberusal for aircraft. Air Cooling Eliminates Winter Worries, the new slogan boasts. 'This is the future,' Viktor explains to prospective customers in his quiet, intense manner. 'The liberation of the working man and his family.' He travels to Berlin, to Paris, to Vienna. Everywhere he takes with him the new creed and proclaims it with all the enthusiasm of a prophet. 'This is where the world of commerce is leading us,' he explains. 'Into a world of peace and trade, where the only battles fought are battles for market share.'

Meanwhile, in the cool and luminous house on Blackfield Road, Liesel grows into her new pregnancy. She has taken to wearing white – white blouses, long white dresses – and walking around the house in bare feet. Mistress of her new domain she floats through the ethereal house just as the house itself, supported by steel and artifice, floats above the city.

'You don't know how lucky you are, darling,' Hana tells her, 'living in this wonderful place when I am condemned to live in a museum. But Oskar won't move. He says he likes four solid walls around him.' She looks at Liesel with that equivocal glance, part envy, part desire. 'And pregnant for a second time! I've been trying for a baby for ages—'

'You've been trying to get pregnant?'

'However much I try nothing seems to happen. I have even' – Hana whispers it as if someone else might hear, although they are alone together in the white and liberating spaces of the Glass Room – 'tried to get pregnant by Němec.'

'Hana!'

She makes a face, that down-turn of the mouth that frightens men and fascinates them. 'But nothing doing. I'm as sterile as a *babka*.'

Liesel relates the conversation to Viktor with a note of amazement in her voice. 'Can you imagine trying to get pregnant by one man in order to please another? How fantastic she is!'

But to Viktor it is Liesel who now appears fantastic, a shining refulgent creature whose swollen belly seems to elevate her from the floor of the Glass Room, as though, when she crosses it on her long, naked feet, in fact she is floating a few inches above the shining linoleum. In his mind her pregnancy, born in the physical and erotic, elevates her above mere flesh. How strange, this metamorphosis from flesh to spirit, mediated by the frame of the Glass Room that is intended to be so literal and exact and yet has become sublime. By contrast the compartment of the Vienna train is closed and dark and battered by noise as it rattles through the bleak borderlands. He buries himself in his paper and tries to think of other, neutral things – markets and investments and recession – while the train crosses over the brown slick of the Danube and edges cautiously past tenements and marshalling yards before sliding into the Nordbahnhof. The station is a racket of sound, a great drum of a place. People push past him indifferently as he walks towards the barriers and the post office with its fetid little telephone cabins. The graffito cut into the wood is familiar now: *My little crocodile, I love you.* Her voice whispers in his ear, as though confiding a great secret. 'I got your note.'

'I worried that you wouldn't pick it up.'

'I'm reliable like that.'

'So are you free?'

'Of course I'm free.'

She is waiting at the Goldene Kugel, amid the anonymous

bustle of the café, the coming and going of customers, the waiters in their aprons cruising between the tables with trays held upwards on the palms of their hands like circus performers bringing off a deft trick. He sits down at her table and watches her fingering the stem of her wine glass. She never seems nervous, and yet there are those bitten fingernails. 'How are you doing?' she asks, and smiles at him as though she means it.

'I'm fine. Business is all right, we're keeping our heads above water. What about you?'

She shrugs. 'All right. You know.'

But he doesn't know. She comes out of the anonymous world of the city, out of the mix of German and Slav and Magyar, and there are things he knows about her and things he doesn't. He knows her taste in chocolates and coffee and wine, her love of popular music and operetta – they have been to the Carl-Theater together and seen something by Lehár – and her views on politics. But he does not know anyone she knows, or where she works, or what she does when she is not with him, or where she lives. She comes whenever he calls her, but from where she comes and to where she returns he has no idea. He guesses only that she has other 'friends' like him, but who they are and how often she sees them he does not know. Only once he didn't send a note in advance and when he rang he found that she couldn't see him. On that occasion he spent the night alone, consumed by anger and jealousy. But the next time they made an appointment he asked no questions and she told him no stories. She never enquires about his life, so why should he know anything about hers? Their relationship, part venal, part affectionate, exists only in the brief moments when they are together.

'What do you want to do?' she asks.

'I just want to be with you. Isn't that absurd?'

She puts her head on one side. She is wearing one of her hats, a small thing of black felt with a red feather. 'Why should it be absurd? It's nice. I like being with you.'

They book into a different hotel from usual, still one of those that proliferate around railway stations, but where the gilt is a little less faded and the carpets a little less threadbare. They book in, as always, under the name Richter, a name chosen at random on the very first occasion but one which now, with its hints of rightness and rectitude, seems to Viktor to have acquired a certain irony. When they have sex it is with a peculiar intensity, a passion bordering on the very edge of anger. And afterwards she sleeps in his arms, with an innocence that could not be feigned.

Martin was born, there being some problem with his presentation, by forceps delivery. For days after the birth Liesel lay in hospital with a high fever, at times slipping into delirium, sometimes conscious enough to call for her child or her husband or Hana, but often merely there on the mysterious borderline between sleep and unconsciousness. The nursing staff and doctors spoke in hushed voices as though they were already in the presence of the dead. At her mother's instigation a Catholic priest was even brought in to pray at the bedside and perhaps administer – the matter was never clear – the last rites. Viktor visited as frequently as was possible but it was Hana who devoted herself to Liesel through the dangerous crisis of her illness, thus showing herself, against Viktor's expectation, to be far more than a fair-weather friend. 'I almost feel she's one of the family,' he confessed when Liesel was on the mend, still bedridden but able to receive visitors. 'I don't know how I would have managed without her.'

Liesel regarded her husband from the depths of her pillows. Her face was sculpted into angular and rather intimidating contours by the receding illness. The baby nuzzled hopefully at her breast, trying to suck at milk that wasn't there. 'I hope she doesn't seduce *you*, Viktor.'

Viktor was horrified. 'Do you really think she would attempt such a thing? And at such a time? I thought she was your closest friend.'

She shrugged. 'She has a very different way of looking at things from us. Haven't you understood that yet? She'd probably tell me all about it, and call it sharing.'

'And what would you feel about it?'

'*Are* you interested in her?'

'Don't be ridiculous.'

She looked away, out through the window where there were trees and a fragment of anonymous sky. 'Then why ask?'

Starved of its feed, the baby began to cry. A nurse took the baby away. Viktor felt a need to explain, to justify his feelings.

'Hana is like a sister to me, that's all,' he said.

Liesel smiled. 'Don't think fraternal love is any protection, my darling. Hana would have no compunction about sleeping with her brother.'

Attenuated by the fever, tall and gaunt like a prisoner of war returning after liberation, Liesel came back home. She had a nurse to tend her during her convalescence. Viktor's dressing room now became his bedroom so that Liesel could continue her recovery in peace and the nurse could attend her as needed. By day she walked, a cool white ghost, in the open spaces of the Glass Room; by night she lay alone, motionless beneath a sheet. People treated her as though she had come back from the dead, a Lazarus who had no real right to be walking on the earth. With the baby in a bassinet by her side she sat in front of the great glass windows and looked out on the view of the city with the distracted expression of someone who doesn't quite recognise where she is. Her voice had changed during her illness. It had become soft and melodic, almost ethereal. 'I almost left you, didn't I, Viktor?' she said. 'What would you have done without me?'

'I have no idea.'

'I think you would have soon found another woman. I only hope that you would have chosen wisely.'

'Why on earth are you talking like this?'

'Coming close to death changes one, do you know that? That's what Benno told me in his letters and that's what I've learned now. You consider things that were unthinkable before. I think you would have gone with Hana.'

'Don't be absurd.'

'Oh, you'd have got on well together as long as she stayed with Oskar. You share the same tastes – modern art, music, literature, all that. And Hana would have kept you from falling victim to any pretty woman with a sympathetic smile. She would have been ideal.'

'You are my ideal,' he said.

That made her laugh. It was difficult to read her laughter these days. There was irony there, and a certain bitterness. 'Of course I am, darling. Of course I am.'

*

86

In the spring Liesel and Viktor made a return visit to Venice. It was their first holiday alone since Ottilie's birth and they stayed in the same hotel as they had on their honeymoon, in the very same suite they had had before, attempting – the motive was never expressed openly – to recapture the past. But beneath the calm surface of their affection there was this new remoteness. Perhaps it had to do with the difficulties of the birth and the subsequent illness. Perhaps it was something in his own behaviour, a distance of mind even when there was no distance at all of body. These things are subtle. Whatever the cause, the effect was clear: Liesel, who had once, in that very room in the Venice hotel, arched her back at the surprising moment of orgasm and cried out in an ecstasy as intense as pain, now seemed to have the even tenor of her being barely disturbed by the act of sex. Perhaps this was what one expected as a relationship matured: love translated into affection, and lust into a kind of placid contentment.

A Day in the Life

A day in the life of the Landauer House. The parents wake early, at six o'clock, the windows of their rooms black with night or flooded with light depending on the season. Make it spring. Dawn is breaking. When the curtains are pulled back and the shutters raised (an electric motor whirrs quietly) they each look out across the terrace and the shadows of the children's sandpit. One of them – usually it is Viktor – comes through into the other's room. They talk a while. He bends to kiss her. Once this brief morning kiss would translate into something else, a quickening of the flesh, a quick and affectionate conjunction. But that has become a rare event these days. Soon there is the sound of movement from elsewhere on the same floor: Liba, the nurse, has woken the children and hurried them, grumbling, to their own bathroom.

Liesel and Viktor's bathroom is cool and spare, like a sunny day in late autumn. Their voices echo against the high tiling as they wash. Liesel takes her bath in the evening, while Viktor has a morning shower. By the time they have finished, the dumb-waiter has rumbled up from the kitchens to present them with a tray bearing coffee. Viktor sips the coffee as he dresses and talks about the coming day, the meetings, the tour of the factory that is scheduled for the afternoon, the telephone conversation he must book with someone in France to discuss the possibility of a joint project – something to do with aircraft, a passion he has. A light-weight, cheap cabin monoplane, ideal for businessmen. The planned partnership with Dornier fell through a few months ago and now he is talking with the Société des Avions Marcel Bloch.

Once dressed Liesel goes to see the children, already awake and dressing under the devoted eye of Liba. Martin is being taught to do up the buttons of his shirt. Ottilie is sitting on the floor to show him how shoe laces are tied – a skill she has only recently acquired and is now trying to diffuse amongst lesser beings with all the enthusiasm of a prophet. She is light and skinny, a proto-beauty whose looks will remain unformed for some years, so much so that throughout her childhood she will consider herself ugly and indeed by most people will be considered plain but interesting until, at the age of about eighteen, it suddenly becomes clear that the solemn structures of Liesel's face and the austerity of Viktor's have been melded into something that borrows from each and yet gains some indefinable quality of grace and softness all of its own. But for the moment she is just a little girl with an insistent voice, pale, ill-formed features and awkward legs. 'That's not a very elegant way to sit,' her mother remarks as the girl sits to tie her laces.

'Liba gave me clean knickers.'

'That, my dear, is hardly the point.'

Liesel speaks German to the children, while the nanny, Liba – Liběna, Liběnka, the language abounds in diminutives – speaks Czech. The result of this is that both children, particularly Ottilie, move easily from one language to the other. 'They mustn't be labelled,' Viktor has always insisted, 'not by language, nor by culture, nor family or anything. They must be brought up as citizens of the world.'

Once they are dressed, Liba and Liesel take the children downstairs where breakfast is already laid out in the dining area. Viktor greets them in the library where he is drinking a second cup of coffee and glancing through the newspaper. The children are noisy and enthusiastic around him, while he is quiet and thoughtful, probably as a result of what he has been reading in *Lidové Noviny*.

'Leave Tatínka in peace,' Liba says, ushering the children to their breakfast.

Liesel glances at the story that Victor has been reading – Jewish doctors in Germany are forbidden to treat non-Jewish patients or something similar – and shakes her head. The story is there, not here. It is over the border in another country, another world, another universe. 'Surely it'll all blow over.'

He doesn't answer. Whether or not it will all blow over is not the point. The point is, this is happening at this very moment, to fellow Jews. In the last few years, since the building of the house in fact, Viktor has come to feel his Jewishness. This is not some atavistic rediscovery of his origins but the acceptance of a simple fact of inheritance, like having a quirky familial deformity, a Habsburg lip perhaps. To some people, to some members of the Deutsches Haus for example, this fact of inheritance marks him. He is a Jew, *ein Jude*, *Žid*, a Yid. And now in Germany they have written this identity into law. Were he in Germany he would have to rearrange the ownership and management of Landauerovy Závody so that only Aryans appeared in the executive posts and on the board. Were he in Germany he would have to get another doctor because their family doctor is a gentile. Were he in Germany his marriage to Liesel, while still being valid, would yet be an anomaly because all further marriages of such a kind, between Aryan and non-Aryan, are now illegal. Were they in Germany, Ottilie and Martin would be officially classified as *mischlingen*, half-breeds, lesser beings.

It is absurd; but it is happening.

'Oh, I forgot to tell you yesterday. I've been invited to join the committee of the Human Rights League.'

'And will you?'

'I think so.' He returns to the newspaper. There's a story about the recent influx of refugees from Germany, Jews most of them. 'And the president asked about raising money. That's why they approached me, I expect. Landauerovka will give something, of course. And I thought we might use the house.'

'The *house*?'

'Some kind of charity thing. A recital, who knows? You know how everybody seems to want to see the place. What about asking Němec? A short recital, sixty people at some ridiculously inflated price per head. It might do some good.'

'Do we really want to open the house to the public?' Liesel did not enjoy the aftershock of their housewarming party, the speculations of journalists, the intrusion into their family life. With all that attention, she felt there was something vulnerable about Viktor's and her presence there, as though they were evanescent creatures within the transparent walls of glass, like summer mayflies with their gossamer wings and delicate tails and ephemeral lives.

'Not really. On the other hand . . .' He goes back to his reading. It is a habit he has, of inviting a discussion without pursuing the counter-argument. She imagines him doing this with his managers, hinting at something with that infuriating smile and then leaving them to find the solution to the puzzle, so that when it occurs to them they feel that they have thought of it themselves. 'On the other hand, what?'

'On the other hand, my darling Liesel, we have to do something. Now I really must be off.' He folds his paper and goes across to the dining area where the children and Liesel and the nanny are having breakfast. 'Laník will be waiting.' He says this every morning, as though it is the driver's regular appearance with the car outside that determines his routine, whereas the opposite is the truth: his own routine is what determines everything in what he laughingly refers to as *die Landauerwelt*, the Landauer world.

He stoops to kiss Ottilie – she rises in her chair and throws her arms around him – and then Martin, who barely acknowledges his presence, so intent is he on manoeuvring a piece of bread roll into his mouth, and finally Liesel. As he kisses Liesel on the forehead he is suddenly ambushed by the thought of Kata. It has become a tic, this mental reference to Kata. Perhaps it is something to do with guilt after all, although he feels no shame about it. Perhaps it is nothing more than an irrational gesture of the mind, an association of thoughts that would intrigue that other Moravian-German Jew Sigmund Freud, at this very moment at work in Vienna on the first draft of what will be his final book, *Moses and Monotheism*. Perhaps Viktor needs analysis in order to root out the concatenation of mental processes that lead to this small and fleeting evocation of the woman. But that assumes he would wish to be rid of the thought of her, when the fact is plain: he is quite happy to think of her. Indeed, there are times when he deliberately courts the memory of her, turns it over in his mind with care and attention, listens to her voice, touches her, smells her, tastes her, watches her taste him. This is something that Liesel will never know. No one will ever know. The only person who might know it is Kata herself. And this thought evokes a small stab of pain. What is she doing right now? Does she think of him as he thinks of her, or is she even now waking up in the bed of some other man for whom she evinces exactly the same counterfeit affection as she does for him? Questions that lead one to the next in that moment of saying goodbye to his family and bring with them something more than mere anguish – an intense desire to see her again.

With a cheery little wave to Liesel he makes his way upstairs. Outside, sure enough, the car is already waiting, a Landauer Prezident, a gleaming black limousine with the characteristic curves of the Landauer design team. Laník is there, holding open the door. Liesel does not like Laník, he knows that. 'He's sly,' she complains. 'And he looks at me.'

'A cat may look at a queen. Perhaps he's in love with you.'

'And he's always speaking in slang, and then grinning at me because I don't understand. And he keeps annoying Liba.'

Viktor slides into the shadowy leather interior of the motor car. 'The office,' he says through the small hatch in the panel that separates driver from passenger. Then he sits back and contemplates the thought that has been growing like a pearl in the closed oyster of his mind: Kata.

As Viktor drives away to work, the women of the house set about what they have to do – Liba to take the children upstairs to brush their teeth, Liesel to have a word with Laníková about the day's routine. Today *Paní* Hanáková is coming for lunch; this evening there will be guests for dinner, a business group of some kind. Laníková tuts, tight-lipped, at the prospect of all the fuss and confusion.

While the discussion goes on and Martin plays on the floor with his model cars – tinplate replicas of Landauers – Liba takes Ottilie to school. It is a fifteen-minute walk to the Montessori school that takes up one floor of a late nineteenth-century villa on Parkstrasse. When she returns, Liba takes over the duties of childcare while Liesel goes into the garden. The garden is her particular delight. Viktor tends the conservatory, the so-called Winter Garden that spans the east wall of the Glass Room, while Liesel looks after the garden with the help of the gardener, an ancient and arthritic Czech who calls her *milostivá paní*, your ladyship, as though any German-speaker with property must be a ladyship of some kind. Then there is the piano practice that she does every day, according to the strict regimen of her teacher who comes once a week for a two-hour lesson. Exercises – arpeggios and scales, with the metronome ticking away – precede a Chopin étude and then the indulgence of the piece she is working on, the liquid notes and the painful silences of Janáček's *On the Overgrown Path*. It astonishes her how significant silence can be within the context of a piece of music. The piece seems so suited to the space and elegance of the Glass Room, to the light and shade and the subtle reflections.

Dinner

One of the dinner guests that evening is wearing a small badge in the left lapel of his jacket. The man has come as the head of a Stuttgart consortium that is interested in building the Landauer Popular in Germany under licence, as a rival to the KdF-wagen that Porsche are constructing. Schreiber is his name. He is tall and elegant, exquisite in his impeccable double-breasted suit. He bows over Liesel's hand and clicks his heels and murmurs *küßdiehand*, *gnädige Frau* as his lips come to within a breath of her skin, and *zum entzücken*, charming, when he looks into her eyes. But the lapel badge that marks his jacket like a seal of authenticity is a tilted *Hakenkreuz*, black on white, ringed by a band of blood-red enamel and the words National-Sozialistische-D.A.P.

Herr Schreiber walks round the Glass Room like a visitor to an exhibition, his head turning this way and that, his hand touching the surfaces as though caressing the face of a loved child. He recognises the Maillol as soon as he sees it, knows of Loos's architectural work in Vienna; and he loves the Glass Room, sees it as the epitome of all that is best in German culture. 'You employed a German architect, of course.'

'Not "of course",' Liesel corrects him. 'There are fine architects here in the city. Fuchs, Wiesener, others.'

Schreiber smiles. 'Nevertheless you chose a German. And anyway, they sound German to me.' Does the fact amuse him? Certainly he is amused by something as they sit round the dining table – extended by one section to accommodate ten guests. Perhaps it amuses him to discover this small island of German culture in the midst of a Slav lake. They drink Moravian wine which he pronounces 'promising' and he raises his glass to Liesel and Viktor. 'To German culture and German business, wherever it may be found,' he says. The maid brings the soup. *Bramboračka*, potato soup, of course. He sips appreciatively. 'But tell me, Herr Landauer, how do you find working with this other language, this Slavonic tongue? And with the Slavs themselves? I mean, if you were in Pilsen all your workforce would be German, of course. Yet here you have a mix. Are there not difficulties, conflicts?'

'Not any that matter.'

'That is not the experience of the Germans in Pilsen. They are, of course, asking for autonomy – if not actual absorption into the Reich.'

'They are just victims of political agitation.'

'Is that so? Or are they merely demanding their rights?'

'In a democracy, rights also involve duties.'

Schreiber sighs. 'Ah, democracy. Of course, democracy. It is such a tricky concept, isn't it? I mean, democracy pure and simple would never have allowed you to build this house, would it? Imagine putting such a proposal to popular vote! Your neighbours would be jealous and vote against you! And yet your German sensibilities have driven you to ignore such democratic reservations and realise your vision. Isn't that it? Over and above democracy, don't German people everywhere have a duty to their German blood? That is what National Socialism means.'

'Are you implying that such a duty falls to me as well?' Viktor asks.

Schreiber shrugs. The other guests at the table look embarrassed. 'It falls to all Germans, doesn't it? Does a Czech German have any less duty towards his national culture?'

Viktor attempts to mirror the man's smile, an expression that is replete with detached superiority but quite without humour. 'But I am not a German, Herr Schreiber,' he says. 'I am a Jew.'

Memories

'That woman has the brain of a sparrow.'

Hana, her face bruised with tears, is pacing back and forth in the Glass Room, talking of Němec's wife. 'And yet she keeps her hold on him. She blackmails him, really. He's frightened of her. God knows why but he's frightened.'

There is a Christmas tree in the south-east angle of the room where the plate-glass windows meet the Winter Garden, a Christmas tree decorated with tinsel and candles and ringed already with wrapped presents. Hana paces between this tree and the open space beyond the Maillol, while Liesel sits in one of the chairs and smokes and watches her friend helplessly. 'I love him!' Hana cries, weeping. 'Don't you understand that? I love him. I want him with me every moment of my life. And what do I get? The occasional night. A few days when his wife is away on one of her shopping expeditions. She knows about me, that's what makes it so shitty.' She uses the Czech word, *posraný*. When talking to Liesel in German she often resorts to Czech when she wants a vulgarity, as though the language gives her more scope. And anyway, the Glass Room has that effect, of liberating people from the strictures and conventions of the ordinary, of making them transparent. 'She's always known about me and up to now she hasn't given a damn. But now she has told him that he's got to choose, either her or me. And he's chosen *her*. My God, he's gone running back to her *kunda*.'

'Hana! Ottilie might hear.'

She stops her pacing and puts her hand to her mouth. Her eyes, red from weeping, are suddenly wide and bright. There is a bubble of laughter behind the tears. 'Oh God, do you really think so? Auntie Hana teaches her goddaughter naughty words? But she's upstairs, isn't she? She won't have heard, will she? Oh, dear, I hope not.'

'I'm sure she hasn't heard. But you've got to be careful. And anyway there's Laník's sister. She's often in the kitchen.'

'And *she* doesn't know what a *kunda* is?'

Suddenly they are laughing. Of course she knows. That's probably what Laník calls her. The laughter does something to restore normality for a while, but soon they are back to Hana's problem. Liesel feels helpless. Her own life – Viktor's constancy, her two beautiful children, the beautiful house – is almost an affront to Hana. She seems to have everything, while Hana, once again pacing up and down in front of the onyx wall while sleet beats against the windows, feels she has nothing. 'Do you know, I told Oskar? About Němec, I mean. And do you know what he said? He said, if he's the one you really want, then I'll let you go. Can you imagine that? If that's what you want, I'll let you go. And then he sort of shrugged and held his hands open like this. "But," he added, "I'll always be here to pick up the pieces." That's what he told me.' And there are the tears once more, not for herself this time, nor for Němec, but for her own husband, the squat, unattractive, wealthy Oskar who loves her more completely than anyone but Liesel herself.

Later that evening, when the children have gone to bed, Liesel and Hana sit together on the sofa in the library area and listen to the radio. Viktor is away on some business trip in Vienna, returning in two days. So the two women sit together on their own, Hana with her head in Liesel's lap while Liesel strokes her friend's temples in an effort to bring peace and calm to her, and the radio tells them what was surely expected and inevitable, that the President of the Republic, Tomáš Garrigue – 'Isn't *garrigue* a kind of vegetation?' asks Hana – Tomáš Garrigue Masaryk has stepped down from office to make way for a younger man. Masaryk is eighty-five years old. His successor a mere fifty-one. Times are changing. 'I'll miss the Old Man,' Hana says, attempting to distract herself. 'I met him once, in Prague, do you know that? At a concert. We were introduced by a mutual friend. We shook hands and he looked at me, and I suddenly felt ashamed. Can you imagine that? It was as though he could see everything about me, and he forgave me.' The attempt at distraction hasn't worked: she begins to weep again, the tears bleeding out of her raw eyes, while Liesel shushes her like a mother with a baby, just as she has done with Ottilie and Martin, a soft sibilant sound to go with the sound of the snow against the windows.

'I'm sorry Liesel, I'm such a wreck at the moment.'

'No you're not.' Liesel bends down and kisses her on the forehead and then on the cheek where her skin is flushed and damp, and then hesitantly, because it is strange and rather miraculous, on the hot pulp of her lips. Couched in the only intimate part of the Glass Room, freed by their surroundings from all strictures, the two of them talk in whispers.

Recital

All the tickets for the charity recital – sixty-five in total – have been sold within a few days of the announcement. The chairs are set out in arcs on either side of the onyx wall and the piano has been moved so that the focus of the room is changed, directing people away from the glass walls towards the interior of the space. People enter the room making that little gasp of admiration or surprise. Many of them have come to see the place itself as much as listen to Němec's playing. Hana, her face drawn and solemn, sits at the back, in the library area, while the pianist's wife, Milada Němcová, takes her seat, triumphantly, at the front. Viktor makes a short introductory speech in which he welcomes everyone and assures them of the value of their support for the Human Rights League, and warns them that, of all the people of Europe, the citizens of their young democracy must look beyond its borders at what is happening to their neighbours. 'At present it is others who are being oppressed,' he warns them, 'but if we stand idly by, it may one day become ourselves.' Then Němec comes down the stairs to appear like Mephistopheles in the entrance to the Glass Room, bowing to the applause and taking his seat with a dramatic flip of his coattails as though he were on stage at the Stadt-Theater rather than in someone's living room. For a fearful moment he crouches like a demon over the keys. Then he begins to play, softly, mellifluously, caressing the instrument as Hana claims he once caressed her, a Brahms intermezzo to soothe the flustered souls of those who have heard Viktor's opening speech. To follow that there is the Janáček piano sonata *From the Street*, and finally, after an interval, a Schubert sonata played with all the pianist's legendary verve and attack, his crouching figure like some bird of prey – 'a vulture,' Hana whispers to Liesel – clawing the notes from the body of the instrument. All three pieces are interpreted with that accuracy and sensitivity that puts Němec, so the music critic of *Moravské Noviny* will write in the next edition, among the foremost interpreters of the time. The event will even merit a mention in the cultural pages of *Prager Tagblatt* under the title Human Rights Bring Cultural Bonus. The evening has been, as the chairman of the League claims in his closing words, both a resounding artistic success and a mark of solidarity with oppressed peoples everywhere.

The Glass Room remained indifferent, of course. Plain, balanced, perfect; and indifferent. Architecture should have no politics, Rainer von Abt said. A building just is. Below it, lapping up to the foot of the garden, were the rough tides of those political years, while the Landauer House stood beached on the shore above the tidemark like a relic of a more perfect golden age. That summer there were graffiti on the walls in Marienbad, where the Landauers went for their usual holiday. *SdP* was the slogan, painted in red letters that dripped blood. Elsewhere there were swastikas, as black as death. Despite complaints, the graffiti remained for days before workmen came and painted them out. That summer Viktor and Liesel went to the cinema and saw in the newsreel a man in pale grey ranting at ten thousand torch-bearing soldiers. Perhaps it was that year, the autumn of that year, that Viktor began, without ever telling his wife, to transfer funds from his bank accounts in both Prague and Vienna into a new account in Switzerland.

Love

She is waiting for him in the shadow of the big wheel, a small, bright figure in her cheap clothes, a flame among the grey coals of the crowd. She laughs as she kisses him, a laugh of something close to happiness. 'You got my note?' he asks.

'Of course I did. That's why I'm here.'

'What shall we do?'

'Let's go for a ride.' She takes his hand and drags him protesting towards the queue. 'Do you remember the first time?'

Of course he remembers the first time. The Riesenrad is like a talisman for him. Whenever he sees its arc above the houses of the city, he thinks of her. The wheel of fate. The metaphor is obvious.

'You were so stern, I thought that I had done something wrong.'

'It is me that is doing something wrong.'

'And do you regret it?'

'No. No, I don't.'

They edge towards the front of the queue. This time their cabin is crowded. A fat *Hausfrau* and her four children push and shove around them, the children quarrelling, the woman apologising for their bad behaviour. Kata looks at Viktor and makes a little grimace, but it gives them an excuse to stand close together, Kata at the window looking out, Viktor pressed behind her. The cabin rises into the air, with the children moving from one side to the other and making it swing. 'Keep still, you little buggers!' the woman cries, and apologises again. 'Kids these days,' she says. Two hundred feet below the crowds in the Haupt-Allee are like lice crawling across the back of a dusty animal. Kata points out the Danube, and in the distance, the hills behind Pressburg, where she lived before coming to Vienna. He bends to kiss her neck where there are wisps of hair and her strange, warm, mammal smell. The children giggle and point at this public display of affection. 'She your sweetheart, Mister?' one of them asks. It must be a dare. The mother clips him round the ear – 'Don't you be cheeky!' – while his siblings watch with bated breath for any reaction from their victim.

'Yes,' Viktor answers them, 'she's my sweetheart. I love her very much.'

'Love!' the children exclaim as though it were a shocking word. Their mother tries to hush them. 'Lovey, love!' they say, giggling with delight.

After the ride they stroll through the Prater and drink beer at one of the cafés. Kata seems distracted. She watches the antics of the sparrows that skip around their feet, pecking at the crumbs she throws for them. One bird is bold enough to come onto the table and watch the two of them with curious, bright eyes, almost as though it knows what is going on. 'What you said, to that kid . . .'

'On the wheel? It was a joke.'

'Of course it was a joke.' She looks away across the expanse of grass towards the Riesenrad turning slowly in the evening air. 'But it was a cruel one.'

'Don't be ridiculous. It doesn't mean that I don't feel for you.'

'*Feel* for me? That's a consolation.' She taps her finger on the table and the sparrow hops nearer, expecting food. 'You know, I think about you often, Viktor. It's stupid of me, but I do. I think about you and wonder what your life is like, your wife and your children, that kind of thing.' She gives a little shrug, still watching the sparrows, reluctant to meet his eyes. When she looks up there is that glacial light in her blue eyes. 'I don't even know your real name, do you realise that? I just wait for you to send me a letter or give me a call. Look.' She opens her handbag and takes out a fold of paper. It is the note he wrote to her three days before, poste restante at the Nordbahnhof post office, a note like many others – just the date and the scribbled lines: *My darling, I will be in the city on the 23rd. Can we meet? At the big wheel at 4.30? Yours ever, V.*

'You see?'

'See what?' There is something inside him that isn't anger but is much like anger. It is focused on this woman in front of him, with her pretty little face and her bitten fingernails and her liberal body. 'What are you trying to make me see, Kata?'

'The words you write. I keep them because I know I'll never hear you *say* them.'

'What on earth are you talking about?' He reaches out and takes her hand and draws it towards him. 'Do you want me to say "darling"? Is that it?' He kisses her fingertips, which seem childish and artless but are, in fact, skilful and inventive. 'My darling Kata. There you are, I've said it.'

Petulantly she pulled away. 'Don't make fun of me. I don't mean *that*. I mean, "Yours ever".'

'Yours ever?' He laughs. 'It's just an expression you use at the end of a letter. *Immer der Ihrige*. Just an expression.' But she doesn't share the joke. There is something disconsolate about the cast of her head and the way she holds herself. Her expression is bleak with unhappiness. And suddenly he understands what his own emotion is, this thing that seems something like anger, an emotion that takes command of his mind and his body and makes both of them obey orders that appear not to be his own. 'Come,' he says, getting up from his seat and taking her hand. 'You're going to ruin things. We're going to say things we shouldn't.'

'What things?'

'I said we shouldn't say them. Don't you see? There are always things that couples mustn't say.'

'Are we a couple? Or just a convenience?'

He puts his arm round her, hoping to break the mood and put the meeting back on its even keel. 'Where shall we go?' he asks as he leads her away through the strolling people, dodging the bicycles and the children and the dogs, towards the entrance of the park. What would happen if someone recognised them, someone from Město, or from the Landauer office in Vienna? But the people passing by are anonymous and indifferent, barely glancing at the two of them, unaware of the small, intense argument that has sown seeds of disruption and disquiet.

'Where are we going?' she asks.

'Where do you want to go?'

'What about my place? It's not far. What about going there?' She shrugs nervously at his silence, as though the question should never have been broached. 'It's just a couple of rooms, but it's all right. Cosy.'

'Fine. That sounds fine.' But it is the first time she has ever made the suggestion.

Her apartment is in a building only a short walk away, in a side street off the Praterstrasse. They must have passed the place before but she never mentioned it. Although it is obvious that she lives somewhere round here, the two worlds, her own and their shared one, have never intersected before. Jews live in this quarter, plying their trade in the narrow streets and huddling together in the cramped tenements. Next door to her block is a *kasher* butcher's shop with a menorah painted on the window and a mezuzah nailed to the doorpost. An old man with a skull cap and ringlets watches from the doorway as they pass by. Perhaps he is the *shochet*, the man who knows how to hone his knife so that the blade is perfect, the cut is perfect, the draining of blood perfect.

Kata unlocks a street door and leads the way in, out of the light and the expressionless eyes of strangers. There is the smell of boiled cabbage and damp in the stairwell. She climbs the stairs towards the attic, chatting all the time, a thin, nervous chatter: Frau So-and-So lives there, and an old couple who used to work at the theatre lived over there; no one cleans the stairs, although they are meant to take it in turns, and so she does the job herself when she can find the time. Once a fortnight or the place would become unbearable. The muck they leave for someone else to clear up! So he mustn't find it too filthy.

'It's fine,' he assures her. 'It's fine.'

At the top of the main staircase she knocks on one of the doors and calls out, 'It's me. I'm back,' through the wood. And they go on, up narrower stairs to the very summit where there is a small landing with a window that looks out onto the roofs, and a narrow doorway that opens into her room. Inside, beneath a ceiling that slopes with the pitch of the roof, is a tight, organised personal world, replete with the mysterious signs of Kata's presence – her clothes, her trinkets and ornaments, all the artefacts of her own, hidden life. There is a bed along one wall and a sofa and armchair on either side of a gas fire, cheap ready-made furniture with velour upholstery and antimacassars on which clients, presumably, might rest their oiled heads. Dormer windows give a view across the Prater towards the river; and there is the Riesenrad, picked out in electric lights now, like a great Catherine wheel, the wheel of fate rotating in the darkening sky.

She stands close to him, sharing the view. 'See what I have to look at? I always think of meeting you there. No one had ever asked me to do something like that.'

'I was nervous. I needed time to think about what I was doing.'

She slips her hand in his. The gesture seems natural, devoid of the artifice that there was when they first knew each other. 'You're never nervous.'

'I was then.'

'And now? What do you feel now?'

He turns from the view and looks at her, taking both her hands in his. He feels a need to explain, although explanation isn't clear even to himself. This simple commercial undertaking has metamorphosed into something else, mere physical need becoming the underpinning of what is now a kind of fulfilment.

'Content. I feel content.'

She's about to say something – what would it be? – but before she can utter any words the door opens. They turn. Viktor expects some intrusion from the adult world but there is only a child standing in the open doorway, a little girl about six years old – five or six, younger than Ottilie for sure: a small, solemn creature in a plain nightdress and with her hair done in pigtails.

Kata slips from his grasp. 'What the devil are you doing up? You know you must stay in your room.'

'I couldn't sleep.'

'Well, you just go back and try.'

The girl's eyes are fixed on Viktor. 'Are you one of Mutti's friends?' she asks.

He doesn't know how to answer. Interrogated by a child, he is speechless.

Kata picks the girl up. 'Of course he is. An old friend. This is Herr Viktor. And' – she turns towards Viktor to show her daughter – 'this is Marika. Now you, young lady, must go back to bed.'

The girl clings to her mother, her pale legs wrapped round Kata's waist, her eyes watching. There is something simian about her, something quick and canny. 'If he's an old friend why haven't I seen him before?'

'You haven't met all of Mutti's friends. Why should you? Now you come along with me.' The door closes behind the two of them and the incident, the unexpected visitation is over.

Alone, Viktor wanders indecisively round the room, looking at the bakelite clock on the mantelshelf and the pictures on the wall, fashion plates from magazines showing women in cloche hats and narrow dresses. In one of the photos there is a car in the background – a Landauer. On the chest of drawers against one wall is a tray with Kata's things in it – a string of small, uneven pearls, some lipsticks, an enamel box with a vaguely oriental design, a scattering of hair grips. He picks through these items as though he might find something of value. A glass bottle of strange, organic shape holds some inadequate fraction of her scent. What else does he not know about Kata? What else is about to walk through the door into his life?

'You never told me you had a daughter,' he says accusingly when she returns.

'Does it matter?'

'Of course it matters.'

'That's why I never told you.' She stands in front of him with that childish defiance. 'I wanted to say, but then I was frightened that it might scare you off.'

'So why now?'

'I don't know.' She shrugs. 'I thought, let him see. Why should I hide? Let him see.'

'But you bring other people here.'

'A few, sometimes. They don't mind, do they? They like to give her sweets and things, pretend they're in a family, really. Uncle Hans and Uncle Josef, that kind of thing. It's nice for her.'

'How can you leave her all alone?'

'I don't leave her alone, do I? There's the woman downstairs. She keeps an eye on her when I'm out.'

'Who's her father?'

'What the hell has that got to do with you?'

'Nothing. Nothing at all.' He casts round for what to say,

sitting disconsolately on the bed, with his hands hanging between his legs and his head down. 'Look, maybe I'd better go.'

'Then go if you want to.' She turns away looking for a distraction. There's a sink in the corner and a gas ring. She puts some water on to boil. 'I'd appreciate something for taking up my time, but that's up to you.'

They have never spoken like this, never had an argument of any kind. What he wanted, she did for him. And when they talked it was in evasive generalities, about life, about their likes and dislikes, about her absurd dreams. Never about the reality of his life, never about hers.

'I don't want to,' he says. 'I want to stay with you.'

She doesn't look round. 'Right. I'll just wash a bit. The bathroom's on the floor below, I'm afraid. There's just this basin if you want it.' She takes off her dress and leans over the basin, and he almost laughs at the emotion he feels at the sight of her, her breasts hanging loose inside her slip, the satin clinging to her buttocks, and the compulsion he has to touch her. 'I'll have to wash my shirt,' he tells her. 'Can we do that, and dry it overnight?'

'I'll see to it. We'll hang it in front of the fire.'

He sits in his vest and watches her as she does the small domestic task. There is something touching about the scene, some quality of light that reminds him of a painting by a French artist that Liesel admires. Not Degas. Someone more modern, but not unlike. Bonnard. None of the pure lines that von Abt applauds, that Viktor himself admires, but instead the broken, refracted shapes of light and colour, the shameless curves of a woman unobserved. But Kata isn't unobserved. She is watched by him closely, for every minute movement and gesture, as though he is a connoisseur and she a work of art.

She glances round and smiles, and in that moment he considers telling her what he is thinking. It would be ridiculous of course, but he considers it just the same: I could love you. The careful conditional tense, even in his thoughts.

When she has finished at the basin she fills a tin bidet with water and squats to wash. As she towels herself dry he takes off his trousers and, blatantly erect, shares her water, washing himself in the cloudy suds that have cleaned her. She laughs at the sight.

'Our dirt together,' she says, touching his shoulder. He reaches up and pulls her head down towards him and kisses her ear, the little, tight curl. Things have changed. The moment of altercation has passed and they have come through, strangely, into a different world. The sex they have that evening is quiet and particular, close to lovemaking, a thoughtful ritual in which they talk together, and smile, watching each other with careful eyes, and kiss, mouth on mouth, which seems an intimacy greater than the other, shameless things they do. The gas fire sounds in the background like a continuous intake of breath and Viktor experiences a strange elation, the sensation of completeness, of being truly alive. 'I could love you,' he murmurs in her ear.

Her reply is a soft breath against his cheek. 'Men always say that kind of thing. Only usually they never have any doubt.'

'Maybe it's the doubt that makes it dangerous.'

Later they sleep, Kata with her back to him, the curve of her body moulded into his, his arms around her.

Viktor dreams. Vienna is the city of dreams, but not the kind of dreams that comfort. It is the city of incubus and succubus, the creatures of nightmare. He dreams of Liesel and Kata. He is standing naked before them, but of course they don't notice his nakedness or the incongruity of their own presence together. In fact no one notices anything, neither the witnesses, nor the judge, nor the jury, nor the people in the public gallery who laugh uproariously at him, not at his nudity but at the absurdity of his situation.

Some time during the night he awakens. Kata is getting out of bed and crossing the room to the door. He waits for her to return, and folds her into his arms when she does.

'Is she all right?'

'She's fast asleep.'

His mind drifts in the border territory between sleep and waking. Lying there in the darkness with Kata, he has the vivid sensation that this cramped little attic room is at the axis of a great wheel, a Riesenrad that is the whole of his world. And everything else rotates slowly round it – the factory, the house on Blackfield Road, Liesel, Ottilie, the whole of his existence, which is the whole of existence itself, the whole world slowly orbiting him and Kata lying there amid the hot sheets.

When he wakes the next morning the flood of milky light from the dormer window washes away all memories of dream and fantasy and leaves only a sense of disquiet. He sits up and rubs his eyes. Kata is already over by the washbasin in the corner, ironing his shirt. She is wearing a cotton housecoat. She tosses water on the fabric of the shirt and picks up the flatiron from the gas ring. The water seethes as she presses the iron down. Steam rises around her.

'You'll have to get dressed quick,' she warns when she notices he is awake. 'Marika'll be up soon.'

He throws the sheet aside. 'I must go.'

'It's all right, if you're dressed.'

'No, I must get out of your way.' He washes in the basin and pulls his clothes on. She hands him the shirt. 'You're still angry,' she says, but he shakes his head in denial.

'Then what?'

'Bewildered. Confused.'

'I'm sorry.'

'It's not your fault, it's mine.' He struggles to adjust his tie. 'I'll need to get a shave.'

'There's a barber just round the corner.'

He takes out his cheque book. 'I want to give you something. For you, for the girl. I want . . .' What does he want? She is looking at him with concern, as though he has done something bizarre. 'Do you have a bank account? Can you use a cheque?' The idea seems plain now, as obvious as the nose on her face.

She shrugs. 'I s'pose so.'

He takes out his pen and writes, quickly, barely thinking but absurdly pleased with his idea: *Katalin Kalman*. And the sum: *fifteen thousand Schillings*. 'It's drawn on my Vienna bank. The Wiener Bank-Verein. Is that all right?' He watches the ink lose its gleam as it dries, then tears the cheque out and hands it to her.

'It's a fortune,' she says, staring at the piece of paper. 'I can't take that. It's more than I earn in two years.'

'It's yours, Kata. For you and your daughter.'

'They'll think I stole it.'

'You couldn't have stolen it. It has your name on it.'

'Maybe I forged it.' She looks at the thing as though to see whether it is genuine, turning it over as she might examine a dubious note.

'They'll probably clear it with me, but that's all right.'

She looks up, and those pale eyes ambush him. 'And what do I have to do to earn it?'

He laughs. It seems the most obvious thing, the simplest thing. 'Just don't go with men.'

'And what about you?'

'That's for you to decide.' They watch one another. He feels this absurd excitement, like a child with a new idea, bursting to tell people, dying to explain. 'That's entirely up to you.'

She shakes her head as though in refusal, but puts the cheque on the table underneath a small vase. 'We'll see,' she says.

'I'll come again soon.'

'Of course.' She reaches up to adjust his tie. He examines her closely, almost as though consigning her features to memory, the cast of her eyes and lips, the way her skin creases at the corners of her mouth, the set of her cheekbones and the dome of her forehead. Her hairline is ill-defined, with a line of soft down before the main growth of hair. There is something endearing about that; and the fact that he hasn't noticed it before makes him panic, as if there may be other things that he has not noticed and will therefore not remember. He bends to kiss her there, among the soft down where she smells warm from sleep and entirely without artifice. The kiss transfers to the smooth texture of her forehead, and then to the palpitating presence of her left eye where her eyelid flutters like a trapped moth. And then down her cheek to her lips. He tastes the sourness of the morning on her saliva.

'I'll bring a present for Marika.'

'That'd be nice.'

'And one for you.'

And then he leaves, thinking, as he goes down the stairs, of what might have been and what might still be, thinking of the pure caprice of life. Sitting in the train on the journey home Viktor Landauer, the man of quality, of qualities, attributes and gifts, feels elation no longer but only a deep and unfocused remorse, like the sadness that comes after coitus, an emotion for which he has a Czech word that he cannot translate into German with any exactness: *lítost*. Rue, regret for a whole universe of things, the irrevocable nature of one's life, the unbearable sorrow of being, the fact that things cannot be changed, that love, the focused light of passion and hunger should be centred not on the figure of his wife but on the body and soul of a half-educated, part-time tart.

Ecstasy

'Have you ever been unfaithful to Liesel?'

The question is a shock, but that is Hana's manner.

'What an extraordinary question to ask.'

'But have you?'

There are just the two of them waiting for the appearance of Liesel from her preparations upstairs and for the arrival of the other dinner guests. They are standing before the windows, looking out over the evening garden, sipping their drinks – under Hana's tuition Viktor has mixed cocktails – and chatting quite idly about things. She has been relating some gossip about the Kaprálová girl – Vitulka – whom she bumped into at a café in Montparnasse on her recent foray to Paris. 'Do you know who she is with all the time? You'll never guess.'

'Then tell me.'

'Martinů. You know, Bohuslav Martinů, the composer. People say they're sleeping together.'

'And what did she say?'

'I didn't ask her directly, Viktor. Don't be ridiculous. But she never stopped talking about him and that's usually the sign.' And then, unexpectedly, she comes out with that question: Have you ever been unfaithful to Liesel?

There is jazz on the gramophone, a record Hana herself has brought them as a gift from Paris: a Negro playing the saxophone. The instrument talks to the listener in tones that seem so close to the human voice that it's almost like having another person in the room, commenting on their conversation. Hana smiles, listening to the music, sipping her icy drink and watching the sunset. The expanse of glass emboldens, makes plain and transparent, opens up the mind and maybe the heart.

'My dear Hana, why should you want to know? And why should you expect me to tell you if I had?'

'That's as good as an admission.'

'Don't be ridiculous.'

'You're an attractive man, so why shouldn't you have a fling or two, something discreet on one of your business trips, perhaps? Opportunities come the way of attractive men. Particularly rich ones.' She is teasing, of course. That is how their friendship manifests itself, in her teasing him and his not taking offence. It's the only way to bridge the gap between their disparate characters.

He draws on his cigarette. 'Would it make you feel happy if I did have a mistress?'

She shrugs. 'Happy, no. But at least Liesel wouldn't seem so bloody fortunate in everything.' The record comes to an end and the needle remains clicking in the inner groove. She goes over to put on something else, glancing sideways at him as she does so, that down-turned mouth curving upwards in her surprising smile. She is good at such smiles, the small expressions of innuendo. '*I* wouldn't mind sharing you.'

'That's more or less what Liesel said you'd say.'

For a moment she seems thrown off balance. 'You've *discussed* having a fling with me?'

'A long time ago. She wondered whether you'd ever made a pass at me.'

'My God! Was she angry? She's so funny about things like that. All that angst . . .'

'She said you have different standards from us. I said that our relationship was more like brother and sister—'

'How sweet.'

'And she added that that wouldn't put you off.'

Hana laughs. There is a gleam of pink gum. 'Darling Liesel, she knows me too well. And you haven't answered my question.'

'It doesn't need answering.'

She is about to reply, but whatever she is going to say is interrupted by the sound of the doorbell upstairs, the front door opening and people coming in. She drains her drink and hands the glass to Viktor. Then unexpectedly she leans towards him and for a moment her face is touching his, cheek to cheek, as though she is going to give him a kiss. He can feel a breath of perfume underlaid with the scent of cigarettes. 'What's her name?' she whispers.

Viktor has come to recognise the signs when visitors enter the Glass Room for the first time. There are those little gasps of admiration, those exclamations of surprise. They've come down from the quiet and intimate enclosure of the top floor and they stand on the edge of the space, unsure at first where to focus their gaze. The impact of the place overwhelms visitors, especially those who are used to riches being expressed in things, possessions, the ornamental bric-a-brac of the wealthy, and instead discover here the ultimate opulence of pure abstraction. *Glänzend*! they exclaim, a word that has both the literal and figurative meaning of brilliant, and thus encapsulates within its gleaming glance exactly what strikes the newcomer about the room.

'Quite a house, Herr Landauer,' this particular guest observes as he advances across the floor. 'Your lovely wife has been telling me about the place. And now, coming into this room. I can see what she was going on about.'

Fritz Mandl is a businessman from Vienna, the head of the armaments company Hirtenberger Patronen-Fabrik. There have already been a couple of meetings to discuss his idea that there might be a joint venture with Landauerovy Zádovy in the burgeoning market for military equipment. The man has suggestions, projects, contacts. 'The Germans are hungry for this stuff,' he has assured Viktor. 'And the Italians as well. Armoured cars are the latest thing. You want to move quickly before someone else steps in.' But it is not Mandl himself who draws the attention as he crosses the room to shake Viktor's hand: it is Mandl's wife. Seemingly very young, she is blessed with looks of the most flawless symmetry. Dark shoulder-length hair frames a perfectly heart-shaped face. Her eyebrows are exact arches stemming from a nose of exquisite delicacy. She has grey-green eyes, watchful and nervous. Her mouth has a vulnerable quality to it, as though she is uncertain whether to smile or cry. She is, quite simply, one of the most beautiful women Viktor has ever seen. The chrome pillar nearby throws multiple distorted reflections of her beauty around the room with the careless abandon of a child. Very gently she inclines her head as she shakes his hand. 'Your house is very beautiful. Modern, it is very modern.'

'I like modern things.'

'So do I.'

She turns to greet Hana. 'Please call me Eva. Frau Mandl makes me seem so old. You do speak German, don't you? Here it is so difficult with Czech. I haven't a word of the language, really. *Dobrý den* is about my limit.' Other guests are coming in and being introduced: a lawyer and his wife; a couple from the motor racing world who have driven Landauer cars in competition; a university professor and his daughter; and Oskar, of course. But Hana seems transfixed by Eva Mandl's appearance. 'Haven't we met before?'

Frau Mandl frowns. 'I don't think so.'

'Eva doesn't get out of Vienna much,' her husband says. 'We have a very busy life there.'

'Maybe it was in Vienna then. I'm sure we've met somewhere.'

'I doubt it.'

Drinks are served. The guests exclaim at the spectacular view through the windows, at the Maillol sculpture, at the beauty of the onyx wall and the elegance of the Glass Room, and in the midst of all this Mandl's voice is loud and congratulatory, somehow taking the credit for himself: 'I like this place. Away with all the nonsense of the past. You seem to have what it takes in this city, Landauer. A good business culture and a modern outlook on life. Not like Vienna. Vienna is hidebound by tradition and cursed by Communism. Maybe I should move here. You've got the factories, all you need is the contacts.'

And then Hana exclaims, 'I know!' and just as she speaks there is an unexpected hiatus in the conversation so that her comment, intended only for Mandl's wife, becomes general. People turn to look at her. What does she know?

'I *know* where I've seen you before,' she explains hastily.

Eva Mandl glances anxiously at her husband. Her eyes – green or grey? – are transfixed, like those of an animal caught in a snare.

'You were in films, weren't you?' Hana cries. 'Machatý's *Extáze*. Oh my God, you're Hedy Kiesler!'

For Hana this is nothing. So the young and beautiful wife of the principal guest has run across the screens of countless cinemas of the world stark naked. So she has bared her breasts – lovely, girlish breasts, so Hana assures Viktor and Liesel later – to the audiences of all those countries around the world that didn't actually ban the film. So her ample thighs and buttocks, her elusive comma of pubic hair, have been displayed to thousands of breathless men and women in breathless auditoriums from Paris to Berlin. So she has bared that ineffably beautiful face to the camera while rising – in simulation, one assumes, but all too many didn't – to orgasm. For Hana all this is perfectly acceptable. It is what people do and the way that art moves on. For Mandl and his young wife it is, apparently, an intense embarrassment.

'That was when I was very young,' the woman says quietly. 'I'm out of films now.'

'She was just a foolish child,' her husband adds. 'It is not something that we wish to discuss.'

There is an awkward pause. What to discuss if not this woman's celebrated nudity? Hana smiles and touches the girl's arm reassuringly. 'But it's wonderful. *Ekstase* was wonderful. *You* were wonderful.'

'I said we don't wish to discuss it.' Mandl is getting angry, Viktor can see that. It is a low-level kind of anger, a mere tightening of the muscles of his face, a whitening around the edges of his nose.

'What's wrong with it?' Hana asks him. 'Your wife showed us such beauty, such innocence.'

Mandl replies, very carefully, '*Gnädige Frau*, it was a misjudgement. My wife does not wish to discuss the mistakes she made when she was a mere girl. Is that clear?'

Hana laughs. 'But I *love* to be reminded of the mistakes I made when I was a girl. They did involve running around naked, but regrettably never in front of film cameras.'

There is a terrible moment when the party seems about to come to pieces. Then Liesel takes Hana's arm to lead her away and Viktor says that everything is quite all right and ushers Mandl and his wife round the other side of the onyx wall to see a remarkable phenomenon, how the sunlight, shining through the great windows of plate glass and striking the wall at just the right angle, lights an elemental flame deep inside the stone.

'How fantastic!' Frau Mandl exclaims, looking into the fire and clapping her hands in delight. 'How truly beautiful!' There is something childlike about her enthusiasm, as though it is designed to curry favour with her husband rather than to express her true feelings. But the diversion has done its job and the awkward moment appears to have passed. They go through to the dining area and take their seats round the table.

'This would appeal to Herr Hitler,' Mandl observes. 'The Führer is very keen on round tables and knights and all that kind of thing.' Of course he has met Herr Hitler in person on more than one occasion, and *Il Duce*. Remarkable fellows, he asserts. 'We know them all, Goebbels, Göring, the whole gang, don't we Eva? They took quite a fancy to you, didn't they?'

'I like Magda Goebbels,' she says. There is something wrong with her smile, as though there are tears behind it rather than laughter. 'Magda's fun. Some of the others . . .' Her voice trails away. She glances at Hana. At this circular table there is no hiding one guest from another. The further away you are, the more directly you look at one another.

'The Führer's a strange fellow,' her husband asserts. 'Quite the family man when you get him on his own. Loves babies and dogs and that kind of thing.'

'What about the anti-Semitism?' Liesel asks. 'Don't you find that a bit hard to take?

Mandl's laugh is like a shout. 'They made me an honorary Aryan. How about that? An honorary Aryan. On Herr Hitler's orders. They're pragmatists, you see. If they need to deal with a Jew then they'll come to an accommodation. I'm proof of that. Jews can get on with Hitler and his lot perfectly well.'

'And when they no longer need you?' Viktor asks. 'What becomes of your honorary status then?'

'But they *do* need the Jews. The Jews still run most of the economy.'

'Yet Jewish businesses are being put under Aryan ownership.'

'That's the way we've got to play it for the moment. Things will change. They'll get more moderate once they've consolidated their power.'

'It's riding a tiger, if you ask me.'

The man laughs again. Riding a tiger is what he enjoys. It is only Hana who has threatened to push him off.

'But,' says Hana, 'if Oskar and I were living in Germany our relationship would be illegal. A gentile married to a Jew? That's not allowed.'

'The law is not retroactive, my dear,' Oskar points out. 'If you'll forgive me, you have got to stick to the facts in these issues. Marriages already undertaken are not automatically dissolved. The race laws are quite specific on the point.'

'Which is a typical lawyer's way of looking at it. Whatever the detail, the new German state is quite plainly saying that people like us are in some way in an illicit relationship. And Viktor and Liesel.' Hana looks across the table at Mandl, and then turns her gaze back to his wife. 'From now on, it is, quite simply, illegal for Jews and gentiles to have sex.'

The menacing fricatives of the word *Geschlechtsverkehr* circle the table. Sitting between Viktor and Oskar, the professor's wife blushes.

'The whole thing will just blow over,' Mandl asserts. 'There are all sorts against Hitler, quite apart from the industrialists. I spoke to someone in Bremen who claimed that the Army was dead against him. There's even a contingency plan to take power and reinstate the Kaiser.'

'Would that be any better?'

Liesel says, 'Who wants to reinstate a monarchy? And anyway, that would be against the treaty.' Everyone knows the treaty of Saint-Germain, which came out of that great conclave of the victorious where presidents and prime ministers met to call countries into being from the wreckage of empires.

'The treaties,' says Mandl scornfully, 'what are those pieces of paper worth?'

'If nothing else they mean the creation of our own country,' says Viktor. 'Which ensures a stable democracy in the heart of Europe.'

And so the discussion goes on, straws drifting down the stream and being snatched at by desperate hands. After the meal they have their coffee in front of the onyx wall, their reflected images suspended over the darkened lawn. Mandl is describing his work in Italy, selling *matériel* to the Mussolini government. He uses that word – *matériel* – and makes it sound like blankets and bedspreads. For the third time the university professor helps himself

118

to brandy from the decanter. 'What do you think, Landauer?' he asks, his voice unsteady.

What does Viktor think? He has a feeling of detachment from them all, from Mandl and his awful ideas of course, but also from the other guests, from Hana, and even from Liesel. He catches his wife's eye and smiles distractedly. Is it the Glass Room itself that generates this sense of remoteness? In this place, he thinks, almost anything is possible. He looks around at his glass house where there will be no secrets. Standing beside the Maillol torso, Eva Mandl is in deep conversation with Hana. There's a studied theatricality about Mandl's wife, as though she is all the time expecting people to be watching her. Carrying her glass of brandy, she strolls with Hana across the room and out onto the terrace. Mandl watches them go, mirrored to perfection by the plate-glass windows of the room, a virtual image that floats out in space until Viktor, getting up from his chair, presses the hidden button. With the faint murmur of hidden machinery, the glass pane slides down into the basement and leaves behind it no replica of the people in the room but only the blackness of the night outside. Out there on the terrace, shadowed by the light from the Glass Room, are Hana and Eva talking.

'I think,' says Viktor in reply to the question that has almost been forgotten, 'that if you play with mad dogs you are going to get bitten.'

'What a dreadful man,' says Hana.

It is afterwards. The space is empty of guests, the lights turned down. Hana and Liesel are sitting on the Liesel chairs in front of the onyx wall. The curtains are drawn across the windows now, so that the two women are enclosed in their own world. There is a litter of glasses and coffee cups around them. Cigarette ends fill the ashtrays. Hana has decided to stay the night and Oskar has left, perhaps thankful that for once he knows where his wife will be. Viktor has just gone to bed, leaving the two women alone. 'What a dreadful, dreadful man,' Hana repeats. 'Do you know what Eva told me? Apparently he has been buying every print of that film he can find, the one his wife was in. He buys them and destroys them all. It's pure vandalism. He's insanely jealous.'

119

'Is that what you two were talking about? You quite monopolised her.'

Hana smiles. 'That and other things. Her ambitions, her desires, her dreams. Isn't she wonderful? I don't think I've ever seen so much beauty concentrated all in one place. It's almost too much to accept. She wants to get back into films but he refuses to let her. He keeps her under guard twenty-four hours a day so the poor darling is virtually a prisoner. She's desperate to get away. She made a run for it in Paris a little while ago but they followed her and dragged her back to their hotel.' Hana crosses her legs and reaches for another cigarette. 'You didn't see her film, did you?'

'Viktor thought it would be mere sensationalism.'

'Oh, but it was beautiful. She was actually called Eva in the film. That's what she was, a kind of Eve in the Garden of Eden. Naked, she was like . . .' Hana shivers. 'I can't explain. It was like seeing yourself as you ought to be.'

'You sound quite smitten.'

'Maybe I am.' She draws on her cigarette and watches Liesel through the cloud of smoke. There is a long and thoughtful silence. The cool box of the Glass Room seems to wait on her words. 'Could you ever love another woman, Liesi?' she asks. 'I mean wholly, sexually.'

'That kind of love? How awful!'

'Why awful? You see Eva Kiesler naked in that film and you think, *that's me*. My spirit made flesh, perfected. A man might think, "that's lovely and I want to fuck it"—'

'Hana!'

'But if you're a woman you think, "that's an aspect of me and I want to love her just as I love myself". I think perhaps there's nothing more perfect than love of one woman for another. There's a completeness.'

Liesel laughs with embarrassment, feeling affection, warmth, something like amusement, and underneath it all a small tremor of shame. Hana is always saying preposterous things, but never as outrageous as this. Perhaps it's the drink she's had – starting off with those dry Martinis she was teaching Viktor to make before the evening really began. 'Darling, you make it sound as though you are talking from experience.'

'Of course I'm talking from experience.'

Her words are a shock to Liesel, and yet not a surprise. It is as though the Glass Room has prepared her for this, its spirit of transparency percolating the human beings who stand within it, rendering them as translucent as the glass itself. 'What an extraordinary thing to say, darling. Are you going to tell me you've fallen in love with Eva Mandl?'

'Not her, no. Although maybe it wouldn't be difficult. But not her.'

'Then whom?'

Hana lifts her cigarette to her mouth and draws the smoke into her lungs. There is the sound of her breath as she exhales. She frowns, her mouth turned down as though in distaste. 'If I tell you the truth, will you promise not to hate me?'

'Hanička, I could never hate you.'

Hana shrugs. 'I wonder.'

'Well, go on.'

She draws again on the cigarette. Her hand isn't quite steady. Her expression isn't quite amused. 'It's you, of course,' she says.

There is a complete silence. No sound at all in the unequivocal spaces of the Glass Room. No murmur from the garden coming through the velvet curtains. No stirring in the fabric of the building. Cigarette smoke drifts like grey silk above Hana's head. 'I'm surprised you never realised, Liesi. Does it shock you?' A pause. 'Don't go back on your word.'

Liesel searches for something to say. 'Of course I won't. But I didn't expect to have such responsibility all of a sudden. I mean, I don't want to hurt you, Hanička, I really don't.'

'Oh, you won't hurt me, not unless you send me away. Just let it be. We're not like men, are we? It's perfectly possible for women just to remain friends without being lovers. How often has that happened?'

'But darling—'

'I should have kept my mouth shut, I'm sorry.'

'No, of course not.'

Hana gets up and goes over to the record player. She puts on another of the records she has brought from Paris. There's a clarinet playing. '*J'ai deux amours*,' a woman's voice sings, a high, fluting sound, the sound of France, the sound of America. The

121

two women talk some more, in subdued tones now, the laughter and the acting gone. They talk of love and friendship and men and women. They talk of Oskar and they talk of Viktor. Liesel watches Hana as though with new eyes and marvels that the form is the same but not the substance. Hana loves her. The word 'completeness' comes to her mind and brings with it a shade of guilt. *J'ai deux amours.*

'Play something for me, Liesi,' Hana says when the record comes to an end.

'I'm not good enough, not when I've been drinking. I make mistakes.'

'I'll forgive your mistakes. I'll always forgive your mistakes.'

So they go over to the piano and Liesel plays something she has been practising, Chopin's Nocturne in F sharp major, a tender and elegiac piece that seems to express what she feels better than any words. The notes fall softly in the soundbox of the Glass Room, as softly and precisely as autumnal leaves on a still day, and when the piece comes to an end Hana bends and kisses her on the nape of her neck.

Carefully Liesel closes the lid of the piano. 'I think we'd better go to bed.'

Leaving the mess for the maid to clear up in the morning, they turn off the lights and go upstairs. The narrow spaces on the upper floor are clinical and cool, bathed in that milky light that is the mark of this place, whether it comes through the glass panels by day or from the globes in the ceiling by night. They look in on the children and watch them sleeping, they listen at the door of Viktor's room and hear the faint murmur of his breathing, and then they pause outside the door to the guest room. Liesel turns the handle, then looks at Hana. 'We are silly things, aren't we?' she says.

Silly things, *dumme Dinger*. It sounds absurd.

Loss

Vienna had changed. The city of dreams had become the city of nightmares, a city of fear and anticipation. A tide of political violence lapped around the ponderous baroque buildings and although the jolly music, the waltzes and the polkas, continued to be played in the cafés and the ballrooms, the dance was a dance of death.

When Viktor telephoned the Goldene Kugel she had gone.

What did they mean?

She'd pushed off – left the area.

He felt panic bubbling up inside him like vomit. Where was she now?

They had no idea, no idea at all.

What was she doing?

The voice on the other end laughed. 'What does a girl like that always do?'

He hurried round to the street where she had her little apartment. It wasn't difficult to find the place. There was the *kasher* butcher and the pawnshop across the street, and the heavy door with its peeling paint. The climb up the dingy stairwell towards the attic was vividly familiar. There was the same smell of cabbages or drains, the same damp, the same taint of mould, and when he got to the top and peered out the window, he saw the Riesenrad over the roof tops just as before. But it wasn't just as before. This time the door to Kata's apartment was locked and when he knocked the sound was hollow, as though the space inside were empty and he was hammering on a drum.

'Anyone there?' he called against the wood.

123

There was a movement on the stair below. He looked over the banister and saw an old woman peering up at him. 'I'm trying to find Frau Kata,' he told her.

The old crone sucked her teeth and seemed to assess the taste of what she found there. Was this was the woman who looked after Kata's daughter? 'Frau Kata,' he repeated.

'She's not here.'

'Do you know where she is?'

'She's not here.'

'Do you have any idea where she's gone?'

'She's not here.'

'But do you know where she's gone?'

The movement of the lips, the thoughtful assessment continued. The woman's face was shrivelled, like one of those shrunken heads he had seen in the anthropological museum, the skin stretched tight across the cheekbones, the hair scraped up and knotted on the top of the head. 'She's not here,' she repeated.

He came down the stairs. As he approached, the woman backed into the open doorway to her own apartment, slipping behind the door and peering out at him. 'You keep your distance,' she said.

'I just want to know where she is. Do you have any idea where she might have gone to?' He was suddenly inspired. 'I'm Marika's uncle. You know Marika, don't you? I'm her uncle. I've come to bring her a present.'

But the old crone kept chewing on the morsel of whatever it was inside her shrivelled lips, peering at him through the crack in the doorway and repeating, 'She's gone away. She's gone away.'

Hopelessly he went down the stairs and back out into the street. The sulphurous smell of exhaust fumes tainted the air. On the Praterstrasse there was the roar of lorries and cars, the clatter and clang of trams. Pedestrians gathered on the island in the centre and moved across in herds, like people being driven to their fate by unseen forces. Where was Kata? He went round the corner to the Goldene Kugel and found one of the waiters he thought he recognised. Did he have any idea where Fraülein Kata was? But the man hadn't seen her for some time. Weeks, he thought. No idea, no idea at all. He enquired at the bar but got the same response. 'Don't people phone for her?' Viktor asked, but the barman only shrugged and turned away to serve another customer.

Outside on the pavement he stood irresolutely for a while, then began to walk up Praterstrasse towards the railway station. The disproportionate city lay all around him, a city of faded glories and dying significance, a city with a decorative and frivolous surface but with dark secrets at its heart. The slogan *Juden raus!* was painted on a wall, along with a little stick figure hanging from a crudely painted scaffold. Elsewhere there was a black swastika daubed over a poster that showed a hammer and sickle. Above the roofs of the buildings he could see the arc of the Riesenrad turning slowly in the evening air. In the railway station he wrote a letter and posted it at the office from where he had phoned.

My darling Kata, I have been to your flat and discovered that you have gone. Please contact me. Please don't just abandon me.

Then he wrote his telephone number, and signed the note, *With love, Viktor.*

Coda

'It was at the Sacher, darling. Where else?' They were in the Café Zeman, amidst the chatter and the gossip, sitting at their favourite table where they could see and be seen.

'And you arranged it all?'

'A glorious plot, just like spies. The problem was getting her away from her companion. I've told you about her, haven't I? Some dreadful woman with a moustache like a walrus and jaws like nutcrackers. So I waited for her in the café and as she and the walrus came in, I slipped out to the bathroom. That was the plan, that she was to meet me there. But she didn't come. There I was, standing in the corridor for about half an hour and wondering whether to put plan B into action.'

'Plan B?'

'Rush in and push a *Sachertorte* in the walrus's face and just grab Eva. Anyway, just as I'm about to make my move, out she comes, looking as pale as a ghost but many, many times more lovely. It seems she had had a stand-up row with the walrus. "I don't care what orders my husband gave you, I'm going to have a piss all by myself!" That's what she said apparently, with the whole café listening, can you imagine? Poor love, she was almost paralysed with fright. But so brave! So I grab her by the hand and off we go, down the corridor and out of the back entrance, imagining the walrus on our heels.'

'Hanička, this is ridiculous.'

'You think I'm making it up?'

'When was all this?'

'Three days ago. Darling, you knew I was going to Vienna. I told you.'

'But you never told me you were going to meet Eva Mandl.'

'I'm telling you now, darling. You know the back door of the Sacher? The one onto Maysedergasse?'

'I've never used it.'

'Of course you haven't. But it's there sure enough. I had a taxi waiting, with the engine running and the meter ticking over. A get-away car, just like in the films.'

'You *are* making this up.'

'I already had the stuff in the taxi. A black suit from Grünbaum and the dearest little pillbox hat with a veil from P&C Habig. We pulled the blinds down and Eva changed there and then. Can you imagine *that*? Eva Mandl half undressed in a taxi? I had to help her, just had to.'

'Hanička, this is absurd!'

'Liesi, it is *true*! By the time I'd got her to the Nordbahnhof I'd transformed her into the Merry Widow. No one would have recognised her behind her veil. And we had a private compartment booked on the train. The logic was that the first place they'd look would be the Westbahnhof for the Paris trains, but still we had ten minutes to wait, sitting there in the compartment with the blinds drawn. It felt like an execution chamber. And then finally the whistles blew, the train began to move. And Eva burst into tears and threw herself into my arms.'

There was something shrill about her, as though the story of excitement and plotting was thinly painted over a deep fracture. 'Can you imagine? A whole hour alone with Eva Mandl in a compartment! Tell me, what do you think is the most beautiful thing about her? Of the things that one can see in polite company, of course. I'm not talking about what she showed to cinema audiences, although heaven knows, I could. Her mouth or her eyes? It's one or the other, isn't it? I still can't make up my mind. Most people say her eyes, but I am inclined towards her mouth. The way her upper lip comes down at the very summit of its curve in a delicious little pout. I touched it with my tongue and she gave a little cry, just as though I had touched her *piča*.'

Startled by the language, people at the nearest table looked round.

'Hana! For goodness' sake, not here!'

'Where then, darling? In private? With you?' Her laugh was as brittle as overblown glass. '*Dumme Dinger?*'

127

'That's not fair.'

'But it's true, isn't it?'

Liesel began to gather up her things. 'Please stop this nonsense. Let's pay the bill and go.'

'Do you know what she told me?'

'You actually *talked*?'

'Don't be spiteful. It was a confession, really. She told me that when she was at finishing school in Lucerne she was seduced by her roommate. She was a mere fifteen years old, and this older girl slipped into her bed one night and showed her what to do. Georgie, that was the girl's name. Deliciously androgynous, don't you think? Quite an adept she was, apparently. And Eva was a quick learner.'

Liesel left some coins on the table and made for the door. 'Please Hana. I don't like you in this mood.'

'The mood, my dear, is misery.'

They went out into the park, Hana's arm through Liesel's. Other couples strolled in the sunshine. A nanny pushed two little children in a pram.

'You really are impossible at times, Hanička. Why can't we just be good friends, like we always were?'

'We *are* good friends. You know that. But you know we are more than that.'

'Special friends, then. Particular friends. But I have obligations, to my children, to my husband.'

'Obligations sound awfully dull. What about love, Liesi?'

'Love as well.'

'You don't sound very certain.'

Liesel laughed. Once, she had felt childish and naive in Hana's company, but things had changed. Now Hana had become a kind of supplicant. 'When you've had two children things change. There's a different kind of love.'

'And your love for me? You do love me, don't you? Tell me that you do.'

'Of course I do.'

'So why can't you find joy in it? Tell Viktor. Be honest with him.'

'He wouldn't understand.'

'He would understand more than you think. Look at Oskar.'

'Does Oskar know about me? For God's sake, Hana!'

'Of course he doesn't, darling. He knows lots but he doesn't know about you. You are my one big secret.'

They walked on in the direction of the Künstlerhaus. Apparently there was a photographic exhibition that they just had to see – *Fotoskupina pěti*, the group was called, Photogroup 5. Why 5? Maybe there were just five of them. Surrealists. They made you look at objects from a completely different viewpoint: a hand became something of great mystery, a mirror became a philosophical statement, an egg was the birth of the whole world. That was what Hana said. She squeezed Liesel's arm. 'What would you say if you found out that Viktor had a mistress, Liesi? I mean, no threat to you. Just a woman whom he saw occasionally—'

'Please Hana, must we talk about this kind of thing?'

'But how would you feel?'

'I don't even think about things like that. Why should I? I've got my family and my friends and that is all I need. I don't want great emotion.'

'You haven't answered the question.'

'I'm not going to. I once asked Viktor if he had slept with you, do you know that?' Why did she even mention it? Why didn't she just let the conversation die? 'It was when I was ill, shortly after Martin's birth. You and he were alone together a lot of the time.'

Hana laughed. 'And had he slept with me?'

'He said he hadn't.'

'That's what I remember too. But would you hate either of us if we had done so?'

'I don't think I would. Not hate. But I wouldn't have been happy.'

'You're being – what's the word? – *neupřímná*. Oh, *doppelsinnig*, something like that. You know what I mean.'

Liesel didn't understand. The Czech evaded her, while the German escaped Hana. Quite suddenly, over the word 'insincere', they no longer understood each other. 'Please don't talk like this, Hanička. Please. I know what you mean and I know it doesn't make sense, it's a different thing. Why should feelings always be logical or rational?'

'Viktor would say that they must be.'

'But I'm not Viktor. I love him, but I'm not him. I love him and

129

I love you, but I'm neither of you. And I don't love you when you are talking like this.'

Beside the art gallery there was a war veteran begging, holding a tin and waiting mutely for money. His right trouser leg was pinned up to his waist and the space relinquished by his missing limb was startling, as though he had performed some kind of conjuring trick, a thing involving mirrors. Now you see it, now you don't. Liesel found a crown in her purse and dropped it into his bowl. The man registered nothing, no nod of thanks, no glance upwards at his benefactor, nothing. What if Benno had returned from the war like that, ruined physically and mentally but still alive? Some kinds of life were worse than death, weren't they?

They came round the front of the art gallery. The building was a confection of the Vienna Secession, all sinuous window mouldings and exhortatory epigraphs on the walls. *Dům umění* announced a noticeboard, but the frieze above the portal still said *Künstlerhaus* and still celebrated the jubilee of Emperor Franz Josef. They paid for their tickets and went inside. The photographs in the exhibition were strange and disorientating. One was a close-up of a single female eye. It watched you wherever you went. Then there was an abstract photograph in which the artist had apparently used the photographic process itself to create a swirling pattern of shade and shape. Another picture showed a female doll, the kind of thing Ottilie played with. But this doll was naked and starkly lit, with its head broken off, and there was machinery coming out through its neck, clockwork machinery, cogwheels and springs.

'I haven't told you the end of my adventure with Eva Mandl,' Hana said as they stood looking at this image.

'I'm not sure I want to know.'

'Oh but you do, darling. She spent the night in my bed – that was my reward.'

'Why are you telling me this?'

'To try and make you jealous. And the next morning – that was just yesterday. It seems an age. Anyway, the next morning I put her on the train to Prague. Paris, that's where she wanted to go. I offered to go with her but she said no. She'll write, she said she'll write.'

'What does she intend to do?'

Hana laughed bitterly. 'She wants to become a movie star.'

130

Anschluss

The radio is on in every bar, in every café, in every living room across the city. Rumour comes quicker than the news broadcasts, conveyed on its own mysterious ether – the Austrian army has fought back against the invasion, hundreds of deaths have been reported, there are riots in Vienna where the Communists have taken to the barricades. There is fighting in the streets between National Socialists and the police. Almost as quickly come the denials: there is no unrest, the Austrian chancellor Schuschnigg has ordered the army not to resist, there must be no shedding of German blood.

The next day the newspapers print photographs of troops crossing the border, and a line of German police marching into some quaint Tyrolean town with villagers raising their arms in the Hitler salute. One picture shows a peasant woman in tears. The German papers claim that they are tears of joy; the Czech papers opt for tears of despair.

The same morning they tune in to Austrian radio and hear the great sea-sound of the crowd at the Heldenplatz in Vienna, the drums beating and the bands playing and Hitler's voice crackling out through the quiet and calm of the Glass Room, announcing *Anschluss*, union. Austria is no longer an independent republic: overnight it has become an eastern province of the greater German Reich, Österreich become Ostmark.

Where, Viktor wonders, is Kata now?

'It is simply illegal,' he says. He sounds absurd saying that, absurd and impotent. But more than that, he *knows* that he sounds absurd as he paces up and down the Glass Room waving the latest edition of *Lidové Noviny* and talking about the treaties of Versailles and St Germain. Both those accords seem like something out of the history books, like Magna Carta or the Edict of Worms: things that apply to different people in different places a long time ago. 'If he's allowed to do this, what the devil will happen next?'

What happens, like torrential rain after the first crack of thunder, is the arrival of the refugees. They cross the southern border, from Vienna and the other cities, a ragbag collection of men, women and children with whatever possessions they can carry with them. They flood into the country and the city, some by train, some by car, some tramping along the roads pushing handcarts and humping suitcases. The flood runs down streets and amongst the houses, trickling through the alleyways, settling where it can into pools of misery and fear. You cannot go into the city without seeing the human debris washed up against doors and deposited on street corners, the flotsam and jetsam of the new Europe.

'We must do something for them,' Viktor says. The expanse of the Glass Room is a reproach, a space where the refugees won't come, won't find shelter, won't be able to unroll their blankets and sleep.

'What can we do?' Liesel asks. 'This is a problem for governments not individuals. How can we help?'

'It is up to individuals to stir their governments into action.'

Outside in the garden, oblivious to all this, the children are playing. Ottilie is directing Martin in some complex game. Viktor can hear their voices like the chattering of swallows. Ottilie is clearly the wife of their little family, instructing Martin what to do and how to do it. They have her toy pram with them and Martin's pedal car. But the pedal car won't go well on the wet grass.

He turns to Liesel. She is reading a magazine, one of those dreadful fashion things she borrows from Hana, a catalogue of attenuated women with bored expressions and no breasts. 'You know,' he says, 'I think we may have to consider going ourselves.'

She looks up. It is strange how he has never become used to her looks, her features, the elongated bone structure and long nose and compressed mouth. Every time he looks at her he thinks of the first time they met, the first glance, the first small stir of attraction. 'Going? Where?'

'It sounds like running away, doesn't it? But I don't see any alternative if things get much worse. I mean, if you look at the situation—'

The magazine lies open on her lap, showing women wearing peignoirs and negligées. 'Viktor dear, what are you talking about? Where exactly are we going?'

She hasn't understood. He always expects her to understand what he is talking about and usually she does. Usually she follows the flights of his mind. 'I mean leaving the house, the city, the country, Liesel. I'm talking about leaving all this just as these wretched refugees have left their homes.' He looks round as though to emphasise the point: all this, the Glass Room, the quiet and the measured, the ineffable balance and rationality of it all. 'I mean emigrating. We might have to emigrate.'

Now surely she has understood, but she still hasn't said anything. The magazine still lies open on her lap, displaying the languid women.

'At least until all this blows over.'

'Blows over?'

He shrugs. 'Who knows? Someone might shoot him. He might have a heart attack – God knows, he looks likely to when you hear him ranting and raving in the way he does. But you can't rely on something like that, can you? We should at least make plans. Just in case.'

She glances down, and for a moment it seems as though she might continue reading the magazine, but then she looks up again. 'In case of what?'

'In case of war, my dear. Invasion. By the way things are going the next target is going to be this country. Look at what's happening in the border territories already.'

'Are you serious about this, Viktor?'

'Would I joke about it?'

She closes the magazine. There's the faint slap of glossy paper. 'But how could we leave? This is where we belong. This is our home. We don't know anywhere else. Oh, I know what you're going to say. You're going to give me some proverb or other: home is where the heart is, something like that. But home is also this house, this city, our family and friends. And what about the business? How can you suggest just abandoning that?'

He shrugs. 'I'm a Jew, Liesel, whether I like it or not. Ottilie and Martin are Jews – or half-breeds or whatever they call them nowadays. It's not by choice. It's a matter of fact. You can choose not to be a Bolshevik or a homosexual or most of the other things they hate, but you cannot choose not to be a Jew. They decide for you. Jews can't hold down professional jobs, they can't own businesses, they pay extra taxes, they can't marry gentiles, they can't even visit gentiles in their houses. They get arrested and imprisoned on any pretext whatever. What's going to happen next? Compulsory divorce for people of mixed marriages? How about that? Jewish children banned from schools? Jews thrown out of their homes? God knows.'

'But all that's in Germany, not here.'

'Don't be naive, Liesel. It's Austria as well now. The Nazis are no more than fifty kilometres away from us here in our nice safe house, and in between them and us are the border territories – which are already German anyway.' He turns and looks out of the great windows again, as though searching for the first signs of their coming. But nothing has changed. The children are still playing, the city is still there, the air is still smudged with the smoke from a thousand fires. Nothing has changed and yet everything has changed. 'I don't want us to be in a panic to get out like all those wretched people from Austria. I don't want to be grabbing things into a suitcase at the last moment. I don't want my family to be like that.'

'So where are you planning to go? Not Palestine, for goodness' sake.'

'Of course not Palestine. Switzerland. I've been moving funds . . .'

'You've been *what*?'

He looks ahead through the window. What has happened to Kata? He wonders this often. All he knows is that fifteen thousand Schillings were moved out of his Viennese bank account. Nothing more. She just vanished. 'Advance planning,' he says to Liesel. 'Never be caught out without a plan, never be caught out by the market. I've been making arrangements. It's only now that it seemed right to mention it to you.'

Encounter

'I suppose it's not unusual for our part of the world, is it?' Oskar is saying. 'Empires come and go, countries come and go, people come and go.' His bald head gleams in the pale lights of the Glass Room. He is sitting in the front row of chairs, with Hana and Liesel on one side and Viktor on the other. Around them people are taking their seats, the Coordinating Committee for Refugees, a committee of committees, an assembly of the concerned and the self-satisfied, the do-gooders and the worriers, the selfless and the self-serving.

'Look at our own little statelet,' Oskar continues, 'carved out of central Europe like an intricate piece of folk art. Now you see it, now you don't. Here one moment and' – he clicks his fingers – 'gone the next.'

'For God's sake, Oskar,' Hana snaps. 'Have a little more tact.'

'Ah, tact. Like that tactful fellow, Herr Hitler.'

Businessmen, lawyers, academics take their places. Clerics of various persuasions and religions nod cautiously when they meet, like former enemies eyeing each other across recently dismantled barricades. The talk dies away and the chairman of the committee gets to his feet and begins his address.

'So what sort of stunt is this?' Oskar whispers loudly.

Hana tries to hush him to silence. 'They've brought some typical refugees to speak to us.'

'What's a typical refugee?'

'For God's sake shut up and listen.'

Fiddling with his pince-nez, nervously shuffling his papers, anxiously eyeing the bald man in the front row, the chairman

135

endeavours to explain: there is the need for shelter, the need for food, the problem of schooling for displaced children and medical treatment for the sick and care for the elderly, and underneath it all, the pressing need for money. 'But the intention of this meeting is to try to bring the plight of the refugees home to us all, make their personal, human tragedy part of our own lives. We have decided to introduce you to some witnesses of these terrible events, people who can tell you in their own words what has happened, to share with us the reality that has unfolded in Austria. Perhaps like that we can take these tragic occurrences out of the realm of the newspaper and the newsreel and into our own hearts.'

There is coming and going round the committee table. The secretary, a middle-aged woman with the manner of a schoolteacher, whispers something in the chairman's ear. 'I'm afraid there's been a bit of a delay,' the chairman explains. 'But they're coming, they're coming.'

'A nonsense,' says Oskar. 'A refugee's just you and me. There's nothing to see.'

'Their story,' Liesel says. 'They want to tell their story.'

'Their story is anybody's story. That's not the point. The point is, they are here and the government has got to do something about them.'

Eventually the refugees appear. They are ushered in from the dining area – presumably they've been brought down through the kitchens – three adults and three children shuffling round the partition under the direction of the secretary of the committee. With their entry, the Glass Room has taken on something of the quality of a theatre, a small studio theatre of the kind that has become fashionable for avant-garde productions, where the audience sits within touching distance of the actors. No elevated stage, no proscenium arch, just the performance about to begin in the space between the dining area and the door from the stairs. 'Stand there,' the secretary tells them. 'And you, yes, you, go over there.'

The refugees obey dumbly, confused by their sudden appearance before an audience. There is a middle-aged couple, with between them a ten-year-old boy and a fifteen-year-old, bespectacled girl. Their clothes are crumpled, as though they might have spent the night sitting in a third-class railway compartment.

Maybe they have. One lens of the girl's spectacles is cracked, giving her a squint-eyed look. Beside this family of four there is a single woman with her daughter. The daughter is about eight years old, a bright blonde girl in a shabby floral dress. She blushes at the sight of so many people gawping at her. The mother seems to be in her early thirties. She is small and neat, with a sharp, pretty face. Men observe her with close interest. But as she looks back at the audience her expression is one of faint disdain. And those eyes, as pale as the sky at the horizon.

Kata.

The whole essence of the Glass Room is reason. That is what Viktor thinks, anyway. For him it embodies the pure rationality of a Greek classical temple, the austere beauty of a perfect composition, the grace and balance of a painting by Mondrian. There are no disturbing curves to upset the rectilinear austerity of the space. There is nothing convolute, involute, awkward or complex. Here everything can be understood as a matter of proportion and dimension. Yet there, standing mere feet away from him, is Kata.

Her eyes, those transparent eyes, move across the faces in the audience. When they reach him her expression changes fractionally. Is there now a glimpse of fear in her look? He shifts uncomfortably in his chair. The secretary is introducing her guests: a Mr and Mrs Adolf Neumann and their two children, Frederick and Sophia; a Mrs Kalman and her daughter Marika. Mr Neumann is a shopkeeper in the 2nd district. Mrs Kalman is a widow, also from the 2nd district. She has been working in the fashion trade.

'A seamstress,' Kata says. Her voice is quiet but clear, unfettered by any self-consciousness. 'When I can get the work,' she adds, looking directly at Viktor. It is the most open look he has ever received, something between pleading and apology, as though she has, for a moment, opened up her soul to him just as she opened up her body. The same wondrous, glistening vulnerability. 'I had a bit of money put aside in the bank, but I suppose that's gone by now—'

'My shop was ransacked,' Herr Neumann interrupts. That's what it seems to Viktor, that Kata's words have been pushed aside. He looks round to see if others in the audience feel the same, but

137

everyone is merely watching the small drama revealing itself on stage, an act from the theatre of the absurd, a dialogue of the dispossessed.

'Windows smashed, everything thrown out on the street. They took things, of course – jewellery, silver, anything they could lay their hands on. The SS, it was, the Black Shirts. They made us go down on our knees to pick up the mess with our bare hands. And then we had to scrub the pavement clean.' As he talks his wife begins to weep silently. The man breaks off his account to say something to her. They are not words of comfort but words of admonition. 'Don't cry in front of all these people! Pull yourself together, woman.'

Kata seizes the moment to speak for herself. She talks about how the place where she was working – 'It was Jewish, see?' – was invaded one morning by uniformed men. They were Austrians, you could tell that. Uniformed, with armbands bearing the *Hakenkreuz*, but Austrians clearly enough. *Raus, raus!* they screamed. Out, out! Women were beaten up – 'There were only women there' – and the machines were wrecked. Somehow she managed to get away unhurt. She ran straight to her daughter's school, snatched Marika from her class and together they went back to their flat. The Nazis were already at work on the ground floor of the building. There was a butcher's shop and they'd smashed the window and thrown everything out into the street, carcasses and all. 'Someone was pissing on the mess,' she says.

There's a sharp intake of breath at her language. Pissing. The word shocks the audience more than anything else, more than the fact that women have been beaten up or that the butcher was lying there in the gutter, his throat cut with one of his own knives. Pissing on the mess.

'Somehow we got past the soldiers and ran inside. They were laughing, I remember that. They were laughing and calling as we grabbed whatever we could and stuffed it into two suitcases. Then we went back down to the street. One of the men in uniform shouted at us. "Are you Yids as well?" Something like that. But he didn't try and stop us. I just grabbed my daughter's hand and we ran all the way to the railway station.'

It was a decision that was no decision. An instant of caprice.

The trains were all going north, to the border. They were packed and Kata and Marika had to queue for six hours before they found a place.

After the meeting people mill about the six witnesses. Liesel talks to Kata, stooping towards the smaller woman like royalty talking to someone in the crowd, bestowing gracious sympathy and a kindly ear. To Viktor the conjunction seems impossible – Liesel talking to Kata, two women from worlds separated by an unbridgeable gulf, here together beneath the white ceiling of the Glass Room.

Kata looks up and catches his eye. Liesel follows the direction of her glance. 'Viktor, come and meet Frau Kalman.'

He walks towards them slowly. It has all the absurd logic of nightmare, when the things you do are outrageous and yet no one takes any notice. It is outrageous to be reaching out and feeling Kata's small hand in his, yet no one notices. He raises it to within a mere centimetre of his lips. It is clear, isn't it, that he holds it a fraction longer than would seem proper? Surely it is obvious that they share a glance that is theirs alone and excludes the whole of the rest of the world. Yet no one notices. Her hand slips away. The contact was fleeting. He wants to keep hold of her. He wants – in a dream world it would happen – to pull her towards him and take her into his arms and still have no one notice.

'Frau Kalman and her daughter have been put up in a school gymnasium,' Liesel explains to Viktor. 'I suggested that we might do something for her.'

'Do something?'

'Help them in some way.'

He hesitates. He should be in command of the situation, lord in his own house, the man who always has a plan. But he isn't. He feels confused and embarrassed, concerned that matters are out of his control. Control is what he craves.

Kata looks at him with that steady gaze. 'The lady tells me that this is your house. I never imagined . . .' Her words are poised on the brink of revelation. What did she never imagine? When did she never imagine? '. . . that there could be such a beautiful place.'

'I'm glad you like it.'

'It's modern, isn't it? Very modern. I like modern things.

Modern is the future, isn't it?' She looks round for her daughter. 'Come here, Mari. Come and meet these kind people.'

For Viktor it is another dream moment, one amongst many. Will Marika recognise him? But she seems a different creature altogether from the girl he glimpsed on that last occasion, when she opened the door to her mother's room. The child has become a girl, embarrassed by the attention of the adults. She keeps her eyes down and shuffles her feet and says something that may be hello. Liesel crouches down to her and tips up her chin. 'What a pretty girl you are, Marika. Are you happy here? Are people looking after you and your mummy?' She glances up at Kata. 'She takes after you, doesn't she? But she hasn't got your eyes.'

'She got them from her father.'

'Her father?'

'He died.'

'Don't you have any other family?'

Kata shrugs. 'I haven't seen them for years. I was the black sheep who ran away to the big city.'

Liesel turns to Viktor. 'I thought of the *chata*. What do you think?'

He stares at her, his mind blank. 'The *chata*? What do you mean?'

'It's just a hut really,' Liesel explains to Kata. 'We used it as a kind of hideaway when we were children but when I had scarlet fever as a child I actually stayed in it with a nurse. So that Benno wouldn't catch it.'

'Benno?'

'Benno was my brother.' She straightens up and grasps Viktor's arm. 'Why not the *chata*? There's even a cooker, or at least there used to be. And a bathroom of course, but only with a shower. The place is too small to turn round in but you'd manage for the time being.'

The absurd dream continues: Liesel is suggesting this. She seems to like this woman in her dowdy clothes, the refugee who yet hasn't acquired the manner of a refugee, the listlessness and the air of defeat that seems to infect most of them. Liesel is fired with enthusiasm and looking round to tell Hana, and taking Kata's and Marika's hands, as though by grasping their hands she has grasped an opportunity of doing something concrete for these people. 'You'll be your own mistress while you sort yourselves out. And I'm sure we can find you some work. I mean, a dressmaker is always in demand. What do you think, Viktor?'

'I don't know what to say.'

Kata's transparent eyes are turned on him, letting the sky into the room as clearly as the glass windows themselves. 'It seems too much. We're only two out of thousands. Why should we get special treatment?'

'What do you think, Viktor?'

Insensible to the fate of thousands, Viktor looks out through the windows into the garden. The silver birch is still bare after the winter, but there is the most delicate dusting of pale green over the tips of its branches: a pollen of new growth. Beyond it the lawn slopes down towards the rhododendrons. And beyond that, among the bushes, is the *chata*. He tries to breathe in. Something seems to be suffocating him, starving him of air. 'You'd have to ask your parents.'

'I'll ring them straight away, and then we can go down and see it. Just wait there.'

Excited by the prospect of doing something other than merely talking about matters, Liesel goes to make the call. For a moment Viktor is standing there alone with Kata and her daughter. 'What do you think?'

'You want me to go, don't you?'

'No. No, I don't.' Someone comes up to say goodbye. The group is breaking up. 'Viktor,' Hana calls, 'there's someone you must talk to.'

'I'm busy,' he replies, turning back to Kata. 'Let me show you the garden. You may be able to get a glimpse of the place. It's very small. Just a summerhouse really.'

Hana reaches out and touches his arm as they go past. 'There's a problem here that you might be able to solve.'

'I'm just going to show Frau Kalman and her daughter the garden. We'll only be a moment.'

They go out through the dining area onto the terrace. It's a kind of escape, a sudden rush of freedom. Like waking from the claustrophobia of a dream into a world of normality and logic: the cool of the outside air, the hard touch of the concrete steps that go down to the lawn. Marika runs ahead as though she too has been released from some kind of stricture.

'She didn't recognise me,' Viktor says.

'I don't know. She's a secretive girl. Keeps her thoughts to herself.'

A breeze shifts the branches of the birch, a cool breath of spring after the heat of the Glass Room. Viktor wants to say a dozen things, dangerous things, the kind of things that leave you open and vulnerable. But he finds only something banal. 'I didn't know you were Jewish.'

'I didn't know you made motor cars. There's a lot we didn't know about each other, isn't there? Landauer, for God's sake.' She glances at him and there's that look in her eye, and for the first time a smile at the corners of her mouth. 'But I *did* know you were Jewish.'

Her words and her glance evoke a small rise of anticipation. Before he can say anything Marika calls, 'Look, Mutti, a hideout!' She has gone in amongst the bushes and found traces of Ottilie's presence amongst the rhododendrons, things that she has taken there to make a house: a couple of old pots, a toy pram but no baby in it, a bucket.

'It's the children,' Viktor explains.

'Where are they?'

'With their nanny. Where did you go? I went to look for you at your flat but there was no one there, and no one seemed to know anything about you. Where the hell did you go?'

'With your fifteen thousand Schillings, you mean?'

'I don't mean that.'

'There's a path through the bushes!' Marika calls. She's there amongst the shadows and the branches, a small, white-limbed elf.

'Come back, Mari! You'll get dirty.'

'You haven't told me what happened.'

Kata ducks into the shadows of the rhododendrons, following Marika. 'Where the hell has she gone?'

He goes after her, following her stooped figure. 'It's quite safe. You can see the *chata*. Just the roof.'

Kata peers, crouching to look through the leaves. He touches her waist, holds her for a moment. That firm waist, those hips that seemed surprisingly full when she was naked. She moves out of his grasp. 'Please.'

And then he makes his confession, his sacrifice, a deliberate demonstration of his weakness. 'I've thought about you every moment of every day since we last saw each other. I know it's idiotic, but it's true. And now you're here . . .' He looks back. Liesel has appeared on the terrace looking blindly over the garden, calling his name. She can't see them, of course she can't see them, not without her spectacles.

'Marika, come here at once!' Kata says sharply. The girl stops, arrested by her mother's tone. 'Come out here. There's no time for this. We've got to go.' She holds out her hand to take the girl's. The moment is over. They step out of the shadows and into the pale afternoon sunlight, blinking up at the house.

'We're here,' he calls. 'We were trying to spot the *chata*.'

Liesel runs down the steps. She's a girl again, excited by her new idea; a large clumsy girl running down the lawn towards her husband and the dowdy woman with her little daughter. 'It's fine, Mutti says it's fine. She says it would be an act of Christian charity.'

Chata

She's there. He doesn't see her, but he knows that she is there. Down through the garden, through the shadows of the rhododendrons, following the sinuous path that Ottilie has made right to the fence that delineates their garden from that of Liesel's parents' house below. She's there.

He doesn't see her but he senses her, smells her almost, her scent coming on the air like the smell of spring, something crisp and fresh mingled with the damp perfume of moss and leaf mould. Standing at the windows of the Glass Room he draws on his cigarette and looks out on the view and wonders whether, climbing up the slope behind the *chata*, she might be able to catch a glimpse of him, and if she does, what does she think? And if she doesn't, the question still remains: what does she think?

'I'll go down and see how she's settling in,' Liesel suggests. 'Do you want to come with me?'

He blows smoke out in a thin stream. 'It's all right. She's your guest.'

'I think perhaps,' she says, 'that I might take Ottilie to play with her little girl. What was her name?'

'I don't recall.'

'Maria, that was it.'

'I think it was Marika.'

'Yes, Marika. I think it would do Ottilie good, to see how others less fortunate than her live. What do you think?'

'Fine,' he says. 'But not as an exercise in social education, for God's sake. Just to make friends.'

'Of course.' So she calls Ottilie down, and the two of them go

144

out onto the terrace together and make their way down the garden.

Watching them cross the lawn Viktor contemplates chance. It is nothing else. The coincidence might seem some kind of predestination but he knows that it is not so – it is pure caprice. You can call it malicious if you like but in fact it is neutral. Things just happen. One country occupies another; people flee, scatter across the countryside, some here, some there, like thrown dice. Contingency. One fetches up amongst thousands at the railway station at Město; helpers try and organise them; do-gooders do good; and there she is. What was one chance in a million suddenly becomes a certainty. Because it has happened.

And life goes on. That is the astonishing thing. As normal. Streams are an obvious metaphor – currents, turbulence, dark depths beneath the surface wavelets, drowned bodies out of sight amongst the mud and the weeds. The possibilities of metaphor are almost limitless.

'There's a piano recital tomorrow evening,' Liesel tells him a few days later when he's sitting in the library, reading the newspaper. A radio is on but for the moment there is no news, just some discussion about gardening. When is the best time to take cuttings from fuchsias? It seems absurd to be talking about fuchsias when the world is falling to pieces. 'Oh?'

'Hana has got us tickets. That Kaprálová girl, you remember? Kundera is giving the première of one of her works. Variations on something or other.'

'They are always variations on something or other. Must we go? I suppose we must.'

'Hana tells me she's trying to renew her scholarship, to get back to Paris.'

'Hana is?'

'You're not paying attention, are you? Kaprálová. Vitulka. You know she got that scholarship to study in Paris. You remember. Now she's trying to get it renewed.'

He folds his paper and puts it aside. 'She's probably seen the writing on the wall. I'm going to have a word with your father.'

'Papi? What about?'

'The business, the company. Just a chat. I think we must consider getting Landauerovka out of my ownership. If they come . . .'

'Oh, Viktor. Not that again. You are such a pessimist.'

'I'm a realist. Look at what's happening. The so-called Sudeten German Party makes absurd demands and the Hitler government just eggs them on. German troops are massing on the border. We could have a war on our hands within days, Liesel. Read the papers, for God's sake!'

'I do read the papers.'

'You read the fashion pages.'

He walks round to his father-in-law's house. The exercise will calm him down. He might have picked his way down through the garden, the path past the *chata*, but he chooses not to and instead goes round by the streets, along Schwarzfeldgasse, Černopolní, Blackfield Road, to the street of steps that leads down to the park, Lužánky Park as it is called now; the Augarten as it used to be and will doubtless be called again when disaster strikes. In the park there is a group of children with their teacher. Maybe they are from Ottilie's school. He stands at the railings for a while trying to see her. Children concentrate the mind wonderfully. He watches them laughing and chasing each other. Three of them are on the swings, with others waiting their turn. 'You must wait patiently,' the teacher tells them but they push and shove just the same. None of them seems to be Ottilie. Maybe it isn't even her class. Maybe it isn't even her school. They chatter like swallows, he thinks, and turns away to cross Parkstrasse and walk up the drive to the front door of the big house where a maid answers and shows him into the study where the old man is reading the newspapers and smoking.

Liesel's father is always welcoming. There is none of his wife's peculiar reserve, none of her sideways glancing at Viktor as though to reassure herself that Jewishness is a not a blemish that you carry, visible, like a birth mark on your face. 'Viktor, how *lovely* to see you,' she is wont to say when they meet, but always with that faint tone of surprise, as though she was expecting much worse. 'Viktor, how *good* to see you,' her father says, and appears to mean it. The old man tries to settle him down in one of the leather armchairs, offers him a cigar and calls for some coffee. 'What's it all about, my dear fellow? Tell me what it's all about. This stuff' – he waves his copy of the *Prager Tagblatt* – 'looks pretty grim, doesn't it?'

Viktor declines to sit. Despite his walk he is still impatient, even agitated. He wants to pace about the room, from library shelf to window, back and forth as he does up and down in front of the windows of the Glass Room; but instead he feels that he should appear calm and collected. 'I'm thinking about the future.'

'The future?'

Viktor stands still for a moment, staring through the window at the fine slope of lawn and the trees, at the rise of ground that leads up steeply to the house, his and Liesel's house that you can't quite see from here because of the trees. 'A *possible* future.' The *chata* is couched amongst hedges so that only its roof is visible. 'As you know we have both families' interests represented in the firm at present. I think that it ought to come entirely under your control.'

The old man coughs on his cigar. He seems startled, but surely it is obvious, isn't it? 'How can that be so?'

'I've spoken to my father and he agrees. And my lawyer. Oh, I'd continue to run everything, but it would be under your ownership. Legally speaking. I'd just be an employee. It's just that as things stand, I fear . . .'

'We all fear, don't we old fellow? We all fear.'

'But this isn't irrational fear, is it? If the Germans come . . .'

'Come?'

Viktor stops his pacing and turns to the old man. 'Invade. If there's a war. If there's a war I think that I may have to leave. As a Jew, I mean. Liesel will of course be in a different position.'

'But isn't that a bit pessimistic?'

'Is it? Look at Austria. Next it'll be the border territories. What's the difference between the borders and the rest of the country? In the eyes of the Nazis, I mean.'

'Have you discussed this with Liesel?'

'Briefly. Like you, she thinks I'm being pessimistic, but I think you have to be pessimistic at this point. And plan. You have to have a plan.'

'And your plan is . . . ?'

'I've just told you. I'll have the company lawyer draw up an instrument for the transfer of ownership . . .'

The conversation goes on. It is one of those conversations that

are the norm these days, partly apocalyptic, occasionally opti-
mistic, usually full of foreboding. 'We'll come through,' his
father-in-law decides in the end, and Viktor has to agree with him.

'I'm sure we will. But who knows where we will be by then?'
He is still standing at the window, looking out on the garden. He
asks, without turning, 'How is that woman getting on in the
chata?'

'The Viennese woman? She's one of yours, isn't she? *Žid*.' The
old man uses the Slav word but his grasp on the language is uncertain. *Židovka*, he should say. Jewess. 'I hardly notice her. She
seems a bit surly to me. The little girl's enchanting though. Calls
me Opa.' He laughs. 'Theresa got quite indignant about such
familiarity but I said, let her be. The little mite probably never had
a grandfather of her own, so let her be. She's a bastard, you know
that? Maybe you don't.'

'No, I didn't.'

'Theresa asked her mother point blank – where is the father?
what's he doing about looking after you? – and the woman must
have got angry because she snapped back that there was no
father, that she had never been married to him and she had no
idea where he was. And furthermore it was nobody's business but
her own. Which made Theresa's eyes water a bit, I can tell you.'

Viktor turns from the view. 'I thought she was a widow.'

'That's what they all say, isn't it?'

'Is it?'

'So I've heard tell.' The old man grins at him through his moustaches. He is a figure from the past, from the days of the
Monarchy – bearded and stiff-collared. Women are something to
be hallowed or despised; there isn't much in between.

'Heard tell?'

'You know what I mean.'

But Viktor doesn't. He doesn't understand any of this, the
jovial exchange of confidences, the sly and off-colour jokes.
'Maybe I'll walk back through the garden and see how she's
doing. I can report back to Liesel.'

'She's probably not there. She seems to go out early and doesn't
come back until lunchtime when her daughter gets back from
school.'

'You've been watching her?'

148

'Theresa tells me.' He laughs gruffly, puffing on his cigar. 'She reports everything to me. Even what I'm doing myself.'

'I'll go and see.'

He finds his own way out, through the French windows that open onto the grass. Who, he wonders, is watching his progress across the lawn? But when he glances back at the house the windows merely reflect the plain white of the daylight. One window is open, high up beneath one of the turrets. A maid's room, perhaps. He turns and continues towards the tall hedges that hide the *chata*. Liesel and he used to come there when they were courting. They'd let themselves into the summerhouse and kiss and cuddle a bit while he hoped, vainly, for something more. 'Not here, not now,' she'd whisper, putting his hand aside.

He rounds the end of the hedge and there is the building. It's the kind of construction you might come across in the country, one of those holiday cabins that are so popular these days. Brick footings and dark, creosoted wood and a tarpaper roof. The place is silent in the morning air, and somehow threatening, like something from a fairy tale or a half-remembered dream, a cottage inhabited by a witch who eats children. He goes up to the door and knocks.

'Anyone there?'

There is no reply. He looks round. The hedges cut him off from view of the downstairs windows of the house. Only the top storey is visible, and the grey roof with its twin cupolas. A maid has hung bedding out of the open window.

He knocks again – 'Anyone at home?' – and then tentatively turns the handle. The door opens. The atmosphere inside is warm and resinous, replete with the heat of distant summer days.

'Frau Kalman?' But there is no one there, just two low beds, neatly made up, and on one side, opposite a small gas stove, a cane table with two chairs.

The floorboards creak as he crosses the cabin. Her things are all around – some dresses hanging over the chairs, shoes on the floor. A piece of string has been fixed across the room as a washing line. Two pairs of knickers hang from it, and a vest with tawdry lace trimming and a brassiere. He pulls one of the knickers towards him and presses the gusset to his nose, but it gives him nothing more than the smell of clean cotton. It is the pillow on one of the

149

beds that holds the smell of her, a warm and complex scent that he recognises instantly. He straightens up and stands there indecisively, part intruder, part acolyte, wholly captivated by the small hints of her presence.

At that moment there is a footfall outside. He turns to find Kata standing in the doorway. There is a hiatus, a pause in the whole progress of time, while they watch each other.

'I was wondering when you'd come,' she says. 'Please, make yourself at home. Don't worry about me. After all—'

'I'm sorry. I found the door open—'

'It doesn't matter.'

He's confused, like a child caught entering his parents' room. 'I just wanted to see how you are getting on.'

'I'm sure you did.' She closes the door behind her. She's wearing a plain coat, the same coat she wore on that first day in the house, and the same lace-up shoes. Her hair is gathered up anyhow, stray wisps framing her face. Her delicate jawline and the impudent ornament of her ears give her a beauty that belies the dowdy clothing. Ornament is crime, he thinks.

'I gather that Ottilie has been to play with Marika.'

'Once or twice. They get on well together.' She lifts a shopping bag onto the table and begins taking things from it. A jar and some tins go into the wall cupboard. There is a loaf of bread, a bag of potatoes, some vegetables. She takes her coat off and hangs it on a peg behind the door, then turns to the washing line. 'I'm sorry if it's a bit of a mess in here. It's not that easy keeping things in order in such a small space.'

He watches the reach of her arms, the quick, efficient fingers. 'You've stopped biting your nails,' he observes.

She glances at them, almost as though surprised at the discovery. 'You told me to.'

'I'm surprised you took any notice. How are you for money?'

'All right.'

'I can give you some if you need—'

She looks round. 'I'm all right, thank you. The committee gave me something to start, but now I'm earning a bit. Your wife has helped. She's given me things to do, adjusting some dresses, things like that. And recommended me to some of her friends. She's been very kind.'

150

He takes one of the chairs and sits down. There is something domestic about the scene: his sitting there watching while she sorts out the laundry. He never sees the laundry being done at the house. It is the province of Laník's sister, down in the basement. Occasionally they encounter each other as he is coming out of the darkroom. Laníková blushes and apologises for her presence and Viktor feels awkward at invading her territory. But there is no such awkwardness now, more a kind of uncertainty, as though the actors don't quite know their lines or understand the thrust of the plot.

'Does she know you're here?' she asks.

'My wife? I told her I was going to see her father.'

'Be careful with your alibi.'

'It's not an alibi. It's the truth.'

She finishes folding the clothes and looks round for somewhere to put them.

'Didn't you get my letters?' he asks.

'I got them.'

'But you didn't try to get in touch.'

'No.'

A cat, he thinks. The same introversion, the same precise quick movements disguised as languor. 'I've missed you more than I can say . . .'

She turns. She has something in her hand, a black dress, one of Liesel's dresses that she is adjusting, something sheer and silk with a label that proclaims Schiaparelli. Hana brought it back from Paris, insisting that it was just perfect for Liesel. 'Isn't all that over? It was a piece of business, and you were very kind to me and gave me the possibility of escape, and now it's over.'

'It's not like that.'

'Oh, it *is* like that. It's exactly like that, Herr Viktor. You may pretend to yourself that it's not but believe me, I know. Look, I haven't got much time. Marika comes back from school soon and I've got lunch to prepare. And anyway they'll get suspicious if they see you coming here. I can't risk that. The old lady watches like a hawk to see what's going on. I think she's worried about her husband. As well she might be.'

'Her husband?'

'You look surprised. He's been round as well. Wanted to see

151

how I was doing just the same as you. Called me pet and patted me on the bottom and said he'd look after me.'

'And you—?'

'I told him that he could keep his hands to himself or I'd tell his wife.'

'Am I any different?'

She looks at him without expression. 'You're younger.'

'Is that all?'

She thinks for a moment and then says, 'No, it's not all,' and turns away and finds something to do, some vegetables to put in the basin to wash, a tin of meat to open.

'What else?'

'Never you mind.'

'But I do mind. I mind a great deal. Why didn't you answer my letters? Why did you just drop me?'

She stops her work, bending over the basin with her hands in the water and her head down. 'Look, everything I did was for Marika. Going with men, going with you. You know that, don't you?'

'Yes.'

'So that's it really. I just needed a bit of money, and the best way to get it—'

'I know all that. But you still haven't answered my question.'

'I did what you told me. I stopped seeing men. Including you. Wasn't that allowed in the contract? You told me. That's up to you, you said.'

'Of course it was allowed. It's just . . .' He cast around for the right words. 'It seemed different between us.' He laughs softly. 'I must sound very naive.'

She says nothing for a while, and then she speaks very quietly, still without looking round. Her voice sounds tired, as though she has battled against the statement but not been able to suppress it. 'Okay, I missed you. I didn't want to, but I did. I missed you. That's the worst thing that can happen, really. You've got to keep your distance. Otherwise . . .'

'Otherwise?'

She turns and looks at him. Those pale eyes, the colour of the sky at the horizon. 'Otherwise you lose what little power you have.'

152

He nods, he who is always in control, who always has a plan, who is a man of singular qualities – those of reason and decision and power – feels quite powerless now. He reaches inside his jacket for his cigarette case. 'Do you want one?'

'Please.'

His hands are unsteady and he has to spin the wheel of his lighter three or four times to conjure up a flame. He lights the cigarette, takes it over to her and places it carefully between her lips. 'And are you powerless now?'

She speaks through the cigarette, the smoke rising. 'Of course I am. I'm a refugee, depending on charity. Of course I'm powerless.'

'You seemed in control at that meeting. You seem in control now.'

She dries her hands and takes the cigarette from her mouth, blowing a stream of smoke away over the sink towards the open window. 'You learn to hide your feelings, don't you? How would you survive otherwise?' There is a shred of tobacco on her lip which she picks off with a quick dart of her tongue then blows away into the sink. Kata the cat, he thinks, remembering. Yet not a cat's tongue. Not rough, but smooth, licking him. The obstruction swells in his chest. It is a kind of pain, a physical pain centred somewhere behind the breastbone, a swelling growth that threatens to cut off his air supply. But the physical sensation is coupled with a perception of the most sublime happiness. Suffocation and joy, a strange dyad of sensation. With an unsteady hand he takes the cigarette from her fingers and lays it on the side of the sink. Then he leans forward and kisses her. The texture of her lips is familiar, as though it belongs to him. There is a moment when they are like that, just touching. And then she turns her head away. 'Please,' she says and moves away to distract herself with arranging things.

'I'm sorry. I just feel . . . I don't know. Helpless. I feel helpless.'

'*You* feel helpless!'

'And a bit of a fool.'

'Look, you've got to go. Marika will be back any moment. You've got to go.' And for once he is devoid of words, empty of any plan. He has always prided himself on his ability to manage situations, on his negotiating powers. 'You could find your way through a minefield, Viktor,' Oskar said to him once when they were involved in some particularly difficult discussion over import quotas or something. Through a minefield perhaps, but not through this involvement with this creature of flesh and blood, a small thing whose limbs and body he knows more perfectly than he has ever known anyone, a person whose inner sanctum of identity he has never approached.

He turns to the door, then pauses and looks back at her. 'I thought I'd get over you,' he says. 'When I found you'd gone and no one seemed to know where to find you, I thought I'd forget you. It would have been a relief. I could go back to being what I was before, a faithful husband and father. And I found I couldn't get you out of my mind. Those letters. You say you got them.'

'Yes.'

'Well then. You know. That's all.' He stands with his hand on the doorknob, trying to gather his thoughts. 'Look, you're not safe here.'

'Not safe?' She looks round the small cabin, at the innocent clutter of her things and Marika's. 'What do you mean, not safe?'

'I mean in this country. You think you're safe here but you're wrong. No one's safe. I'm planning to take the family to Switzerland. There's going to be an invasion.'

'Invasion?'

'Don't you listen to the news?' This is something he can deal with, a matter of facts and opinions, of judgement and decision. 'Henlein has a secret pact with Hitler. Don't you know who Henlein is? He's the leader of the Sudeten Germans. He's got the German army at his back and he's demanding self-rule for the border regions. If the government does agree then Henlein will invite the Germans in; if it doesn't the Germans will use the so-called oppression of the Sudeten Germans as a pretext for invasion. I can't see any way out of it. One way or another the Germans will be here just as surely as they are in Austria.'

'And you're going to leave?'

'Not immediately, but I'm making arrangements. So that we're prepared.'

'Will Switzerland be safe?'

'Who knows? We might have to move on. To the United States perhaps.'

'And what'll happen to me and Marika?'

'I'll think of something. I won't leave you here.'

'We don't have any papers. Marika has her birth certificate but I don't have anything.'

'We must see what we can do. There's the refugee office. They issue papers for people without anything. We'll work something out.'

Outside the air is cool and fresh. There is a sensation of relief. How long has it been? He has lost all sense of time in the close confines of the *chata*, in the presence of Kata. The upstairs window in the big house is closed now. The garden, the hedges and the trees are empty. Not even Marika has appeared. He glances at his watch and sees that it has only been a few minutes. Fifteen, maybe. A part of him, that part that always has a plan, always considers and calculates, tells him that little or no damage has been done. He just dropped by to see how things are going, how the Kalman woman is dealing with life in exile, how she is making ends meet. One has an obligation, just as one has an obligation to one's work force. But it is a frail voice, barely heard above the storm that is raging in his head. He turns and makes his way up the slope towards the trees that cut off the top of this garden from the bottom of his own property, the trees and bushes that cut him off from Kata. He knows there is a way through the dense undergrowth, the jungle of clutching branches and shielding leaves.

Robots

Fuchsias are in bloom, so the gardening programme on the radio says. 'We ought to have fuchsias,' Viktor suggests, against his better judgement. Fuchsias are ornament and ornament is crime. 'I like fuchsias. The Berchtolds out near Slavkov, they breed fuchsias, don't they? We should pay them a visit and get some.'

'The Berchtolds are a bore.'

'Who tells you that? Hana?'

'Have you seen the news?'

'Of course I've seen. I always see the news.'

The news tells of German troops massing on the border. The Czechoslovak army has been mobilised, sabres are rattling, hearts are beating, engines are roaring, boots are tramping, all that kind of thing. He remembers it all from last time, the last war where he occupied a bureaucratic position behind the front line – some military headquarters in Graz just inside the border from Italy – and watched the thousands go marching off to death. One of them was Liesel's brother. They met up – the purest chance, the caprice of war – on the edge of a parade ground where Benno's unit was mustering.

'My God!' they both exclaimed as they caught sight of one another. 'I don't believe it!'

That is the kind of thing you say, but of course you do believe it. Coincidence happens. Paths cross, journeys meet, lives intersect, like the various progressions of articulate but entirely automatic animals, ants maybe, weaving around on a table top, moving, searching with no more sense than robots. 'Robot' was Čapek's word, the linguistic gift of the Czech language to the

156

whole world. Robot, from *robota*. Hard labour, drudgery, the slave labour of the serfs. They talked a bit, those robots called Benno and Viktor, they talked about home, about parents and family, about Liesel who was then no more than a young girl – fourteen, fifteen – with, so Benno said, a crush on Viktor. It was that that turned Viktor's head. He'd never imagined the possibility that Benno's sister could admire him, love him even. Being loved was a new experience. Then Benno had to go because his unit was waiting for him and Viktor watched him clambering aboard one of the lorries and turning to wave. The engines roared and off they went, robots climbing up the hill away from the army camp. And that was the last anyone from home saw of him.

And now Viktor can hear the same sounds, the same preparations for war, as though they are being carried towards him on the breeze from the other side of the hill. But the strange thing about this new season of danger and dissolution is that he has almost ceased to care. Or at least he cares far more about what is going on in the *chata*, whose tarpapered roof he can just glimpse if he goes upstairs to the terrace. Or what's happening down there on the lawn, where, in the evening sunshine two days later he watches Liesel and Kata playing with the children.

He stands and smokes and watches. They are both wearing white, Liesel tall and narrow, slightly stooped, and Kata smaller and vivacious, running with the two girls, then turning and crouching down to encourage Martin, who follows with all the determined clumsiness of a five-year-old. As the little boy runs into her embrace she straightens up and hoists him above her head. Viktor can hear the shrieks of laughter.

Can they see him standing at the windows of the Glass Room? It depends on the light, and your point of view. Sometimes from the garden you can look up and see someone standing there beyond the windows as plain as daylight; sometimes only milkily, through the pale reflection of the day; and sometimes not at all, for there is only the view of sky and the clouds in the whole expanse of glass, so that you seem to be looking through the building, as though the house itself were transparent.

The two women are making their way up the lawn and onto the terrace. Only then does Liesel notice her husband. 'I didn't see you there, Viktor. You're back early from work. Katalin and I have been entertaining the children.'

Kata is looking bright and happy. Her face has taken colour, a faint flush in the cheeks, a smooth, buttery tan from the summer sun. 'Good afternoon, Herr Landauer,' she says, and he inclines his head in acknowledgement, watching the sky in her eyes. 'Frau Kalman,' he replies. But he wants to call her Kata. He wants to cry out loud, Kata!

The children sit at the table, Martin determined to be as grown up as the two girls. Ottilie and Marika patronise him, tell him to sit properly at the table, not to talk with his mouth full. Marika is a beautiful child, more beautiful by far than Ottilie, a radiant genetic reflection of her mother, except for her eyes, which are dark. She glances at Viktor with all the indifference of a child perceiving an adult to be nothing of importance in her world. There is apparently no memory of that man standing in her mother's room, no record of clinging monkey-like to her mother and watching him and asking, 'Are you one of Mutti's friends?'

'I'll leave you ladies to it,' he says, and retreats to the library where he can read the papers and listen to the noise of the children and hear, just once, Kata's voice raised to stop the girls doing something that annoys Martin. He wants Kata. More than anything in the world, he wants her.

The next day he goes down to the *chata* again, but this time she's not there. He finds some paper and a pencil and scribbles a note. There is the question of whether to make it cautious and safe or open and incriminating. *I want to see you*, he writes, *but cannot find the way*.

The weasel words of a coward.

Gossip

'It's a matter of perspective,' Oskar says. They've finished dinner and are sitting in front of the onyx wall. They come together these days for mutual comfort. The house has become a refuge for them, the Glass Room, that least fortress-like of constructions, bringing the consolation of reason and calm, while outside the confines of their particular lives, the world is crumbling. There are riots in the border areas, demands from the German-speaking groups for autonomy, the massing of German troops along the Austrian border, cries for rights, shouts for independence, shouts for secession.

'What do you mean, perspective?' Viktor asks. He has returned late from a visit to Prague, where there is panic and treachery in the air.

'Historical perspective.' The ceiling lights gleam on Oskar's bald head. He holds out his hands, as though to display perspective, an abstract idea resting between his palms. 'After the war we – that is the poor benighted inhabitants of this country – thought ourselves to be at the culmination of some historical process. But we were wrong. Actually we find ourselves in the middle of a process with no idea what the end will be.'

'What process?' Hana asks. 'Darling, you are being opaque.'

'The dissolution of the Empire, of course. We thought – we were naive enough to think – that it was all over. The Emperor has gone, Woodrow Wilson has spoken, the principle of self-determination has been established, and that's it. Bye bye the dual monarchy and all that went along with it; welcome Czechoslovakia, Hungary, Austria and goodness knows how

159

many other little statelets. But we were wrong. We weren't at the end of a process, we were merely in the middle. That's what I'm saying. It's like a happy couple strolling through the countryside. They think they're in a pretty little piece of woodland and after a while they'll break out onto a sunny pasture. But actually they have entered a dense forest and it stretches hundreds of miles ahead. And they have no idea of the end.' He lifts his brandy glass to his mouth. 'If there is an end.'

Liesel gets up and walks over to the windows. 'An end to history? Of course not.' She presses the button and waits while the central pane slides gracefully down into the basement and opens the room to the cool air of the evening. 'Let's talk about something else. It's always politics. Politics, politics, politics. Let's talk about people.'

'We *are* talking about people,' Oskar insists. 'Politics is people.'

'How's your refugee lady?' Hana asks, ignoring her husband. 'Katalin?'

'It's Katalin now, is it? Should I be jealous?'

'Don't be silly, darling. She's a common little thing but really quite bright. And tough. When you think what she's been through. She has done some wonderful work for me. You know she used to work for Habig? Making hats. And then dressmaking with Grünbaum or someone. One of those houses. I mean, quite a talent. And then all this happens and she's just thrown on the mercy of others . . .'

Thus set on a new course, the conversation shifts, first to the contingent trials of Katalin and then, to Viktor's relief, to the self-imposed trials of another pretty little thing, Vitulka Kaprálová. 'Have you heard?' Hana asks. They haven't, of course. They wait on Hana for gossip, for distraction, for delicious morsels of scandal. 'Well, you know about her affair with Martinů, don't you?'

'Only because you told us.'

'Don't be silly, darling. Everyone knows it. So she's there in Paris in the arms of the doting Martinů, leaving his wife all alone in their country house, and then something happens – we know not what, perhaps the wife cut up rough – and she's off on an extended holiday with a new boyfriend.'

'A *new* one?'

'Some unknown engineering student she met. His name is

Kopec, apparently. From Prague. Anyway, off she goes, to Italy and the south of France, abandoning poor old Martinů to his wife.'

'How do you know all this?' Liesel asks.

'A little Parisian bird tells me. Then, apparently, she gets back from her holiday and falls straight back into Martinů's arms again. And now – well you've got to hand it to her – now the little *koketa* sets off, with Martinů in her baggage, to London, to that music congress. You heard about that from Kaprál himself, didn't you? Everyone was there. Hindemith, Britten, Bartók, the American Aaron Copland, all of them. And our little minx actually opened the congress with the 'Military Sinfonietta', the piece she conducted in Prague last winter. Can you believe it? Taking the music world by storm and Bohuslav Martinů by the balls.'

'Hana!'

'Well I don't know how else to put it. The poor man's completely infatuated. They say the stuff he's writing now is full of coded references to her.'

The gossip goes on, the suggestions and the intimations, the life of a young country stumbling to its death. People and politics dissected and discussed in the cool spaces of the Glass Room, while outside the storm gathers.

'By the way, there's a problem with Liba,' Liesel says, later when Oskar and Hana have gone and she and Viktor are upstairs. They are in her bedroom, the quiet box of her bedroom, the plain white box which contains the most intimate secrets of their marriage, the delights and disappointments, the silent revelations that they share but never talk of.

'You're avoiding the issue,' Viktor says. 'The issue is what is happening to this country. It will affect us all, Liesel. We must talk seriously about leaving while there is still a chance.'

He's in his pyjamas, sitting in an armchair smoking. She is standing in the doorway to the bathroom, her head wrapped in the turban of a towel. She is naked. There is something clumsy about her nakedness, the wide hips, the rough beard of dun-coloured hair between her thighs, her breasts like wayward eyes. Once she had been shy of his seeing her like this. Now she doesn't even realise she is doing it.

'I'm not avoiding any issue. You see, Liba's engaged to be

married. She told me the other day. It's all a bit of a rush and I think she's pregnant although she denies it. Anyway, the point is, not only would she not be able to come with us to look after the children if we did leave, but she's actually handed in her notice. She was awfully upset about it, said how much she loves the children and all that kind of thing, but Jan – that's his name – works in Prague. I mean he's with his regiment at the moment, of course. But he lives in Prague and she feels duty-bound to be with him.' She towels herself dry, briskly rubs her head and stands there with a frizz of damp hair about her face. 'And so I thought, what about Frau Kalman?'

Viktor is dumbstruck. What exactly is his wife suggesting?

'Ottilie and Marika get on remarkably well, and Katalin is a wonderful mother despite all her trials and tribulations. Martin adores her. What do you think?'

What does he think? He thinks the immediate thoughts of a liar: how to react appropriately, how to make the unnatural appear natural, a process that carries with it the seeds of its own destruction, the premeditated act betraying itself as unnatural precisely because it is premeditated. A conundrum.

'Don't you like the idea?'

'I didn't say anything.'

'I can tell by your expression. You're not impressed.'

'Well, does the woman have any experience?' He is not used to dissimulation but he discovers a natural talent for it. 'I mean, we're talking about a nanny, aren't we? Does she know what's involved? What is she? A seamstress? Hardly a qualification. And does she have references?'

'You make it sound like a job application.'

'It is precisely that.' It is precisely something imprecise: it is a whole universe of possibilities. The possibilities confound him. His wife shrugs her way into a silk nightdress. The material – pale ivory – clings to hips and breasts and belly. He senses, as though it is something that operates independently of his mind, something extraneous, the growing insistence of an erection. How curious that arousal should come when she dresses rather than when she is naked.

'There's also the question of what happens to Katalin and her daughter if we do leave.'

'Do we have an obligation to her?'

162

She looks at her husband with an expression close to outrage. 'Sometimes you appear so heartless, Viktor. Of course we have an obligation. In abstract terms we have obligations to all refugees, and we try to discharge those obligations by supporting the various organisations that we do. But we also have precise and personal obligations to those we know and hold in regard.'

'You sound like a moral philosopher.'

'You sound like a cold fish.'

'So you hold Frau Kalman in regard?'

'Don't you? I think perhaps you do.'

'What do you mean by that?'

'She's an attractive woman. Men like attractive women. I have noticed the way you look at her.'

He laughs. 'Ergo I should want Frau Kalman to become the children's nanny? Don't be ridiculous. Liesel, I don't know enough about her to judge one way or another. I know that she has been living in the *chata* for the last few months and I know that your mother doesn't like her. And you apparently do.'

'My mother didn't like you either, at first. So that puts you in the same boat. Anyway, what do you propose doing about her and her daughter? Are you happy to abandon them? All these things that happen to the Jews – that's why you are talking about going, isn't it? Are you happy to leave those two and have such horrors happen to them? Could you face yourself? Look, why don't you go and have a word with her? Talk to her a bit. See what you think.'

He considers this possibility amongst the galaxy of possibilities, a universe of possibilities greater than anything he might have imagined. 'Have you mentioned this to her?'

'Not specifically. We've talked in general terms of what she might do, where she might go. I suggested Palestine. She says she's looked into that. Apparently there are Zionists trying to drum up support amongst the refugees – the Germans and Austrians are even encouraging it, did you know that? Apparently they even have an office for Jewish emigration in Vienna. But she says that the British have quotas and it's not easy to get in . . .'

'I'll go and have a word with her.'

'But be kind. You're not interviewing someone for the firm. You're looking for someone who might be an addition to the family.'

Proposal

The *chata* stands quietly in its envelope of hedge and grass. Beyond it lie the gardens of the big house, and the house itself staring blindly out at the silent morning. Behind him, from the upper garden, comes the distant noise of the children playing – Ottilie and Marika, and Martin's voice raised in some kind of protest against the girls.

She gives a start of surprise when she sees who it is at the door. 'What are you doing here?' she asks and there is almost panic in her tone, as though he might do her violence.

'Liesel suggested I come. So I'm here by right, as it were. She has a proposal to make.'

'Proposal?' She stands aside for him to come in. There is an awkward moment when they pass in the cramped space, their hands almost touching, her face looking up at him as though she might be offering it to kiss. Then she moves away from him to sit at the table, quiet and composed, her hands folded in her lap, while he remains standing. If someone were to come in now they would never guess that anything has ever passed between them. It looks like an employer about to question the maid. 'What did she want you to tell me?'

She refuses his offer of a cigarette, but he takes one for himself. It interests him to see that his hands are quite steady, the flame of the lighter quite still as he raises it. 'What do you call her?' he asks through the smoke. 'Frau Landauer? Or Frau Liesel?'

'I suppose, Frau Landauer. I don't really know.'

'Frau Landauer wants to take you with us.'

'With you? What do you mean?' She frowns. 'Where to? Where are you going?'

164

'I've already told you. We're going to Switzerland. We've just discovered that Liba is leaving us to get married, and Liesel had this idea that you could take her place looking after the children.' He sits opposite her across the table. 'What do you think? Come with us when we leave. You and Marika of course. Would you do that?'

Bewilderment, suspicion, a whole cluster of confused emotions cloud her face. '*She* had this idea? Or was it yours?'

'Hers alone. I had no part in it. I promise you that. It was her suggestion.'

She looks away, out of the window at whatever lies beyond, a stretch of lawn, the tall box hedges that cut the *chata* off from the main garden. He has never been able to get the measure of her. What does she want? What will make her happy? 'I've told you that we don't have any papers.'

'I'm sure something can be done. They can give you something they call a Nansen passport. I've already spoken to people in Prague. The Human Rights League can organise things.'

'You've already done it?'

'Just in general terms, just to see if it is possible. Look, Kata, I want you to come with us. I want to help you.'

'Is that all you want to do?'

'You know it's not.'

'Then what?'

'You know what. You know what has been between us. You cannot just pretend that it didn't happen'

'And you want that again? A little bit on the side whenever your wife is out of the house?'

'Don't speak like that.'

'But it's true, isn't it?'

'It's more than that. It's . . .' His fluency deserts him. He fumbles for words.

'What is it, then? Love? Is that what you're trying to say?'

'Yes, perhaps that's exactly what I'm trying to say.'

She laughs. She is bright and sharp, that is what he loves in her. Her mind is as quick and neat as her body, the two things united into something he has never met before. 'If it's love then leave your wife and come away with me.'

'You know I can't do that.'

She gives a bitter laugh. 'I know you *won't* do it. I'm trapped, aren't I? I tried to escape, but I failed.'

'You're not trapped. You're as free as a bird. I promise you that. Whatever you want to do, I will pay for it. I paid you once to walk out of my life. I'll do the same again if that is what you want. But I'm asking you to come with us.' He pauses, and corrects himself. 'Begging,' he says. 'I'm begging you.'

Ship

Viktor stands in the Glass Room looking out at the view that was once a wild hilltop panorama and now is something framed and therefore tamed, in the way that the ocean appears tamed when viewed from the bridge of a ship. He has always liked the ship analogy. Despite being a citizen of a country that has no shoreline, he feels an affinity with the sea. The Glass Room is the bridge and the floor above a promenade deck, with cabins for the passengers. The sound of the wind in the trees is a sea sound and the house itself is a ship pitching out into the choppy waters of the city with the wind beating about the stanchions and bulkheads. And ahead is the storm.

He turns away from the view, crosses to the door and climbs the companionway to the cabins, from the expanse of one space into the narrow constrictions of the upstairs. In the hallway he pauses and listens. Here everything is silent, bathed in the still, amniotic light from the glass panels. Along the corridor, past Ottilie's and Martin's bedrooms he waits at the furthest door and listens again, fancying that he can hear the quiet interior breath of expectation. 'Come in,' she says when he knocks.

She's standing by the window looking out onto the steep slope and the jungle of trees and bushes. The room itself is bare except for the bright splash of a František Kupka abstract painting on one wall. There are only a few of Kata's things, those that she managed to take with her in flight from Vienna, things she could cram into the single suitcase, and those she has managed to buy since coming here. On the chest of drawers there's a photograph of her and Marika in a park, perhaps the Augarten in Vienna, perhaps the Prater. Mother and daughter are smiling and squinting against the light, and Viktor wonders – a small pulse of jealousy – who held the camera.

'I came to see how you are.'

She turns and accepts his awkward kiss. She's wearing a plain white blouse and black skirt, the uniform of a governess or a female companion or something. 'I'm fine.'

'You're happy?'

'I'm confused. So much has happened. I feel that it's going to go wrong.'

'It's not. It's not going to go wrong.'

There is nothing much more to say, really. Whether it is going to go wrong is not up to her or to him. The wrongness or rightness of the future is a matter of the purest contingency. Viktor has always worked on the principle that the future is there to be handled, manipulated, bent and twisted to one's own desires but now he knows how untrue that is. The future just happens. It is happening now, the whole country poised for disaster; it is happening now, his standing there confronting Kata.

Out of the window through the dense fretwork of branches he can just see the sky, small pieces of sky like fragments of a mosaic. Turquoise blue, winter blue, a deeper blue than Kata's eyes. He wonders what lies beyond the horizon of her gaze. 'I love you,' he thinks, and finds the assertion as thrilling as anything he has known, as enrapturing as, say, flying. There is the sudden elevation, the unexpected lightness of spirit, the same sense of your whole material existence being predicated on nothing more than a whim. But he daren't say it out loud.

'Everyone seems to be out.'

'Yes.' She knows that well enough. She has been party to the fact, walking with the children down the hill to the Montessori school near the hospital, where Martin has just started in the kindergarten. Liesel and Hana are at some organising committee setting up a concert in aid of refugees. They'll be there all morning.

'So,' he says, and there is a moment of indecision, as though, despite both knowing what they are about, there is still some uncertainty about how to proceed. What, in this novel puzzle, are the necessary moves? Then she begins to unbutton her blouse and it is just like it ever was: the quiet matter-of-factness of her gestures as she puts the blouse aside, and shrugs off her brassiere as one might shrug off an inconvenience.

'We'll have to be quick,' she says.

He watches, breathless, as she steps out of her knickers and stands naked in the small, spare room. She has, he realises with a small start of recognition, exactly the body of the Maillol sculpture downstairs in the Glass Room, the same loose breasts, the same swelling to her belly, the same firm thighs and plump shoulders. 'One of my men-friends only wanted to look,' she told him once. 'All he wanted was that I undress and lie down so that he could look at me. He never touched me. I had to do various things – open my legs, bend over, that kind of thing – and he just looked. He must have been short-sighted, I think. He'd look so close that I could feel his breath on me. But he never touched me. Wasn't that strange?'

But Viktor understands the remote desires of that anonymous *Freund*. He feels that he could spend whole days just looking at the marbled whiteness of Kata's body, at the curves and creases, at the deft folds of flesh and the sinuous hair. What could be more perfect than to look? And yet mere looking is not enough: while the Maillol torso stands forever motionless and detached in the cool and rational space of the Glass Room, upstairs in the small cabin of her bedroom Viktor goes down on his knees before her. He feels neither fear nor shame: there is only this compulsion filling his whole being so that for those few moments he is helpless. Afterwards, after the convulsions of mind and body, comes the anxiety, the fear of discovery, that razor's edge of panic. They pull their clothes on, adjust hair and skirt and collar and tie, prepare to return to that ordinary world of convention and decorum. 'How can this go on?' she asks.

He doesn't have an answer to her question. Deception in the Glass House is a new experience for him. He has no idea how to go about it. 'I think we should all live in glass houses,' he said years ago. It was at the housewarming party they gave when the house was newly completed. Hana was there, and Oskar probably, and Liesel of course. But there had been others listening. Rainer von Abt himself. And Professor Kundera and the composer Václav Kaprál. And that journalist who had come uninvited with one of the other guests. And the pianist Němec. Dozens and dozens of them all looking up to him and listening to his brave words. 'If we all lived like that there would be no more secrets, no more deceit. We could all live openly and honestly.'

The little speech amused Hana. 'You are a spoilsport, Viktor,' she accused him. 'I love deceit. Everyone loves deceit. Without deceit there would be no art.'

Leaving Kata in her room Viktor makes his way – feeling light and yet replete – down to the Glass Room. He feels no shame. He has new memories to treasure, new thoughts and sensations to augment the miserly store that he keeps from previous times with Kata. He has love – sexual, spiritual, total – to elevate him above the downward pull of guilt, like a bird rising against the earthly tug of gravity. He feels immensely and illogically happy. Illogically because all this is threatened, this house and the life within it, their presence in this city, in this country. The world is crashing down around them, pulled down by the gravity of events, yet he feels only elation.

He comes through the door and finds Laník standing there in the middle of the Glass Room. 'What are you doing here?' he asks sharply.

'Looking for you, Herr Viktor.'

Is there a sly insolence in the youth's expression? Liesel says there is, and now Viktor discovers it as well. 'Why? Why were you looking for me?'

'I wanted to know if you need me this afternoon. Otherwise I was going to visit my cousin in Šlapanice.'

'Go,' Viktor said. 'Take the afternoon off. If I need to I can drive myself.'

'Unless . . .' Laník pauses. Is that a smile? He seems to consider his words.

'Unless what?'

'Unless Fraülein Kalman needs to go anywhere.'

'*Frau* Kalman,' Viktor corrects him. 'And I don't imagine that she does.'

'And if she did, you could drive her, Herr Viktor, couldn't you?'

The Last Year in Marienbad

That summer the Czechoslovak army became Landauer Motors' largest customer. The contracts were for military vehicles – the Popular car converted for army use and one of the production lines turned over to making lorries. That summer, as always, the family took a holiday at Marienbad, staying at the Hotel Fürstenhof. They took two suites, one for Katalin and the children, the other for Viktor and Liesel. It was a week of fine weather, with crowds thronging the Kolonada and the bands playing Strauss and the illusion of being projected back into the past, when things were settled and the future seemed assured, when King Edward VII was in residence in the Weimar and Emperor Franz Josef was at Klinger's and all was well with the world. But there were shadows behind the confectionery façades: graffiti on the walls called for *Anschluss*, union, and the flags flying over the spa gardens were the red and black of the Sudetenland. On a drive to the monastery at Teplá the Landauer party encountered a column of army trucks making its way towards the border.

'Are they going to fight?' Martin asked his father.

'They are just on manoeuvres,' Viktor replied.

That evening a parade of young people – men in lederhosen and knee-length socks, women in dirndls – passed directly below the windows of their rooms. The marchers were watched by an applauding crowd. *Ein Volk, ein Reich, ein Führer*, a banner proclaimed. A band marched with them and the marchers' voices were raised in song. *Die Fahne hoch*! they sang, *Die Reihen fest geschlossen*! Further down the road there was an encounter with the police, some shouting and a scuffle which ended with the banner being smashed. But still the parade went on. 'The flag is high! The ranks are tightly closed!' they sang and the people on the roadside cheered and waved.

'What will happen?' Liesel asked.

'How the hell do I know what will happen?' Viktor snapped.

Next morning the town awoke to find itself daubed with swastikas.

Small Issue

'Tomorrow,' the voice from the radio says, 'parliament is going to meet and I shall be making a full statement of the events that have led up to the present anxious and critical situation . . .' It is a thin, precise voice, the voice of a cleric enunciating points of theological exactitude. It speaks in English and Oskar frowns, understanding little of the language.

'Shh,' Hana says when he complains. 'Let's listen.'

They are in the library area behind the onyx wall, Oskar, Hana, Liesel and Viktor. Outside it is evening, a cool autumnal evening, the trees in the garden illuminated by the backwash of light from the sky.

'An earlier statement would not have been possible,' the voice goes on, 'when I was flying backwards and forwards across Europe and the position was changing from hour to hour, but today there is a lull for a brief time and I want to say a few words to you men and women of Britain, and the Empire, and perhaps to others as well.'

Viktor is standing with his back to the others, smoking and looking into the conservatory where cacti and rubber plants take up stylised positions. Hana and Liesel are sitting together on the sofa, holding hands. Oskar is in an armchair, smoking a cigar and frowning as he struggles to grasp what the voice is saying. The Glass Room is immensely still, a space of quiet and calm around them, a barricade against emotion.

'And first of all I must say something to those who have written to my wife or myself in these last weeks . . .'

'His wife!' Hana exclaims.

'. . . to tell us of their gratitude for my efforts and to assure us of their prayers for my success. Most of these letters have come from women, mothers or sisters of our own countrymen; but there are countless others besides, from France, from Belgium, from Italy, even from Germany, and it has been heartbreaking to read of the growing anxieties they reveal and their intense relief when they thought, too soon, that the danger of war was past.'

'The danger is past?' Liesel asks, misunderstanding the awkward academic construction.

'Shh!'

'If I felt my responsibility heavy before, to read such letters has made it seem almost overwhelming.' Here the voice pauses, and when it continues there is a sudden and unexpected catch of emotion, even revulsion: 'How *horrible*, fantastic, incredible it is that we should be digging trenches and trying on gas masks here because of a quarrel in a faraway country between people of whom we know nothing . . .'

Hana gives a cry of disbelief, and Oskar asks, 'What did he say?' but the voice doesn't wait, doesn't pause for the listeners to take in the import of its words. It continues, thin, exact and pusillanimous, 'It seems still more impossible that a quarrel which is already settled in principle should be the subject of war. I can well understand the reasons why the Czech government have felt unable to accept the terms which have been put before them in the German memorandum. Yet I believe, after my talks with Herr Hitler, that if only time were allowed, it ought to be possible for the arrangements for transferring the territory that the Czech government has agreed to give to Germany to be settled by agreement under conditions which would ensure fair treatment of the population concerned. You know already that I have done all that one man can do to compose this quarrel. After my visits to Germany I realise vividly how Herr Hitler feels that he must champion other Germans . . .'

'Turn it off,' Hana says.

But Liesel doesn't move and the voice continues, cutting through the thin rush of the ether, 'He told me privately, and last night he repeated publicly, that after this Sudeten German question is settled, that is the end of Germany's territorial claims in Europe.'

Finally Viktor reacts. He laughs. 'That's it, then, isn't it? That is the end.' He crosses over to the radio and reaches out to turn it off.

'Wait!' cries Hana.

'What for? To hear more of this drivel?'

An argument breaks out between them, a ridiculous dispute about whether they should prolong the agony, whether this irresolute man, who holds the future of their country in his hands, should be allowed to continue. 'Don't be childish!' Hana cries in frustration and fear, and Viktor stays his hand, just in time to hear the voice express its careful anguish over the death of an entire nation:

'However much we may sympathise with a small nation confronted by a big and powerful neighbour, we cannot in all circumstances undertake to involve the whole British Empire in war simply on her account. If we have to fight, it must be on larger issues than that . . .'

Viktor turns the radio off.

'That's us,' Hana says. 'Do you realise that? Us. A small issue. People of whom they know nothing.'

The fact is, she is in tears. Oskar pats her shoulder in a vain attempt to comfort her. But the tears continue.

How do you dismember a body? There are two fundamentally different approaches – that of the surgeon and that of the mad axeman. The one is cool and calculating and progressive, with the application of bone-saw, scalpel and shears. The other is a frenzy of hacking and tearing, with blood everywhere and the taste of iron in the mouth. But whichever way you do it the result is the same – dismemberment. That autumn the Great Powers assisted at the dismemberment of the country. They witnessed the cutting off of limbs from the body, the severing of arteries, the snapping of ligaments and tendons, the sawing of bones. That autumn the Czechoslovak army stood down and watched while men in field grey tramped into Eger and Karlsbad, into Teplitz and Liberec. In the north, like a vulture taking an eye from a dying man, the Polish army snatched part of Czech Silesia. In the east Hungary took parts of Slovakia. Everywhere refugees fled from the advancing soldiers like herbivores scattering before a pack of predators. They shuffled along roads and across fields, pushing handcarts with their belongings, humping sorry bundles on their backs. The trains were packed, the roads crowded. It was the effect of war without the fighting, a kind of rehearsal for the future.

By the end of autumn, shorn of its limbs, only the ruined trunk remained. The Republic of Czechoslovakia had ceased to exist and in its place was born a hyphenated, hybrid cripple, Czecho-Slovakia, destined for the shortest of lives imaginable.

'Surely this is the moment for Prince Václav to wake up and come to the rescue.' Oskar is referring to a popular and ancient legend, the awakening of Good King Wenceslas who lies with his knights beneath the Blaník Hill near Prague awaiting the call to save the homeland.

'I wouldn't bet on it,' Viktor replies. 'The twentieth century is not a time for miracles.'

He and Oskar have been going over some of the points connected to the transfer of ownership of Landauer Motors. They are on one side of the onyx wall; the children are on the other, with Liesel and Hana and Katalin, decorating the Christmas tree. Marika has never had a Christmas tree before. She has seen Christmas trees, but they have never been part of her life. Not part of Viktor's life either, until his marriage. Hanukkah was the winter feast celebrated in his family, a feast that commemorates the kind of thing that he detests: a miracle.

Oskar gathers up his papers and stuffs them in his briefcase. He looks up, his expression difficult to read. There's regret there, and fear. Viktor has seen fear before of course, during the war, when men were going up to the front; but it is strange to see fear in a man's face when there doesn't appear to be any outside reason. Yet that is what you see everywhere these days, fear on the peaceful streets. 'Do you think they'll invade?' Oskar asks.

Viktor laughs. 'Invade? They won't invade because they won't need to. They'll just walk in when it suits them. Be realistic, Oskar. We have a puppet government, no defences and an army that was ordered not to fight at the only moment when it might have held its own. We've no more chance of surviving than an overripe plum has of staying on the tree. Even *Lidové Noviny* has advocated accommodation with the Germans. They'll wait for spring, that's all.'

The children are laughing and arguing. Something about the star on the top of the tree. Hana says there should be a fairy, but a fairy seems absurd. 'She'd fall off,' says Martin's voice.

'But fairies can fly,' Hana points out.

The laughter comes round the onyx wall, the delight of children discovering the stupidity of adults. 'Not *really* they can't. Auntie Hana, you are so silly. Fairies aren't real!'

'Are you really going to leave?' Oskar asks. The conversation has slipped into Czech. They discuss legal issues in German but they talk in Czech.

'I don't think there's any choice, but Liesel does. We're still in negotiation.'

'It's the other way round with us. Hana says we should go but I say, what the hell will I do kicking my heels in Venezuela or some place? I wouldn't be able to work, would I? And they'll always need lawyers here, even if it's only for the Jews, don't you think?'

'I don't know what to think.'

'What'll you do with the house?'

'We won't sell it, if that's what you mean. We'd never sell it. Liesel's people will look after it. They think we're mad, of course. Running away, they say. So the place will become Germanified again, what does that matter? That's their attitude. It's always been a German city anyway.'

'Maybe they're right.' Oskar hesitates, briefcase packed, business over, but still with something holding him back. His voice is lowered even further, to make certain that it cannot be heard on the other side of the onyx wall. 'You know, I used to think that you and Hana . . .'

'Me and Hana?'

'Keep your voice down, old fellow. You know what I mean. I thought that you were one of her men.'

Viktor smiles at the man's confusion. It is not often that he sees a lawyer embarrassed. 'Don't be absurd.'

'I don't mind her having her men friends,' Oskar explains, 'but I don't like to *know* them, if you see what I mean. It got quite difficult when she had a crush on that piano player. Anyway, it makes things easier now I know that you are not.' He smiles, as though delighted to have got that over with. 'Shall we join them?'

So they go round to where the women and children are standing round the tree admiring it. 'Look, Tatínku!' Ottilie cries as they appear. 'Isn't it wonderful?'

Viktor stands by the Maillol torso and looks at the decorated tree and the three children standing round it, and the three women with them. Beyond the glass wall snow is falling. It is falling over the whole city, out of a sky as heavy and sombre as a funeral shroud. It is falling on the soldiers in the Sudetenland as they establish their new possessions, and the soldiers in the Czech lands as they try to consolidate the hurriedly improvised border. It is falling on the triumphant and the dispossessed, on those that have and those that have not. It is falling on the Hrad in Prague and the Špilas in Město, on the hills and forests of Bohemia and Moravia, snow falling softly through space but giving the illusion, when seen from the Glass Room of the Landauer Villa, that the flakes are stationary and the Villa itself is rising, the whole Glass Room softly rising in the air, borne aloft on light and space.

Will they invade?

They won't invade because they won't need to invade. They'll just walk in when it suits them. They'll wait for spring, that's all.

The next day the sun shines and the children toboggan down the sloping lawn. Their voices are raised in laughter. Katalin has a go as well, shrieking with the delight of it, until the toboggan slews sideways and throws her into the snow. She comes back up the slope to where Liesel and Viktor are watching, her face flushed, her hair damp, her fingers numb with cold. Viktor wants to take them in his hands to warm them, he wants to do that more than anything in the world. He wants to hold her. He wants to press his face against her cold wet cheeks. He wants to take each raw, icy finger in his mouth and suck it warm. But he doesn't move. It is Liesel who clasps Katalin's hands in hers and rubs them to restore them to life.

'March at the very latest,' Viktor tells Liesel. 'If we delay any more it may be too late.'

Storm in March

'Have you heard?' Hana's voice on the phone. The phone hasn't stopped ringing all morning – friends, acquaintances, people from the Human Rights League. Outside there's a blizzard, and then a break when the sun attempts to shine, and then another gust of snow. The weather is as unstable as the mood of the city.

'Have I heard what?'

'The news.'

'Of course I've heard the news. The radio has been on all morning.'

'Can I come round? Are you doing anything? Can I come round and see you?'

'You know what we're doing. We're packing.'

'But can I come round?'

'Of course you can.'

There's something ragged about her, something uncertain. As though she is damaged inside but isn't showing it yet, doesn't even know herself, perhaps. Alcohol or drugs or something? It is only eleven o'clock in the morning and she seems inebriated, intoxicated, riven with misery and chemicals. She stumbles on the stairs down into the Glass Room and crosses the room like the victim of a car crash staggering away from the wreckage. Except that she has staggered *into* the wreckage for it is there all round her as she walks into the centre of the space: the packing cases, the tea chests, all the litter of the removal men. Wood shavings and wood wool on the floor. Rolls of wrapping paper. Two removal men are lifting a chair into a case.

'Hanička, what the hell's the matter?'

179

'I've been drowning my misery, darling. Have you seen? They're everywhere, everywhere. Like a plague of rats. They moved in overnight and the whole city is swarming with them. And that idiot Oskar Judex has taken over the town hall with his mob. That's what they say, anyway.'

'Has there been any fighting?'

'Not a shot fired in anger from what I've heard. The whole country has just lain down and rolled over.'

Liesel watches her. Her love is tempered by something: impatience, fear maybe; and the underlying sense of panic that she has been trying to suppress for days now, ever since Viktor, sitting quietly at the breakfast table and putting his newspaper down, said, 'I've booked the flight. The seventeenth.'

Now it might be too late.

'Is Katalin here?' Hana asks.

'She's gone out to do some last-minute shopping. Look, darling, I'm very busy, you can see that . . .'

'Will you get away?'

'God knows. The weather's even against us now. But we can't change our plans now, can we? Viktor has gone to ring the airport to see if the flight is going to happen. Can they stop an international flight? I suppose they can. I suppose they can do anything they please.'

The foreman of the removal people comes over. 'Is the piano going as well, ma'am?'

She touches the cool flank of the case. She has played her last piece on the instrument. Wherever they are going, if they go, if the bloody weather lets them, if the German army lets them, they will have to hire one. 'You know it isn't. We said it wasn't.'

'Righty-ho.' He has this manner of forced jocularity. What is there to be jocular about at a time like this? There are German troops in the city and fanatics have taken over the town hall and this fool is saying 'righty-ho' and 'okey-dokey' as though the world is going on just as normal.

'Maybe we can go upstairs, Hana. They haven't started on my room.'

So they go upstairs and closet themselves in the bedroom. 'What have you been drinking?' she asks as she closes the door.

'How do you know it's drink?'

'I can smell it on your breath. For God's sake, Hanička. It's eleven o'clock in the morning.'

Outside on the terrace there are the signs of the children – a football of Martin's, his pedal car, Ottilie's pram. They should be under cover in this weather. Surely that's Katalin's job, to look after the children's things. As she stands there, she feels Hana come close behind her, putting her arms round her waist and resting her chin on her shoulder. 'What are you thinking? Apart from my drinking habits? Are you wondering how to get rid of me?'

'I was wondering why Katalin hasn't got the children to put their things away.'

'Ah, Katalin. Is it her you think of now?'

'Don't be silly.'

'Do you love her?'

'Don't be idiotic.'

'And what about Viktor? Does *he* love her?' She nuzzles against Liesel's neck. Her voice, a mere whisper, is loud in Liesel's ear. 'Mm, you smell nice. Motherly, I suppose. You smell like my mother used to. Warm and yeasty, like fresh bread. Does Viktor love Katalin, do you think? Does he . . .' a pause, for courage perhaps, 'fuck her?'

'Hana!' Liesel pulls away. 'If you're going to say that sort of stupidity, you may as well go immediately. Really, you are impossible at times.'

'I'm sorry. It was a joke. One of Hanička's outrageous jokes. You know that.'

They confront each other now, standing opposite each other. No holding hands or standing arm in arm or anything like that.

'You really are going, aren't you?' Hana says.

'If we can.'

'How can you bear to go, Liesi? Your family, your friends, your whole world. This wonderful house, how can you bear to part with that? Me? What about me?'

Liesel shrugs. 'You've seen what has happened. Viktor has been predicting this for months. If he'd had his way we would already be safe in Switzerland.'

'What if the whole country did what you are doing?'

'The whole country isn't Jewish.'

'Oskar's staying put.'

181

'That's his choice.'

'And you're taking Katalin with you?'

'Of course we are. She's part of the household now. Look, Hanička, I've got stacks to do . . .'

'And what about me?'

What about her? That is a question Liesel can't answer, has never really been able to answer. What about Hana, whom she often loves and sometimes loathes, to whom she owes secrets and with whom, in her turn, she shares secrets; what about her? 'I'll write. We'll keep in touch. Maybe you'll come too in a while. Maybe Oskar will see the folly of his ways and you'll join us. We could have a wonderful time together . . .'

Hana laughs. She is sitting on the bed and looking at Liesel with that sceptical expression that is so much part of her. 'You know what a wonderful time is for me? It's you alone. That may sound silly but it's true. All the men, all the women, all the silly pleasures of life, they're nothing beside you. There I've said it. That's what I came to say and I've said it.'

Liesel watches her, feeling a muddle of emotion that is far too difficult to disentangle. Affection, and sorrow, and impatience, and a thin veil of repugnance. And love of course. Of course love. So how can you be repelled and attracted at the same time? She finds a packet of cigarettes on the chest of drawers, lights one and turns to look out of the window. Outside there's another flurry of snow. Out there spring is trying to happen despite the snow, despite the fact that the German army has just marched into the whole country, despite the fact that their homeland is even now disappearing under the flood. Out there the clouds hang low over the city, almost touching the spires of the churches that Hana always says look like hypodermic needles. Out there men in grey are tearing her whole world to pieces. 'It's eleven thirty in the morning,' she remarks, inconsequentially.

Hana laughs. 'I told you once that things couldn't last. Do you remember?'

'You always say that kind of thing.'

'And now it has happened.'

Flight

The Glass Room is almost empty. The piano stands where it has always stood, in the space behind the onyx wall, but except for that and a couple of chairs, all the rest has gone. In some ways this has returned the room to its moment of birth, when the builders and the decorators left it and the furniture had yet to arrive. Just the space, the light, the white. Just the gleaming chrome pillars. Just the onyx wall and the curved partition of Macassar wood. The cool, calm rationality of the place undisturbed by any of the irrationality that human beings would impose upon it. They pause for a moment and look.

Is it rational to have a sentiment about a place? A place, a room is just space enclosed, volume sequestered by concrete and glass. 'Does it break your heart?' she asks, holding his hand and glancing at him.

He doesn't reply directly. 'It's still ours. We haven't sold it, we haven't given it away. Your parents will keep an eye on it. There's still Laník and his sister.'

'That's not the point, is it?'

'We'll come back.'

'Will we? When?'

He squeezes her hand, and leans across and kisses her on the cheek. 'Come on, they're waiting.' The briefcase he is carrying has everything important in it – birth certificates, marriage certificate, the deeds of the house, all those things that document who you are and who you might be, those scraps of paper that give you existence. Where that goes, they go.

'You haven't answered my question.'

'I'm not going to because I can't. I told you, I can't predict the future. I can't even be sure that the flight will be allowed.'

'They told you it will be.'

'They *hope* it will be. But who can tell for certain? Now come.'

But she stands for a moment, one last moment, looking at the Glass Room. Rain runs down the windows like tears from her eyes. The light is diffused, refracted, blurred by the water; just so are memories distorted by time and mood. This is no place for sentiment. It is a place of reason. And yet sentiment is what she feels, the anguish of departure, the exquisite pain of remembering, the fragility of being. When will she be here again?

Ten minutes later a small convoy of cars heads away from the house down Blackfield Road. Viktor and Liesel are in the front car with the children. Katalin follows in the second car with Marika and the luggage. Oskar and Hana follow behind. They set off on the right-hand side of the road – new regulations have come into force, a new highway code, a new way of driving. The convoy goes down the hill past the children's hospital to the main road, then turns right and heads down towards the Ringstrasse. There is no other traffic around, and few pedestrians. It is like a Sunday morning, but it isn't a Sunday morning. It's a Friday, Friday the seventeenth.

'What's happened, Laník?' Viktor asks through the hatch in the panel between the driver and the passengers. 'Where is everyone?'

Laník glances round. 'Dunno, sir. Who can tell these days?'

They turn onto the Ringstrasse, bump over the tramlines. There's a tram stopped at a light and a thin crowd on the pavement. Another tram passes in the opposite direction, heading towards the north of the city, but there isn't the usual traffic and there aren't the usual crowds. As they reach the Grand Hotel they find military vehicles parked across the wide road, blocking access to the railway station. Soldiers flag the cars down. A few civilians have gathered on the pavement to watch.

Laník winds down his window as one of the soldiers advances. The man looks puzzled, as though he feels he should recognise these people and these vehicles. He's dressed in that uniform that they've heard about but never seen until the last two days: dove grey with a hint of green about it. On his chest hangs a silver breastplate. *Feldgendarmerie*, it proclaims. 'At least he's a German,' Viktor says. 'That must be better than one of the local fanatics.'

The children stare at him with that open curiosity that children have, as though nothing will affect the even tenor of their lives. Liesel grasps Victor's hand for reassurance.

The soldier peers into the car and demands their papers.

'We're heading for the airport, Sergeant,' Viktor explains. 'We have a plane to catch.'

The man shrugs. 'Well you can't pass here. The road's blocked.'

'Why? We'll miss our flight.'

'Orders, sir. An important convoy. You'll just have to wait.'

There's a feeling of panic. The plane won't wait, the world won't wait. They'll be stuck here for ever, held back by a squad of soldiers. Viktor opens his briefcase and hands the documents over. 'There is also the children's governess and her daughter travelling in the car behind,' he explains. 'Her documents are there too.'

The soldier examines the papers with a mixture of indifference and incomprehension. Behind him there's a stir in the crowd. People are pointing and craning to see down the Bahnstrasse towards the ornate station building. A father has lifted his child onto his shoulders. There is a crowd there at the entrance to the station, soldiers drawn up, a banner flying and vehicles waiting.

'Why are these people here, Sergeant? What are they here to see?'

'I can't tell you that, sir. Orders.' He hands the papers back.

'But these people know.'

'Maybe, maybe not.'

There's a distant roar of engines. Abruptly the soldier leaves the window of the car and snaps to attention. One of his colleagues salutes, arm extended in that absurd, histrionic gesture. Viktor climbs out of the car to look. Liesel calls him back but he ignores her. Behind them Oskar and Hana are out of their car. The people on the pavement are straining to see, some with excitement, others looking on with indifference. And suddenly the object of all the interest is there, in an open-topped six-wheel car, driving out of the station forecourt, standing there in the front seat of the vehicle, a figure of inconsequential ordinariness who has never-theless become iconic across the continent, the sallow face with its paintbrush moustache and the eyes that stare out of newsreels and newspapers, gazing into a history that seems already destined and defined. And then the small parade of vehicles has roared away, across the station road and down Masaryk Street towards the city centre. People in the crowd around them are weeping, but whether they are tears of joy or tears of misery it is impossible to tell.

'Did you see?' Hana asks. She has come to the window on Liesel's side. 'Did you see who it was?'

'Who was it?' Martin asks. 'I didn't see the man. Who was the man?'

'Shut up Martin,' Ottilie says.

Hana is tense with excitement, as though she has come out here to wave and cheer. 'How has he done it? They say he was in Prague yesterday. Here today. How does he do it?'

'It's not magic, is it?'

'What's magic?' Martin asks. 'Why won't people tell me? Tell me, Maminko, tell me.'

The soldiers are relaxing. The onlookers drifting away. 'May we continue, Sergeant?' Viktor is asking. His voice is quiet, as though he is confiding something to the soldier. 'We turn left just there, before the station. Otherwise we'll miss our plane.'

The man hesitates. 'You turn down there right away? Is that understood?'

'Of course it's understood, Sergeant.'

'Get in,' Liesel says to Hana, opening the door. 'We can't wait.' So Hana climbs in beside her and takes her hand for comfort and their little convoy moves forward, manoeuvring past the army vehicles and turning left into the tunnel that passes below the rail-way line, away from the city centre and towards Černovice and the aerodrome.

'How did you know he was a sergeant?' Liesel asks.

Viktor looks tense, as though the ordeal is still to come. 'He wasn't a sergeant, he was a corporal. But I always promote a sol-dier if I can. It makes them feel good.'

Hana laughs and the children laugh with her, Martin because he always follows Ottilie. Liesel joins in and the laughter is immoderate, a lifeline they grab to pull them out of their anxiety. The only traffic on the road seems to be military. The whole country is under siege.

'Have you heard?' Hana says, to try to keep the mood light-hearted. 'Apparently they put up curfew notices in Olomouc yesterday – you know, just like the ones here – in German and Czech. Only they got it wrong. The ones they put up in Olomouc were in German and Romanian.'

The laughter starts again, and then dies away. It isn't so funny after all.

'Why Romanian?' Ottilie asks. 'Are there German soldiers in Romania as well?'

'No there aren't,' Liesel assures her. 'But if Auntie Hana's story is true it looks as though there soon may be.'

The airfield lies beneath a plain and windy March sky. Grey vehicles sporting iron crosses are parked round the perimeter and soldiers are patrolling with their weapons at the port. They let the cars through reluctantly, only when Viktor shows them the tickets and explains the problem and they have talked about it amongst themselves.

On the airfield are aircraft of the Luftwaffe, grey machines that look like coffins. Inside the concrete airport building a crush of people threatens the airline desks. Policemen, ordinary Czech policemen, are trying to keep order. Voices are raised in argument. Soldiers stand guard, German soldiers here as everywhere else. Viktor wades into the crowd waving their tickets aloft. A voice over the public address system announces that the Air France flight from Paris has been cancelled. The announcement is in German and Czech, but the German comes first.

Through the windows of the airport building they can see their aircraft on the concrete apron, wings spread, its nose up, its tail like a Swiss flag flung out by the wind. Daylight gleams on the corrugated metal fuselage. The other aircraft on the perimeter are dull grey and bear the *Hakenkreuz* on their tails, and there is a strange antinomy between the two symbols, the straight Swiss cross and the crooked German one.

'Will our aeroplane take off?' Liesel asks a passing official, but he just shrugs. Nobody seems to know anything. She clings to

Hana for comfort, dear Hana who seems so strong now, not the fragile fractured creature of the other day. 'Hanička, maybe it won't go. Maybe we'll have to stay.' And a part of her, an unexpressed, suppressed fragment, hopes that it will be so, that the airport authorities will deny their pilot permission to take off, that they will have to return to the cars and reload the luggage and set off back to Město and the quiet comfort of the Glass Room.

Viktor comes over, with his face stern but satisfied. She knows the look. He doesn't like to celebrate his triumphs. Outside, a trolley loaded with suitcases is being pushed across the concrete towards the aircraft. 'I'll tell Laník that he can go,' Viktor says. 'We'd better get a move on before they change their minds.' And there is the announcement over the Tannoy, that the Swissair flight to Zurich will be departing in fifteen minutes.

Liesel shepherds her children towards the gate. 'We're going to fly!' Martin says. 'We're going to fly!'

Viktor walks behind, with Katalin and Marika. Hana and Oskar follow like a couple at a funeral – the same drawn faces, the same searching for things to say and failure to find them. At the doorway a border guard checks documents. Katalin and Marika's Nansen passports are glanced at, then passed back with a shrug. He asks Hana for hers. She shakes her head. 'We're just friends,' she tells him. 'We're just the people left behind.'

At the door they say their farewells, exchange kisses and hugs. Hana clings to Liesel and whispers in her ear, *Miluji tě*, I love you, and then lets go and stands there bereft. They go out into the cold, uncertain day, Viktor leading the way across the concrete. 'We're going to fly!' Martin announces to the hostess who stands at the foot of the steps. Holding her hat on against the wind, she bends towards him. 'You're a very lucky boy,' she says.

They climb the steps and duck in through the door. The cabin is a narrow, sloping tunnel with seats on either side and a dim twilight coming through the windows. It seems the very antithesis of the Glass Room, with no sense of design but instead a hard, factual functionality. Above the seats there is netting for hand luggage and behind each seat a paper bag for vomit. At the summit of the tunnel is an open door and a glimpse of daylight where the pilots and navigator are at work.

The other ten passengers are already settled into their seats.

The Landauers strap themselves in, Viktor and Liesel across the aisle from each other, Ottilie and Martin behind them, Katalin and Marika just ahead. The pilot appears at the door at the top of the slope.

'We must apologise for the delay, ladies and gentlemen, but as you know these are unusual times.' He has the jovial manner of a sea captain about to set off on a cruise. He even uses the word: 'We'll be cruising at an altitude of three thousand metres. And an estimated flying time of three and a half hours. The weather seems to be improving a bit, but be prepared for a bumpy flight.' He says *bockig* for bumpy. Martin and Ottilie giggle, and look over at Marika. '*Bockig*,' they whisper and make the gesture of a bucking horse.

'Are there many first-time flyers?' the captain asks. 'Well, you mustn't worry about it. It's what the birds do. Quite natural. If you do feel sick there's a bag in the pocket opposite you. There will be a bit of a bang when the engines start, but don't worry, it's quite normal.' He returns to his cockpit, closing the door behind him.

'Will we be sick?' Katalin asks. She looks round at Viktor. He is the expert, the only one of their party who has done this before.

'Some people are, some people aren't. It's a bit like a fairground ride at times.'

'I went on the Riesenrad once,' Liesel says. 'With Benno.'

'A bit more than the big wheel, I think. A roller-coaster, maybe.'

The passengers wait expectantly. But still they jump when the explosion comes and the engines start. The cabin is flooded with noise, like the inside of a drum when the drummer beats a military roll. Katalin looks round and tries to smile. Liesel pulls the curtain aside and peers out of her window at the aluminium wings and the shining disk of the propeller. It seems an insubstantial thing, a ghost of something that cannot possibly pull them up into the sky. Are they really going?

'We really are going, aren't we?' she says, not to Viktor, not to herself but somehow to the low line of hills she can see out there beyond the limits of the airfield.

The engine note rises in pitch and the aircraft begins its move forward, swinging its tail from side to side, bumping over the grass. '*Bockig*!' Martin shouts above the engine noise. '*Bockig*!'

189

Liesel tries to shush him to silence but the endeavour is futile. The racket of the engines drowns everything including his child's voice. She reaches out and holds Viktor's hand across the aisle and wonders whether this is usual, this monster of noise, the cabin shaking, the aircraft snaking forward, the lurching and bumping.

'Everything's fine,' he mouths when he sees her expression. 'This is what it's like.'

At the far end of the airfield the aircraft turns and settles for a moment, the cabin shaking. Then the shaking becomes a shuddering and the engines roar against the brakes, and abruptly the passengers are thrown back into their seats as the machine moves forward, faster and faster, the wheels rumbling beneath them, the grass rushing by, the airport buildings and the fuel trucks and the grim grey military aircraft all rushing by, and a small crowd of spectators at the windows of the terminal building, among whom, Liesel presumes, are Hana and Oskar. And then there is something magic, a sudden lightness, a last kiss of the earth, and they are free, detached, floating up into the *Raum* above them, the ground dropping away, the aircraft rocking and the engines shouting in a call of triumph. Liesel looks down on buildings and streets and the sinuous line of the river, the Svitava, there like a snake winding through the undergrowth. Then more houses, and a factory, surely the Landauer factory, and dense clusters of houses, like decorative stones embedded in concrete, slipping beneath the wings and falling away behind. 'Oh, Viktor, it's wonderful!' she cries, overwhelmed for a moment by the pure sensation. 'Oh, do look! Do look at that!'

And then there is a line of buildings and a street that somehow she recognises even from this unaccustomed angle: the bulk of the hospital and then a slope of grass and trees, and there, outstanding on the lip of the hill, the long low shape of the house itself, her house, hers and Viktor's, the pure dimensions of von Abt's vision drawn with a ruler across the land, the blank wall of glass, the Glass Room, *der Glasraum*. And suddenly she weeps, that she might never see the house again, that all that has happened is past and that the future is uncertain and full of fear.

Laník

Laník stands in the centre of the Glass Room examining the place, the chairs that have not yet been packed and sent to storage, the glistening flooring, the wooden partition of the dining area and the honey-coloured partition of the onyx wall, the chrome pillars and the milk-white lights and the plate glass. He feels an immense relief. They have gone. He is his own master. Not that he covets the house in any way. In fact, he dislikes it. 'Can't see what they see in the place,' he has said often enough to his sister. 'More like a fish tank than a house. And if it's a house it certainly isn't a home.' But whether or not he likes the place, he prefers it to be within his own sphere of influence.

He walks round the room fingering the fittings, running his hand – they all do that, he has noticed – over the surface of the onyx wall. 'I think you had better board that up,' Herr Viktor said to him as they were preparing to leave. It was almost the last command given to him before they went to the airport. 'Plasterboard either side, turn it into an ordinary partition wall. See to it, will you?'

For the moment the matter can wait. The place is his. The sensation is not of unalloyed contentment: he feels like someone in the audience who has suddenly been invited up on stage but then discovers that the set has been abandoned, the actors have all departed and there are only the props left behind. Still, there's something of the magic of the performance hanging round the place. Faint echoes. Memories of listening from behind the door to the kitchen and occasionally sneaking out for a peep, and hearing things, even – occasionally – seeing things that he can mull over in his mind.

He pours himself a whisky (the glasses have been packed away and shipped, but the drink is still there in the library area) and walks over to the front of the onyx wall to sit in one of the chairs. A Liesel chair, he happens to know. It's not the kind of chair he likes – much better to have something with proper padded arms, something you can nod off to sleep in, listening to the wireless – but it's funny to sit in a chair she sat in, her round arse against the same leather. That gives a small stir of pleasure. Paní Landauer. Paní Liesel. As he lights up a cigarette and contemplates the view through the windows, he says the name out loud, savouring it. 'Liesel.'

There's a footfall behind him. He turns to see his sister coming out from the kitchens, wiping her hands on her apron. 'I thought I heard someone in here. What you doing?'

'Just sitting. I thought I owed it to myself.'

'It's not your place to sit, is it?'

'Isn't it? Do you reckon it's theirs still?'

'Well, it is, isn't it?'

'You think they'll be back? They'll settle in Switzerland or wherever, won't they? People like them never really have a fixed home, do they?'

'What do you mean, "people like them"?'

He sniffs and turns back to the view. 'Yids.'

'*She* wasn't a Yid.' It has become the past tense now. 'I'll miss her, you know that? Miss her, I will.'

'Not him?'

'You know I didn't like him. Cold fish. You said so yourself.'

'I told you, he's a Yid. That's his problem.'

'You were happy enough to take his money.'

'He's got enough of it, hasn't he? Look at this place.'

She stands in front of him, between him and the windows, her bulk blocking the light. 'Your tea's going to be ready soon. You'd best go and wash.'

He looks at her with a sly smile. 'You know I saw her once? In her bedroom.'

'What are you talking about?'

'It was almost dark. I was doing something on the terrace, unblocking a drain or something. And I saw her in her room. No clothes on.'

She laughs. 'You dirty old thing.'

'I couldn't help it, could I? The curtains weren't properly drawn and I just looked round and there she was, naked as the day she was born. Looking at herself in the mirror. Small tits.' He grins. 'But a nice bush.'

'You're making it up.'

'No I'm not. She touched herself, you know that? She touched herself *there*. Swear to God.'

'Since when did you take any notice of God?'

'Got me stirred up, it did. Like a bloody bargepole—'

She turns to go. 'I haven't got time to stand around listening to your dirty talk. I've got to get tea ready.'

'Let's eat at their dining table,' he calls after her. 'No reason why we shouldn't use the place if we want to.'

'There's more,' he tells her twenty minutes later, when they're sitting at the round table eating.

'What do you mean, more?'

'About them. There's more about them.' He lifts food to his mouth and talks through the chewing. When he was a kid she used to stop him doing that but now he's his own master and he'll do what he pleases. 'You know that refugee woman? Kalman. You know her?'

'Frau Katalin, you mean?'

'Call her what you like, she was being fucked by him. I'll bet you didn't know that, did you?'

'You just talk dirty. It's disgusting really, what you say.'

He laughs through his mouthful of pork and potato dumpling. 'It might be disgusting but it's true. I caught them at it. One morning when there was no one around. The kids were at school and Frau Liesel had gone somewhere and I went looking for him. Wanted the rest of the day off, I did. Anyway, I go up to the top floor—'

'You're not meant to do that.'

'Well I did it, didn't I? And I caught them at it in her room. I listened outside the door and they were going at it hammer and tongs, I tell you. Like he was strangling a pig with his bare hands.'

'You're lying.'

He laughs again. 'What do you think, that they're all like you? These people love it, I tell you. They play the respectable but really they love fucking each other. It's what they do.'

193

Exile

The villa resembled a small castle, complete with turret and crenellations and a front door that looked as though it would keep out a siege army. A monstrosity in the Wagnerian style, Viktor called it. They settled in amongst the heavy drapes and the heavier furniture and felt like raiders camping in the abandoned ruins of the enemy.

'It's only for the time being,' Liesel told herself. 'Soon it will all be over and we'll be able to return.'

At first she tried to imagine it like that, as a holiday, one of those summer vacations when they rented a villa on a lake and spent the days in an idle simulacrum of domestic normality: visiting local sights, taking a sailboat, feeding the ducks, walking in the hills. But holidays are circumscribed by the inevitability of their ending. You know you are going home to pick up those threads of a life that has merely been suspended. This was different. Life had not been suspended, it had been ended and a new one had to be constructed out of a poverty of component parts: this house, this garden, this view of the lake and the mountains, these three adults and three children. Six characters in search of a home.

She wrote sitting at the desk in her bedroom with the view of the lake before her. She wrote in the strange abstraction of exile, talking to people who no longer existed except in memory: her mother, a favourite aunt, an old school friend of Benno's who wrote to her saying how sorry he was that they had found it necessary to leave and how things were not so bad and at least all that was finest about German culture was being preserved. And Hana.

My Darling Hana,
How are you and Oskar? And how are all our friends? And how is the dear house managing without us? You must go round and see it from time to time. I told Laník that you would, so don't accept any nonsense from him. I feel quite strange thinking of you being there without us, but you are so much part of me that in a sense it would be me, wouldn't it? Me by proxy. I miss you, Hanička. Of course I miss you. But I truly believe it won't be long. This awfulness cannot continue.

But it was not long before the idea of return came to seem absurd. The children were found places in schools nearby and settled in quickly, and Viktor was making plans. His latest project involved the manufacture of instruments for both cars and aircraft. It would combine traditional Swiss expertise in clocks and watches with his own knowledge of the motor industry. During the day-time he was often in Zurich, occasionally in Geneva, meeting people. There were potential investors to persuade, partners to coerce, contacts to establish.

Liesel waited patiently for his return from these outings to the city. There wasn't much else to do except wait, Katalin doing some needlework and Liesel writing letters or practising the piano. Almost the first thing she had done on arrival was to hire a piano – a Bösendorfer grand just like the one in the Glass Room – and find a piano teacher. Piano teachers were two a penny here, Jewish refugees struggling to make a living.

Right at the start she had invited Katalin to come down from her room and join her in the sitting room. It seemed absurd to pretend that she was a mere employee, a servant of the family. 'We might as well keep each other company,' she suggested.

Katalin had seemed hesitant, but perhaps that was to be expected. She came from a different world, and had to adjust to this new experience. They talked about the places they had left behind, about the dream of return, about all those vague aspirations that are symptoms of ennui and exile. Outside a thin rain was smudging the view of the lake.

'Maybe we'll be back home before Christmas,' Liesel suggested. It was always she who suggested the possibility of return. 'Maybe everything will settle down.'

'But you can't go back, can you?' the younger woman said. 'You can only go forward.'

Liesel gave a small, humourless laugh. 'Goodness, we sound like two characters from Chekhov.'

'What's Chekhov?'

'You don't know Chekhov?' She didn't meant to sound so surprised, but Katalin's manner sometimes belied her ignorance, that was the trouble. It was easy to forget that she did not possess the same *qualities* as their other friends. Qualities, *Eigenschaften*, was a word Liesel liked to use. Viktor was a person of *Eigenschaften* and so, of course, was Hana. The qualities were implied rather than defined: a level of intellectual understanding, a high degree of culture, a certain liberal attitude, a delight in the modern and a loathing of the bad things of the past. *But Katalin is a charming companion for all her limitations*, she wrote to Hana, *and we get on very well*. For they did have things in common and, thrown together by circumstance, were happy enough in each other's company, going round the market in Zurich together, or taking a steamer trip on the lake with the children, or swimming from the landing stage at the foot of the garden. Katalin turned out to be an excellent swimmer. The first time she ventured into the water she surprised them all by diving off the end of the jetty with a sudden fluid grace that had barely disturbed the water: just a liquid plop! and there she was beneath the surface, swimming strongly and silently towards the shore. The children had clapped as she emerged, as though the dive had been quite unexpected and remarkable; but Liesel saw that Katalin had that about her, something sleek, like an otter.

Summer passed, the first summer in exile, and when the first snowfall came they took the children tobogganing in the hills behind the house. Later, before Christmas, there was the first trip to the ski slopes where Ottilie could show off her skills already learned in the Tatra Mountains. She and Marika were almost inseparable by now, a pair of precocious young females with budding breasts and knowing smiles. Marika had taken to calling Viktor *Onkel*.

He seemed to find that amusing. 'Show me how to ski, Onkel Viktor,' she would cry. 'Please show me how to ski.' Or, 'When are you going to take us tobogganing, Onkel?' Or, 'I want to do ice skating, Onkel Viktor, please come and watch me ice skating.'

'He has become like a father to her,' Katalin confided to Liesel. Her face was flushed and her eyes shining, happiness and cold conspiring to make her seem so young. 'You don't know how much we owe to him.'

But Liesel did know. There were signs, of course there were signs, small hints, like the first indications of age in a someone's face, changes that you don't notice if you are living together until you wake up one day and there they are: the greying hair, the crow's feet round the eyes, small creases of disapproval at the corners of the mouth. In retrospect she realised that she had noticed them even before they had left Město. It wasn't the way that Viktor and Katalin looked at each other, it was the way they didn't look. It wasn't the notes, it was the silences between the notes. Some music is the very enemy of silence, keeping the sounds coming so that the listener has no time to reflect. But other music, the music she played for herself, was different. In that music – the music of Janáček, for example – the silences matter. They are silences of foreboding, anticipatory echoes of the sounds that are yet to come.

Viktor bought a sailing boat and taught himself to sail on the lake. Once or twice Liesel went with him but she didn't enjoy the experience. Absurdly – it seemed absurd in such a small craft – it made her feel sick. So it was Katalin who crewed for him, with one of the children as a passenger. They couldn't take more than one passenger, there just wasn't room. And sometimes they just went on their own and Liesel looked after the children. She wasn't a fool. She saw the laughter in Katalin's eyes when they came back, and something else as well, a hint of shame.

Then one night when she couldn't sleep because of a headache Liesel opened the door to Viktor's room. She was in search of aspirin and there was none in the bathroom and she knew he kept a bottle at his bedside, so she crept into the bedroom like a shadow, determined not to wake him. But in the event there was no risk of that happening because he was not in his bed.

She whispered his name, ridiculously she whispered his name. 'Viktor? Viktor?' Whom was she hoping not to disturb? Anyway, there was no reply. The bed had been occupied, but not for a while. The sheets were cold. She waited but he did not appear. So she left the room and crept, breathless and fearful like a child, up the stairs to the attic floor. The corridor was silent, illuminated only by a night light at the far end where the children's rooms were. The first door was Katalin's. For long minutes Liesel stood with her ear against the door, listening. What she heard was the breath of slumber, the mutter of sleep-talk, the moan of nightmare and then a voice crying out in despair or pain, Katalin's voice crying *Oh*, *oh*, *oh* in short, staccato bursts, as though her very life were being shaken out of her. And then a quietness that held within its embrace a low mutter of contentment.

Liesel turned and went back down to her bed. She slept fitfully for the remainder of the night, her sleep disturbed by dreams in which they were back home in the house on Blackfield Road, and she was standing outside on the terrace looking in through the windows into the Glass Room and seeing Viktor making love. The object of his love was Katalin, was Hana, was herself, the three women metamorphosing one into the other, then becoming one, a chimera, and the man becoming Hana, Hana with a penis, Viktor with a vulva, the act of love transformed into something that people watched, crowds of people packed into the space between the onyx wall and the windows, an audience that laughed and applauded as the protagonists performed, giving and receiving sperm that was like rice thrown at a wedding.

She woke to a pale dawn and the grey lake beyond the garden, and a misery that remained ill-defined until she remembered what she had discovered during the night. She sat in her room listening to the familiar sounds – footsteps on the floor above as Katalin got the children up, the running of a bath in her and Viktor's bathroom, the door opening downstairs as the maid let herself in, all this domestic familiarity standing as sharp contrast to the silence of the night and the dark shadows of suspicion.

Over breakfast she watched Viktor and Katalin for signs. There were none. No glance exchanged, no secret contact. Life, domestic life, went on as normal.

Viktor glanced up at her from his paper. 'Are you feeling all right, my dear?'

'I'm fine,' she replied. 'I just didn't get much sleep last night.'

He smiled and nodded and went back to his reading. The *Neue Zürcher Zeitung* was the usual catalogue of disaster – Jewish refugees being held on the border, questions being asked in the assembly of the League of Nations, people being arrested in Prague, German forces massing on the Polish border this time, nobody doing anything effective. The meal continued, the cook hovering, wanting to ask about lunch, Viktor reading, Katalin talking to the children, explaining to Martin how he should eat a good breakfast, how it would set him up for the day. 'What's "setting up" mean?' the boy asked in the manner of children, who will ask a question even when they know the answer.

'Can I have a word with you, Viktor?' Liesel asked. She felt like a supplicant, bereft of the natural authority that she should feel in her own household. What would Hana have done in such a situation? How would she have behaved?

He looked at her over his paper. 'Really?'

'If you don't mind. In the study, perhaps.'

The idea of leaving the breakfast room for a private discussion seemed both surprising and amusing. He folded his paper open at the place he was reading and got up from his chair. 'If you wish. I have to catch my train in twenty minutes. I have a meeting in Lausanne.'

'Perhaps it won't take long.'

Katalin watched as they left the room. The children were arguing about the meaning of 'setting up'. 'Setting down' they knew. 'Setting up' was surely the opposite. '"Settling up" is when you pay your bills,' said Ottilie, who knew more than the others.

'Tell me,' Viktor said as he closed the study door. The study had become his territory ever since they moved into the villa. When Liesel wanted to write letters she went to her room looking out over the lake. Here, on the other side of the house, with a view of the front garden and the road, it was a male refuge, all heavy oak panelling and leather-upholstered armchair and a wide desk with a leather skiver.

'It's about Katalin.'

'About Katalin?'

199

Carefully, she paused. 'Is she happy?'

He seemed surprised by the possibility of happiness. 'Happy? I don't really know. I think so. You speak to her more than I do. What do *you* think? Goodness, she has enough to be thankful for. I mean, what would have happened to her if she'd stayed behind?'

'Of course there's that. But what kind of future does she have here?'

'With us, do you mean?'

'I suppose with us. She doesn't have anyone else, does she? And no way of supporting herself.'

He looked puzzled. 'What are you driving at, Liesel?'

She shrugged. She didn't really know the answer to his question. What *was* she driving at? The expression implied intention, a target, an aim, and in truth she had none. There was just the dull notes of accusation. 'What do you think of her?' she asked. 'Do you find her attractive?'

'Certainly she's attractive.' It was impossible to read his expression. Just a faint smile, as though the question revealed more about her than it did about him. 'Eliška, I do believe you are jealous.'

He never called her Eliška, not these days. 'Do I have reason to be?'

'Of course you don't.' He paused, considering. There was nothing in his expression, no guilt, no shame. So much so that a small part of her wondered whether she had imagined the whole thing last night, whether it was all part of her dream. 'We can be honest with each other, can't we?' he asked.

'Can we?'

'I think we can. I think we ought to be.' He seemed to be thinking about the form of words he might use, like a chess player wondering how his move would affect his opponent, how that move would affect the next, how the single first step would reverberate on throughout the game. But it wasn't a game, was it? There were no boundaries and no rules. 'Nothing that is due to you is compromised by Kata being here,' he said. 'Whatever is mine is yours, you know that. And if you were to say that Kata must leave, then she would have to go. Is that what you want? Is it?'

'I don't know what I want.' She turned away and looked out of the window. She needed a cigarette. She rarely smoked so early in the morning but she felt the need now. Her hands were trembling as she dealt with cigarette packet and lighter. She drew on the cigarette and felt the smoke in her lungs, consoling her. Out there beyond the window, beyond the limits of the garden and the boundaries of this country everything was happening: politicians were ranting, troops were massing on borders, people were being shipped off to camps, the whole world was coming apart. And here there was this intestine, undeclared conflict.

His voice came from behind her. 'You can tell me that she must go and there will just be the two of us. If that's what you want. Look, I'll miss my train. We'll talk this over when I come back. Is that all right? Until then I suggest you say nothing to her. Will you do that for me?'

She nodded at the window. Perhaps she nodded. Anyway, she felt that she nodded, and then he was gone: the door had opened and he had gone. She could hear the children, and Katalin hurrying them up to get ready for school. And soon she saw him walking up the drive with his briefcase in his hand. What would Hana have said? What would Hana have done? She felt that strange longing for the familiar and the unexpected, those demon things that she had known with Hana. Nothing more perfect. A completeness of body and soul.

Dearest, darling Hana, she wrote, *I have no one else to confide in here, and of course you are the one person I would tell if we were still at home . . .*

It was fruitless, of course. The letter wouldn't get there for more than a week, and it would be more days before the reply came back. But she could talk to the page, and talking would make things clear. *I know what you'll say. You'll say I told you so. You'll say, men are like that. You'll say all those things that you warned me of. As you make your bed, so you must lie on it. Literally, I suppose. And now I have to lie on it without my Hanička by my side . . .*

She didn't come down from her room until the middle of the morning. Out in the garden there was a fresh breeze from across the lake, a feeling of open sky and air. Sunlight glittered. There were sailing boats on the water, a small regatta like something in a painting by Raoul Dufy, all bright colours and cheerfulness. She walked down to the water's edge where there was the landing stage and Viktor's little sailing dinghy moored, and Katalin, standing there.

'I think we need to talk,' she said.

The girl didn't turn. Was it absurd to think of her as a girl? Young woman, then. She was watching the boats and her profile was presented to Liesel, the curved nose, the childish forehead, the prominent lips. Very lovely, of course. Alluring. And those eyes, their startling pale blue, paler by far than the sky. She spoke to the lake. 'You know, don't you?'

'Yes, I do.'

'It's stupid, isn't it? After all you've done for me, to let this happen.'

'But it has happened and now we've got to decide what we do about it. It had better be us to decide, don't you think? We are the vulnerable ones. Viktor's going to be all right whatever happens so the question is not what is *he* going to do, but what are *we* going to do?'

Katalin shook her head. 'Do you mean which of us wins and which loses? I'll lose. How can I do anything but lose?'

'I'm not talking of winning or losing. I'm trying to suggest a resolution. Viktor always has a plan. Maybe he's even got one now. But I've been thinking as well. I've been writing letters and I've been thinking. All the possibilities. For example, I could just leave, return home. I'm not a Jew. My family isn't threatened.'

'The children?'

'I could take them with me.' She paused. Ducks had appeared on the water before them, three pairs of mallard. They lived in the reed bed just along the shore and when anyone appeared at the water's edge they congregated, expecting food. There was the soft chuckle of their laughter, as though the humans on the bank were performers in some comedy of the absurd. She wished now that she had brought some bread for them. Uxorious birds, she thought, content in their couples. 'Or I could leave them with you and Viktor.'

'But you're not going to do that, are you?'

'It's tempting. Even with all that's happening at home, it's tempting. But I think you are right. I don't think I'll run away.'

'And where does that leave me?'

The ducks chuckled softly. 'I should have brought something to

202

give them,' she said, lighting a cigarette. She was smoking too much. Her fingers were tinged yellow. 'When did you first meet Viktor?'

The girl looked round. 'In your house, of course. That meeting. It was awful, really. Like being something in the zoo with all those people watching.'

'I don't think that's quite right, is it? That wasn't the first time. I've only just put everything together. I think he recognised you the moment that you appeared in the Glass Room.'

The girl hesitated, looking for a way out of this confrontation and finding none. 'It was in Vienna,' she admitted. 'I used to . . . go walking in the Prater. You know the Prater? The gardens, the cafés, the big wheel, all that stuff . . .'

'Of course I know the Prater.' Liesel drew on her cigarette. The sensation of shock was as much physical as emotional: a lightness of head, a sensation of nausea, almost the feeling that she had had in that aircraft as they took off from Město. It was strange how the emotional could manifest itself so clearly in the organic. That connection between mind and matter. But she was going to keep calm. She was going to embody reason and balance. 'So you were walking in the Prater and Viktor picked you up? Is that it? Or did you pick him up? Did he pay you?'

Katalin shrugged. 'He helped me from time to time. It was difficult to get by sometimes.' And then she looked up, suddenly defiant. 'Do you want me to say that I'm ashamed of taking money from him? Well, I'm not. You've never had to worry about where you're going to spend the night, have you? Or where your next meal's coming from. Or how you are going to buy clothes for your baby. But when you can't find a job and you can't afford the rent, then things look very different.'

'And when was this?'

'A few years ago.'

The girl looked as though she was about to cry, that was the absurd thing. She made a small, sorry figure standing there looking at the ducks, her face pale, her eyes glistening, her mouth drawn down in childish misery. Like Ottilie when she was about to burst into tears, but not Ottilie now – Ottilie when she was six. A child. 'I'm sorry, Frau Liesel, but I don't want to lie to you.'

'In a way you already have, haven't you? Did you plan it all?

Coming to Město, I mean. Did you think you might find him and inveigle your way into his family?'

Katalin shook her head vehemently. 'I had no idea where he lived. I didn't even know his name. Only Viktor. And we'd not seen each other for some time. I'd got frightened, see.'

'Frightened?'

'Of what I felt for him. The occasional pick-up was easy to forget. But not him.' She blinked the tears away. 'I moved away from my place and got a job and I never expected to see him again. He'd given me a bit of money, for Marika really, and I thought we could make a fresh start with that. Look, I'm sorry about this, Frau Liesel, it's not what I wanted to say but you really surprised me with that question. You'll probably throw me out now, won't you? What'll I do then? I can't get work here, can I? I'll have to go back . . .' She was weeping now, like a child faced with some impossible demand. Liesel watched her, barely comprehending.

'I'm not saying that at all, Kati. I don't really know what I *am* saying. Or what to think.' But she *was* thinking: she was thinking an image, just an image that shifted across the screen of memory: people crowded into the Glass Room. And the noise, the talk and the laughter, she heard that; and the sound of metal – a knife – against glass, and Viktor being helped up onto a chair and standing there and calling for quiet, and an approximate hush descending so that his voice could rise above the residual chatter to talk of transparency and clarity and how he wanted his house to be like that – transparent and full of light. And all the time he was going on business trips to Vienna and fucking Katalin in the shabby opaque world of some hotel bedroom.

She drew on the cigarette. And yet she had known, hadn't she? From the moment that Katalin had stood there on the stage in the Glass Room and he had looked at her with shock, with horror even, she had known.

She looked round. 'Are you in love with Viktor?'

There was a long pause. 'Yes, I think I am.'

Liesel thought for a minute. It seemed very important that she get this right, use the right words, say the correct things. Which weren't *correct* at all, not in that sense. Most incorrect, in fact. The kind of thing she would only have dared say to Hana. 'You don't speak Czech, do you? Of course you don't. Well, in Czech we have an expression, *propadnout lásce*, to *fall* in love. You can't do that in German, can you? In German you just come into love. But in Czech you can *fall* into it. Am I making sense? Well that never happened to me. I never fell in love with Viktor. Came into it, perhaps, but never fell. And then when Martin came along . . .' She drew on the cigarette and held the smoke in her lungs before letting it out in a thin stream. 'The birth was very difficult. I lost a lot of blood and was very ill afterwards. When it was all over things had changed.'

'Changed?'

'Between us. It's difficult to explain. My need for him had gone. Isn't that strange? I found him . . . intrusive. I mean physically. Can you understand what I'm saying, Kati?' She glanced round. 'I don't even know whether I should call you that. Kati? Kata? Which? What does Viktor call you?'

'Kata's fine. Or Kati.' The girl looked ahead across the water, with a faint frown, as though she was trying to understand which should be her name. 'I don't mind which, Frau Liesel, really I don't.'

Captivating, Liesel thought. She understood exactly what Viktor saw in her: that pliancy of body, the scent of her skin and her hair, the neat symmetry of her face, the swelling of her bust, much fuller than her own. But something else as well, the hint of blatant sexuality beneath the sleek innocence, the knowledge that she had of men. 'I like Kati. And that strange Magyar sound you give to it. *Koti*. Maybe you should call me Liesel now, when we're alone together.' And then, 'I'm sorry, I shouldn't confide in you like this. And yet I have no one else. I'm here on my own and I've no one to whom I can tell these things.' And quite unexpectedly both to herself and, presumably, to Katalin, she was in tears, tears running down her cheeks, tears threatening to dissolve the fragile fabric of her face, tears racking her body. 'I'm sorry,' she said through her weeping. 'I've never spoken to anyone like this, Kati, and somehow telling it has made it all the more real.' And Katalin turned to her and put her arms around her, the smaller woman comforting the taller. It was ridiculous really, Liesel thought. Height should give you some kind of defence, make you less vul-nerable, make you able to control your life and your love and your destiny; but it doesn't. A tall person in tears somehow seems, and feels, ridiculous.

On the surface of things little appeared to change, but that evening Katalin joined Liesel and Viktor for dinner when previously she had always eaten earlier with the children. Viktor didn't remark on the change. Did he even notice? He was full of his account of meeting Fritz Mandl at lunch in Zurich. Mandl was going to South America, to make his fortune – his third or fourth fortune, Viktor couldn't be sure which – and maybe that was where they should go, Venezuela or Argentina or somewhere. Mandl was looking for partners. 'Do you know what happened to his wife? Apparently she left him; apparently she's making a career in Hollywood.'

'I told you that, Viktor. Hana helped her, don't you remember?'

'Did she? How strange . . .'

The conversation died away. It was like a family meal after the announcement of a death, stories started but not completed, comments stillborn. 'How are the children getting on at school?' he asked, which was not the kind of thing that usually concerned him. But the question was treated like a serious enquiry, each child's progress analysed, teachers discussed, progress dissected. Katalin thought that Marika needed some help with her Latin – she hadn't studied Latin before – and Viktor thought that it might be arranged. Some private tuition, perhaps. The cost? The cost would be no problem.

After the meal Katalin left them alone. 'Perhaps we should talk,' he said. 'About that business this morning.' He had spoken to Katalin, she knew that. His face betrayed him: anxiety, distraction, the knowledge that a life that had been disrupted by circumstance could now be blown to smithereens. The roles, she understood, had neatly reversed.

'Why didn't you do what I asked? Why did you speak to her?'

'Why should I do what you ask? Because you're my husband? It's been going on for years, hasn't it? We've been sharing you for most of our married life.' She lit a cigarette. 'All those trips to Vienna when you could so easily have come home. Oh yes, I know all about them. At least, I can imagine all about them. I thought it was just women, tarts, whatever. What men do. But it wasn't tarts, was it? It was her. No, she hasn't told me anything but it doesn't take much to work it out. I tried to contact you once at the Sacher and they were most apologetic that you weren't there. As though it was their fault. You weren't at the Bristol either. You weren't anywhere I knew.' She gave a bitter laugh, lighting a cigarette and drawing the smoke deep into her lungs. 'I suppose it happens all the time. I suppose the hotel staff are used to it.'

'You never said anything.'

'I didn't want to believe it myself. We spend much of our lives not wanting to believe it ourselves, don't we? When did it start?'

He shrugged but didn't answer. She tapped cigarette ash onto her plate, something that he loathed. 'Years,' she said. 'Before Martin? I suppose so. Did you love her as much as you loved me? Or maybe you never loved me. Maybe that's it. I suppose she does things for you that I won't do? Is that it? What does she do, suck your penis, is that it?'

'Don't be vulgar.'

She laughed, but the laughter didn't really work. It seemed more like a cry of misery or pain or something. 'You know what Hana always says? The way to a man's heart is through his cock. She's right, isn't she?'

'No, she's not.'

'Anyway, I don't want to talk about it, Viktor. I don't want to hear mention of it again, nor do I ever want to be embarrassed by it. And it goes without saying that the children must never, ever know. Now, if you don't mind, I must go to bed. I was up most of last night and I feel very tired.'

Dispossession

The man from the planning department examines the hallway suspiciously, then glances at the plans that he has just taken out of his briefcase. He frowns, as though he expects to find inconsistencies between reality and the official documents. 'Five bedrooms?' he says, tapping with his finger. But he doesn't wait for an answer as he sets off down the corridor, opening doors as he goes. Except for the odd bit of furniture – a bedframe in one, a cupboard in another – the rooms are bare.

'These are the children's rooms,' Laník explains as he hurries along behind.

'*Were*,' the man says. 'They *were* the children's.'

'Were. And the nanny's room at the end. They had a nanny to look after the kids.'

The man writes something in his notes. 'And the master bedroom?'

'Two bedrooms, either side of the main bathroom. Back there.'

They examine those equally barren spaces. 'This one was hers,' Laník says of one of them. His tone is soft and affectionate. 'She was all right. Lovely woman really. But *he* was a bastard. Arrogant, you know what I mean?'

'A Jew,' the man says, his tone implying, what do you expect? He opens the door onto the terrace. Outside it's like the wreckage of a seaside holiday cottage – the pergola bare and rusting, the semicircular bench in need of a lick of paint, the sandpit empty. There are even some weeds growing round the edge of the sand, ragged, thrifty plants finding some kind of living in that unpromising soil. 'Where the kids play during the summer,' Laník explains.

208

'Played.'

'Played. That's what I meant. Look, if they're not coming back—'

'I've told you, they no longer own the house. So even if they were to come back they wouldn't come back here. Not without taking the matter to court. And they're Jews. Jews aren't going to win any more cases now.'

'But what about me and my sister? That's what I want to know. We live here as well.'

'That remains to be seen. It all depends what we do with the building. But for the moment . . .'

'But we need to live. We need a roof over our heads.'

The man ignores him. 'Now the lower floor, I think.'

Laník shows the way, back inside and down the stairs. At the entrance to the Glass Room the surveyor pauses and glances at the plans once more. 'Open-plan living space, eh? Very classy.'

'They were classy people.'

'But not very practical.' He stalks around the Glass Room, tutting all the time. It's a habit he has. The tut of bureaucratic disapproval. When he passes the piano he lifts the lid and plays a single note. The note does nothing in the place, just dies away amongst the chrome and the glass. He sniffs, looking round the empty expanse. 'Where has all the furniture gone? Back in the office they said that it was all specially designed for the place, all of a piece. Where is it?'

'Where is what?'

'The furniture.'

'Oh, that. They took it. Virtually all of it. Stacks of money, you see. So they just shipped it all out. Except for the piano. As you can see.'

The man glances in at the kitchens. 'What's downstairs?'

'The basement. Pokey little rooms – laundry, storerooms, boiler, that kind of thing. Do you want to see? It's not really worth it.'

The man opens the plans on a table. He points. 'This is the garage?'

'That's right. Empty of course. Used to have a couple of Landauers, but they've gone too. And that' – he gestures over the man's shoulder to indicate the rooms behind the garage – 'is where me and my sister live.'

209

The man isn't really interested. He looks at the plans with an expert eye. 'What is it? Sixteen by thirty-two, something like that. Over five hundred square metres per floor and not a lot you can do with it.' Shaking his head he folds the plans away and returns them to his briefcase. 'You can hardly put people in here, can you? It's more like a gymnasium than a living room. What a waste.'

'So what d'you think'll happen?'

'No idea. They'll probably pull the place down.'

'What about us? What about me and my sister?'

The surveyor shrugs. 'In the meantime there needs to be somebody on site. I'll have a word back at the office, see if I can fix you up as caretaker.'

The letter from the lawyers in Město reached the Landauer breakfast table days later. The mail – delivered promptly at seven o'clock by the celebrated Swiss postal service – was always placed beside Viktor's plate. There were the usual bills, letters addressed to him about various business concerns, sometimes a letter for Liesel from home – perhaps from her mother, rarely from her father, occasionally (as this morning) from Hana. But this time there was also one from the family lawyers, a letter distinguished from the others by a certain gravity, as though the law firm's legal fees could somehow be sensed by the weight and texture of the paper. Viktor glanced at it and then looked at her with a bleak expression that she did not quite recognise. But then there were many things she did not recognise about Viktor nowadays. 'It's from Procházka.' Procházka was the partner who always dealt with personal matters of the family.

'What is it? Oh God, not a death?'

He made a small sound that may have been a sign of disapproval, may have been a deprecating laugh. 'Not exactly a death.' He passed her the letter. 'It seems we no longer own the house.'

'What on earth do you mean?' She peered at the sheet. Without her glasses the words were no more than a blur.

'Procházka informs us that it has been confiscated by the government. Taken from us, expropriated, whatever you want to call it. Stolen.'

'Why?'

'*Why?*' He looked at Liesel in astonishment. 'Because I am a Jew, Liesel.'

'And they've *taken* it? But it's not theirs to take. It's ours. We built it, we own it. It's yours and mine, and Ottilie's and Martin's when we go.'

'Where are you going?' Martin asked.

'Nowhere, darling.'

'What's happened to the house?' Ottilie's tone was sharply admonishing, the tone of her mother when she was telling the children off.

It wasn't often that Viktor addressed the children at breakfast but he turned to her and explained. 'I'm afraid it isn't ours any longer, Ottilie. Now it's theirs, the property of the so-called Protectorate. The decree has been signed in the name of the Reichsprotektor of Bohemia and Moravia himself.'

'Is that Hitler?'

'No it's not Hitler, but it is Hitler's representative.'

The girl was angry. 'But it's our house. It's ours!'

'Otti,' Katalin said quietly, 'you mustn't shout.'

'Isn't there any redress?' Liesel asked.

'Redress?' Viktor laughed. 'How quaint. Of course there's no redress, Liesel. These people write the laws to suit themselves.'

'What will they do with it?'

'God knows. Pull it down probably.'

'*Pull it down?*'

It was only at the suggestion that the house might actually be demolished that Liesel finally broke down and wept, not only for the beautiful house on the hillside in Město, but for her lost life and her lost love and because of the whole world of exile in which reality is elsewhere and the life you live seems to be something happening to someone else, a dream world that hesitates on the edge of nightmare. The children had never seen their mother weep. They watched in astonishment at this display of emotion, while at the head of the table Viktor looked impatient and help-less, as though she had done something silly but he didn't know how to explain the right way to do things. It was Katalin who got up from her chair and came round the table and put her arms around her shoulders to comfort her.

2

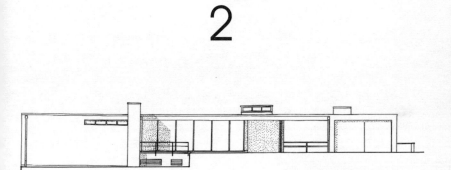

Occupation

Stahl calls for the car to stop.

'I'll get out here and walk,' he tells the driver. 'You go on and wait for me.'

He climbs out and lets the car pull away up the hill ahead. You aren't advised to do this, to appear alone on the streets in uniform, but on this quiet road with no one about and the sun beating on the asphalt he is prepared to dispense with caution for a moment. Walking is what he likes – hiking in the Kaisergebirge or walking along the dunes of Usedom island on the Baltic coast – and he has had all too little opportunity to stretch his legs in recent weeks. He strides up the hill enthusiastically. The road climbs. It is hot in the sunshine. There are trees and birdsong, the mundane things of suburban life. Houses hiding behind carefully trimmed vegetation. A dog barking in some garden nearby. The road reaches the brow of the hill and widens out and there it is, on the left-hand side with the view of the city beyond it – the Landauer House.

Startling, the reality, although he knew what to expect from those photographs and plans that he saw in an architectural journal some years ago: a long, low, almost featureless pavilion, somewhere that you might store sports equipment or furniture. A kind of stylish anonymity. The architect's name was Abt, he knows that as well. There is a story going round that Speer tried to persuade Abt to work with the Party on their new vision, their new aesthetic, but seeing this example of his work one wonders what the point would have been. The Party's vision is one of triumph and grandeur, not this kind of understatement. What happened to the man? Detention, probably. It isn't worth being lukewarm towards the regime. He who is not for me is against me, that is the watchword.

By the time he reaches the gate the driver is already inside the fence and arguing with someone. 'Is there a problem?' Stahl asks.

The man turns and salutes. 'Herr Hauptsturmführer, this fellow refuses to open to us. He says it's council property. I'm not sure if he really understands what's going on.'

Stahl smiles. He looks round at the houses across the street. They seem deserted, indifferent to his presence there in the fore-court of the Landauer House. Does a curtain twitch? He turns back to the problem at hand. The custodian is a surly looking Slav with the typical broad features of the race, the wide nose and blue eyes. Young. Couldn't be more than thirty. Not unintelligent. The Slavs aren't unintelligent of course, just emotionally unstable, liable to great heights and great depths. That is what science tells one. Look at Tchaikovsky. Look at Dostoyevsky.

'He understands all right.' He smiles pacifically at the fellow and tries to cajole him into acceptance of what is a fait accompli. 'Now come on my man, we don't want a silly argument, do we? Everything is above board. Legal.' He enunciates the word precisely, in case it is not understood. *Rechlicht.* 'We are possessing the property for purposes to do with the war effort. It's all written here in black and white.' He points to the foot of the document that the driver is trying to push into the man's hand. The requisition order – transfer of ownership from the Municipality of Město – is in German but there cannot be any doubt in the man's mind, can there? The former owners were German speakers so he must know the language well enough. 'Signed by the Secretary of State of the Reich Protectorate. See? Stamps, signature – Karl Hermann Frank – everything. My name's Stahl, by the way. Hauptsturmführer Stahl. And yours is Laník, I believe. Isn't that right? Look, *Pane* Laník, why don't you just show me round – as a visitor, if you like – while you think things over?' It is important to understand how to treat these people. What is the point in coming over all arrogant when all that is needed is a bit of per-suasion? 'I mean, we're going to get inside one way or the other, aren't we? So why not make it peaceably?'

Laník sniffs, looking from the officer to the driver and back.

Finally he shrugs and leads the way across the pavement towards the building. Stahl follows. The custodian opens the door and stands aside. Nodding approval, Stahl steps in and finds himself in a vestibule like the waiting room to a medical studio, all sterile white and gleaming chrome and dark wood panelling. Appropriate for what is planned for the place. The floor is pale limestone of some kind. There's a table where a dentist might have put a pile of magazines, copies of *Illustrierter Beobachter* and *Frauen Warte*, that kind of thing. A stairwell on the left leads down to the floor below.

'The rooms?'

Laník opens doors in the panelling. It's almost a conjuring trick, mere flat panelling – one expects a cupboard – opening to display entire rooms. The rooms are bare, stripped of furnishings, except that one of them still has a bedframe and a set of fitted bookshelves. There are two bathrooms, tiled in white. One of them, a children's bathroom presumably, has a row of small rubber mats on the floor depicting a family of ducks advancing towards the bath from the door: mother and father duck and a trail of four ducklings.

'Where are the original owners?' Stahl asks.

'Away.'

'I can see they are away. Where have they gone?'

Laník shrugs. 'Abroad.'

'And you're not going to say where?'

'I don't know.'

'You have no contact?'

'No.'

Stahl contemplates the Slav thoughtfully. 'They were Jews, weren't they?'

Again, that shrug. It borders, just borders on the insolent. That is the mood of the whole, damned country: indifference bordering on the insolent. The universal shrug. For the most part the Germans are enthusiastic enough, of course, like converts to a new religion. It's the Slavs that are the problem. He looks into the man's eyes and wonders what is there behind them. They are Aryan blue, but it is well known that the inheritance of eye colour is not an infallible guide. 'Are *you* a Jew?'

'I'm a Catholic.'

'That means nothing.'

'I don't like Jews,' Laník offers.

'Neither does that. Didn't you like your employers?'

'They were all right.'

'Ah. Bad Jews in general, good Jews in particular, is that it? The usual story. Show me downstairs.'

They go down, Laník leading the way. Twelve steps down to the turn, then a further nine, and a door opens onto the living room. Laník stands aside and lets him go through first.

Glänzend! Even more impressive than the photographs: a great open space of a place, almost the entire floor area of the whole building. Open plan. Stahl likes that. Ideal for a laboratory. Clean and bright, with those huge glass windows shedding the cold light of reason into the place. None of your Bohemian *Gemütlichkeit*, thank God. He finds it difficult, when the future beckons, to applaud the Party's obsession with the past, all that mystical folk-lorish stuff.

'What happened to the furniture?'

'It went.'

'All of it? I've seen photographs. Good modern stuff.'

'All of it except the piano.'

'A pity.' He walks round the room like someone looking to rent a property, running his finger along a surface, tapping the wooden panelling, touching with his palm the cool stone of the partition that crosses the room and divides part of the space in two. What stone is it? Alabaster or something. The tortuous veining resembles the contour lines of some remote countryside, twisted hills and sudden, surprising gorges. 'Remarkable, this.'

'It was chosen by *Pani* Landauer herself.'

'Where did it come from?'

'Africa, they say. I don't know.'

He lifts the lid of the piano that stands there in the shadow of the partition. 'A Bösendorfer. Who played?'

'*Pani* Landauer, a bit. But they used to have recitals sometimes. Public, like. For charity and stuff.'

'Patrons of the arts, were they?' He sits at the instrument and plays some notes, listening to the sounds with a practised ear. 'It needs tuning.'

'*Pani* Landauer used to see to that.'

Then Stahl begins to play, picking out the main theme of Smetana's *Moldau*. The trills, the flurries, lap around the Glass Room. 'Do you recognise it?'

Laník shrugs.

'It's one of your Slavic composers. Smetana. "*Ma Vlast*" or "*Mein Vaterland*". Which should it be?'

'I don't know anything about that. I'm not political.'

Stahl shuts the lid of the piano and stands up. 'Everyone's political these days, Laník. Being non-political is a political act.' He walks round the stone partition into the sitting area where the glass windows look out over the sloping lawn and across the rooftops of the city. There's the Špilas fortress in the distance.

'Where she is now, your *Paní* Landauer?'

'I told you, I don't know.'

Stahl laughs. 'Why are you so suspicious of me, Laník? I'm not concerned with tracking her down or anything. Scientific research, that's what I'm here for. Anthropology. Biometrics. The measurement of man. You, Herr Laník. We'll measure you. And tell you whether you are a Jew.'

The next day lorries draw up outside the Landauer House and men begin to unload – chairs, shelving, desks, filing cabinets. A wooden guard hut is assembled inside the gate and two soldiers erect a notice, a metal sign capped with a wreathed *Hakenkreuz*:

Rasse- und Siedlungshauptamt
Forschungsstätte für Biologie
Biometrik Abteilung

Neighbours peer through lace curtains at the work going on. A group of children gathers at one of the barricades and is chased away. Meanwhile the two houses directly across the road are requisitioned, one of them as a staff hostel. There is work to be done, bedrooms to be set up, kitchens to be equipped. No-entry signs abound.

A week later the scientific staff arrive, a dozen of them, three women and nine men, all of them young, all of them in civilian clothes, the women plainly dressed, their hair gathered back severely from their faces emphasising their good bone structure, the men wearing jackets or suits, with their hair cut military short. They stop first at the hostel and settle in, then they cross the road to the Landauer House.

There is uncertain laughter as they look round their new workplace. It is like the start of term, the same nervousness, the same exploring of new acquaintances. 'What a place!' one of them exclaims. 'Just like a clinic.'

'Is this a Jew house?' another asks.

'More like an art gallery.'

A voice, heavy with irony, says, 'Degenerate art,' and there is more laughter, confident laughter now as they begin to sense each other's views. Stahl is delighted with them. Perfect examples of the finer points of the Teutonic race. His children, he thinks, although they are barely younger than he is; his flock. Two of them, a man called Weber and a woman called Elfriede Lange, worked under Fischer at the Kaiser Wilhelm Institute in Berlin where Lange was a pupil of the redoubtable Agnes Bluhm. Lothar Scherer and Ewald Amsel have come from Jena, from Karl Astel's Institute for Human Genetics and Racial Policy. There is a representative of Fritz Lenz's group in Berlin and another from Reche's Institute for Race and Ethnology at Leipzig University. Three others come from the newly established Institute for Racial Biology at Charles University in Prague and bring with them the advantage of speaking Czech. 'We must look upon ourselves as pioneers in this great endeavour,' Stahl tells them. 'Remember, always remember, that we are first and foremost scientists. It is as scientists that we shall comport ourselves in this delicate work.' He talks to them in inspiring terms, of science, of discovery, of the frontiers of knowledge being pushed forward even as the armies of the German people push forward the frontiers of the Third Reich. 'We live,' he tells them, 'in historic times.'

By now the house has been transformed. The upstairs rooms have become offices and the kitchens are being converted into a laboratory. In the basement one room is being prepared to receive an X-ray machine. Another room is already a photographic darkroom, left by the original owners. Curtains have been drawn in order to divide one section of the Glass Room from another. There are anthropometrical devices in front of the onyx wall, scales for weighing, a vertical stand for measuring height, a chair that resembles a dentist's but with a construction of steel rulers suspended above the head rest, tables with callipers lying ready. Drapes have been hung in front of the semicircle of Macassar panelling and lights erected to shine on the focus of the curve, converting the dining area into a photographic studio. A camera – a Rolleiflex twin lens reflex – stands ready on a tripod. Only the piano, incongruously, remains from the past. Stahl has seen to it that a piano tuner, a Jew, has done his work and restored the perfect tones of the Bösendorfer.

After the furniture comes the documentation equipment. A lorry draws up outside and heavy machines are unloaded into the garage. Workmen undo the packaging and stand back to examine what they have been carrying: great black contraptions in steel and Bakelite with the name of the manufacturer on brass plates, Deutsche Hollerith Maschinen Gesellschaft mbH. One of the machines resembles a mangle. Another has a typewriter keyboard but the machine itself is out of all proportion to a typewriter, as large as an upright piano; a printing machine, perhaps. The whole space that once housed two Landauer motor cars now takes on the aspect of the print shop of a newspaper. There is the same hum of machinery, the same smell of ink and ozone. Soldiers carry boxes and boxes of files into the main building, all the documentary evidence that has been collected so far in Vienna and is forming the basis for the most important catalogue on human variation that the world has ever seen.

And then the subjects begin to arrive.

A bus offloads them at the gate, no more than a dozen at a time. There is a uniformity about each group – either a dozen males or a dozen females, all of approximately the same age. The soldiers on the gate watch as the visitors are ushered across the pavement to the front door. There is no shouting, no military coercion, just the quiet, polite indication of where they should go and what they should do. Czech or German is spoken as required. 'We are scientists,' Stahl has reminded the staff. 'Zoologists treat animals with due respect. So as anthropologists we must treat our human subjects with due respect.'

The subjects are taken by the receptionist down to the lower level, into the Glass Room. Details are filled in on a form: date of birth, place of birth, first language, second language, other languages, religion, race, nation. There are other matters – a record of diseases suffered, of conditions present in the ancestry: mongolism, alcoholism, criminality, mental retardation. It is all confidential. It is all in the interests of pure science.

Clutching their files the subjects move into the library area. Here there is a series of tests to perform – shapes to match, series to complete, patterns to identify. Then they move to one of the cubicles to change into medical gowns. From there they move to a desk where a needleprick – a sharp intake of breath, sometimes a small cry – reveals blood groups, and a sphygmomanometer measures blood pressure.

Stahl watches.

In the measurement areas the staff work in pairs, a recorder and an examiner, the one positioning the subject at the stadiometer – legs fractionally apart, heels, buttocks and shoulder blades in contact with the back board, heads held in a grip, chins horizontal with the ground – while the other waits, pen in hand. The examiner kneels down, pushing and pulling, adjusting and cajoling. It all has to be just right, standardised, exact. Measurements are taken: total height, hip diameter, chest diameter. Then sitting: leg measurements, arm measurements. Then the dentist's chair: head dimensions, the callipers holding the different crania in their cool jaws. The smooth girls, the grizzled men, the matrons and the husbands. Skin colour is assessed, the inside forearm compared with a von Luschan chromatic chart. Eye colour is recorded, rows of glaucous model eyes staring back at the examiner to be matched with those real ones, wide and anxious, in the subject's own face. 'It's all right,' the examiners reassure their subjects, 'there's nothing to worry about. No pain, no discomfort.'

Stahl watches.

Precision, the cool gaze of scientific objectivity. The measurement is as perfect as the dimensions of the Glass Room itself.

'Now we will just take some photographs, and then everything is done. Please take off your gown and hand it to the assistant. This is a scientific examination. We are all scientists here. And the records are entirely confidential.'

Stahl watches.

222

Gown handed aside, the subject stands naked under the lights and before the judgement of the camera. Sometimes they are as white and pure as alabaster, sometimes mottled or brushed with hair, sometimes creased and sagging like old cloth, sometimes firm and youthful, some bellies bloated, some mere cushions, ribs visible in some, breasts sagging like bladders or sharp and prominent like fruit, penises hanging, strangely ageless, like the probosces of blind, hirsute animals. The whole gamut of human variation.

Stahl watches, enthralled by the systematic measurement of what defines human and subhuman, of what makes *Herrenvolk* and *Untermenschen*.

Rainer

Switzerland was an island in the midst of disaster. All around swirled the floodwaters of war, fetid and dangerous, carrying with them the wreckage of lives and places. They heard on the wireless and read in the newspapers of armies marching, of men dying, of refugees fleeing, of Paris itself disappearing under the flood.

Have you heard about Kaprálová?, Hana wrote. Nowadays the letters always came with official stamps – the eagle with the *Hakenkreuz* in its talons – and a sticky label holding the flap down and announcing *Geöffnet*, opened. Liesel imagined bored men and women glancing over the banalities, missing the little bits of personal code, peering dully into other people's private lives, seeing everything and understanding nothing.

You know she dropped Martinů and married this fellow on the rebound? Perhaps you don't. Jiři Mucha, Alfons Mucha's son, would you believe! Well, she fell ill and was in hospital just as the Germans were approaching Paris. Can you imagine the panic? Apparently – I got this from Kundera who heard it from old Kaprál himself – her husband managed to get her out of the city just in time. They fled south, to Montpellier, I think. But there was nothing to be done: the poor girl died in hospital two days after the fall of Paris. God knows what it was. An ectopic pregnancy? Anyway, the lovely creature is dead, and Kaprál and his wife distraught.

Liesel looked up from the letter. Kaprálová dead! Another part of the past dead. The young dying as often as the old. Out of the window the sun was bright on the lake, but she saw the wreckage of lives all around her, and herself cast up on this island of safety. How long would it last, she wondered?

We ourselves are as poor as church mice nowadays, Hana continued. She wrote that bit in Czech – *chudý jako kostelní myš*. That's what she did, mixed her German and Czech, perhaps to make it difficult for the censors. *All O's money is frozen – some new move against his people – and we are living hand to mouth. Darling, you cannot imagine how dreadful it is becoming . . .*

'His people' was code, Liesel had worked that out months ago. It meant the Jews.

I think I may have to look for work, can you imagine?! God knows what I'll do – walk the streets, probably!

She smiled at Hana's exaggerations, folded the letter back into its envelope, put it away in a drawer and hurried downstairs. The reply would have to wait. It was almost midday and they had a guest for lunch. 'Are the children ready?' she called to Katalin. 'I want them to look presentable.'

Then she hurried around, putting things right in the sitting room, going in to the kitchen to make sure that the cook was prepared. They saw so few people these days, and this was a very special person, a link with the past, a link back to the house. He would bring with him that air of bullish self-confidence that would put everything else in perspective for a few hours.

'There's the car! We must all go and greet him. Hurry, let's hurry.'

They came out to welcome him as the taxi drew up on the gravel, Martin, Ottilie and Marika standing in an obedient line in their Sunday best with Katalin behind them and Viktor beside Liesel. And their guest played the part to perfection, almost as though he was inspecting a guard of honour, bowing solemnly to Marika and her mother, shaking Martin's hand and proffering a cheek for Ottilie's kiss. 'I remember when you were just a little baby,' he told the girl; and Liesel remembered too. She remembered baring her breast for the baby to suck, and Rainer watching, his cheeks flushed, perhaps with embarrassment, perhaps with desire, maybe both. Liesel felt something like that now, a flush of something that was not quite embarrassment.

225

'I see you've betrayed the cause, Landauer,' he said, looking up at the front of the villa, at the ogive windows and the crenellations, at the tower with its pointed turret. 'If ornament is crime then this house is a capital offence.'

Viktor smiled. 'We are beggars now, von Abt. Beggars can't be choosers.'

'They can always choose the bridge they sleep under.'

'Let me show you the garden,' Liesel suggested. 'You may loathe the house but you will love the garden. Viktor, are you coming?'

But Viktor was going to see about the wine. He had a particularly fine Montrachet, something that Rainer would surely appreciate. Not quite beggars yet. So Liesel and Rainer walked down the lawn to the lakeside together, Liesel with her arm through his, the children running on ahead. She hadn't expected to be so delighted with his visit. He reminded her of the excitement of those early days, the days of optimism when they were planning and building the house, when there was hope and confidence and the storm clouds were so far away on the horizon that it was possible to ignore them altogether. 'How do you enjoy the life of a refugee?' she asked. 'Are you like me, in danger of dying of exile?'

But he insisted that he was not a refugee. He had a project in Zurich, some bank that wanted a new headquarters. And then the German government wanted him to go back and design entire towns. 'That fellow Speer has been begging me. He's not a complete fool like some of them.'

The idea was shocking. 'But you won't accept?'

That loud and roguish laugh. 'Certainly not. They can do their own dirty work. When I'm finished here I'm off to America.'

'America!'

'They've offered me a post at one of their absurd universities that no one has ever heard of. The Michigan Institute for Science and Technology. It is known to one and all as MIST. How do you like that? Out of the European mess and into the American muck.'*

She laughed at the joke and hugged his arm to her. Rainer gave

---

* German *Mist* is 'muck' or 'manure'.

her hope, a sense of possibility. He talked of steel and glass, of light and volume, of buildings soaring up so high that clouds obscured their summits. America! Apparently this institute of the future wanted him to redesign their whole campus. It seemed incredible: in Europe they were destroying but in America they were building.

'You know the house is no longer ours?' she told him. 'They took it from us, stole it. Because Viktor is a Jew.'

'That means nothing. When the war is over . . .'

'But will it ever be over? That's what I want to know. Will it ever be over? It was terrible when we left, you know that? Our beloved house. Viktor's and mine, but yours as well. It was like having a limb amputated. We were so happy there. You know I compose it in my mind? It's like recreating it in a dream. I walk round the terrace and pick up the children's toys. I go inside and walk into the rooms, Ottilie's, Martin's, and their bathroom with the ducks – you'd be appalled to see them, Rainer, a line of rubber duck silhouettes following their mother across the tiles and into the bath. Then I go down into the Glass Room – twelve steps to the curve, and then round and down nine more, and the space opens out around me just as it really was. I'm there, right there, where we were so happy.'

'And you're not happy now?'

She wanted to tell him. She wanted to explain about Viktor and Katalin and the awful penalty of isolation and indifference. Surely Rainer would understand. 'I don't feel I belong here. Viktor says he belongs anywhere. He claims to be a citizen of the world, but I miss home and friends much more. And everything is so uncertain. He always talks of going to the United States, but it's not that simple for people like us, without work, without relatives there. They have quotas. He says that one way of doing it is via Cuba, but who wants to go to Cuba?'

'Why don't you come with me?' he suggested. 'Leave Viktor and run away with me to America.'

For an ephemeral moment his tone seemed serious, and the very idea possible, this man snatching her away from enigma into certainty. Then she laughed – 'Don't be absurd' – and he laughed with her and they strolled along the lakeside and onto the landing stage, laughing at the idea of her running off to America as though it was the greatest joke imaginable. She hadn't laughed like that in years.

Lunch was eaten on the terrace at the back of the house in the pale sunshine, the three of them together at one end of the table, Katalin with the children at the other. The conversation was about the past because that is what exiles talk about, what was and what would never be again: the house in Město, the light and the balance and the beauty; and the people who had inhabited it, creatures of light and beauty as well. 'Sometimes I feel that the place never existed,' Liesel said. 'That it's no more than a figment of my imagination. Can we really have been so happy there?'

'That is why I built it,' Rainer said. 'To make you happy.'

'But now whom are you making happy? Banks in Zurich and universities in America? Why not stay here? We'll knock this pile down and you can build another house of glass and make us happy again.'

Rainer laughed and caught her hand across the table. 'Viktor,' he said, 'you don't know how lucky you are with your wife.'

Viktor's expression was of detached amusement, like an adult with over-enthusiastic children. 'What makes you think it's luck? It's all planned.'

And Liesel thought, watching Katalin at the foot of the table talking to the children and only occasionally joining in the adults' conversation that, yes, it was a plan, all of it was a plan. While the world itself was thrown around in the storm, Viktor had managed to plan the little world of his family down to the smallest detail. When Rainer came to leave after lunch she found herself absurdly close to tears. Somehow he represented the truly uncertain, the capricious and the dangerous. It was only in the unknown that hope lay. 'Maybe we'll meet up in the United States,' she said as his taxi drew up.

'And then I will design you another house,' he assured her.

She had to bend to kiss him goodbye. She'd forgotten that, that she was taller than he. Somehow being with him, you forgot a simple physical fact like that.

Encounter

He sits at a window table in the café, watching. The place seethes with talk and laughter, an inchoate sound that reminds him of the noise from some animal colony. Men and women, hooded crows and parakeets, as though a species boundary is being crossed – crows and parakeets mixing together against the laws of nature. He remembers hours, days spent in a hide on the Baltic coast near Peenemünde watching terns nesting – the chattering, the raucous calling, the manoeuvring for mates and territory. Later, in the ornithological section of the Kaiser Wilhelm Institute, he chloroformed his samples and handed them to the taxidermist for skinning and preserving. The skins lay in drawers, their feathers bright and sharp as though they were still alive; but each with a small inflorescence of cotton wool poking out of its eye sockets. As with these women in the café the faint smell of mothballs clung to their plumage.

'May I join you, Herr *Oberst*? All the other places appear to be taken.'

Stahl looks up. A woman, perhaps in her thirties, certainly older than he. Her eyes are blue, and bright with something like amusement. Mockery, perhaps. Her hair is just the pale side of chestnut. She is dressed in black, with a small blackbird's nest of a hat perched on her head. Half rising to his feet, he offers the chair. '*Bitte*.'

She sits and orders something called a *turecká* and a small slice of *Sachertorte*. Despite the fact that her German is perfect, she is clearly a Slav. As she speaks to the waiter he examines her, focusing on her mouth, looking for curves and corners, wondering if clues lie there. And her ears, where they are visible beneath her careful hair: the convolute sculpting, the cartilage joining smoothly into the line of the neck. No lobes.

'So tell me, Herr *Oberst*,' she asks, turning her eyes on him. 'To what do we owe the honour of your presence here in our city?'

He smiles, embarrassed by her attention. 'I'm afraid I cannot claim to be an *Oberst, gnädige Frau*. I am a mere Hauptsturm-führer.'

'*Mere* Hauptsturmführer? Hauptsturmführer sounds dreadfully important. But then all Germans are dreadfully important, aren't they? Anyway, I always promote soldiers. It makes them feel good.' She peels off her gloves, folds them into her bag and takes out a silver cigarette case. He declines her offer of a cigarette but reaches across the table with his lighter.

'Is your husband not with you?' he asks, noticing her wedding ring.

She blows smoke away towards the window, as though with it her husband. 'I always leave him behind. This café is where I meet my friends, and I'd hardly include my husband amongst my friends, would I? My friends spend money; my husband makes it. The opportunity for a conflict of interests is evident.'

Her order comes. She sips and eats carefully, endeavouring not to touch either coffee or cake with her glistening, scarlet lips. 'And what about you? Is there a Frau Hauptsturmführer somewhere in the background?'

He hesitates, wondering whether to lie. 'There was. But now she is dead.'

'Oh, I'm so sorry.' But she doesn't seem sorry. She seems merely thoughtful, as though she is trying to assess the truthfulness of that answer. 'You haven't told me what you are doing here. Or perhaps you can't tell me. Perhaps it is terribly secret.'

'No secret at all. I'm here in the name of science. Beneath my uniform beats the heart of a scientist.'

'How remarkable. I always thought that scientists were heart-less. What kind of scientist are you?'

'Zoologist, anthropologist, geneticist. I am director of the research centre at the Landauer House.'

Which is when the brittle banter, part sexual, part social, the

230

one shifting over into the other, stops. She holds a forkful of *Sachertorte* suspended in mid air, her lips open. 'The Landauer House?'

'You know it?'

'Very well.' The chocolate cake goes into her mouth. She lifts her napkin and touches crumbs from her lips. 'Liesel Landauer was a great friend of mine.'

'What happened to her?'

'She went away. Surely you know that, otherwise why should you be in her house?'

'And you have no contact with her?'

She looks at him thoughtfully. 'Am I being interrogated, Herr Hauptsturmführer?'

'I am asking a question about your former friend.'

'Why should you wish to know?'

'Because I am intrigued by the house and the minds behind it. The Landauers must have been unusual to build such a place.'

She shrugs. 'They were people of imagination and culture. They wanted a new life, a modern way of living. That is all. And they had it for just ten years before they were forced to abandon it.'

'Why?'

'I am sure you know why, Herr Hauptsturmführer. Viktor Landauer is a Jew. No, that's not quite right. Like his nominally Christian wife, he is in fact an atheist; but he has what you would term Jewish blood.'

'I dislike the term "blood". There is no racial identity in blood. In the genes, perhaps. Jewish genes.'

'The words don't matter. The concept does. That is why they left.'

There is a small hiatus in the conversation, a pause while the two of them assess what has been said and what has not been said. 'Perhaps we ought to introduce ourselves,' she suggests carefully. 'I know this is hardly the normal thing to do in polite society, but then we don't live in normal times, do we? Or maybe even polite society any longer. My name is Hana Hanáková.'

'Werner Stahl,' he says. There is a solemn shaking of hands across the table.

'So what exactly are you doing with the Landauer House?'

231

'Would you like to see?'

'Is that an invitation?'

'Certainly. Perhaps you could take part in our survey of the human species?'

She considers the suggestion. 'Only if you'll treat me to dinner afterwards,' she decides.

'Won't your husband object to that?'

'My husband,' she explains, 'lets me do exactly as I please. Tell me what I would have to do to be part of your survey.'

'There would be some tests, some photographs, some measurements. It is all very straightforward.'

She looks at him, right at him with those constant and striking eyes. 'But human beings are not straightforward, Herr Stahl. They are very complex.'

Swimming

Dearest, lovely Liesel, she read, *I hope this reaches you quickly. How long the post seems to take these days. To think you are only a day's train journey away and yet your last letter took three weeks! I suppose they have to read our prattle, but why should it take so long?*

They had carried wicker chairs down the lawn to the lakeside, and a large umbrella with panels of red, white and blue, like a national flag. This was how time passed – not the fleet and nimble time of home but the leaden time of exile, measured not by hours but by the changes in the surface of the lake, from the quiet reflections early in the morning with the far shore flung upside down into the depths, through the daytime when the breeze stirred it to a brilliant, metallic blue, to the violet of evening and the black of night. Sometimes rain turned the surface to beaten silver but now there was some kind of sunshine and the surface was a ruffled azure. Their third summer lived in this limbo that was neither paradise nor hell.

So, I have made the acquaintance of the new occupant of your house. You may be interested in this! The place is being used for official purposes and the man in charge is a 'dish', if you know what I mean. *Fešák*, as we used to say. Young and good-looking and strange: rather reserved and shy, and, of course, dumb. He calls himself a scientist and I suppose he is in some way – an anthropologist or something.

Dumb, *němy*, was the word that gave *Němec*, German. Liesel could imagine Hana's delight at the little joke enshrined in her

233

code word. She looked up from the letter. The three children were already in the water, with Katalin. Viktor was reading the paper. Other newspapers lay on the grass around him. The breeze lifted the corner of one page, alternately obscuring and revealing a map of eastern Europe pierced by black arrows. The headline shouted Invasion. The name BARBAROSSA marched across the page like some bearded monster on the rampage.

He was sitting, would you believe it, in our window seat at the Café Zeman! and so I went over and sat down and introduced myself (there wasn't a single free place in the whole café – really!) and found him quite charming and we got to talking and of course he mentioned the house and I said that I knew it. So he invited me to have a look round the place and maybe take part in the investigation that they are doing there – it's an anthropological survey or something (have I spelled that right?), nothing to do with the current situation really, and I thought, well why not? I'll be able to report back to you on the goings on there.

How are you, and how is the Cuckoo? Write soon and tell me everything. Give Viktor a kiss from me (the devil!) and especial hugs to the children from their Aunt Hana, and an extra one to my goddaughter. And one to you, of course. Many to you my sweet. Let me know how things are going. You seem so very far away.

'Come in with us!' Ottilie called.
Liesel looked up. 'When it's a bit warmer. Ask your father.'
'Tatínek is useless. He can't even swim.'
Viktor lowered his paper and looked at his daughter. 'Frau Katalin is an excellent swimmer. Why do you need my help?' Then he tossed the newspaper aside and got up from his chair. 'I'm going to listen to the news. Find out what's happening.'
Liesel put on her spectacles. She had to squint against the light to look at Katalin standing there in the water with the children playing round her. The young woman's hair was slicked back and dripping so that you could see the perfect oval of her head. What did she think as she watched Viktor walk away up the lawn? The fact was he almost never looked at her, barely ever acknowledged

her presence. When he did he always called her Frau Kalman and always addressed her as *Sie*, never *du*.

'It's bad, isn't it?' Katalin called, seeing Liesel watching her.

'What's bad?'

'The news.'

'Of course it's bad.' The fall of Paris last summer paled into insignificance compared with this latest development – the German armies plunging into the Soviet Union, three million men, so the reports said, thousands of tanks, a front of two thousand miles. It seemed incredible. Armageddon, the end of all things. Only the literal part of the brain could assimilate it, not the imaginative part. The imagination could only encompass the personal – Vitulka Kaprálová dying in a hospital in Montpellier; Hana stuck in Město with Oskar; the house on Blackfield Road abandoned to its fate; and the six of them here, in this incongruous place of peace, where there were boats on the water, where the sun shone during the day and the lights shone at night and people went about their business as they always had with only the newspapers and the wireless to say that the world outside was coming to an end.

Katalin walked out of the water and came over for her towel. Her wet skin was puckered with cold. 'Should we be frightened?' she asked, quietly so as not to be heard by the children.

'I think perhaps we should.' Liesel looked up at her and put her hand against her thigh. 'You'll catch your death. Do you want me to dry you?'

She smiled, and stood willingly, like a child, like Ottilie, while Liesel rubbed her legs; then knelt on the grass to have her hair dried. It seemed absurd that they had this closeness, as though intimacy with Viktor tied them to each other. 'My mother used to do this,' Katalin said. 'We'd have a bath in the kitchen and then I'd sit in front of her and she'd dry my hair just like this.' She frowned, as though bewildered by circumstance. 'I haven't seen her for years, you know that? Not since I left home for Vienna. I don't even ...' she paused to consider '... know if she's still alive.'

The children started shouting, the girls ganging up on Martin. Liesel called out to them, 'You mustn't fight. If you fight you'll have to come in and there'll be no more swimming.'

'It's Ottilie,' Martin insisted, standing defiantly in the water between the two girls. 'She says I can't swim but I can.'

'He's only pretending,' Marika said. 'He's putting his hands on the bottom.'

'Maminko, can we take him further out so he can't reach? Then we'll see.'

'No you can't, Ottilie. Of course you can't. You must stay in your depth.' She turned back to Katalin, kneeling there on the grass, with her hair plastered against the smooth oval of her skull and her cheeks white with cold and her blue eyes the colour of ice. For a moment she looked like the young girl who had run away to the big city and cut all ties with her family. Liesel wrapped the towel round her and rubbed her shoulders. 'Do you want to go back home or something? Is that it?'

'It's not that.'

'What is it then? Look, you should get out of that costume or you'll get cold. Let me hold the towel for you.'

Katalin hesitated. And then, as Liesel took hold of the towel, she pulled her costume down to her knees. 'There,' she said, and for a moment she was naked between Liesel's outstretched arms. Liesel looked at the curve of her hips and the hang of her breasts, the dome of her belly and the delta of dark hair that nested there between plump and childish thighs. Her skin was marbled with blue. 'You mustn't catch cold,' she said, wrapping her in the towel and hugging her tight. For a moment she felt the cold touch of Katalin's hair against her cheek, and something else moving beneath the surface of her maternal concern, a sleek shark of desire.

'Martin's swimming!' Ottilie cried out. 'He's really swimming. Maminko, come and look. We've taught him how to swim.'

'Well done,' she called, letting Katalin go. 'Five more minutes and then you must come out.'

Katalin sat back on her heels. 'Is it true what Herr Viktor says? That we will go to America?'

'Have you discussed this with him?'

The young woman looked embarrassed. It was part of the tacit agreement between them that nothing was ever mentioned, no reference was ever made, however oblique. 'He said something.'

'It seems he has decided that Europe's finished and the only hope is America. You know what he's like.' And that was an admission too, that Katalin might possess knowledge of Viktor that was equal to her own. Things were shifting on this summer day of sun and wind, with the sailing boats crossing to and fro and the children splashing in the shallows.

Katalin hitched her towel over her breasts and stood up. 'I never thought that this would happen. I mean, I thought we would wait here for a while and then it would all be over. I never thought we might be going to the other side of the world.'

'Would you rather stay here?'

She shrugged. 'I don't have any choice, do I? I can't stay here on my own.'

Far out towards the distant shore there were sailing boats, triangles of white and red passing and repassing. And beyond those the houses along the opposite shoreline, and then the hills, dark with trees. 'Then that makes it easy.'

'And you? Do you want me to come?'

Liesel looked away. 'Of course I do. Now let's get the children in and the things cleared up. It's almost lunchtime.'

Examination

She arrives at the house exactly on time. Someone from reception brings her to his office and when he looks up from his work there she is standing in the doorway, wearing a grey suit with wide shoulders and a short sharp skirt, looking like the kind of model that you might find in a fashion magazine. Her hat is a neat grey pillbox, set at an angle on her head.

He's not used to this. He is used to the milk and honey girls of the farming community where he grew up, or the earnest plainness of the women – many with a hint of Jew about them – that he encountered in the university world. And Hedda, whom he loved and who loved him in return until that love was murdered by circumstance. But never this elegance and urbanity. He rises from his chair and comes round the desk to take her hand and raise it towards his lips.

'*Küßdiehand, gnädige Frau,*' he says.

She looks round, her expression difficult to read. Regret, perhaps. A hint of sadness. 'This room used to be the guest room. I spent the night here sometimes, can you imagine? There was a painting on the wall just there, an abstract by František Kupka. Do you know Kupka? Bright, pastel colours.'

He doesn't know Kupka. He knows little of abstract painting. All he knows is that now where she points above his head there is a tinted photograph of the Führer gazing towards an unseen horizon. 'So you knew the family well.'

'Very well. Liesel Landauer was my greatest friend.' She turns away and looks out of the window across the deserted terrace. Her face is broader than he recalls from that meeting in the café, her zygomata wider and more accentuated. 'The children used to play out there. Dolls, cars, that kind of thing.'

'How many children were there?'

'Two. A boy and a girl.'

'And is Frau Landauer a Jew like her husband?'

She smiles warily. 'She is a German, my dear Hauptsturm-führer. As beautifully, sleekly Germanic as yourself.'

'Then the children are *mischlingen*.'

'They were wonderful. They *are* wonderful.'

'Miscegenation is not a wonderful thing. It is a terrible curse on our species. Hybrids between the races are unfit.'

'Ottilie and Martin aren't unfit. They are normal, healthy children.'

He shrugged her assertion away. 'We are gathering evidence to prove it. We are striving to find what characteristics define each human race so that the purity of the races may be preserved.'

'And which race do I belong to?'

'You?' He considers the question seriously. Perhaps it was intended as a joke but that does not concern him. What concerns him is scientific truth. He reaches out and takes her chin to turn her head this way and that so that he can see all the angles and curves. 'Of course you are fairly characteristic of the western Slav racial sub-group. But I would have to make a more detailed assessment to be certain of details. Eye colour and hair colour are obvious enough. And at a guess I'd say that your zygomatic arch is strongly Slav.'

'I didn't even know I possessed a zygomatic arch.'

'Of course you do. Everyone does. The orbit to zygomatic arch ratio is a measure that I developed when I was at the Kaiser Wilhelm Institute in Munich. It has considerable correlative potency.'

'Potency, indeed! Doesn't it repel you that I am Slav?'

'Certainly not. I am a scientist and I must be objective. Objectively Slavs may be people of great talent and great . . .' he pauses '. . . beauty.'

'Are you trying to flatter me?'

'I am merely saying what is true. So, let us go downstairs and see the work, shall we? As I suggested, maybe you can become one of our subjects. I must warn you that you will have to undress. For the photographic record.'

'Undress?' The mockery is there, in her smile and in her

manner, as though somehow she is above all this. 'Is undressing the cost of a dinner? You *are* taking me to dinner, aren't you? Wasn't that the agreement?'

'Dinner wouldn't be a cost, it would be a pleasure. And the photography is for scientific purposes only. If we were to publish any of the pictures the eyes would of course be blacked out so that you would not be recognisable.'

'And what about private use?'

'How do you mean, private use? The researchers—'

'I mean *you*, Herr Hauptsturmführer.'

She is difficult to read. Usually he can assess people immediately. Usually they surrender to the demands of medicine, motivated perhaps by something close to anxiety, like patients who have been told they have a fatal disease and who submit to treatment unthinkingly, placing themselves in the hands of the medical profession without thought. But this woman is different, distrustful and sardonic. And intelligent. 'I am a researcher like the others. Let me assure you of my absolute discretion.'

'I'm not sure that discretion is what I am looking for,' she replies.

They make their way downstairs into the measuring room. At the entrance she stands still for a moment, evidently amazed by the transformation that has taken place. People bustle around her. Three women are waiting at the stadiometer. Another couple are performing tests at a table. There is that atmosphere of focus and discovery, the sensation that the borders of knowledge are being moved back.

'I don't know what Liesel Landauer would make of it all,' the Hanáková woman remarks. 'The only thing she would recognise is the piano.'

'Does it seem out of place?'

'It is the only thing that is *in* place. Is it just for show or does someone play?'

'I was at the Munich conservatory before I felt the call of science. I still try to keep my hand in.'

She looks at him in surprise. 'You must play for me some time, Herr Hauptsturmführer.'

One of the workers, the milk-white girl called Elfriede Lange, hands her a form to complete and, when that is done, directs her to one of the changing cubicles, from which she emerges wearing a green gown and looking somehow smaller and defenceless, stripped of artifice. 'I feel like a lamb going to the slaughter,' she remarks as Elfriede prepares to take her blood.

'It's just a prick,' Stahl assures her. 'There will be a mild discomfort, nothing more.'

'But I'm not used to discomfort of any kind.' Yet when the needle jabs she doesn't flinch, doesn't move, doesn't register anything at all, just watches Stahl as blood grows like a bead of ruby on the tip of her finger. Elfriede manoeuvres her hand over the row of sample tubes, then adds test solutions and holds each tube of clouded red against the light, watching for coagulation. 'AB,' she announces. 'MP negative.'

'What does this show, Herr Hauptsturmführer? Whether I am *Mensch* or not?'

Der Mensch – human being; *das Mensch* – slut. Which does she intend? They usher her on to the stadiometer to have her height measured, then onto the scales for her weight, then into the dentist's chair to have her legs and arms measured. Stahl takes on this task himself, bending the callipers towards her, touching her heel and knee; knee and iliac crest. Close to her he gets a faint drift of her scent. If only, he thinks, it were possible to measure smells. Surely there would be a means of classification: a Jew smell, a Slav smell, a Teutonic smell. This woman's smell, only partly disguised by some Parisian perfume, makes him imagine the steppe in summer, the miles and miles of wheat fields, the scent of hay, the scent of crushed grass. Coumarin. Vanilla. And something darker underneath.

'Am I in good shape?'

'Fine shape,' he says. 'A most beautiful shape. Now the cranial measurements.' Her eyes follow him as he moves above her, touching her temple to place the jaws of the callipers exactly. Her smile reveals even, perfect teeth. There is a faint warmth from her breath. He turns the callipers to measure from the frontal to the occipital, then crown to chin. Then the length of her nose and its width across the base. Then the orbit, with the jaws of the callipers coming close to the egg white of her eye and the staring blue jewel of her iris. 'Just keep quite still.'

She blinks. 'How did you get into this kind of research?' she asks him.

He measures the curve of her cheek, the zygomatic arch. Her

hairline comes down into a distinct widow's peak. He notes this on her form. 'I used to work on birds,' he tells her. 'Capturing and measuring tern on the Baltic coast. There are five species all of the same genus, *Sterna*, and I was interested in the problem of hybridisation.'

'And what did you do with your poor captives when you had finished with them?'

He smiles at her concern. 'Most we released, but some specimens we chloroformed and skinned. You need to preserve the evidence, you see, for the future.'

There are moles: one on her left cheek, another just inside the right-hand wing of her nose. He notes the finely sculptured ears, their lower margin curving directly into her neck without any lobe. Then skin colour, the flesh of the inside of her arm compared with a von Luschan colour chart.

'Then I transferred to Ernst Rüdin's team at the Kaiser Wilhelm Institute for Genealogy and Demography in Munich, specialising in human hybridisation; and then I began this task.'

He turns to her eyes, to match them with the samples that sit like a row of boiled eggs in a tray. His eyes go from one to the other, from the real things to the simulacra, before lighting on the colour of his choice. He writes on the form and then closes the file. The real eyes follow his movements. Her gaze is disquieting. 'And will you release me back into the wild when you have finished with me, Herr Hauptsturmführer? Or will you chloroform me and skin me?'

'I do not think you are captive, Frau Hanáková.'

'Oh, but I am. I am captive, the whole damned country is captive. The question is, will we ever be set free again? Or will we all be chloroformed and skinned?'

Elfriede Lange looks shocked. Stahl laughs.

'There is no question of anything like that,' he says. 'We've finished here. Now just the photographs.'

'Ah, the photographs. Do you watch?'

'Not if you don't wish me to. If they wish, subjects may request only people of the same sex. But I must emphasise that I am a scientist.'

'So is Doctor Mabuse.'

'I can assure you that I am no criminal genius.'

'That's what he would say.'

They cross over to the photographic area. Stahl holds the curtains aside for her to go through, then pulls them firmly closed and ties the tapes behind him. Within the enclosure the air is warm and bright. In her green gown she stands at the focus of this semicircular space and looks around, apparently unconcerned at the lights and the photographer examining her in the viewfinder of his Rolleiflex. 'This is where we used to dine. There used to be a circular dining table right here.' There is a hint of accusation in her tone, as though he might have been responsible for some kind of vandalism.

'It was in the way so we moved it downstairs into the basement.'

'Parties – Christmas, New Year. It was fun.'

'Christmas isn't Jewish.'

'I told you, Viktor Landauer was never an observant Jew. They were modern people, agnostics, free-thinkers. I am more of a believer than they were.'

'And what do you believe in?'

She smiles, that slanted, ironical smile. 'Not the compassionate God of the Christians. Some kind of malign life force, I suppose. Something that is always ready to trip you up just when you think things are going all right.'

The photographer signals that he is ready and Stahl holds out his hand for her gown. She looks him straight in the eye. 'I was expecting to do this in less clinical conditions,' she says as she undoes the tapes. She slips the gown off and hands it to him with no more concern than if she were handing her coat to a servant.

He looks away from her eyes, away from her smile, at the body. She is a specimen, a type, perhaps even an exemplar. On the form there are boxes to check. Skin colour: ivory. Breasts: pendulous but turned upward at the nipples. Left breast larger than the right. Areolae: oval, earth-brown in colour, nipples pinkish and erect. Some small moles on chest, another below left breast. Belly faintly convex, umbilicus hollow, hips wide, thighs narrow, knees not quite touching. He has noticed that when they are naked, men and women are transformed from what they appear when clothed. The athlete may turn into a plump sybarite, the frump into a sensual fertility figure, the sylph-like beauty into a scrawny

243

scarecrow. Hana Hanáková too has metamorphosed, from sterile elegance into something uneven and erotic. The word *Scham*, shame, sounds in his mind, a cultural parapraxis such as the Jew Freud talked about when he uncovered human shame of everyone for everyone to see. She shifts her legs slightly apart, her eyes fixed on his, watching where he looks. Most women hold their legs together and, like Eve, try to cover their *Scham* with their hands. But not this woman. Her pubic hair is a flock of curls, darker than her head hair, an arrow blurred faintly into her groin; and at the point of the arrow is a glimpse of pink lips.

'Legs together please. Stand as straight as you can with your arms by your side.' The camera emits a small, decisive click.

'Please turn sideways to your right.'

The sinuous arabesque of her back and her buttocks presents itself. Another click.

'Please face the wall.'

And now there are the complex planes of her shoulders and back, the scapulae visible beneath the flesh, the faint serration of spinal vertebrae curving down between the corrugations of her ribs to the cleft of her buttocks.

'Thank you.'

She turns to face the camera again, looking him up and down as though he, not she, is the specimen.

'That is all,' he tells her.

Again there is that smile. 'I very much doubt it,' she replies.

He sits at his desk, fiddling with paperwork. There are returns of ethnic minority groups in the Carpatho-Ruthenia zone, a report by the Bratislava unit working under the aegis of the Slovakian government. For a moment, just a moment, he can forget her. The Bratislava unit has processed one hundred and ninety-three gypsies, from ages thirteen to eighty-seven. The unit is, apparently, to be congratulated.

Afternoon sun bathes the terrace outside. Light pours in through the windows where Hana Hanáková stood. He shifts awkwardly in his seat, crosses and uncrosses his legs, and considers the returns for the month of April: six hundred and seventy-two people assessed, of which three hundred and sixteen Slav, two hundred and thirty-nine Aryan, one hundred and twelve *mischlinge* of various degrees. Roma and Jews are accounted separately in the addendum. The contemplation of these figures does not hold his attention for long. Impatiently, he gets up from his chair and goes down the corridor to the administrative office. 'The file for the Hanáková woman,' he asks the filing clerk. 'Can I see it as soon as it's ready?' Then he returns to his work, signs off the month's returns and hopes that he has not made any errors. The latest punched cards are all being duplicated, stacked in boxes for the courier that will run them to Prague. From Prague they will be sent to Berlin. In Berlin the sorting will take place, the great black machines whirring through the night, sorting, assembling, analysing, fingering through the records at a rate of one hundred and fifty cards per minute. Patterns and correlations will be revealed. The keys to human race and identity will be discovered.

He puts the returns into the out-tray and turns to the final task, an easy one, a letter from the company that manufactures and maintains the machines themselves, DEHOMAG, the Deutsche Hollerith Maschinen Gesellschaft. They wish to reschedule their weekly maintenance visits. Wednesdays rather than Tuesdays.

There is a knock at the door and an assistant comes in with the file he has requested: a plain buff folder with the eagle on the cover, its talons grasping a wreathed *Hakenkreuz. Rasse- und Siedlungshauptamt, Forschungsstätte für Biologie, Biometrik Abteilung*. And the name, written in ink: *Hanáková, Hana.*

'Has this been through the Hollerith section yet?'

'Not yet, Herr Hauptsturmführer.'

'Very well.'

The girl goes. He lays the folder down and opens it. There are Hanáková's details, the centimetres, the kilograms, cranial index and facial index, the shades of eye colour and hair colour, the trivial and the momentous. Mid-phalangeal hair: present; ear lobes: attached; widow's peak: present. All the quirks and traits that will be measured against the catalogue, counted and sorted so that she will become just one amongst the thousands, a nameless cipher in the racial catalogue, a single drop of water in the great ocean of statistical significance.

Nothing on the form gives the essence of the woman.

He turns over the page to the photographs. From the glossy emulsion Hana Hanáková looks back at him with a faint smile, as though she knew, at that moment of exposure under the lights, that he would be sitting here looking at her image.

She is so unlike Hedda as to seem a different species. Hedda had the delicate look of a child; this woman seems supremely adult. Hedda's face described the almost perfect oval of the Nordic; this woman has the square jaw line and high zygoma of the Slav. What subtle detail of mind or body makes Hana Hanáková a Slav and made Hedda Nordic? Is it merely a matter of measurement? Is a cranial index of 88.3 and a facial index of 83.5 sufficient? He recalls Hanáková's smell – that amalgam of things artificial and natural, of scents and perfumes. Is that a Slav scent? He tries to recall Hedda's smell, but it is as elusive as a dream. Yet if the differences between the races are chemical as well as structural and if every feature of a living organism ultimately comes down to its chemical composition, then surely there must be a way to identify Slav or Nordic or Jew by pure chemistry.

He turns to the photograph of the side view, then to the rear view, to her heart-shaped rump, soft and white, with two dimples on either side. He moves uncomfortably in his chair. Back to the frontal view. Her breasts have the shape of teardrops. What are the laws of physics that determine the hang of flesh and fat, of muscle and ligament and adipose tissue? Her nipples are pointed, asymmetrical in their gaze, like someone with a slight, amusing squint. He shifts his legs. And the faint dome of her belly and the flock of hair with its trace of shadow on the inguinal surface of the thighs. A hint of . . . he picks up a magnifying glass and holds it over the photograph . . . yes, a hint of inner lip, *labia minora*, the pliant membrane pushed out of her sexual mouth.

After a while he stands up and returns the file to the registry.

They meet that evening in the café of the Grand Hotel opposite the railway station. The choice is his but it suits her well enough – it is the kind of place where people come and go, where no one is a regular any longer, where she is not known. They sit in the Winter Garden among potted palms and rubber plants, while a quartet plays selections from Strauss and Lehár and couples shuffle round on the exiguous dance floor. He has never encountered anything like this before – this woman with her wit and knowledge, this casual encounter across a dinner table, the unspoken possibilities. She talks of herself, of musicians and artists she has known, of Paris and Vienna, of an intellectual and cultural society that used to exist in this city but is now, she says, dying. And then she asks about him, about his family, and he finds himself telling her about Hedda. 'She was a violinist. At the Munich conservatory. We used to play together.'

'You were a musician?'

'The piano. I played the piano. But I was not a true talent, not like Hedda's. She was very brilliant. We . . .' he hesitates . . . 'had known each other all our lives, played together since we were little children.'

'Childhood sweethearts? How touching. Was she beautiful? I imagine you with a beautiful woman.'

'I found her beautiful. She was blonde and blue-eyed, a typical Nordic type.'

'Were you happy together?'

He toys with his food, wondering how to get out of this interrogation that he has brought upon himself. 'Very happy. We knew each other so well, you see. All those years, as long as we could remember. We were . . . always very close. But when we married there were difficulties. We were under great pressure.'

'From whom?'

'Our family.' The singular is there. Has she noticed?

'Tell me.'

He looks down at his plate, at the debris of the meal, the scattered crumbs, the bowl smeared with the traces of fruit and artificial cream. Why should he tell her? Why should all this be known to someone whom he has just met, someone with whom, if the logic of things works out, he will shortly have sex? But it is easier to confess to strangers. 'Hedda and I were cousins.'

'Cousins? Is that bad?'

'We were first cousins. Relatives of the fourth degree. There were people who said that our love was unnatural. Incest, they said it was incest.'

'But it isn't.'

'Not legally, no. But my family is Catholic – Bavaria, you see – so we had to obtain a dispensation from the bishop to marry. And even then there were people who were scandalised. And then . . .' He looks away from her and round at the other tables, as though he might find escape. 'And then she died. It was an accident . . .'

'How very sad. Do you have children?'

'No. No, we do not have any children. Look, I don't want to talk about it.'

At that moment, mercifully, there is a distraction. A singer appears in front of the band, some refugee from the Vienna cabarets, all brassy hair and scarlet lips. She begins to whisper into the microphone, a Mimi Thoma song called '*Märchen und Liebe*', 'Fairy Tales and Love'. Stahl lets Hana lead him onto the dance floor. She is almost as tall as he and he feels awkward as they come together, like a young boy at dancing classes. But as they shuffle round he discovers that contact with her is a palliative, that thoughts of Hedda retreat to the back of his mind, and that Hana Hanáková is not disconcerted, merely amused – he feels a breath of laughter in his ear – by his growing erection pressed hard against her.

'I think we should go upstairs, don't you?' she whispers, 'before it becomes embarrassing.'

So they abandon the table and go up to one of the anonymous bedrooms on the first floor, that costs, so the concierge informs him when he books it, eighty crowns. It is a room that has become used to such assignations, a tawdry place of heavy velvet drapes and shabby furniture. The lighting comes from a few table lamps with weak bulbs. It emphasises the shadows, sculptures the curves and declivities of Hana Hanáková's body as she undresses for him and lies down on the ornate and forgiving bed.

'What do you want to do?' she asks. There's a hint of impatience about her tone, as though he ought to have made up his mind by now and she doesn't have much time. But what *does* he want? He bends over her. There is that Slav smell, elusive and evocative, the scent of steppe and forest, of earth and moss. Her hands are on his head, pulling him down to her breasts. 'There,' she says as though she has guessed something. His mind wavers. His grasp on scientific truth slips. She is pushing him down over the contours of her body, over the slight swelling of her abdomen and the pout of her umbilicus, down into the froth of hair between her legs. He has never done this before. Never with Hedda, never with anyone. It is a mystery beyond his experience, almost beyond his imagining, something at once tantalising and threatening. She moves her legs apart. The scent is almost

248

overwhelming, an amalgam of things recognised and things unknown. Woodruff and vanilla. The warm perfume of musk. A hint of fruit. A faint breath of ammonia. Hesitantly he tastes the strange flavours, the dark mystery of the Slavic *Scham*, the shame that is always there, the bearded mouth that seems, even as he kisses it, to poke its insolent tongue out at him. He feels faint, his head swirling with scent and taste and touch. And though he tries to move away, her hands are on his head, holding him there, pressing his face into the darkness.

Outside in the corridor there are footsteps and talking, and a woman's voice raised in a shrill laughter. Doors open and bang closed. Inside the room Hana Hanáková is standing in front of the wardrobe mirror in her skirt and brassiere, doing her hair. Stahl watches. There are deft flocks of hair in the hollows of her armpits. Her fingers work neatly and quickly, as articulate as lips.

'How much do I pay you?'

She pauses, looking at his reflection. 'For God's sake, you don't *pay* me. That'd be far too sordid. You give me a *present*. A gift. Some mark of your gratitude and admiration.'

He takes some notes from his wallet and puts them on the table. Eighty crowns.

'I don't think that's quite enough admiration, *meine Schatz*,' she says, watching him in the mirror.

Meine Schatz. My treasure. There's sarcasm in the word. He loves her and loathes her, a strange dichotomy of emotion, the one balancing the other. How might it be if the scales tipped decisively one way? Feeling like a child who doesn't know the value of adult things he takes some more notes out and adds them to the pile. She turns from the mirror, picks the money up and puts it in her handbag. 'You've never tasted a woman like that before, have you?' she asks.

The memory is still vivid in his mind. It is more than taste alone. There is scent and touch and a sensation of transgressing boundaries, a blend of sensations that he has never imagined. She snaps the handbag shut. 'I thought not. It is very special, isn't it? Unique.'

Hedy

Dearest Liesel,

So, the house, your lovely house. The Glass Room. I've been to see it, as I said I would. The place has been converted into a kind of clinic, laboratory, something like that. Don't worry – nothing damaged. Upstairs, your rooms have been converted into offices, and in the garage some sort of counting machinery and downstairs in the Glass Room they are measuring people. That's it. A sort of ethnic record – they measure everything, everything, my dear, including the inside of your ears, can you imagine? – and then they photograph you, first your head front and side close up, and then the whole of you, front, side and *zadek*. Yes, darling Liesel, all in your *birthday suit*. With my scientist fellow watching me I gyrated in the nude and felt a bit like I did when posing for Drtikol to take those photos. But it was amusing in its own way, so medical and serious we were. 'I am a research scientist' he said as if he thought that was some kind of assurance. Anyway, there I was showing my gifts to him and I could tell that I was getting through, if you see what I mean. Well, it was a trifle *obvious* – and all that talk about being a scientist!

You'll think me awful saying all this, but perhaps you'll also say, 'she's my old Hana! At least some things haven't changed!' Anyway, we went to dinner afterwards and my doctor was very stern and rather offhand, as though he didn't know how to deal with the situation. He is rather strange. He told me he had a little wifey but that the family didn't approve because they were cousins. But weren't Jaromil and Federica cousins? I don't remember any problem with them. Afterwards . . . well, you may imagine. One day I'll tell you all.

As for the Cuckoo – when we get to join you, you can let her fly away with him and I will comfort you! Darling, don't show *any* of this letter to Viktor. He'd never speak to me again. And I do hope to be able to see you soon, all of you. But you in particular Liesi, *always you*.

Hana

She folded the letter away and slipped it into the drawer of her desk. It was already over a month old and yet it had only just arrived. By now Hana's *affaire* with the soldier had already advanced far beyond this vague hint. Or perhaps it had come to nothing. How was she to know? That was the irony of exile – the disparity of time. What was happening now still lay in the future. She looked out of the window, at the sunshine on the lake. It was difficult to imagine the house on Blackfield Road. Three years, almost. The detachment of exile, recorded scenes blurring at the edges so that they lost their context, memories becoming imagination. She remembered how Viktor showed her the trick of taking photographs with soft focus. 'This is how they do it for the film stars,' he had said – and put a faint smear of Vaseline on the lens. That was how fact became memory, by blurring the edges.

She took paper and pen to write a reply. Outside on the lawn the children were playing, Ottilie and Marika teasing Martin as they so often did. She would sometimes lose her patience and shout at them, and shout too at Katalin for not keeping them better behaved. After all, wasn't it her job to look after the children? And then there would be tears – Katalin coming to protest, standing in her room and saying that she didn't want to be here, that she had not chosen to be here, that Herr Viktor – always 'Herr' Viktor – had determined that she should be here with them, stuck in this place that was little more than a prison for her. Things like that. And then the making up. Kisses and hugs, and whispered apologies.

The tedium of exile is unbearable, she wrote.

We play cards, and chess, and there is a game that Ottilie has discovered called Lexicon, where you have letter cards and make words with them as in a crossword, so we play that. In English, because that is what the children must learn now, if we are to make a new life in America. And there is swimming and Martin has become quite a little sailor with Viktor. It must sound like a holiday, but really it is not. Oh, I long for Město and our friends and family. Viktor is often away, working on various projects but determined now that we leave this place for America. He says it will not be long.

One thing reminded me of you. *Everything* makes me *think* of you, but one event in particular brought you to mind. We went into town to the pictures. A great excitement, some new film from America. And then, after a few minutes of a rather dreary story that was meant to be set in the Kasbah (have I spelt that right?) of Algiers, in she walked. Eva Kiesler! Yes, that is true. She has changed her name but it is she plainly enough and looking as beautiful as ever she did. And I thought of my wicked Hana who behaved badly with her just to spite me. And I wish now that we could have that time all over again and I would never give you reason to go with anyone else. Oh Hanička, if you were only here I would run into your arms and never let you go. There I've said it.

She sat back and read the words through, and wondered whether to send the letter.

Concert

The theatre is full, a packed crowd milling around the foyer beneath crystal chandeliers. Despite the early hour many of the men are in tailcoats and white ties, the women in long dresses. Hana Hanáková finds him where he stands watching on the edge of the crowd, modest in his grey suit and stiff collar. She takes his arm to hurry him through the crush, nodding and smiling towards acquaintances, waving to friends, calling out something in Czech to someone who hails her. 'Thank God I didn't miss you,' she says. 'I don't want to be seen talking to you in German. Just at the moment it is a most unfashionable language.'

They climb the stairs out of the crowd. The upper foyer is plush and red, like the inside of a blood vessel. An usher bows obsequiously and greets her by name. He leads them along a curving corridor past numbered doors, opening one to reveal dark shadows, six chairs upholstered in red velvet, and a balcony overlooking the auditorium. 'Our box,' Hana explains as she closes the door, then adds, in case the statement might have been ambiguous: 'My husband's and mine. Don't worry, he's away. We won't be disturbed.'

Standing in the shadows Stahl looks down. Plaster caryatids frame the view of the stage where the orchestra is assembling in that casual manner that they have, musicians wandering in to take their places, fiddling with their instruments and their music stands, blowing or bowing a few notes, anticipating the arrival of the conductor who, like a schoolmaster entering a classroom, will bring them all to order.

She takes a cigarette case from her bag. 'Do you mind if I smoke?'

He doesn't, of course. Smoking is against the teachings of the Party, but he is a tolerant man. He takes one of the chairs and sits apart from her, perhaps to distance himself from her and her smoke, perhaps to see her better. She is wearing black, a calf-length cocktail dress hung about with jet beads. Her legs too are sheathed in black, as slick and lucid as oil. He watches her profile as she smokes and stares out across the auditorium. In the close space, despite the drift of smoke from her mouth, he can smell her scent.

What is she thinking?

And what would Hedda have thought?

Below them the orchestra has finally assembled and the audience has taken its seats. The instruments are warming up, a shrill, discordant cacophony that precedes order and certitude. Then the conductor emerges from the wings to take his place on the podium, and silence descends. The musicians seem suspended from his raised arms as though by puppet strings. He moves and they move, the liquid runs of the woodwind introducing the first piece on the programme, the swirling waters of Die Moldau, Vltava, the ripples and whirlpools of the young river that grows with the entry of the strings and finally becomes old and pompous as it passes Prague and loses its identity in the Elbe. Surely, Stahl thinks, there is a moral there for this absurd island population of Slavs adrift in the German sea: Germanisation is the only hope for them, the integration of those who are close enough to the German race and the corresponding removal of those who do not qualify.

When the piece comes to an end there is a storm of applause, as though the musicians have done something extraordinary, heroic, a feat of arms. People stamp their feet on the floor so that the whole auditorium resounds like a kettle drum. The clapping goes on and on, everyone washed along on a tide of emotion until finally, like flotsam, they are deposited on the dull tidal flats of catharsis.

Hana stubs her cigarette out in a shower of sparks. 'How do you like our Czech protest?'

'It seems harmless enough.'

'Harmless! It's pathetic. Our enemy marches in with soldiers and we protest by playing tunes.'

'Do you think of me as an enemy?'

254

She doesn't offer an answer. Below them there is a distraction. A man – Miroslav Němec, so Hana says – has walked out on stage. He stands beside the black coffin of the piano, illuminated by spotlights as though under some kind of interrogation. '*Dámy a pánové!*,' he cries. Ladies and Gentlemen! There follows a rapid scurry of Czech plosives and fricatives in which Stahl grasps only a name: Pavel Haas.

'What was that all about?' he asks when the speech comes to an end.

'He said that he was ashamed of his name.'

'Why should that be so?'

'It means "German". He is Miroslav German. And he said he was sorry that a friend of his could not be here in the audience today, the composer Pavel Haas. He said we should all be thinking of him.'

'Why isn't this Haas here?'

She sits back in her chair as Němec settles down to play. Silence has fallen once more. 'He is a Jew,' she says.

At the end of the concert they leave hurriedly, before the applause for the final piece has ended. The foyer is deserted. Out in the evening light they look around, blinking, at ranks of policemen ranged in the square. Parked up sidestreets are army lorries filled with troops. They cross the square to Stahl's car. 'Where do we go now?' he asks.

They stand irresolutely on the pavement, each unsure of the other's motives. Behind them the concert audience begins to stream out into the evening, stirred by thoughts of national redemption and collective shame. She lights a cigarette and draws heavily. 'You tell me, Herr Hauptsturmführer. I just want to be normal for a while. Even if I am going with a German and getting paid for it, I want to be something other than a whore.'

'You are not a whore.'

She glances back at the dispersing crowd and the ranks of policemen. 'Oh yes I am. Everyone here is a whore in some way. The whole damned country is reduced to whoredom.' She tosses the cigarette down and treads it out. 'Let's go to the house. The sun will soon be setting. Let me show you something.'

*

The Landauer House is quiet and still. Stahl takes out his keys, opens the front door and stands aside to let her go through. 'We shouldn't be doing this,' he says. 'People will talk. The guards will make a report.'

'What are you afraid of? A mere woman, and a Czech woman at that?'

'I'm not afraid of anything.'

'Oh yes, you are. Everyone is afraid of something.'

They descend into the Glass Room. The place is empty, like a stage after the actors have left, with all the lights off and the curtains drawn and the props standing there ready for the next performance. 'Now watch,' she says, and presses a button on the wall. With a faint purr of a hidden electric motor the curtains draw apart along the whole length of the windows. Desks, chairs, the various measuring devices are flooded by evening sunlight.

She points. 'Look.'

Something remarkable is happening to the onyx wall: slanting through the great windows, the light from the setting sun is gathering in the depths of the stone, seething inside it like a fire, filling it with red and gold. This concurrence of sun and stone seems elemental, like an eclipse or the appearance of a comet, some kind of portent. Or hell. The fires of hell.

'It wasn't planned,' she tells him. 'No one had any idea about it until it happened for the first time. Like looking into a furnace.' They stand watching for a while. The whole of the library area is suffused with red; even their faces are tainted with the colour. She walks over to the piano and raises the lid. 'So what are you going to play for me? Didn't you say you used to play?'

'I'm very rusty.'

'That doesn't matter. Pretend that you are all alone. Isn't that what you do, Doctor Mabuse? You come down here to play to yourself and pretend that none of this is happening.'

'None of what is happening?'

'The war, the occupation, the deportations. Pretend that we live in a time of peace. A time without fear.'

Reluctantly he sits at the piano and puts his hands together and flexes his fingers. Then he begins to play, quietly and hesitantly, a piece he used to play with Hedda. The notes punctuate the stillness of the place, intense, melodic phrases, meditative passages, solemn echoes – and as he plays, and as the fire in the onyx wall slowly dies, he hears the notes of the missing violin part, as a bereaved twin may sense the presence of his sibling.

'You are very good,' the woman says when he brings his playing to an end.

He shrugs. 'I'm good enough to know that I'm no more than adequate.'

'And your wife – how good a musician was she?'

'Did you recognise the piece?'

'It was part of the "Kreutzer Sonata", wasn't it? Did you use to play it with Hedda?'

'Yes, I did.'

'What happened to her? How did your lovely violinist die?'

Softly, as though lowering the lid of a coffin, he closes the keyboard. The Glass Room is still.

'She killed herself.'

'Why? Was it something to do with being cousins? Was that it?'

The light may have died in the onyx wall, but through the windows the sun is still hanging on the lip of the world, blood red and ominous. Hana Hanáková stands silhouetted against this light, an anonymous shape like the figure of a confessor behind the grille. If he tells her she will know everything. There is nothing more than this. There are no armies on the march, no guns firing, no bombs exploding, no people dying. There is only this, his own personal disaster.

'I told you that there was no child, but that was not the truth. We had a daughter. We called her Erika. I don't imagine you know babies very well . . .'

'I knew Liesel Landauer's babies. I watched them grow up and I love them still.'

'So imagine a baby like they were. Beautiful, perfect, the loveliest baby you could imagine. Hedda seemed to have found something beyond mere music, a fulfilment she hadn't ever thought possible. Our perfect baby, born out of a love that some said had crossed forbidden boundaries . . .'

'And then?'

'And then things began to go wrong – various things, small things at first. This piano – I press a combination of keys and it plays a chord. The correspondences are exact.' He lifts the lid and

257

does that very thing and the chord of C sharp minor, clear and harmonious, sounds through the proportions of the Glass Room. 'Well, for six months Erika seemed like that: perfect. She grew and developed, smiled and laughed. Knew us, reached out for us as we stood over her cot. And then, like a piano going out of tune, she began to deteriorate. She used to smile at us; and then she couldn't. She looked at us; and then she didn't. She used to grasp toys, her rattles, things like that; and then she couldn't do that either.'

Hana waits, standing there by the windows. There is this compulsion to tell her what he has never told anyone else. He doesn't know why. He doesn't understand how the armour of his defences has been breached by this woman whom he has paid for sex. It seems absurd. Yet she holds comfort in her arms and between her legs.

'The condition is known as infantile amaurotic congenital idiocy. That's the medical term. Amaurotic means blindness. That was just one of her symptoms.'

'She went *blind*?'

'There were the signs on her retina. Cherry spot, they call it. Gradually she lost control of her head – it just lolled about. She couldn't hear, she couldn't respond to anything. She had learned to grasp things and was just beginning to crawl and then all that stopped. She went from being a happy, smiling, funny child to being completely unresponsive. Then came the spasms and convulsions.' He gestures, as though to conjure up the whole gamut of symptom and syndrome, the various tricks by which a single mutation can wreak havoc in a human body. 'It was like winding the clock backwards, unlearning all that she had learned to do. We were told that she would eventually lose all bodily functions, and then finally she would die. The average life of such children is four or five years. There is no way out, no possibility of a cure. Not even a miracle.'

'What causes it?'

He sits there in the Glass Room among the trappings of scientific measurement, in the pure proportions of the place, and talks of irrationality and senselessness. 'It's to do with a chemical, a particular kind of fat that the body makes when it shouldn't. It accumulates in the brain and somehow turns the nerve cells off, that's what the specialists say. It's what they call an inborn error of metabolism. Inside me, inside every cell in my body, there is this genetic mutation. Recessive. You need one from each parent before you have the disease.'

'So Hedda had it too.'

'Of course she did. The same mutation, running in our family, but brought together by our union.' He pauses. 'It's one of the Jew diseases.'

'A *Jew* disease? Is there such a thing?'

'Jews particularly suffer from it, along with many other diseases of that kind. Degeneracy, you see. They are a degenerate people.'

'And does having it make you a Jew?'

'It doesn't make me a Jew, but some Jew introduced the disease into the family four generations ago. A great-great-grandfather. That is what I believe.'

She comes over from the windows and stands beside the piano. 'And the baby? When was this? I mean, is the baby still—'

'Do you know how such children die? Finally they lose the ability to swallow. You try to feed them but they just choke everything up. Either they starve to death or they die of pneumonia. There's nothing anyone can do. Nothing.'

'And that's what happened?'

'No, that's not what happened.' He hesitates, looking up at her. Her expression is full of compassion, compassion tinged with horror. He doesn't mind the horror; it is the compassion that he resents, the pity that he loathes. He looks around the Glass Room, illuminated at that moment only by the backwash of light from the set sun, and he tells her about the Castle.

The Castle stood on high ground on the edge of a village, a quiet and peaceful village in Upper Austria. It was tall and hunched and secretive, with high walls and windows like small, surprised eyes. There were corner towers with pointed tops and a clock tower with an onion dome and a steeply pitched, grey-tiled roof. It was there that they took Erika.

'She was four years old by then. We drove from Munich. It is not far but it was winter and the roads weren't easy. When we arrived everything lay under snow. We parked the car outside the main gate and carried Erika up to the entrance. An orderly came almost immediately when we rang the bell, as though they had been waiting for us. I suppose they had been. They knew we were coming.'

'A clinic?'

'A kind of clinic. It was very quick and efficient. Of course there were a few forms to sign but everything had already been taken care of so they only really wanted to confirm our identity. Then we were shown into a waiting room where we could do whatever we wished – say a prayer or something. We tried to say goodbye to Erika, but there was no point by then. The way I look at it, we had already said goodbye to our child months ago. After five minutes a nurse came and took her away.'

Outside the windows the sun has settled below the horizon, the blood-red bladder suddenly bursting all over the sky in a great mess of crimson. Hana is very still. 'What for?'

'They took her away to kill her. Painlessly and quickly, an injection of morphia and scopolamine to put her out of her misery. I think . . .' What does he think? He thinks that science holds the key to everything, that science will ultimately reveal all the answers and solve all the problems. 'I think it was for the best.'

'I don't know how to take this,' Hana says quietly.

'Who does? There aren't any easy answers. Hedda didn't find any. A few days later she came back early from the conservatory, ran a bath, climbed in and cut open her veins with one of my razors.'

Why ever did he do it? Why did he tell her? Knowledge is power, and she now has power over both his body and his mind. She knows everything about him, every shadow and every light, every small particle of fear and every minute focus of gratification. She knows how to evoke memory and how to bring, for a moment, forgetting. 'Stop,' he tells her, but she doesn't stop for his words have no power over her. He lies there helpless, on the unforgiving floor of the Glass Room, while she kneels astride him. Her hands are on his throat. Above him the dark maw of her shame threatening him with ecstasy.

'Please,' he begs her. 'Please.'

She lowers her hips. There is no world beyond her. There is no light, no smell, no taste, no touch that is not hers. The Glass Room is not there. The balance and the reason has vanished.

There is only her shame enclosing him, suffocating him, enveloping him, her choking fingers bringing sensation and oblivion in equal measure.

'Someone might have come,' he says afterwards, pulling on his clothes and trying to find some semblance of normality, some shred of command. 'You must never come here again, do you understand? Never.'

She smiles. This smile is particular. It starts from a downward turn of the mouth that is almost an expression of contempt, and it ends in warmth and promise. She leans towards his face and her tongue laps across his mouth, tasting herself. '"Never" is a word I am not entirely familiar with,' she says. 'If we listened to never we would never have done what we just did. And how would you like that?'

Leaving

They were on the terrace at the back of the house, the girls playing some board game, Katalin helping Martin to draw a picture of
the house. They all looked round as Liesel came out with the post.
'There's a letter from Oma for the two of you,' she said. 'And one
from Auntie Hana for me.'

It was a ritual, the reading of the letters, that fragile thread that
linked them back to home. Ottilie opened the letter from their
grandmother and prepared to read it to Martin. Liesel opened the
one from Hana.

Life here is drudgery, she read. *O can do less and less. You
know how he always liked to wear a buttonhole – a rose or a car-
nation? Well, now things are different and it is impossible to find
any flowers but the Star of Bethlehem, and then only a poor imi-
tation in yellow cloth. So he refuses to go out. If he can't dress
properly then he won't set foot outside the house, that's what he
says. So I have to do everything for him.*

She stopped and looked up. 'The yellow star,' she said, to no
one in particular. 'It was in the papers a few days ago. A yellow
star. And now Oskar has to wear one.'

'Would Tatínek have to wear one if we were still at home?'
Ottilie asked.

'Yes, he would.'

'And would we have to?'

'I really don't know. It just seems . . .' She shook her head in
disbelief, '. . . absurd. Unbelievable. Like branding cattle. Poor
Hana is the only one who goes out now.'

'Doesn't she wear the star?' Martin asked.

'She's not a Jew.'

Money is the difficulty as I told you. I can't really explain the details in a letter but let us say that my scientist contributes to the funds and in exchange I contribute to his well-being. Once or twice a week at the Grand. And once – I'll confess – just once in the Glass Room. He even played for me, and not too badly. There was a wife and she played the violin, so he's got talents other than his science. And he has a little boy's weakness for plums. They cost a lot these days – eighty crowns a kilo. But he gobbles them up.

She stopped reading and looked up, startled, to where bright daylight glittered on the lake. Plums. *Pflaumen*. She felt the blood in her cheeks, remembering laughter in the darkness, a laughter that faded to silence, and strong limbs open and hands on her head, and an intricate perception of touch and taste and scent there at the crux. Ecstasy and shame in intense conjugation.

Should I be telling you this? You'll think me a disgrace but you cannot imagine what things are like here, Liesel. Really. People in Město get by selling whatever they have. That's the way it works. That's what I do. Nothing more than that. Tell me something happy. Tell me all about you and the children, and even Viktor, the old goat, and the Cuckoo whose circumstances I understand a little better now.
    Burn this letter immediately!
    Your loving Hana.

She got up. 'I must go and answer this,' she said. 'I won't be long.'

She was sitting in her room attempting a reply when she heard Viktor's car draw up outside. The car door slammed, and then the front door opened and closed and footsteps came up the stairs. Carefully she covered up what she had been writing. There was a knock and Viktor stood there in the doorway, holding a large buff envelope in his hand.
    'The tickets have come,' he said.

Should she be happy or sad? She felt something physical, a throb of anguish behind her breastbone, as though her heart had stopped. 'They've come?'

'It's a ship called the *Magallanes*. That's Magellan, I think. A Spanish line.' He glanced at the letter in his hand and attempted the Spanish pronunciation. 'Compañía Transatlántica. Return tickets—'

'Return?'

'I told you, that's what the Cuban authorities require. A fee of two hundred and fifty dollars for each visa applicant, a letter of credit for two thousand dollars, a caution of five hundred against the visitor's leaving the country, a one hundred and fifty dollar security against an onward ticket to the country of final destination, and a return ticket so they can put you back on the boat if you can't go anywhere else.' He pulled one of the tickets out, a veritable booklet with a liner steaming across the cover towards a vivid sunset. 'Seven hundred for this alone. It's a seller's market.'

'And Katalin and Marika? Their visas?'

'That's all been taken care of.'

She looked back to the view. The past was slipping away, the coast of Bohemia dropping away behind her, Hana standing on the shore waving, as she had stood that day at the aerodrome. 'We'd better start thinking about packing, then.'

'I suggest we move immediately. We need to be ready to go as soon as the train tickets are confirmed. I suggest we take a hotel near Geneva, what do you think?'

Of course she agreed with him. He was the planner and the driving force. Where would she be without him? Back in Město in all probability. He seemed to be fired with enthusiasm, as though departure for the New World were a good thing rather than a disaster. 'America, you've got it better than our old continent,' he said. 'We're going to leave Europe's useless memories and pointless conflicts behind us.' They were words from a poem by Goethe. He was always quoting it these days. She remembered the first time he had quoted Goethe to her, on their honeymoon when they had just got to Italy and all seemed settled. She turned from the window, from the sailing boats on the lake and the hills in the distance, and looked at him. 'Are memories really useless? They're all we have, aren't they? There's nothing else.'

'There's the future.'

'I'm not sure I believe in the future. What they're doing in our old house, anthropology, race, whatever it was that Hana said. That's the future.'

'It won't last, and at least they haven't pulled it down '

'I was so happy there. Although it was an illusory happiness, wasn't it?'

'Isn't all happiness illusory?'

'How cynical you are.'

He came into the room and put his hand on her shoulder. She liked the contact with him, that was a strange thing. Was it absurd to crave contact and yet feel betrayed? 'You were happy. We were both happy. Isn't that enough?'

She shook her head. 'I don't understand you, Viktor, I really don't. After all these years.'

He smiled, that smile that had captivated her, captivated dozens of women. It was so open, so honest. 'Do you expect to? No one really understands another. I don't understand you, either. You and Hana, for example.'

She looked up, startled, blood coming to her cheeks. 'What about Hana and me?'

He bent and kissed her on the forehead. 'That's exactly the question, isn't it? What about you and Hana?' He dropped the envelope of tickets on the desk in front of her. 'Here, put these somewhere safe.'

Protektor

There is panic in the Glass Room. The Reichsprotektor will be visiting Město. Not old von Neurath, the dear old fellow whom everyone loves, but the new man, the martinet, Obergruppenführer Reinhard Tristan Eugen Heydrich. Telegrams and telephone calls speed here and there. Plans are made and just as soon abandoned. Rumours trample over speculation. The Reichsprotektor will be visiting the Biometric Centre; he will not be visiting. He will come in the morning; he will come in the afternoon. He will want to meet with all the staff; he will wish to see the place when no one is around. Eventually, of course, the full itinerary comes, stamped with the seal of the Reichsprotektor's office in Prague Castle, and there is no longer any question or argument: the Biometric Centre will be available for his inspection at eleven o'clock in the morning, with all the staff on parade.

The visitor's convoy arrives exactly on time. There is the distant rumble of motorcycles and then a sudden proximal roar and the vehicles come into view from the direction of the children's hospital. Motor bikes are followed by a closed car containing officials, and then a dark green Mercedes convertible with the *Hakenkreuz* flying from the front mudguard and SS–3 on the number plate. It takes little to understand where this man stands in the hierarchy of the state. The Führer is SS–1; Reichsführer-SS Heinrich Himmler is SS–2; this man is SS–3. The father, the son and the holy ghost. A trinity. The hood of the car is down so that the people may see him sitting in splendour in the back and indeed he looks like something ghostly, pale and solemn, rising to his feet as the car draws to a halt. Medals and badges glint in the sunshine: the eagle on his left arm, his pilot's wings on his left breast, the golden badge of the Party, the ribbon of the Knight's Cross. His face is long and immobile, with pale eyes and a proud prow of a nose, reminiscent of an Aztec mask that Stahl recalls seeing at the Kaiser Wilhelm Institute. What, he wonders, does it say about the man's genealogy? His ears are lobed, his hair is blond, his mouth is full and sensual and pulled for the moment into a bleak smile. He has wide, almost feminine hips.

Standing there with all the staff, Stahl raises his right arm and pronounces the clarion call '*Heil* Hitler!' The Reichsprotektor steps down on to the pavement and gives a jaunty acknowledgement of the salute, a mere wave, as though he has privileged knowledge of the man who is being invoked and therefore may treat the matter with some familiarity. 'Stahl,' he says holding out his hand. 'I have heard about you and your work.'

For a moment Stahl is overcome. 'Herr Obergruppenführer Heydrich, you are ...' What is he? Welcome? Feared? Impressive? '. . . most gracious to favour our small outpost of scientific endeavour with your presence. As humble warriors in the battle for truth and understanding we—'

The Reichsprotektor cuts him short. 'I'm sure everything you say is quite laudable but I'm afraid I don't have time for that kind of thing. I wish to see what you people do, not hear what you may or may not think about my visit.'

'Of course, Herr Reichsprotektor.' Stahl turns to where the scientific staff are waiting. 'May I introduce you to my fellow researchers—'

The Reichsprotektor nods at the line of scientists. 'That's fine. I am sure they do their work well. Please show me the way.'

And so they move on, ten minutes ahead of schedule, with people scattering before them. 'What kind of building was this?' Heydrich asks as they descend towards the Glass Room.

'A private house.'

'How could people live in such a place? Were they Jews?'

'I believe so.'

Heydrich pauses on the stairs. The hooded eyes are an ambush. 'This work you do here. Does it mean that you can identify Jews?'

'We are making inroads into the problem. For example, hair colour—'

'I have heard that there are Jew diseases.'

'They are a degenerate race and like all such races they may carry certain genetic diseases, what one expert has called "inborn errors of metabolism". Sachs's infantile amaurotic idiocy, for example; and the so-called spongy degeneration of the brain that Canavan identified. Then there is Gaucher's disease, and one or two others. They all appear to be inherited in the Mendelian fashion.'

There is a moment of stillness in the narrow space. 'Is this what we have been looking for?'

'It's not that simple, Herr Reichsprotektor. Not all Jews have the diseases, and conversely, not all people with those diseases are Jews.' Stahl pushes open the door and stands aside for Heydrich to go through. 'Here we have adopted a different approach. In this laboratory we are trying to measure the most minute variations of phenotype, and then we search to see whether particular *combinations* of characteristics can lead to a racial diagnosis. That is what the Hollerith machines are for, to sort out all the data that we collect. Herr Reichsprotektor will see them later.'

In the Glass Room the staff wait nervously. The visitor looks round, at the semicircle of expectant scientists, at the onyx wall and the open space, at the glass plates of the windows and the view across the city. 'And this is where these Jew owners *lived*? It looks more like a fencing salle than a living room.'

'They were very modern people, Herr Reichsprotektor.'

'What happened to them?'

'They emigrated.'

'Excellent.' He nods at the scientists, as though the emigration of the Landauer family were their merit. And then he notices the piano. 'What is *that* doing here?'

'It was left behind by the owners. We have chosen not to remove it.'

'Why? Why have you kept it? Do you play?'

Is there some Party ordinance that forbids such things? 'I play a bit, Herr Reichsprotektor. I thought, some German culture might not be amiss.'

'So it is in tune?'

'Yes.'

There is a pause. People stand watching, uniformed men from the Reichsprotektor's party, the scientific staff in their white coats, all wondering what will happen. Heydrich lifts the lid of the instrument and moves his fingers fluidly across the keys. A few notes spill out in the silence, the opening bars of one of Mendelssohn's *Songs Without Words*. 'Spring'. The Reichsprotektor's mouth moves in what might be considered a smile. '*You* don't play Mendelssohn, I hope?'

'Liszt. Beethoven,' Stahl says. 'Not Mendelssohn. Mendelssohn was a Jew.'

'Does his being a Jew make his music any worse? It's a shame I don't have my violin with me. We could have played together, perhaps some Mendelssohn just to put him to the test. Now show me the measuring.'

The wave of relief that overcomes Stahl is almost orgasmic. 'Perhaps the Obergruppenführer would consent to be measured? It will give him a clear idea of our methods.'

The Reichsprotektor hesitates. Hesitation is something he rarely discovers in himself; often in other people. It seems like a weakness, the first symptom of a degenerative disease, like those the Jews suffer from. Surely you can will weakness away? 'Why not?' he agrees finally. 'I am sure we have a few minutes. Why not?' He hands his cap to a minion and consents to be led into the mensuration area. Blushing Elfriede Lange indicates where he should stand, where he should sit, where he should lie down. The man's body is long and languid on the couch. His boots gleam in the lights. His medals shine. He smiles up at Elfriede and she blushes more deeply. 'You are of fine, Nordic stock,' he tells her.

'Thank you, Herr Reichsprotektor.'

'You shouldn't thank me, you should thank your parents.'

She calls out the measurements and Stahl himself writes them down on a blank form.

'So you say you have no single character to distinguish a Jew from someone of Nordic stock?' Heydrich asks.

'No single character,' Stahl agrees.

'But a combination?'

'It is a possibility, Herr Obergruppenführer. That is what we are working on.'

269

'And the Slavs? We are also interested in the Slavs. It is a question of whether they may be racially assimilated into the German stock or not. You understand?'

'We are working on both problems, Herr Obergruppenführer.'

'Then I suggest you hurry up. The work is vital.'

Elfriede moves to the final measurements, the crucial ones of the cranium. As she adjusts the callipers, Heydrich grabs hold of her wrist with all the speed and precision of a fencer. The woman stands quite still, like a white rabbit caught in a snare. 'When you have finished I will take my file with me,' he tells her. 'As a souvenir.'

'Of course, Herr Obergruppenführer.'

'And you will keep no record of my measurements.'

'Of course not, Herr Obergruppenführer.'

Wide-eyed with fear she completes her task. The Reichsprotektor stands up, smoothing down his jacket and adjusting his tie. 'Fascinating,' he says to Stahl. 'But it is a shame that you have not found a Jew character that is beyond argument. You should work on it. It seems to me a matter of priority. And the same with the Slavs. Some of the Slavs are no less degenerate than Jews.'

'Of course, Herr Obergruppenführer.'

And so the visit continues, brisk and businesslike, people scuttering around, Heydrich looking this way and that, probing, smiling, frowning. His smile is worse than his frown. It is the smile on the face of a corpse.

The staff members are going round putting things in order. 'How did it go?' they ask one another anxiously as they work. Stahl stands by the windows looking out on the afternoon view, the sun descending towards the horizon, preparing to pierce the onyx wall with that lance of fire. They'll all be gone when it happens. Only he will witness the marvel.

He thinks of things that happen in the Glass Room: the precisions of science, the wild variance of lust, the catharsis of confession and the fear of failure.

'Did I do everything right?' Elfriede asks. Her smooth brow is creased with anxiety.

'Of course you did.'

'And did he like our work?'

'Who can tell?' She reminds him of Hedda, that is the problem. Hana Hanáková is so different as to seem an altogether separate species, but Elfriede Lange is from similar stock as Hedda. 'Tell the others they can go. I will close up.'

'Are you sure?' She has that look of concern, as though she is responsible for his well-being. The same expression that Hedda wore.

'Of course I'm sure. It's an order. Do as I tell you.'

And when they have all gone he stands in front of the windows and looks out on the city and wonders about Hana Hanáková. Looking out of the windows his gaze encompasses the whole city. She is somewhere there, waiting. He thinks about her, what she knows and what she thinks. She seems a danger to him, a threat to his very existence. He wants the oblivion that she offers, but at the same time he would be happy never to see her again. Perhaps this is like addiction to a drug. He has known people like this with morphine, craving it and loathing it at one and the same time.

This is not love, it is the very antithesis of love: it is hatred made manifest.

Léman

Dearest Hana, Liesel wrote, *I received your number eighteen just before we left the house in Zurich. So there's only number fifteen that seems to have gone missing. Who can wonder these days? Please note the new address, for the moment at least. Where we will be a week from now, I cannot imagine. I have given them instructions to forward anything that comes in the meantime but I will let you know as soon as I am able.*

So after the stasis of Zurich they were finally on the move westward, the children fretful at leaving new friends behind, the adults hopeful. This time there was to be no permanence: a hotel not a house, a grand hotel in the Biedermeier style, Le Grand Hôtel Vevey, with striped awnings that flapped in the breeze and an expansive terrace where Swiss families congregated for lunch and congratulated themselves on being neither German nor French, neither conquerors nor conquered. Again Liesel had a lake view from her window, but it was a different lake now, a bigger, darker lake with another country on the far side. The mountains of the French shore were black with forest; above them you could see the snow on the high peaks hanging over the haze like clouds. The shore might be only a few miles as the crow flies, but of course they wouldn't be going by boat when the time came. It would be a train, from Geneva all the way across France to Bilbao. That was where the transatlantic liners left from. Further and further away from what she knew.

There are always delays with the bureaucrats and it's uncertain exactly when we will travel. We go by train, via Lyon, in

272

five days' time. I can actually see France from my room. The place feels so French after Zurich – you know, old men wearing berets and drinking red wine at breakfast and that kind of thing! Viktor says it is better to be here. He wants, he says, to shake off the past, all that Germanic nonsense.

So our strange life together continues, a kind of dance in which the steps are instinctive more than learned – one of those Moravian folk dances we used to laugh at! In some way Kata and I can share things that we cannot even talk about. Should I feel anger towards her? Well I don't. Affection, in fact. Perhaps we are both victims of a kind. The children are flourishing, of course, although they miss their friends. Poor Martin is bossed around by the girls. Anyway, they send their Auntie Hana big kisses and Ottilie tells you to be good. She doesn't quite know what she means by that, but I do! I laughed when I pictured you entrapping your brave scientist, and then felt shocked, and then jealous. How is O? You mentioned him only in passing – I hope he is well.

Your loving,
Liesel

She folded the letter in the envelope and sealed it, then took it downstairs to the concierge's desk. Just as she was walking away towards the terrace and the sunshine a voice called her back. 'Madame Landauer!'

It was the concierge himself, resplendent in uniform – a Ruritanian lance-corporal Viktor had described him – coming round the desk, bearing a letter on a silver salver. 'This has just been delivered, Madame.'

It was stamped and taped and bore the familiar word *Geöffnet* across the flap, and the well-known handwriting on the front. 'It's from the person to whom I have just written,' she said. 'Perhaps I can have the letter back so that I can reply?'

But there was no possibility of such an irregular action. The post box was the property of the Swiss post, to be opened only by an approved operative. And letters therein were property of the addressee not the sender. He seemed upset that she should not know such things. 'Such is the law of the land, Madame.'

'Of course.' She took the letter with her onto the terrace. It was a bright, breezy morning. Ottilie sat with her sketch book. The wind lifted the corner of the page she was drawing on and she spoke to it harshly, as though it was a deliberately recalcitrant child. Martin was immersed in a book and Katalin was sewing, embroidering initials onto the corner of a linen handkerchief. MK. Her daughter sat and watched the creation of this small tribute to herself.

Liesel took the chair that had been left for her. 'A letter from Auntie Hana,' she told them as she sat.

'Read it to us,' Ottilie said. 'Read it to us please. I miss Auntie Hana so much.'

She tore the envelope open, took out the letter and unfolded it. '"Darling Liesel",' she read out loud. And stopped. *I really don't know how to tell you this, but I'll try . . .*

Storm

He is called to the gate. There's a woman asking for him, insisting on seeing him, won't take no for an answer. Apparently she knows him, which is why they didn't just send her packing.

It is her, of course. She is wearing an old grey coat and plain walking shoes that make her look like a refugee, standing in the driving rain and looking like one of the thousands of displaced people who throng the city. Perhaps that is intentional, some kind of disguise. He hurries her across the forecourt, hunched against the wind, away from the curious gaze of the soldiers. 'What the hell are you doing here?'

'I want to talk.'

'Not here, for God's sake.'

'Where then? How else do I see you when I want?'

He hasn't seen her for over a week. She hasn't been in the café where they first met, she hasn't been answering the phone number that she gave him, she hasn't been at the Grand Hotel when he went there for a drink. And now here she is, coming suddenly and unexpectedly out of the storm. He shows her into the building and down the stairs into the Biometric Centre. Mercifully, the place is deserted. She kicks off her shoes and crosses the room to the windows. There's something unsteady about the way she moves, as though a piece of the machinery inside had broken. Beyond the glass it is a ragged autumnal evening, the clouds battering fast across the sky over the castle, gusts of rain thrown like pebbles against the windows, the occasional shaft of sunlight breaking out of the cloud. 'Where the hell have you been?' he demands. 'I've been trying to get in touch

275

with you but you weren't answering the phone at the number you gave me.'

'I've been busy.'

'Doing what?'

'That's my business.'

'And now? Am I your business again? I told you we shouldn't meet here. Once is enough. People will see you. Questions will be asked. I cannot allow my work to be compromised by your presence here. You must never do this again. If you do—'

'*What* will you do, Herr Hauptsturmführer?'

'I'll have the guards arrest you.'

She laughs. Perhaps she's drunk. She seems wayward and dangerous, liable to do anything. Outside, the wind hammers at the windows. 'How was your visitor?' she asks.

'My visitor?'

'Our Lord and Protector. How did you find him? Is he the monster that they say he is?'

'Who says that?'

'Everyone says it. Even the newspapers imply as much. Arrests, disappearances, deportations. Thousands of Jews have been rounded up in Prague and sent to Poland. Five thousand, they say. You must know something about it. There's a rumour—'

'There are always rumours.'

'They say the fortress at Terezín is being turned into a ghetto. The Jews are to be concentrated there, that's the story.'

He shrugs. 'Perhaps they are. Who knows? It would be a practical solution.'

She walks round the room, touching things as though to assure herself of their reality – the examination couches, the measuring callipers, the desks and chair – and speaking thoughtfully, as though trying to work things out for herself. Is she perhaps a Jew? The thought brings a shiver of revulsion to him, that what he has done with her might have been with a Jew. But the measurements deny it. She's a Slav, a typical, emotional, unstable Slav lurching from one thing to another, her mind as varied as the storm outside.

'They've been forbidden everything, haven't they?' she says. 'The Jews, I mean. They can't use shops during normal hours. They can't travel on the trams. They can't go into a café or a hotel, they can't even enter a public park. They can't own a pet or a telephone. They can't hold down a decent job. They have to wear a label as though they have the plague or something. And now they are being rounded up and deported. Surely you know something about it. Surely all this' – she gestures at the whole room, the apparatus, the devices – 'means that you know what is going on.'

He picks up some files, taps them into order and puts them in one of the drawers. He feels anger towards her, anger for her insistent interrogation, for her knowledge of him, for having allowed her to look into the depths of his past. He slams the filing cabinet closed and turns. 'It's a plague in our midst affecting everyone. For God's sake, it has affected my own family. You know that. And now every mile we advance into Russia more and more of these people come under our control. We cannot just stand back and do nothing. We have to find a solution.'

'And the solution is to persecute them?'

'To isolate them, yes. Why are you so concerned?'

She looks him straight in the eye. 'Because my husband is a Jew.'

He looks around the room, the Glass Room, at the beauty and the balance of it, at the rationality. Then back at her. She's laughing at him. It's the laughter that's disturbing. Like the laughter of an idiot.

'Does it disgust you, the thought of sharing me with a Jew? The idea that there's been a Jew prick inside the cunt you like to suck so much?'

'You'd better go,' he says. 'You'd better leave at once.'

But she's staring at him, her face taut as though braced against the gale that is blowing. 'There's something else,' she says. 'To do with your damned miscegenation. Something else that you should know about.'

'What? What else is there?' She's mad or drunk, or perhaps she's under the influence of some other drug. He has heard about it, women of her kind taking things. Morphine, playing with morphine, the morphine that is needed in the front line to deal with genuine pain, being used by them to treat their own imagined pain. How he can get rid of her, get her out of this place to somewhere where it doesn't matter, the hotel where they have always met, that anonymous room with the subdued lighting and the trams clanging outside the windows, not this place of cool and objective measurement? Should he call the guard? But that would only lead to complications, problems, questions. 'Look, just wait for me to clear these things away and we can go. I won't be more than a few minutes.'

But she stands there before him without moving. 'I'm pregnant,' she says.

Behind her, beyond the windows, the trees are throwing caution to the wind. The panes shudder. The whole room seems to be a soundbox for the gale, a chamber that resonates with outside forces. Where has the wind come from? All the way from the Atlantic ocean, right across France and Switzerland and the Alps, ignoring borders and territories, wars and occupations, ignoring everything to do with humans.

'You are *what*?'

She nods. 'You heard what I said. I've had the test done. The rabbit test. I got the result yesterday, and it's positive. I'm pregnant.'

'Why are you telling me this?'

'Because the child is yours.'

'Mine? What about your Jew husband? Why should it be mine?'

'It's not his, believe me. I told you, he's much older than me. We have a different relationship.'

'And the other men you've been with?'

'There are no other men, dear Hauptsturmführer. There is only you and it's your child.'

'And you want me to give you money to get rid of it? Is that the idea?'

'Well, you shouldn't have much compunction about that, should you? Killing babies is in your nature.'

That is when he hits her. The blow, a heavy slap across the side of her face, is sudden and shocking, surprising him as much as her. She gives a gasp of outrage and pain and backs away from him, but he reaches out and grabs her by the wrist, pulling her towards him. 'What do you mean by that?'

'Let me go!' she cries, struggling in his grip.

'What do you mean, killing babies is in my nature?'

'Werner, let me go!' She calls him by his first name. Always it has been Stahl or his rank, or something mocking like Doctor Mabuse; but now it's Werner. 'Werner, you're hurting! Werner!'

But he holds her tight, drawing her closer, wondering if he can smell alcohol on her breath, wondering if she is lying or if all this is true. She turns her head away. There's a weal across her cheek and a swelling in her upper lip and a trace of blood from where one of her teeth has cut the inside of her mouth. 'You're drunk. I can smell it on your breath. You're drunk and you're lying.'

'That's not true. I swear. The child is yours.' She tries to drag her arm down but he doesn't let go so she drops to the floor like a child trying to pull away. She's sitting on the floor at his feet, her legs splayed. He can see the tops of her stockings and the whiteness of her thighs, that marbled flesh whose texture and scent he knows.

'You're trying to blackmail me.'

'No, I'm not.'

'Yes you are. You're trying to blackmail me with your half-breed child.'

'I'm not, I swear I'm not. I wanted to discuss it with you. I wanted to see what we could do about it. Now let me go.' She puts her hand to her mouth and brings it away with a smear of blood and saliva. 'You've hurt me.'

'It's nothing.' He releases her wrist but still stands over her, wondering about the foetus that may or may not be swimming in the salty amniotic ocean of her uterus. The thought excites him, that is what is so strange. That he has impregnated her. His tainted seed, those millions of swimming cells, half of them carrying the gene that killed Erika, meeting this woman's own Slavic egg. Maybe his seed is only good for someone like her, an *Untermensch*. A slut.

He reaches down to pull her to her feet but she backs away like a hit bitch, cowering in front of him. He follows her as she moves across the floor towards the windows. Something is rising inside him like gorge, a compulsion born of disgust and delight. She's powerless there on the floor, trapped against the glass. No longer is she the sharp and sarcastic woman who knows how to sell herself and, worse, knows what he wants. Suddenly she's a victim, unsteady and unclean. He reaches down and grabs her knees. She

279

thrashes her legs, trying to twist out of his grip but he holds on, laughing at the sight of her caught like a mammal in a gin trap.

'Let me go,' she cries. The demand carries no weight. He twists her legs and turns her over, surprised at how light she is, how easily he can move her this way and that. Her face is pressed against the window and her hands are spread out on the glass and he takes her by the scruff of the neck to hold her steady. With his other hand he lifts her skirt and pulls her knickers down, and suddenly she is naked, humbled, the pale globes of her buttocks there in front of him.

'Werner,' she cries, 'what are you going to do?'

It's an interesting question. What is he going to do? What does this creature, to whom he has opened up the secrets of his own life, merit? What does this *Mensch*, who claims to be carrying his own child, deserve? He kneels down and unbuttons his trousers, then spreads her buttocks apart so that she is open to his gaze, the dark valley, the tight mouth of her anus, the dark fold of her shame. What does she deserve?

'Werner, please,' she says. 'Someone might come.'

But no one might come. The doors are all locked, the staff dismissed, the Glass Room silent and reserved, observing impassively whatever might happen. Rain dashes against the other side of the glass, running in rivulets down the reflection of his own face floating above her. He holds the head of his penis against her and presses in.

It's a sudden thing, the resistance breached and a void beyond, the dark void of her humiliation. Everything is over in a moment. She gives a cry of outrage and pain and he knows an instant of irrational ecstasy more intense than anything before. And then it's over and she is crouching against the windows, pulling at her clothes and trying to restore some semblance of decency. The swelling of her lip is as thick as a finger. 'You hurt me,' she says, her words dulled by the bruise.

'You'll be all right.'

He reaches out to take her hand and pull her to her feet, no longer feeling anger towards her, or even fear. It's the variance of emotion that is so disturbing. He even feels pity, that emotion that you must learn to expunge when working with animals, when chloroforming or skinning them. Or when taking your child to

Hartheim Castle. He reaches out to touch her swollen lip. She's still cowed, frightened of him, flinching when he moves. And now he sees her clearly for what she is – a degenerate Slav, a beautiful but alien creature cast up on the shore of the Aryan world, a thing of unknown provenance and uncertain nature, tainted by her genes and the manner of her life. Behind her the glass has changed, lost all its transparency, closed off the world so that it only reflects the interior, the two of them standing there like figures on a stage. And there on the glass are the prints of her hands, the fingers spread like the petals of two flowers, and a smear of blood.

'Come,' he says, suddenly sorry for her. 'You can wash a bit and then you'll have to go.'

She's shaking, touching her lip and shivering like someone with a fever. 'You hurt me.'

'You'll be all right.'

'Why didn't you ask? Why did you have to hit me? If you'd asked I'd have let you do it.'

'It doesn't matter. It's over now.' And he feels in control of her. No longer her victim. There's something almost loveable about her, something small and fearful. He takes her to the bathroom and splashes water on the bruised lip. And then bends and kisses it, feeling its heat, tasting the metallic flavour of her blood.

'There's a curfew on,' she says, turning her head away. 'I can't get home by myself. You'll have to take me.'

'I'll take you. Don't worry, I'll take you.'

They leave the house and hurry through the rain past the guard box. In the car she fumbles with cigarettes, striking three or four matches before she gets one to light, her hand still shaking. She smokes it awkwardly, on the opposite side of the mouth from where he hit her. 'What about the baby?' she asks.

He drives by the thin pencils of headlight that are all that the regulations allow. Tramlines run like nerves along their route. There are few vehicles on the blackened streets, only an army truck grinding past, its gears grating as it turns a corner, its engine revving like a blasphemy in the cold wet evening. 'Were you telling the truth?'

'Of course I was telling the truth.'

At the end of Franz-Josef-Strasse is a roadblock where callow youths who have yet to be moved to the Eastern Front flag the car down. They shine a torch in Stahl's eyes and up and down the form of Hana Hanáková in the seat beside him. 'Papers,' they say, snapping their fingers in the torchlight. Hana looks straight ahead, ignoring them, not trying to hide her bruised face.

'Are you all right, madam?' a voice asks. But when they see Stahl's identity card with the twin Sig runes and the eagle bearing the *Hakenkreuz* in its talons, they douse the light and salute sharply and pull the barrier aside to allow the car on its way. They drive on into the old city, Staré Město, the Altstadt, across tram-lines and over cobbles, past church and convent and the slope of the Krautmarkt, Cabbage Market Square, where the stalls are shuttered and closed.

At the head of the square is a ponderous block of a building with columns on its façade. 'You can stop here,' she tells him. Slivers of light leak out of blacked-out windows. Cobblestones glisten in what light there is from the sky. A shadow hurrying away down an alleyway is a curfew-breaker scurrying to safety.

'I want to keep the baby,' she says, sitting there without moving.

Does he believe any of this, or is it all a charade to get more money from him? 'Then keep it. It's yours. Keep it.'

'But I'll need help. We have no money, you know that. I told you, my husband's a Jew. They've frozen all his bank accounts, everything.'

'And you want me to pay for it? How do I even know there is a baby, never mind whether it is mine or not?'

'Because I don't lie.'

'How do I know that?'

'Because,' she says, sounding like a child holding on to an argument that it knows is nonsense. Then she shrugs. 'You'll have to trust me.'

He laughs. 'How much do you expect? What do you expect? An open cheque?'

She doesn't know. She knows everything but she doesn't know this. He finds some notes in his pocket and hands them to her. 'That's all I've got for now,' he says.

She glances at the money and then stuffs it in her coat pocket and climbs out into the damp, cold evening.

'I'm sorry,' he calls after her, but exactly what he is apologising for isn't clear.

She turns and looks back into the car. It astonishes him how things can change, how she has changed from the woman who first picked him up in the café, the woman who knew things that he had barely imagined, into this fragile creature begging for money. 'I want the baby, Werner,' she says. 'It's the only future I have.'

Departure

She read the letter for the fourth or fifth time. Times without counting. Sixth? Seventh? Remembering her own pregnancy and Hana's attentions, her closeness, the wonder of it all, and that time they had divined Ottilie's gender, successfully, with the pendulum. And Hana kneeling there as though at an altar, her hands on the swelling of her belly, and her small gasp of amazement. And now this.

I thought I couldn't have children. The doctor said so. Barren. It's a terrible word isn't it? But now I know I'm not. The terrible thing is, I want the baby, Liesi. I want him or her or whatever it is.

There was a knock on the door. Hastily, she folded the letter away and called out, '*Hereinkommen!*' and turned to find one of the porters there in the doorway. 'I've come for the luggage, Madame. Monsieur said to tell you that the cars are ready.'

Her suitcases stood ready in the middle of the carpet. Her other things, the trunks and the packing cases, all of them marked Not Wanted on Voyage, had already gone ahead. 'I'm coming,' she said. 'Tell them I'm coming.'

What could she do? Hana was there, on the far side of whatever divide it was that separated them, and she was about to go even further away. A rail journey across the continent. She would see the ocean for the very first time. She would cross the ocean to another world.

Turning back to the writing desk she picked up her pen. There was no time to write anything more than a postcard. The photograph showed the hotel itself bedecked with awnings and flags like an ocean liner. There was barely space on the other side to write anything.

Darling Hana,
We're going at last. I've received your number 19. Goodness knows, I want to be with you but I cannot. I've only time to write this and pray that things work out. Go ahead with what you want, please go ahead. I'll write as soon as I am able. Bilbao, maybe.

She signed off and hurried downstairs. Outside on the fore-court there were two motor cars drawn up, two Citroëns piled high with luggage and people, Katalin with two of the children in the rear car, Ottilie in the front one and Viktor waiting impa-tiently by the door. 'Where have you been? We've got a train to catch.'

'I was just writing a card. I must leave it at the desk.'

'For God's sake get in and let's go. We can post it at the station.'

Geneva station was a great noisy rattling drum of a place. Trains seethed at the platforms, venting steam from their joints and snorting like vast dormant dragons. There was the smell of carbon and sulphur in the air. It stung the eyes and the back of the throat and seemed to penetrate whatever clothes you wore. The plates on each carriage of their train said SNCF and people were already leaning out of the windows of the third-class com-partments, calling and waving. Others on the platform passed suitcases up through the windows. There was the sound of panic in the air, passengers arguing with officials, papers being scruti-nised, tickets being examined, passports and visas being waved like weapons.

Viktor led the way, pushing through the crowds, followed by a porter and a trolley piled high with suitcases. Liesel remembered the station in Město, when they had met Rainer off the Vienna train, when he came to survey the site for the new house. And now the house was no longer theirs and Rainer was in America and Europe was dying beneath the burden of war, and Hana was pregnant, and she was hurrying after Viktor towards escape.

285

'The next carriage,' he called, turning to let his flock catch up. 'For God's sake get a move on!'

They clambered on board, one of the porters going ahead with the luggage. 'Will we have a bed?' Martin asked as they edged along the corridor.

'Of course we'll have a bed,' Ottilie told him. 'How else will we sleep?'

Other compartments were full, people standing in the corridor, people talking, people arguing. Someone had found his place already taken and a row flared up in German and French, two people fighting over the same exiguous sleeping space. Mercifully their own compartment was empty, six bunks folded down, their cases dumped on the floor. 'Not quite what we're used to,' Viktor said as they crowded in. But then nothing was what they were used to. War and exile wasn't what they were used to. The attendant took their papers – tickets, passports, transit visas for l'État Français, entry visas for el Estado Español – and apologised that there was no restaurant car on the train. He shrugged helplessly. No wagons-lit, no restaurant car, but what could you expect? Things were not what they used to be.

'Will we all be in here together?' Ottilie asked.

'Of course we will. This is how you travel on trains if there aren't any sleeping-cars.'

'I want to go on the top,' Martin said. 'It's just like camping, isn't it, Tatínku?'

Katalin was organising the children. Ottilie would take the other top bunk. She wasn't afraid of falling. Viktor and Liesel would have the two bottom bunks. Katalin would sleep above Liesel – the alternative was too embarrassing to contemplate – and Marika would be above Viktor.

Liesel sat on the bottom bunk and looked out of the window at the grimy station. Doors banged and whistles blew. The engine bellowed, an explosion of steam, and slowly, like the hands of a clock moving, the train began to slide forward. 'We're going,' she said. 'Finally we are really going.'

'Will we sleep?' Marika asked. 'Mummy, will we be able to sleep?'

'Not if you don't all quieten down.'

French border guards were coming down the corridor and

286

sliding open doors. They flicked their fingers insolently. 'Documents!' they called. 'Passports, visas.'

And Liesel suddenly remembered that she hadn't posted the card to Hana. The train was sliding through the shunting yards, rocking sideways as it went over points, trundling towards the border and she still had the postcard in her bag.

'Too late now,' Viktor said.

'Won't we stop at the border?'

He indicated the police pushing along the corridor, *gendarmes* wearing their absurd kepis. 'This *is* the border. You'll have to post it in Bayonne or somewhere.'

'But it's got Swiss stamps.' It seemed to worry her, the matter of stamps.

'We can get stamps in Bayonne. Or in Spain. We can always get stamps.'

The carriage swayed and rocked. Officials stood at the open door and examined their documents, the passports, the tickets. Finally they handed them back and moved on to the next compartment. There were houses passing by and neat, Swiss fields. Then a glimpse of the river, the Rhône, on their left. She was in tears. They were going. Lyon, Montpellier, Toulouse, Bayonne and Biarritz; and then Spain and Bilbao where they would board the ship. They were going for ever.

'But how will it ever get to her? How will it ever reach her?'

Město was slipping away behind them, far behind them. The Ocean lay beyond. And America. She was in tears, holding the postcard and weeping. 'It'll never get to her,' she said through her tears. 'She'll never know.'

Decision

He ponders the problem, standing in the Glass Room while the measuring goes on around him: Slavs, Germans, Jews all going through the mill. Getting Jews isn't easy these days. The teams have to scour the streets during the two hours in the afternoon during which Jews are permitted to shop, but how can you find enough people when they skulk in doorways and scurry along streets, keeping close to the wall and looking out for official vehicles?

Elfriede Lange approaches him, blushing prettily. 'We have a group coming from Trebitsch this afternoon, sir.'

'A group?'

'Of Jews. And there are a few from the Old Town coming down now.'

The landscape outside is calm after the storm of last night, a landscape of placid trees and lawn, of rooftops and church spires and the distant block of the Špilas fortress. He ponders the problem of the Jews. If only they possessed some clear characteristic, some marker like the wide nose and thick lips of the Negroids or the epicanthal fold of the Mongoloids. Then it would be easy. For a moment his eyes focus closer, not on the distant view but on the window pane itself: down there at the level of his knees, as though etched into the glass, are the prints of two hands, narrow female hands, fingers splayed, and a streak of rust brown. You can see them only if the angle of the light is right, but they are there nevertheless. They recall the decorations in one of those palaeolithic caves discovered in Spain, the imprint of a human hand pressed in pigment on the wall. But these two hands are momentary and evanescent, witnesses of a moment that has not lasted. They will go with the wipe of a cloth. He calls one of the staff over and points out the problem – 'Have it cleaned' – and the woman cancels the prints with one stroke.

A short while later the Jews are shown in. There are two men, and a woman with a four-year-old boy. They look around the place as though trusting nothing. It is in the Jewish nature to be suspicious, but can you measure suspicion? The woman keeps complaining that she must telephone her husband, she must let her husband know; and one of the men protests about this act of detention being against the law, being tantamount to kidnapping, in fact. He is well into his sixties and smartly dressed in stiff-collared shirt and rather threadbare suit; the kind of man who might once have worn a flower in his buttonhole but now has only the yellow star as a decoration. Stahl strolls over to the desk as they are filling in the forms. This particular man is writing with a fountain pen that is clearly a personal favourite. He has an old-fashioned, elegant hand, the kind that used to be drummed into children in the old days before the Great War. *Oskar Hanák*, he writes.

A small shock of recognition. Is it just a coincidence of names? Stahl asks, 'Do you know this building?' and the man looks up, startled to be addressed in this manner. Go there, sit there, do this, people are saying to him, and then this officer who looks to be in charge strolls over and asks a civilised question.

'Of course I know it,' he replies. 'It's Viktor Landauer's place.'

'Was he a friend of yours?'

'Business associate, friend, yes. Why do you ask? Do you know them?'

The man has a fat, heavy face. A typically sallow Jew complexion. A momentary sympathy is replaced by repugnance. 'I'm interested.'

'They went abroad.'

Stahl nods. He watches while they process Hanák, take his blood, measure his dimensions, enter his numbers onto his form. In the photographic area Stahl observes him with the detached eye of a scientist. He sees the paunch, the clumsy paps, the brushwork of black and grey hair across his chest and down his belly, the dark phallus that hangs like a mushroom between his thighs, and he tries to work things out, matters of attraction and repulsion, the urge to hybridisation, the desire for purity and defilement. Naked, the man revolts him. Perhaps all Jews revolt him, but how can you measure revulsion?

Afterwards he goes up to his office and calls down to the registry for that file they put aside for him. *Hanáková, Hana*. The file comes within minutes, delivered by Elfriede Lange. He holds her look for a moment as she hands him the folders. She blushes. She is a perfect specimen, with the exact facial proportions of the Teutonic people. Like Hedda. When she has gone he locks the door, then sits at his desk and takes out the photographs. He lays them out on the desk and examines them for a while. If she wasn't lying, this woman is carrying his child. It seems extraordinary. But how do you measure the extraordinary? How do you measure any of this, the attraction and the repugnance? He remembers the birds on the Baltic coast, the five species of terns. Beautiful, sleek animals, designed for speed. White and grey and crested with black, lying palpitating in the palm of his hand. Fragile, insubstantial things, they watched him with a terrified eye as he put them into the chloroform. You had to steel yourself to do it.

He lifts the telephone receiver and phones one of the departments in the Špilas fortress. Amt IV. There is someone he knows there, a fellow Bavarian, not the kind of person he would call a friend but a contact nevertheless. 'It's Stahl at the Biometric Centre,' he says. 'Yes, Werner Stahl. How are you?' Then he explains the problem. 'She's subversive, yes. She has been asking questions. And Jew-friendly.' *Judenfreundlich*. 'Hana Hanáková.' He repeats the name, and then dictates the spelling in case the man on the other end should make a mistake. The address? Yes, he has her address.

He feels much better now, as though something that was blocking his airway has been removed. He gets up from his desk and walks over to the window. Out there on the terrace the children used to play. Dolls, cars, that kind of thing, that's what she told him. Two of them, a boy and a girl. *Mischlinge*. Where are they now, he wonders? Later he returns the file to the registry, and takes out another one. *Lange, Elfriede* it says on the cover. He opens it and lays those photographs out on the desk. Pale and

290

perfect, her image blushes prettily back at a point just to the right of the camera, the place where he himself had stood watching. He wonders about that cloud of pale hair between her thighs, the texture of it, the scent.

Ocean

The rhythms of the carriage had become part of their conscious-
ness. It was any break to those rhythms that disturbed them
during the night – a half-hour when the train halted somewhere
south of Lyon, another pause in an unnamed station where they
watched a man attach water hoses to the train, and another near
Avignon when the guard passed along the corridor blowing a
whistle. An air raid warning. Viktor climbed out of his bunk and
let the blinds up but there was nothing to see, just the black of
night and, in the faint backwash of light from the sky, an anonymous signal gantry. Cool air came in through the open window,
but there was no sound of aircraft, no distant exploding bombs,
just the muttering of nighttime and the noise of people in the next
compartment talking with subdued voices. In the upper bunks the
children slept on.

'What time is it?' Liesel asked.

'Half past two.'

They dozed, and then another whistle sounded the all clear
and the train gave a jolt and edged forward and the rhythms
were restored and they slept once more until dawn came and
they woke finally to a cool, bright morning with the train
trundling along through the French countryside – low, scrubby
hills, isolated farms, the occasional village. Viktor was standing
at the window in his shirtsleeves, looking crumpled from the
night. There was rough stubble on his chin. She had not seen him
unshaven for years. The train rattled over points and they were
passing through another station and this time there was a signboard visible: MONTPELLIER.

'This is where Vitulka died,' Liesel said. 'You remember, Kaprál's daughter. She married Mucha's son, you remember? Hana told us in one of her letters. I suppose Mucha had the same idea as us. Getting her to Spain.'

This tenuous coincidence with Vitulka Kaprálová seemed important. It was a thread that stretched across a hostile continent and linked them with home. Reduced to this exiguous compartment, this enforced intimacy, she clung to this thread of association, back through the years, back through different lives, all the way to the Glass Room, and Němec surrendering the piano and Vitulka sitting at the keyboard to play.

'What was the piece she played? "Ondine", wasn't it?'

'I don't remember.'

'Of course you do. Ravel.'

The train rumbled on, away from the sea now, towards the other side of the country, towards the Atlantic. While Viktor went down the corridor to the bathroom and shaved in cold water, Katalin and Liesel folded the bunks away. There were some bread rolls for breakfast and some milk for the children. 'It's sour,' Ottilie protested.

'It's not sour,' Liesel told her. 'It's perfectly all right. Anyway, it's all we've got. There are plenty of people who have nothing.'

Once they had finished, Katalin organised the children with some kind of game. It involved spotting objects in the passing countryside – sheep, rivers, villages – and scoring points if you guessed correctly what would come next. Later in the morning they discovered another landmark. 'A castle, a castle!' cried Martin, and when they looked out of the window there were the walls and pointed turrets of a medieval town that Viktor could name. 'Carcassonne,' he said. Later they went at a walking pace through Toulouse where the platform was lined with uniformed police. People pushed past in the corridor, straining to see out of the windows. Stories went back and forth. They would be changing trains at Biarritz. They would go straight through to Spain. They'd have to get off at the Spanish border and walk over to another train. Papers would be checked. Papers would not be checked because the train was sealed: in effect they were already in Spain. There were as many theories as people you asked, but in fact no one knew.

293

In the afternoon the train slid slowly into another station. 'Soldiers!' Liesel cried, looking out of the window. The word struck a chill.

Katalin peered over her shoulder. 'Germans,' she whispered, as though she might be overheard through the window and over the grinding of the brakes. 'I thought the Germans were in the north. I thought it was the French in the south.'

But they were Germans, a motley collection of the young and the middle-aged, the lucky ones who were not on the Eastern Front, stern in their grey-green uniforms.

BAYONNE, a signboard said. The train stopped. There was shouting, the banging open of doors. '*Raus! Raus!*' Someone hammered on the window with a cane. '*Raus! Alle raus!*'

Liesel and Katalin gathered their things. 'Do we take our suitcases? Do we take everything?'

People pushed and shoved along the corridor, some with bags, some without. Passengers climbed down onto the platform, blinking like animals emerging from a stable. An old woman had to be helped down the steps while people behind her urged her to hurry, shouting at her as though it was all her fault.

On the platform, Liesel grabbed Ottilie and Martin and held them tight. 'What's happening?' she asked Viktor. 'What are they doing? Why Germans?' She suddenly had the terrible fear that they would be separated, that women and children would go one way and men would go the other. 'Stay with us, Viktor,' she pleaded, as though he had any power over such matters.

'Line up!' an officer called in French and German. 'Get in line! Papers! Have your papers ready!'

Some of the passengers struggled back on board to retrieve their documents. There was more shouting and pushing. German voices railed. Eventually queues formed, awkward, shifting queues, like sheep jostling at a gate. At the head of each queue was a desk, where a pair of officials sat in judgement. They wore uniform and silver gorgets hanging round their necks like symbols of some arcane priesthood.

'Silence!'

There was a smell amongst the waiting crowd, the smell of stale sweat, of unwashed bodies. 'People pong,' exclaimed Ottilie. Talk died down to a low muttering. In the sky above there was something new, great white birds circling and calling, a mocking, jeering sound that reminded Liesel of summers spent in Nice. 'Seagulls,' she told the children.

They edged forward, the children wedged in behind Viktor, with Liesel and Katalin standing behind them. Katalin was trembling. Liesel grasped her hand for comfort. At their backs soldiers were going through the train. They could hear them banging around, opening doors and pulling luggage down from racks. Some kind of disturbance broke out at one of the carriages. A man shouted and there was a scuffle as a figure was dragged away. Outside the station an engine revved. The story diffused amongst the waiting passengers, people muttering to one another out of the hearing of the soldiers. Chinese whispers. There were people on board without papers. Stowaways. The Germans had caught them and taken them away.

The queues shuffled forward. Passports were being stamped. Passengers were climbing back on board. Once they had got past the desks, people were going back on board! But some were being taken away, off the platform into one of the station buildings. Problems with papers, questions of identity, that kind of thing. Some were taken away but most were being let through. Relief spread though the crowd like something palpable, a kind of joy, a kind of ecstasy; but it was relief mingled with the fear that when your turn came you might not pass the test.

'Documents,' the man said, snapping his fingers under Viktor's nose. He was stout and middle-aged, with a poor complexion and thinning hair slicked over a bald head. The master race. What had he been before the war? A minor civil servant in Darmstadt or something. Now he had a uniform and a silver plate on his breast with an eagle with wings outspread and the title *Feldgendarmerie*.

Viktor laid their papers out on the desk in neat piles. 'My family – me, my wife and two children. And the children's nanny. And her daughter.'

The man turned over the pages, glancing up every now and again. Passports, French transit visas, Spanish visa. He pursed his lips and nodded at the display of documentation, then snapped his fingers again. 'Tickets.' The tickets were laid out before him, like someone disclosing a winning hand at poker. But the stakes were high and victory wasn't guaranteed.

'Jew?' he asked, looking up.

Viktor was impassive. He still had that ability, the business negotiator, keeping his cards to himself. 'Czechoslovak,' he said.

'Czechoslovakia no longer exists,' the official said. 'Now it is the Protectorate of Bohemia and Moravia.'

'Moravian, then.'

The man sniffed. 'And this one?' He tapped Katalin's temporary passport, her Nansen passport, a desolate, homeless document. Liesel could feel Katalin's fingers tighten around her arm.

'That is our nanny, the children's nanny. And her daughter.'

The man considered. He was one of those people who has been reared on the importance of pieces of paper. Official stamps were ranked in front of him like stormtroopers in the victory of bureaucracy. 'Come forward, woman,' he said.

Katalin stood in front of him, trembling. He looked her up and down, as though what he saw there might be reflected in some aspect of her dubious papers. 'What is this document?' he asked.

'It's what it says,' Viktor pointed out. 'She has no passport. The League of Nations issues these—'

'I didn't ask you.'

Katalin shrugged. 'It's all I have.'

'She's in our employ,' said Viktor.

'I didn't ask you to speak, sir,' the soldier repeated with elaborate politeness. He held up a hand to call another official over. There was a moment of consultation. They examined the passport and the various visas while Katalin looked on with terrified, rabbit eyes. And then things happened with a disturbing rapidity. A uniformed figure took her by the elbow and led her away towards a nearby hut. Marika shouted, 'Mama!' and Liesel grabbed her and pulled her closer. 'It's all right,' she said, 'It's all right.'

'Is this the woman's child?'

'It's all right,' Liesel replied. 'She's with us. We'll look after her.'

'She must go with the mother.'

'What the devil's going on?' Viktor demanded.

The official gathered up their documents and handed them to him. 'A procedural issue. The rest of you may move on.'

The soldier led Marika away, pushing her towards her mother. As they were shoved into the hut Katalin gave a desperate glance over her shoulder. 'Viktor!' she cried.

Viktor was shouting. His face was contorted with fear and anger and he was shouting: 'Her papers are in order! She's travelling on a refugee passport, a Nansen passport.'

'I suggest you move back into the train,' the official said. 'Unless you wish to find yourself in detention.'

'We left Czechoslovakia like that. She has everything that's needed! It was all right for entering France. It's all right for Spain.' People were pushing from behind. The crowd was stirring with something animal and feral, the desire to survive, the desire not to be one of the unlucky ones who were taken away, a desire to have the little incident forgotten.

'Move on, Herr Landauer,' the German said quietly. 'For your own sake, move on. Maybe the delay will only be temporary. Maybe all will be well. Just be patient.' The official was looking past him to the next family, holding out his hand for their papers, wanting to get the job done. A soldier, a mere child, it seemed to Liesel, pushed them away towards the carriage, pushed them as you might push cattle. He came into the carriage and took Katalin's and Marika's suitcases away.

'What are you doing?' Viktor demanded. 'They'll be coming back. They're coming with us.' But the youth just shrugged as he humped the cases out into the corridor.

In the compartment, Martin was crying and asking what had happened. Ottilie was telling him not to worry. 'It's just a procedural issue,' she said, not knowing what the words meant but liking the sound of them. Overhead the sound of gulls seemed jeering and malevolent.

They settled down to wait like a family in a funeral parlour, talking in whispers, breaking off sentences to stare away out of the window. Outside on the platform the queues shifted forward inexorably towards the desks, souls queuing to cross the Styx. Viktor went down the corridor to see what was happening, while Liesel sat with her arms round Ottilie and Martin, as though comforting the bereaved. Viktor was down on the platform talking to someone in uniform. Would he do something stupid, say something stupid, he who was always so balanced and thoughtful, always in possession of a plan? He was gesturing and arguing, and the official shook his head and held out hopeless hands.

'It'll be all right,' Liesel assured the children, while feeling no assurance herself. 'You know how it is with documents. Things get muddled, mistakes get made. Tatínek will sort things out.'

And then the two figures out on the platform moved. It was a sudden thing, a rapid dance of violence. Viktor made some gesture and the official shouted. A soldier ran across, unslinging his rifle and holding it across his chest. There was a moment of argument and then he drove the butt into Viktor's body. Viktor staggered backwards. Liesel cried out. Ottilie screamed. The soldier advanced, pushing and shoving with his rifle, driving Viktor back to the steps of the train. A moment later he came into the compartment with blood on his face and on his hands.

'What were you doing?' Liesel shouted at him. 'In God's name what were you doing?'

He dropped down onto the seat, shaking his head. It was as though the answer to her question was as difficult to understand as the reason for Katalin's arrest. Just a shake of the head and his fingers touching the swelling on his cheek where the rifle had hit him. 'Your responsibility is to us!' she screamed. 'Your duty is to your family! What the hell happens to us if you get taken away?'

But he sat there, shaking his head and looking at the blood in his hands, as though oblivious to his wife standing over him and screaming. 'You silly fucking bastard!' she yelled. 'That whore is more important to you than your wife and children! You silly fucking bastard!'

And then came the aftermath of the storm and they sat and waited in a strange, ethereal silence. Ottilie wept quietly in the corner. Martin turned away to look at a book. And Liesel and Viktor sat side by side, as far apart as they could get, as far apart as they had ever been, while soldiers walked up and down the platform in that mindless way that they have, striding back and forth, going nowhere. From the corridor windows you could see others down on the track, looking up at the windows of the crowded train as though peering into another world, a civilian world that they did not, would not understand.

Then the engine gave a snort of steam and the carriage jerked forward.

'We're going!'

Liesel gave a small cry, of shock, of fear. 'Where's Marika?' Ottilie cried. 'Mutti, where has Marika gone?' But there was no answer. The carriages clanked together, jerked and shuddered, and then began to move more smoothly, out of the station area, through a short tunnel and then curving past dilapidated buildings and trundling across a bridge. There was a stretch of brown water below them and then more houses and open fields.

'We're going,' Viktor said. His tone was incredulous. He looked at his wife. The blood had dried on his face, streaks of rust red down his forehead and on his cheeks. 'What could I have done?' he asked her. 'What else could I have done?'

Liesel shrugged and looked away. Suddenly she felt the dreadful enclosure of the compartment. She stood up at the window and put her face to the small opening to breathe in the outside air. There was something new borne on the breeze of their passage over the top of the pungent fumes from the engine. 'Do you smell it?' Liesel asked, turning to the children. 'Do you smell it?'

The breeze came from the west and it carried with it the scent of the ocean.

Later they talked, in hushed tones so as not to wake the children, in allusive tones, in case they were awake and listening. The train trundled on through the darkness. They were in Spain now and there was no longer the constraint of the blackout. Looking out of the window you could see the lights from the neighbouring compartments falling onto the embankment, throwing rough grass and sere trees into momentary life, like frames from an old film.

Viktor sat hunched in the darkness on the lower bunk, and she knew that he was weeping. She knew it by the set of his shoulders and the manner of his breathing and the hesitance in his speech, even though she had never known him weep before. It made her angry. 'For God's sake, pull yourself together. You'll be no use to anyone in this state. You've got to pull yourself together and think about what we might do when we get to Bilbao. You'll be completely useless like this.'

'I thought . . .' he said. 'I thought . . .'

'You don't know what you thought. You haven't known what to think for ages now.'

'I thought everything would be . . . all right. Her papers, this journey, the whole thing.'

'And us? Would *we* be all right?'

'What do you mean by that?'

'You know what I mean.'

One of the children stirred. It was Ottilie, on the bunk above. 'What time is it?' she asked.

'It's late. We've got a long day tomorrow. Go back to sleep.'

'What are you and Papi talking about? Is it Katalin? Is it that?'

'Yes, it's that. Now go back to sleep.'

The train trundled on through the Spanish night, and the sour internecine argument continued, a rapid flow of accusation and recrimination with dark currents underneath. 'Why did you do this to me, Viktor? Do you hate me so much?'

'I don't hate you, Liesel. Don't be silly.'

'You must hate me to have done this to me.'

'I loved her. It's different. Love for one doesn't mean hate for another.'

'Did you ever love me?'

'Of course.'

'And now?'

The train rattled on, slipping easily through cuttings and across bridges, passing through darkened stations, sliding through the dark night and carrying with it its cargo of secrets and lies, and silences.

'Would you weep for *me*?' she asked.

3

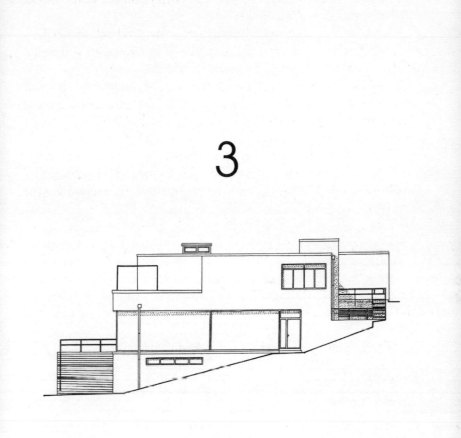

Dissolution

The news comes through from the Reichsprotektor's office: the Biometric Centre is to be closed down and all personnel are to be returned to their former occupations. It seems – a phone call to the head office in Berlin confirms this – that the Reichsprotektor does not consider the research work to be justified. If the centre can find no scientific means of distinguishing between Nordic, Slav and Semitic then the work must be flawed. That a difference exists is patent. Anyone of common sense can detect it. That is the trouble with scientists: they can't quantify and measure common sense.

So the personnel pack their suitcases and draw rail passes for Berlin and Jena and Leipzig and get transport to the station. The measuring instruments and furniture are packed away, the files stacked in boxes for transfer to Berlin, the furniture sent to offices in Město, in Prague, and in Warsaw. Technicians come and unscrew the Hollerith machines from the floor of the garage and load them onto trucks for despatch to an undertaking that will make more fruitful use of them, the new camp complex being established in Silesia near the town of Oświęcim.

She dreams. Her dreams are subtle and elusive, of flesh and hair and glass and chrome, strange chimerical dreams that are peopled by buildings and built of people. When she awakes those images flee from her as rapidly as the shadows of night are extinguished by a hot, tropic day. Outside her room the cicadas begin early in the morning in short rhythmic pulses, like an engine starting. By midday the sound is constant, a steady mechanical scream in the vegetation along the dried-up stream bed beside the garden.

Darling Hana, she writes. *The heat here is of a different order of things from that which we know at home. Dead heat, like someone trying to suffocate you . . .*

But the letters go nowhere. They accumulate in a drawer in her desk. The continent of Europe is sealed off by war, isolated from the outside world, a place of plague. 'What do you think happened?' she asks Viktor. But he can only shrug in reply.

She dreams. She dreams of cold. She dreams of glass and light, the Glass Room washed with reflection, and the cool view across the city of rooftops, the cold view through the trees, the crack of snow beneath your boots. She dreams of a place that is without form or substance, that exists only in the manner of dreams, shifting and insubstantial, diffuse, diverse:

space

glass, walls of glass

a quintet of chairs, placed with geometrical precision

a sweep of shining floor – ivory linoleum

white and black

the gleam of chrome

These things move, evolve, transform in the way they do in dreams, changing shape and form and yet, to the dreamer, remaining what they always were: *der Glasraum, der Glastraum*, the single letter-change metamorphosing from one into the other: the Glass Room become the Glass Dream.

My dear Liesel, her mother writes. Somehow – the stamp and postmarks give it away – it has been taken to Switzerland and posted there. *I can only pray that this reaches you. I can't even say who has taken it for me, in case it goes astray. So, your father and I have moved to Vienna, to be among our people . . .*

'Our people!' Liesel exclaims. 'What does she mean by that?'

Your uncle and aunt, who have stayed behind, send their love, as do the cousins. Except Ferdinand who cannot because he has gone away to war and we have heard little of what has happened to him . . .

'To war? Ferdinand? For whom does he fight? Which side is he *on*, for God's sake? Which side?'

I have some news of the Hanáková woman and her husband. It seems – the story has done the rounds and I heard it
fourth- or fifth-hand – that they have both been arrested. He
was a *Žid*, of course. They say that he has been sent to
Theresienstadt where they are gathering the Jews. Of his
wife there are only rumours. Some that she has been sent to
Germany, others that she went to Austria, to some kind of
work camp. More than that I cannot say. I am sorry not to
be more precise but these are difficult days. Of the house, I
can say that it was used as some scientific laboratory – can
you believe it? – but now it lies empty, looked after by Laník
and his sister but in the possession of the authorities. Before
we left we tried to get access to the building but were not
allowed, although your father spoke with Laník who tells
him that everything is all right.

I do hope and pray that all is well with you and Viktor
and the children . . .

Viktor spends much time away from the villa, in the city. He
visits offices and consulates, he sits at desks demanding that
people write letters, send telegrams. They are looking for a
Katalin Kalman and her daughter, last seen in Bayonne in the
German-occupied coastal zone of France. They may be in Spain,
they may still be in France, they may be somewhere, anywhere.
He doesn't know where. But he wants to find them. And cannot.
When he returns in the evening he has the hopeless look of the
refugee about him. Liesel comforts the children with lies.

She dreams. In the hot night, alone in her bed beneath the heavy
hand of a mosquito net, she dreams. She dreams of Katalin and
she dreams of Hana. And when the heat wakes her in the morning, the joy and the ecstasy of the night vanish as quickly as the
bats that spend the night circling the house in search of prey. In
the day there are only flies and lizards and this box of a room with
the white walls and a French window onto the veranda and cane
chairs and a brightly coloured bedspread in some kind of Aztec
design. Geckos cling to the ceiling as avariciously as she clings to
her memories. But memories are not constant, being, like dreams,
evanescent things that shift and change, metamorphose and

vanish. Flies circle the light fitting in the centre of the room – a hideous thing that the owner claims is Murano glass – while the wind rattles the palm trees outside. Fans whirr behind their metal cages like something aeronautical, like the engines of the flying boat that will take them – Viktor assures her – away. And above all this and below all this is the one constant: the sound of the ocean. How strange that the ocean, that played no part in her life before, that was something imagined, foreign, alien, should have come to dominate it now.

Viktor teaches Martin to play chess. Ottilie, golden-limbed from the sun, finds animals in the garden, in the carefree manner of young children forgetting all about her friend Marika. Liesel reads. Somewhere in the villa she has discovered a cache of paperback thrillers in English – Dashiell Hammett, Raymond Chandler – and she works her way through them with the aid of a dictionary. 'You'll end up speaking like a gangster,' Viktor warns her. He comes to her room and asks if he can spend the night with her. She lets him, but they have forgotten the moves, the things that they do and the things that they don't do. She knows that he is thinking of Katalin.

Storms flicker on the horizon or slam into the coast to deliver rain in torrents. Everywhere grows dank with water. In the worst downpour the roof gives up and a wet patch appears in one corner of her room so that a bucket has to be placed beneath it to catch the drips. The sonorous rhythmic sound of falling water underpins the night. Then the sun and the heat, the shriek of insects in the vegetation and the sound of music blaring from some radio in a room nearby, the strange syncopations of the Latin world, maracas rattling, guitars strumming, and voices wailing about love and loss.

The Landauer House lies empty. It is impractical for housing, although under wartime conditions housing is at a premium, and there is a move to have it demolished. Reprieve comes in the shape of draughtsmen from Messerschmitt AG. Messerschmitt have moved some of their facilities to the local airfield in order to put them as far away as possible from Allied bombing. They test new types there, in particular a fighter with a new kind of propulsion system, a shark of a machine that breathes itself along instead of thrashing at the air with propellers. Turbo, they call it. All summer the strange, elemental sound of this aircraft is heard in the skies above the city, rumbling like distant thunder, or coming nearer with a noise that seems to rupture the very air that sustains it. While draughtsmen pore over their drawing boards, fiddling with details of the aircraft's undercarriage and engine cowlings, the windows of the Glass Room shudder with the aircraft's passage overhead.

Then that project is over and those temporary interlopers collect up their equipment and load it into a truck and the house lies empty once more.

They pose for a photograph on the veranda in front of the French windows and the purple bougainvillea: two cane chairs for Viktor and Liesel, with Martin sitting cross-legged on the ground between his parents and Ottilie on the right beside Liesel. The camera, a Leica equipped with a clockwork timer, is mounted on a tripod in front of them. The timing mechanism gives the camera a personality all of its own: it buzzes for their attention.

'Smile,' Viktor tells them, and they smile self-consciously while Ottilie says, 'You can't smile on demand,' and the camera snaps at them in the manner of an ill-tempered instructor saying 'I told you so.'

Viktor gets up to reset the machine. 'One more. And this time we must try to keep still and look natural.'

'Looking natural's not natural,' Ottilie insists. Martin laughs. The camera begins to buzz and Viktor settles back in his chair. 'Now,' he says.

What the camera sees, what it preserves for posterity, is Viktor in a lightweight suit and a panama hat against the sun and Liesel wearing a floral frock and a straw hat that fails to shade her eyes. She has espadrilles on her feet. She looks rather thoughtful, as though she is considering her position here. The children wear broad-brimmed straw hats, Mexican style. Ottilie watches the camera and tries not to giggle, but Martin is looking to one side, following the sudden dart of a lizard across the floor of the veranda.

'There we are,' Viktor says when the ordeal is over and he is unscrewing the camera from the tripod, 'the last souvenir of our tropical paradise.'

307

Outside the villa the car is waiting to take them to the port, to the flying boat that will carry them to the promised land, to the future.

A house without people has no dimensions. It just *is*. An enclosed space, a box. Wind rattles round the shutters of the building. Rain falls on the terrace and batters against the walls. Snow falls and stays and melts. Water, the death of all structures, the destroyer of mountains, the solvent of the caverns and caves of the Moravský Kras to the north of the city, insinuates itself into the walls. It freezes and expands, melts and contracts, levering apart the material. Paint and concrete flake away. Tiles loosen. Steel is brushed with autumnal rust. Dust settles in the cold spaces and draughts whisper round the wainscot like the hints of what has happened there and, perhaps, may happen again. People walking along Blackfield Road glance indifferently at the long, low form of the building. Some of them wonder what has happened to the owners. Switzerland, people say; others say, Britain; some, the United States. But they don't really care because there is little opportunity to care about anything these days other than the basic worries of survival. Where is the next meal coming from? How will this coat survive another winter? How can these shoes, already wooden-soled, already sewn and patched, survive another walk? When will the war come to an end?

The great plate-glass windows of the Glass Room shake and shudder in the gales. During one storm, suddenly and with a sharp crack that no one hears, the pane at the furthest end near the conservatory is fractured right across, creating a diagonal line of reflection like a cataract in a cornea.

Laník

Laník and his sister occupy part of the house like epiphytes living on a tree, not integral to the place but depending on it for shelter. Sometimes they wander round the main room, the Glass Room, just to check. Occasionally they go through the upper floor and see that shutters are closed and doors are fast. But they live in their own world on the edge of the building, in the two rooms at the back of the garage and in the kitchens where the sister cooks and they eat together, and in the basement. The basement is a warren, a subterranean complex, like something you might discover in the Punkva Caves north of the city. It is the antithesis of the Glass Room. There all is space and light, but in the basement the ceilings are low and the doors narrow. There are dozens of rooms, one leading off from the other, going back underneath the front terrace almost as far as the street: laundry rooms, storage rooms, the boiler room with the boiler that drives the heating system of the house and the compressor that runs the air cooling. The place hums and grunts in the darkness like the engine room of a ship. As you move around you have to duck your head beneath conduits carrying electricity cables and pipes carrying water. There are water tanks and fuel tanks, and, against the front wall, the electric motors that raise and lower the windows of the Glass Room directly above, and the twin bays into which the glass panes descend. In this underground maze Laník has his stores. 'We've got to think of the future,' he tells his sister. 'We've got to think what we can do when it's all over.'

'What do you mean by that? It'll be just like it was, won't it? They'll come back and we'll be here and it'll all be like it was.'

'Don't be a daft cow. I've told you, they're never coming back. For the moment this place is ours and we've got to make the most of it. Nothing is ever going to be the same again.'

His sister is heavy and dull, a peasant woman transposed to the city with all her peasant certainties. It was those peasant certainties that, despite the insistence of uncles and aunts, led her to bring up her younger brother when their parents died within two years of each other. 'I'll manage him,' she told them, and that is what she did. She still feels that maternal devotion, but now it is mixed with something else: pride. He's a clever one, is her brother. He'll go places. 'So what do you propose to do?'

He taps the side of his nose. 'Propose to do? I'm already doing it, aren't I? Building up a little nest egg, that's what. Laying in stock for the future. Accumulating a bit of capital.'

'What do you mean by capital?'

'I mean stuff, that's what I mean. Stuff.'

Stuff, *věci*, conjures up everything that one might want. Food, blankets, paraffin, cigarettes, brandy, beer, chocolate, all the things that matter in life and that have become unobtainable. Stuff is riches. You hoard during a time of plenty and you sell during a time of dearth. That's the way.

The war seems to stretch backwards into memory and forwards into the unknown future. Maybe it will go on for ever. The inhabitants of Město scratch an existence as best they can, living off potatoes and turnips and beets, things grubbed out of the earth and tasting of the earth. They have been thrown back to the ways and means of their stone-age ancestors, hunched forms that scavenge for food, a whole city of hunter-gatherers. German troops appear and disappear, moving eastwards, always moving east. What comes back are the defeated and the damaged, human wreckage being cleared out to make space.

At U Dobrého Vojáka, The Good Soldier, the pub at the bottom of the hill past the children's hospital, Laník hears the news: the Red Army is coming. There's a small group of men – mainly workers at the armament factory down by the river – who gather there when they come off the morning shift. News and rumour battle for attention. The Red Army is coming. But when? How far away are they? Geographical terms mean little:

Carpathia, Ukraine, Belorussia, the Don, the Caucasus, Moldava. How vast the distances and the areas, how huge the numbers – of tanks, of aircraft, of soldiers and civilians, of the dead and the dying. The Russians are coming, the apocalypse is coming, but when? The men congregate round Novotný, who treats every advance of the Soviet army as a personal triumph. He talks of Operation Bagration and can even show a map of the Soviet front line swelling out towards them like a bladder filled with red paint that threatens to burst across the whole of central Europe. The Great Patriotic War he calls it.

Back at the house, Laník muses on this conversation. He may look forward to the coming of the Soviets but he harbours no illusions about them. The onyx wall clearly has value and he doesn't want it stolen. So, finally, he carries out Viktor Landauer's parting instructions, to cover the wall up behind a partition of wood and plaster. Quite what he might do with the wall once the war is over isn't certain. Ashtrays, maybe. Hundreds, maybe thousands of ashtrays.

November. A cold November morning with snow smeared into the corners of the streets and a heavy fog hanging over the buildings, turning the alleys back a century, making every pedestrian a ghost, every vehicle a monster, every building a castle keep. It deadens sound and restricts movement. It carries the cold inside the clothing of every inhabitant, in through the doorways and windows, into the houses with their meagre fires and their spare rations.

In the early morning an air raid siren gives out its call for the dead. People feel their way through the fog to the shelters and the basements. They huddle like souls in purgatory, muttering prayers or imprecations until the all clear sounds. Another false alarm. Cautiously they re-emerge from the shelters and go about their business, the eternal queuing for food, the eternal labour in the factories. The city seems to be at the very bottom of the world, invisible, starved, anaemic.

And then bombs begin to fall. They drop through the fog from nowhere without warning, without the sound of aero engines, without an alarm, without any sign at all. At the very first detonation people think of a gas explosion – sabotage perhaps. But then the explosions continue, trampling over the city like some cosmic child stamping on a nest of ants. They scream fury. If God exists he is a petulant brat. Roads are torn up, paving stones are hurled around, buildings are swept into rubble – churches, houses, shops, part of the railway station. Shrapnel rattles across the tarmac. Dust and smoke combine with the fog to make a denser kind of obscurity. And one bomb falls towards the Landauer House where Laník and his sister are cowering deep in the basement, where she is praying, reciting the litany of the saints, the rosary, anything that will give her an edge on survival; and where he is yelling at her to shut the hell up. Neither of them hear their particular bomb falling, for it is dropping towards them faster than the sound it makes. But they hear the explosion, feel the explosion, absorb the explosion into the very marrow of their bones. The building rattles to its roots. Plaster and cement crack. The plate-glass windows, those walls of frozen liquid with which Rainer von Abt (currently designing the main building of MIST, the Michigan Institute for Science and Technology) created the Glass Room, flex and burst.

As the flying debris settles, brother and sister release each other from their mutual and instinctive embrace. 'Fucking hell, that was close,' Laník mutters. His ears are humming, as though a piece of electrical equipment is being run just near. His sister is weeping. 'You should be laughing,' he tells her. 'You should be happy that we're still alive.'

Cautiously he goes to the door of the basement and looks out into the fog. A fractionally different parabola and everything might have been different. The bomb might have hit the upstairs terrace. It might have plunged through the ferroconcrete and through the white space of the Glass Room, down into the basement. Five hundred pounds of high explosive might have blown the whole perfect construction to pieces together with Laník and his sister. Instead the bomb has fallen into the garden, deep into the wet earth. Where there should be the skeletal frame of the silver birch there is only the edge of a muddy crater from which rises smoke and steam and the sulphurous stench of the underworld.

His sister comes to stand beside him. 'We were bloody lucky,' he tells her.

312

She looks at him and shakes her head. 'I can't hear,' she says, her voice unnaturally loud. She shakes her head again as though she might shake the problem away. 'There's just this noise. Like a train. I can't hear nothing.'

Later in the day Laník ventures further out. He climbs the steps to the terrace and peers inside the house. Scimitars of glass are scattered across the floor. In places the linoleum is torn. The partition hiding the onyx wall is peppered with dirt. Over the next few days he fixes canvas tarpaulins where the windows were. No longer a place of light, now the Glass Room is shrouded in the gloom of dusk. Sunlight, when it comes, cuts through the gaps between the tarpaulins like blades of glass. In the pub they say it was the Americans, the capitalist war machine wreaking random destruction on the working people of Město, but who knows? Just bombs. Random.

Soviets

Spring brings distant rumour of battle, like a storm on the horizon. To the house it is just a melting of the snow, an easing of the frost-hardened joints, a flexing of the concrete shell. People come to do business with Laník, descending the outside stairs down to the level of the basement, bringing their stories of hard luck and destitution. He listens sympathetically. You don't want to antagonise your customers. He gives credit where credit is due and accepts payment in kind. He tries to do his best. Cigarettes, paraffin, powdered egg and powdered milk, they are all there in the maze-like rooms of the basement, carefully hoarded, not like a miser with his gold but like a banker with his investment. 'You've got to take your opportunities,' he shouts at his sister. YOU'VE GOT TO TAKE YOUR OPPORTUNITIES!

The city becomes a ferment of activity – troops coming and going, civilians looking to find refuge. The Soviets have driven through Hungary and taken Budapest after a two-month siege; now Vienna has fallen and the Red Army is turning north towards Město. Over three hundred thousand troops, Novotný tells his audience in the pub. They sit in a fug of cigarette smoke, drinking watery beer and discussing the situation. Nurses often drop in at the end of their shift at the hospital. They have stories to tell of wrecked bodies brought back from the front, of amputations, of burns, of young boys with their faces half blown away or their intestines spilling out over their knees. And they hear things as well, how the fighting is going, where the front line is. The Red Army has tried to cross the Morava river south of the city but has been held up by the flooding of the valley. Cossacks have died in their hundreds.

314

The word 'Cossack' brings a thrill. Taras Bulba is reborn. Next day the nearness of the Soviets becomes a presence: a formation of twin-engined bombers, red stars on their wings, appears over the city. It is a fine spring day, a Sunday, with people walking in the parks and going to church, where they are praying, presumably, for it all to be over quickly. From the upper terrace of the Landauer House Laník and his sister watch the aircraft circle over the city. There are distant concussions and smudges of smoke in the peerless blue sky. A burst of anti-aircraft fire throws clods of dirt at the aircraft, the sound of the flak coming later, detached from the event by distance. Untouched and indifferent, the planes turn away and disappear towards the east, leaving smoke rising over the railway station.

'WE'LL HAVE TO KEEP OUR HEADS DOWN,' Laník shouts at his sister.

'Haven't you always done that?'

'IT'S THE BEST THING TO DO, ISN'T IT? WHEN PEOPLE ARE GETTING THEIRS BLOWN OFF.'

The next day German civilians begin to leave. A loudspeaker van drives through the city, its metallic voice telling them to report to the station or to the local police post, or just to get out, move north, move out into the countryside. The Germans move as best they can, in cars, with handcarts, on foot, in lorries, while the Czechs watch, sullenly.

That night the inhabitants of Město are woken by a new phenomenon, the persistent buzzing of a small aircraft over the centre of the city. It seeds the black sky with flares that cut through the darkness like electric arcs. The light exposes the Špilas fortress and the spires of the churches and the roofs of the old town to a merciless view. Some desultory machine-gun fire comes from the castle hill but the aircraft continues undisturbed in the darkness above the lights, weaving back and forth, round and round, dropping more flares and occasionally conjuring explosions down on the ground. The flares drift on the wind trailing plumes of pallid smoke.

The scene repeats itself the next night and the night after that, the same aircraft buzzing around in the darkness, coming and going as it pleases, casting the same lunar light over the darkened buildings, causing explosions where it pleases. Ivánek, little Ivan,

315

people call the visitor. There is something impudent and quirky about the presence, as though the approaching army has a sense of humour as well as a store of pyrotechnics.

Novotný knows about the aircraft, as he seems to know everything. '"Night Witches", that's what the Krauts call them. They're all piloted by women.'

In the pub, the men look at him in amazement. 'Women?'

'That's right, women. Flying pussy.'

'You're joking.'

'Don't believe me, eh? I tell you, the pilots are women, the mechanics are women, the whole squadron consists of women. This shows the heroic nature of the Soviet woman in her struggle for freedom. It also demonstrates that there is perfect equality of the sexes in the Soviet Union.'

'Equality of sexes? Don't let my missus know.'

Behind the laughter there is something else – admiration and fear. The Soviets have thrown everything into the battle, tens of thousands of tanks, thousands of aircraft, millions of men; and now even their women.

That evening Laník and his sister move all their things down into the basement. Previously they have been going down during raids but now it seems time to take shelter permanently. In the streets of the city the German forces are digging trenches, building tank traps, clearing lines of fire. Tanks and half-tracks rattle over the tramlines. Eighty-eight-millimetre guns appear at street intersections, their barrels pointing like fingers at the direction from which the Slav hordes will come. Reinforcements are coming down from the north, from Ostrava and the Polish border, lorryloads of kids who stare out uncomprehendingly from under their helmets as they pass by the grey tenements. Rumour and report come in their wake: the Red Army is in the outskirts of Berlin, fighting from house to house, from street to street towards the heart of the city; the Anglo-Americans have crossed the Rhine and have reached the Elbe. Hitler is dead.

Except for the machinery of warfare the streets of Město lie deserted. People live a troglodyte existence, scurrying out from cellars and basements into the sunlight when they can. They are on the search for the elementary things of life – candles, potatoes, bread, paraffin for cooking, a piece of soap, a box of matches, a packet of cigarettes. Money has become insignificant: the city has been thrown back a thousand years to the days of barter.

Laník understands the cost of everything. He knows instinctively how much bread you get for how many cigarettes, how much cake buys a candle. When a young woman from a nearby house comes for powdered milk for her baby the calculation is easy. He takes her down the outside steps and into the basement. Jana, she's called. Jana Kubecová. He likes the line of her jaw, the uneven turn of her mouth when she smiles. But she doesn't often smile these days and her grey eyes have the tired look of defeat about them. Six months ago her husband was deported to Germany to work in a factory near Hamburg and she hasn't heard from him for two months now. Perhaps he is dead. Perhaps he is one of the nameless victims of the bombing. Now, just when the country is on the verge of liberation, Jana looks as though she has given up. 'I can't be too long,' she says. 'I've left the baby asleep.'

Laník nods understandingly. 'We'll be quick about it, won't we? And I'll throw in a packet of cigarettes, how about that?'

She smiles her bleak little smile, that twist of resignation. 'Thanks,' she says, looking round for somewhere to put her clothes.

The end, when it comes, takes little more than a day. There is gunfire in the south and the west of the city, and smoke drifting across the skyline. Shells scream overhead to explode somewhere behind them in the northern suburbs. Aircraft fly low over the roofs, all of them with red stars on their wings, the roar of their engines dulling for a moment the chatter of gunfire. In any lull in the racket you can hear the sound of traffic on the road below the house, the rattle and roar of vehicles moving northward.

'They're going,' Laník calls down to his sister. He's standing on a chair to see out of the basement window. There's smoke over the Špilas fortress but nothing else visible. The battle for the city is almost entirely a play of sound, a cacophony of percussion, from timpani to snare drum. More shells come over, tearing the air apart and crashing over the back somewhere. The ground shakes. Plaster falls from the ceiling of the basement. Near at hand there's machine-gun fire, and the sound of an explosion. Perhaps there's fighting down by the hospital. Stuck here in the bunker beneath the Landauer House, shut away from human contact, it's impossible to tell.

'We'd better go right inside, where it's safest,' Laník suggests. He leads the way into the inner rooms of the basement, going by the light of a candle. The power is out and the guttering candle gives mere glimpses of a store room with some furniture inside, a couple of chairs from the living room, a glass-fronted cupboard, a wardrobe. The noise of battle is more distant now, the occasional crump of an exploding shell more of a visceral sensation than a perceived sound.

'What's happened to the rest of the furniture?' his sister asks as she makes herself comfortable in one of the chairs. It's one of those named after Frau Landauer herself: a Liesel chair.

'I sold it,' he says.

'It weren't yours to sell. What happens when they come back?'

'They'll not be coming back. I've told you, they don't belong here.'

'Where do you think they are?'

'The Landauers? How the hell should I know?'

'I do wonder, though. I do wonder where they've fetched up, poor things.'

'Poor things, my arse. They're rich things. Rich enough to get out, rich enough to get to somewhere safe. Why should we worry about them?'

'This is their house, after all.'

The whole building shakes to another explosion, closer this time. 'They're coming nearer!' she cries, forgetting all about the Landauer family. 'Jesus, Mary, Joseph, they're coming nearer.'

And suddenly there are footsteps overhead, the sound of people running, a sharp rattle of machine-gun fire right above them. 'Keep quiet!' Laník urges her. In the unsteady candlelight his face is flabby with fear. There is more firing, and even the sound of shouting, muffled through the concrete roof to their hiding place. They crouch in the darkness like neolithic cave-dwellers and listen to the battle above. She grips his hands for comfort. 'Joška,' she says. It's the diminutive of his name, the way he was always called at home, the name she used when she rocked him to sleep. Above

318

them the battle rages, machine guns rattling, mortars pounding, men running this way and that across the paving stones overhead. Then it falls quiet. Any noise is distant now, a background sound, the rumour of war but no longer the narrative being played out overhead. 'What's happening?'

'Shh!'

'There's someone up there still. Who do you think it is?'

'How the hell should I know?'

And then something more than mere human – giant footsteps, iron-shod footsteps, ringing on the pavement in front of the house and sounding down through the concrete spaces below to where Laník and his sister crouch in the dark. 'The Golem?' Laníková whispers, wide-eyed with fear.

'Golem my arse. That's a horse!'

In this world of mechanised warfare it seems absurd that a horse should intrude. Yet the sound is there overhead, and suddenly multiplied – half a dozen of the animals moving around, the strange syncopation of their hoofs clopping on the stone forecourt. And then something else, someone hammering on the front door two floors above their heads.

'It's the Russians,' Laník says. 'It must be the Russians. Who else can it be?' He takes the candle and heads for the stairs.

'Hey, where are you going?'

'I'm going to see. Come on.'

'I'm not going anywhere. I'm staying here. Leave me the candle.'

'Don't be idiotic. They're our liberators.'

'They're soldiers, that's what they are. Rapists.'

'Well they wouldn't be daft enough to rape *you*, would they?'

In the main room of the basement Laník pauses to rummage in a cardboard box and comes up with a bottle of clear liquid. Hefting it in his hand like a weapon, he climbs the spiral stairs that lead directly up into the kitchens.

All is quiet. The daylight is dazzling after the sepulchral dark of the basement. Cautiously he opens the door into the living area, the Glass Room that no longer is. The afternoon sun is low over the castle hill, its rays slanting like blades through the gaps in the tarpaulin that he rigged. He tiptoes across the linoleum to the stairs, then climbs up to the top floor. In the milky light of the

319

entrance hall he listens. The sound of battle has receded up the hill. Gunfire is only a sporadic sound on the afternoon air but there is a presence on the other side of the glass panels, the incongruous scrape of hooves and a distinctive snort. He thinks of cowboys, things seen in films or read about in Karl May's books, men round the campfire cooking beans. Cautiously he opens the front door.

There's a woman. That fact seems even more fantastic than horses or golems. A woman. She's standing just outside the front door, looking straight at him. She has broad Mongol features and a green forage cap with a red star that gleams like a ruby. On her shoulders – as wide as a man's – are shoulder-boards large enough to take a coffee cup and biscuits. More red stars. And medal ribbons on her khaki blouse, where Laník tries not to look because surely looking at an officer's chest, however prominent and brilliantly decorated it may be, would be disrespectful. And he doesn't want to be disrespectful, not least because she has a pistol levelled at his chest.

'Kamarád,' he says. And then adds soudruh, comrade, just to cover his options. And then tovarish. 'A present to the victorious Red Army,' he says, holding the bottle towards her. 'I give.'

The woman's eyes narrow. She isn't so sure. Without taking her eyes away from Laník's face she calls something to one of her companions. Half a dozen soldiers have come into Laník's field of vision. And horses. There are at least three of the animals tethered to the front railings of the house, contemplatively munching from piles of hay thrown on the ground in front of them. One of the animals opens its anus and, with incontinent generosity, deposits a pile of steaming turds on the travertine pavement.

'Slivovice,' he explains. 'Dobrá. Slivovice.'

'Slíva?' She smiles. Her face lights up when she smiles. From something like a frog it becomes almost beautiful.

'That's right. Slíva! Dobrá slivovice. Slíva!'

Recognisable through the fog of incomprehension are shared words. 'Dóbrá,' she cries, good, and advances on Laník to throw her arms around him and deliver a kiss on each cheek, and then a third as though to confirm the reality of the two. She smells strongly of horses and sweat and ordure. It is not an entirely unpleasant smell. It reminds Laník of his country childhood. Her skin is strangely smooth, like old silk. 'Tovarish!' she cries, 'Tovarish!' And then, disturbingly, she kisses him full on the mouth.

The Russians move in. They are battle-weary and battle-scarred, a dozen young men and three women, all with the look of Asia about their features. Where have they come from, how many thousands of miles have they crossed to reach here, this place at the epicentre of Europe? They mount a guard on the horses and hump their equipment down into the Glass Room. There are two machine guns, a mortar, three or four grenade launchers and several rifles. These they strip down and clean. Oil smears the linoleum flooring. Laník's sister – she has plucked up sufficient courage to come up from the basement – remonstrates with them and they roar with laughter at her protests.

'Your wife?' their commander asks Laník.

'My sister.' There's no misunderstanding there. The words are the same in both languages: *zhena*, wife; *sistra*, sister. The officer nods thoughtfully. What is she thinking? She is square and tough, her face lined and her skin burnished by months in the sun and the wind. You can imagine her standing outside a yurt on a desolate Mongolian plain, or riding a horse bare-back into battle. It's difficult to guess her age. Is she in her forties? Is she that old? '*Starshyna*,' she says when Laník points to her rank badges. It's another word he understands. *Staršina*, sergeant-major. She gives off the smell of stables and ordure, the smell of thousands of miles living with the animals, living in barns, living in trenches, living like a gypsy. 'Rostov, Odessa, Jassy, Kishinev, Bucharest,' she tells Laník. 'Budapest, Bratislava. On, on, on.' She waves her hand at the memory of all those different places. 'Always men and women die but always more come. Patriotic duty,' she says. Laník agrees. He has no choice, really, for she is holding his hand and staring into his eyes and nodding as though she has already made up her mind about patriotic duty.

'She fancies you,' his sister tells him when he gets away for a moment. 'I'd watch it.'

'We've got to get them out of here,' he says.

'I don't see how.'

'At least keep them out of the basement. If they see what we've got down there they'll have it all. What are you going to give them for supper?'

'Dumplings, stew, what do you think?'

'Don't put too much meat with it. It'll make them suspicious.'

'We haven't got too much meat.'

'Keep the *slivovice* coming anyway. It'll take their minds off anything else.'

In the Glass Room the Russians have finished their work and are sitting about smoking and laughing. The two young women are lumping Ludmilas with faces like potatoes and hands like hams. And then there's the sergeant-major with her ripe apple of a face and her leering eyes. She has been in the bathroom upstairs and had some kind of wash. Her hair – as black as axle grease – has been combed. There is even a hint of something red smeared across her lips. When the food is ready she indicates that Laník should sit down beside her. The great circular dining table is lit with candles. It is a feast of the absurd, Laník and his merry men reflected in the blackness of the one remaining window of the Glass Room. There are toasts as they eat, to Comrade Stalin, to the commander-in-chief Comrade Malinovsky, to Comrade Churchill and to the brand new Comrade Truman, to the recently deceased Comrade Roosevelt. After the meal they clear their equipment to the side of the Glass Room while one of the soldiers gets out an accordion and begins to play. Some of them stand up to dance but if the expectation was that they would execute some wild Cossack dance with stamping and leaping the reality is quite different: 'Yes Sir, That's My Baby', the accordionist plays and two couples, two men and the two girls, the two clumsy Ludmilas, begin to shuffle round the Glass Room for all the world like couples in a bar in London or Paris. When the couples swap over, so that the men are each dancing with one of the girls, there are hoots of lascivious laughter and glances in the direction of their sergeant. 'Dance,' they shout, 'dance!' and the word is the same in both languages so that Laník knows his fate even before she shrugs and pulls him to his feet to more laughter.

'Yevgeniya,' her voice says loudly in his ear as she grabs him round the waist. They shuffle across the floor to a storm of applause. 'You call me Yevgeniya.'

'Yevgeniya,' he repeats dutifully.

'And you?'

'Laník.'

She practises the name, her breath hot and alcoholic against his cheek. 'Lyanik,' she says, 'Lyanik.' The dancing goes on and the *slivovice* goes down, and as the music relaxes so does Sergeant-Major Yevgeniya's grip on Laník get tighter.

'You are rich man, Lyanik?' she whispers. 'This big house yours? You are *kulak*?'

'No, I'm poor,' he insists. 'The caretaker, that's all. *Proletář.*'

'Ah! *Proletarij.*' She hugs him tighter. '*Proletarij* is good. You are child of revolution.' After a while she releases him for a moment and claps her hands. 'It's late,' she calls, like a mother with her children. 'There's work to do tomorrow.' Laník tries to move away but she is too quick for him. Her hand darts out and grabs his wrist. The men are laying straw pallets out on the floor of the Glass Room and Sergeant-Major Yevgeniya has become incongruously girlish, pulling Laník nearer and smiling coyly. His heart sinks. 'You come?' she asks.

'Where?'

'With me? You show us the rooms.'

Some of the men are watching, grinning. The two Ludmilas wait with their kitbags over their shoulders and their faces without expression. Reluctantly Laník leads them up the stairs to the top floor where all is quiet and placid, where the candle that Yevgeniya carries throws unsteady shadows across the wall, where the ghosts of the Landauer family walk. 'Here,' he says, throwing open the door to one of the rooms. 'You can sleep here.'

The two Ludmilas hump their kitbags in and close the door. Laník is standing there in the corridor, alone with Sergeant-Major Yevgeniya. 'In here,' he suggests, pushing open a second door. It is Frau Landauer's room, *was* Frau Landauer's room, a space where there once was her dressing table and wardrobe, her clothes, her make-up and jewellery, the very stuff of her life; where now there is only the bare walls and a bedframe without a mattress.

Yevgeniya pushes him in and closes the door. She looks him up and down, her small eyes shining from deep within their folds of flesh. 'Lyanik,' she says, 'I kill many men, but I won't kill you.'

He laughs. It isn't so funny but he laughs all the same. Downstairs in the Glass Room the Russian soldiers settle down for the night. Further down, in the basement, Laník's sister locks her door and climbs into her bed. On the top floor, in Liesel Landauer's old room, Laník is enveloped in the smell of horses and the scent of ordure, gripped by armpits and groin, enveloped by lips and legs. He feels that he might suffocate, that he might explode, that he will die. For the moment it is apparent that the war is finally over, but it is not certain what has taken its place.

4

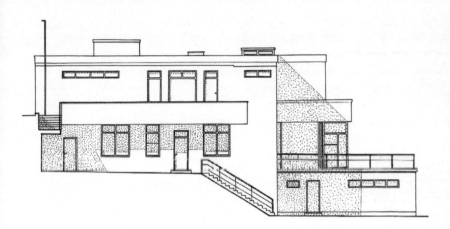

Tomáš

Tomáš stands at the windows, smoking and looking at the view. Behind him the children go through their exercises. A dozen mats are laid out for this purpose along the floor in front of the onyx wall and Zdenka is putting the children through their paces, although 'paces' is rather strong a term for what they do – leg-lifting, leg-bending and stretching, turning this way and that with all the difficulty and awkwardness of geriatrics. When the session is over the children's parents will come and collect them, and Tomáš and Zdenka will be able to talk together for a while.

They will talk about the past or about the future. Tomáš does not wish to talk about the past, or the future, or anything temporal. For Tomáš there is no such thing as time. He is a doctor (a paediatrician at the children's hospital down the road) but a small, hard core of his mind is that of a philosopher rather than a physician. The philosopher has decided that past and future are both illusions, that there is only a continuous present, and the present is this view through the window over the city, this cigarette, this vague and milky reflection of Zdenka walking backwards and forwards behind him urging her charges on: 'Come on, Miloš! You know you can do it. That's right Zdenka,' (another Zdenka, the name is not uncommon) 'show us what you can do. How happy your mother will be when she sees what progress you have made.'

The children are broken approximations of what it means to be a child, polio victims, creatures with twigs and sticks for limbs, and pale hospital faces. In the hospital down the road there are others even worse, one of them in an iron lung, contemplating a future in which the machinery will breathe for her, and people will

327

feed her and the world will be something that she sees inverted, in a mirror. Alenka is her name. The irony is not lost on Tomáš. Alenka is Alice, and her life will be lived through the medium of a looking glass.

If there is no future, Tomáš thinks, then Alenka's life ought to be more bearable.

He smokes and looks. He has opened one of the window panes and can blow the smoke out into the garden, which is necessary because otherwise Zdenka would not allow him to smoke. 'You shouldn't smoke in here,' she said when he first lit a cigarette. 'It is against the regulations.'

Regulations. The city, the country, probably the whole world (having travelled little, Tomáš is unsure about the matter) is pinned down by regulations. His own view is that regulations are designed to control the future and if we all live in an eternal present then regulations are, by definition, powerless. When he tells Zdenka this she sighs impatiently like a mother with an unruly child, and tells him that he'll get himself into trouble one day. It seems absurd that Zdenka should be a mother to him. She is only five foot three inches tall and with a build as slight as a child's. A dancer's body. And yet Tomáš imagines her giving birth to him. Sometimes when he touches her intimately, that is what he imagines: Zdenka as both mother (his own mother died during the war) and lover, *matka* and *milenka*.

Tomáš smokes and looks. He would like to live in ignorance of both the past and the future, forever at the pinnacle of time, the eternal present, this moment in what he calls the Glass Room, with this cigarette and this view over the city.

'Now, one more time,' Zdenka calls to her charges behind him. 'Are you ready?'

He first met Zdenka in this very place, the gymnasium that he always calls the Glass Room. It was two years ago, when he had reason to visit the physiotherapy department to follow the progress of one of his patients and discovered this new member of staff on duty. This was, she told him, her first job since abandoning her childhood ambition, which was to be a ballet dancer. From classical dance to recuperative physiotherapy did not seem too much of a leap (that was her joke) and so here she was trying to help children to walk when what she had wanted to do was fly.

He laughed at her joke. There was something tantalising about this small, energetic young woman. How was it that she had so much energy when he himself felt almost debilitated by his work? She seemed to have an optimism that he did not share, a belief in the future that was quite contrary to his. They discussed his patient and then they talked of other things – her ambitions, his lack of them; her hopes, his despair. She had come from a town in the north towards the Polish border, a place called Hranice, which itself means 'border'. 'It's the border between the north and south of the continent,' she told him proudly when he asked. 'On one side all the streams run north to the Baltic, on the other side all the streams run south to the Danube and the Black Sea. So I was born at the very watershed of the continent.' From that moment on, Tomáš has always associated Zdenka with water. My *rusalka*, my nymph, he thought of her. Within a few minutes of meeting her he had invited her for a drink. Perhaps he wanted more of her hopes and ambitions. Within a few days they were seeing each other regularly. Within a week they were making love.

Ondine

One of the children in the hospital, one of Tomáš's patients, suffers from a condition that no one has ever seen before. This child is incapable of breathing when she is asleep. When she is awake all is well and she can move her ribs, move her diaphragm, ventilate her lungs, but as soon as she falls asleep she stops breathing. The only solution is to have her sleep on a ventilator. If there isn't the ventilator she will die of asphyxiation. This is a mystery to the medical profession. It is known as the curse of Ondine.

Ondine was a water nymph, and therefore an immortal, who fell in love with the handsome, but mortal, Palemon. Although he was already betrothed to the noblewoman Berta, Palemon was prepared to sacrifice his marriage for the love of Ondine. There was, however, a catch. There is always a catch, in stories as in life. For when a nymph has a child by a mortal she has to sacrifice her immortality. Naturally Ondine was afraid of this, afraid of becoming pregnant and thereby losing her eternal youth and beauty. But Palemon reassured her. 'My every waking breath shall be my pledge of love and faithfulness to you,' he vowed. So the two lovers married and in due course Ondine had a child. At first Palemon was delighted. Now he had a son and heir, and also the most beautiful of wives. But with the birth of the child, Ondine began to change. She was a mother now as well as a lover, and the eternal youth of a nymph had vanished. She had become a mortal like any other woman, subject to age and decay.

One day Ondine discovered Palemon lying naked in the arms of his former fiancée. Thus betrayed, she fled back to the river to die of grief, but not before she had summoned her last bit of immortal magic: she woke Palemon and cried, 'You vowed that your every waking breath would be a pledge of faithfulness. So be it. For as long as you are awake, you shall breathe; but should you ever fall asleep, your breathing shall cease.'

That is the curse of Ondine.

Tomáš knew this story because of the affliction that his patient suffered from; Zdenka knew it from the piano piece by Maurice Ravel. 'Show me how you dance,' Tomáš asked her early in their relationship, but at first she refused. That part of her life was behind her, she told him. Teaching dance was all she allowed herself (twice a week in the evenings she conducted classes there in the gymnasium). However he insisted and one day after she had finished work and the others in the clinic had gone home, she produced the gramophone that she used in her classes. The music she chose was the piece called 'Ondine', from Ravel's suite for piano entitled *Gaspard de la Nuit*. 'It's what I danced for my final presentation at ballet school,' she explained.

She placed the gramophone beside the onyx wall and plugged it in, then went to change. When she came back she was transformed. What had been a small, energetic nurse in white coat and trousers had metamorphosed into something mythic and magic – a barefoot, barelegged, gracile creature with white limbs and flowing seaweed hair. She was wearing a shift of translucent green silk and he could see the shadow of her body through the material almost as though he could see her soul inside her.

She curtseyed before him. The music began, a liquid trilling of notes, like water flowing over stones. If Tomáš had never quite believed in her being a nymph, at that moment he was convinced. Zdenka moved, flowed like weed in the stream, like reflections of sunlight on the surface of a pool. And the room in which she moved, the Glass Room with its transparent walls, its chromium pillars, its onyx wall, its pools of light, seemed a kind of tank in which the nymph was trapped. She darted this way and that as though trying to find a way out, but always she came back to the centre of the room, to the onyx wall and to the chair where Tomáš sat. He was entranced. He was also sexually aroused. And it was the moment when he fell in love with her.

Tomáš applauded when the music had trickled away to silence and she had completed her dance. The clapping of a single pair of hands inevitably sounds ironic, but there was no irony in Tomáš's mind. What he had seen was one of the most wonderful visions of his life, a blend of abstract beauty and pure, feminine loveliness, something mythic and yet at the same time physical and real. Zdenka bowed before him, holding out her hands as though to display what little she possessed.

'Come,' he said. She stepped forward on bare, narrow feet and folded herself onto his lap like a cat. He could feel her body through the thin material of her dress – the corrugations of her ribs, the undulation of her spine, the small nodes of her breasts. 'Can we make love?' he whispered in her ear.

'Of course not! How can we make love here? This is where I work.'

'Then where can we go?'

She didn't know. She wanted to make love to him as well, but they had nowhere to go. The housing shortage meant that he still lived in his parents' house, while Zdenka had a room in the nurses' hostel at the bottom of the hill. Men were not allowed in the women's section. So they had nowhere that they could safely go and make the love that was even now spilling out of them. That was why, despite the fact that anyone might come in and catch them, the caretaker maybe, or one of Zdenka's colleagues coming back to check on something, they made love there and then on the floor of the Glass Room.

Tranquillity

Tomáš always referred to the gymnasium as the Glass Room.
There is a language problem here. The word he used for room,
pokoj, can also mean peace, tranquillity, quiet. So when he said
'the glass room' he was also saying 'the glass tranquillity'. Thus
does one language fail to make itself felt in another. He loved the
Glass Tranquillity. The place appeared quite without reference to
period or style – just a space of light and stillness where, when his
work was over, he could be with Zdenka. Sometimes when she
held her dance classes after work he would come and watch. The
classes earned Zdenka extra money. The arrangement was quite
irregular but some of the dancers were children of party officials
so everyone turned a blind eye to the use of a state-owned building for a private enterprise. Tomáš would come down and find a
seat in a corner of the room and watch the young girls going
through their exercises and their routines. He enjoyed watching
their efforts, sometimes ungainly, sometimes genuinely beautiful.
It was a relief from always dealing with children who had been
crippled by disease. He loved the sound of their chattering when
they relaxed. They chattered like swallows, he thought.

After one of these classes, when the children had all gone, he
persuaded Zdenka to dance naked for him. 'I feel shy,' she
protested.

'But that's absurd. I see you naked every time we make love.'

'That's not the same.'

But still he insisted. And, he explained, the Glass Room, the
Glass Tranquillity, demanded such openness and honesty. He
opened the curtains so that the evening light shone in on her and

the roofs of the city lay there as witness. 'I want you to dance before the whole city. Before the city and the world.' Of course this was purely symbolic. Even if they could see the house, no one could possibly have made out the naked figure moving behind the panes of the Glass Room. Nevertheless there was this feeling of total exposure, as though she was dancing naked on a stage before thousands of strangers. This excited Tomáš and intimidated Zdenka. She danced poorly at first, the motion of her pale body out of sympathy with the music, and then the dance took over and she underwent a sea change before Tomáš's eyes. She became – the metamorphosis seemed real – a water creature, her limbs undulating in the flow of music, the sea grass of her hair tossed around as though by waves. Her breasts were medusas pulsating with the rhythms of the ocean, her limbs were tentacles, her eyes were pearls. When she finished she lay down before him as though cast up on a beach, cold and wet; and the flock of hair between her thighs was like a marine organism, an anemone, hiding in a crevice of the rocks, ready to open its mouth and engulf any creature that strayed near.

After that they made love more passionately than ever before, there and then on the floor of the Glass Room, in front of the sightless city and the sightless world.

'Do you know this was a private house once,' Zdenka tells him. Tomáš tries to silence her. He doesn't want to hear.

'It was even famous, in fact.' She is putting away equipment that she has been using with one of the children, an exercise machine for strengthening the leg muscles. 'There's a woman who came round yesterday who told me about it. The Landauer family. You've heard of the Landauers. They used to make cars. Before the war.'

Tomáš owns a Trabant. The Trabant is the present. Landauers are the past, a mythic epoch of luxury and freedom, but the Trabant, small, noisy and with a poor performance, is the present. The future is beyond imagining.

'So apparently this family were very, you know, artistic, and they had this house built by some famous German architect. He builds skyscrapers in America now. And this is the house he built for them. That's what this woman told me.'

Tomáš finds it very disturbing that the Glass Room possesses a past, that it has not always been this sterile gymnasium, this fish tank in which Zdenka dances for him, this room of glass and quiet. Did a family really live here once? Were there children playing games – as opposed to the children who come now with their ruined bodies to do exercises that will never help them play games?

'She's interesting, this woman who told me. Part of some committee. Committee for Heritage or something.'

'I don't want to know.'

'You must meet her.'

'Why should I be interested in finding out about the past? The past is an illusion.'

Berta

Zdenka is not the only woman in Tomáš's life. There is also a woman called Eve (she uses the English form Eve, rather than the Czech Eva or Iva) who is a journalist on a local newspaper.

It is much easier for Tomáš to see Eve than it is for Tomáš to see Zdenka, because Eve has her own apartment in the centre of the city. It is only one room and only has one bed, but that does-n't matter to them because they make love quickly and without particular passion, Eve instructing Tomáš on what she wants him to do and Tomáš enjoying it in a rather detached way, as though it were a medical process of some kind, something that brings physical relief from a kind of pain. But all the time he is with Eve he feels guilt about Zdenka, his Ondine.

'Would you mind if I had another lover?' he enquired once, when he and Eve had just finished making love and were lying in each other's arms, sharing a cigarette.

She shrugged. 'Why do you ask? *Do* you?'

'No. I just wondered.'

'I wouldn't mind at all. In fact I see Oddball occasionally.' Oddball, *podivín*, was her nickname for her editor. It was quite a surprise for Tomáš to hear this. He had met Oddball a few times. He seemed middle-aged and rather unprepossessing.

'You do?'

'Once or twice a month, maybe. The poor fellow's marriage is finished and he's quite appealing and when he made a pass at me I thought, well why not? He's very considerate, he's never going to cause any trouble, and besides, it helps in my work.'

'How does it help?'

'He gives me the assignments I want, the stories that interest me. And when I go away on a job he always gets me the best hotel.'

As Tomáš had accompanied Eve on a number of these trips he realised that he was in some way compliant in this clandestine affair with Oddball. The thought amused him, and spurred him to confess: 'Actually there *is* another woman.'

Eve took the cigarette from between his lips, drew on it and blew smoke towards the ceiling. 'I assumed there was.'

'She works in the hospital. A physiotherapist. And a dancer.'

'I bet that makes her interesting in bed.'

He laughed. Eve was so much a woman of his type. There was none of the usual jealousy and envy, nothing underhand about her. Now that he knew about Oddball and she knew about Zdenka he felt even closer to her. Yet none of this affected Tomáš's sense of guilt because the point was not so much whether Eve minded his having another woman, as whether Zdenka would mind. He didn't dare ask Zdenka the question he had asked Eve because he already knew the answer – she would be destroyed. Like Ondine, she would die.

So why, Tomáš wonders, does he betray Zdenka? Perhaps, he reasons, because by risking the curse of Ondine he can inject some meaning into his life. It is the curse of not breathing that attracts him. Breathing is so fundamental to human life, as fundamental as the heart. The words involved in the act of breathing sound in his mind: inspiration, respiration, expiration. Birth, life and death. So Tomáš thinks of Zdenka as Ondine, with all the undulating beauty of the name, but above all he courts that dreadful curse, and fears it if Zdenka ever discovers his unfaithfulness with Eve.

Paris

In the Glass Room, Zdenka marshals the children with great skill. Having no child herself she seems to consider all her charges to be in some way her own children. She lives their moments of success, feels their moments of despair, provides the necessary impetus to pick themselves up and continue in the face of adversity.

'You shouldn't allow yourself to get so involved,' Tomáš warns her. 'In this business you must keep your distance. Otherwise you won't be any use to them.'

But she cannot keep her distance. Each child's tragedy is her own. Sometimes, after working with the children, she is in tears. But only ever when they have gone. Never does she allow them to see her upset. Tomáš, on the other hand, is never in tears. 'My job is to try to mend,' he says, 'not to weep.'

One day he came to the gymnasium to find Zdenka in a state of great excitement. She had just been nominated to attend a conference in Paris on polio and its treatment. It was a large international gathering of experts from around the world and to be selected to go was a great honour.

'But that was what *I* came to tell *you*,' Tomáš said.

'What do you mean?'

He waved a piece of paper. '*I* have been selected to attend a conference on poliomyelitis in Paris.'

She looked at him in amazement. 'The same one?'

Her naivety amused him. She was brisk and energetic at her job, fragile and sylph-like in her dancing or in his arms, and credulous in her dealings with the world. She believed in progress. She thought the Party had the best interests of the people at heart. She

338

thought that the future would exist and it would be better than the present; and that the past had existed and it was worse. She thought that there was meaning in life. And she thought that there might be two different poliomyelitis conferences at the same time in the same city. 'I'm sure there's only one,' he insisted.

'Then what a wonderful coincidence that we've both been selected.'

That was another mark of her naivety: she assumed that their both being selected was purely fortuitous, but in fact it had all been arranged by Tomáš. His own attendance was almost automatic: he was the leading expert in polio at the hospital and as two doctors would be going it was inevitable that the Head of Paediatrics would want to take him along. Albert Sabin, an American of Polish origin, would be talking about his trials of an oral vaccine against polio. This was a live vaccine, which promised to be more effective in developing immunity in the subject than the Salk vaccine. But a live vaccine also brings the danger of inducing a real infection in some children. It was a matter of balance: of balancing the many protected lives against a few that might be destroyed. That was what particularly interested Tomáš. How do you make such judgements?

'There's quite a lot about physiotherapy on the programme as well,' the professor added thoughtfully when they were discussing the conference. He turned over the pages of typescript that he had received from the organisers.

'Physiotherapy is very important,' Tomáš agreed.

'Perhaps someone from the Physiotherapy Department ought to go?'

That was Tomáš's opportunity to suggest that a certain Zdenka Vondráková, being responsible for most of the remedial work with the polio patients, might be an appropriate delegate. He smiled as he told the professor this. It was a knowing smile, which made the situation clear without mentioning anything specific.

'That sounds a good idea,' the professor agreed. 'She's a Party member, isn't she? That'll be a help in getting an exit permit for her.'

Tomáš never told Zdenka that he had made her attendance at the conference possible. He preferred to preserve her belief in the wonderful, fortuitous coincidence of existence, the miracle of contingency.

The trip to Paris was Zdenka's first time out of the country and only the second time that Tomáš had been to the West (the other time was to Vienna when it was still a divided city and he was in the army). They found the city bright and colourful, whereas their home town and their country seemed dull and monochrome. The hotel was magnificent. 'Each room has its own bathroom. And there's free soap and toothpaste,' Zdenka cried, as though bathrooms, soap and toothpaste were the height of capitalist luxury. They also discovered that it was easy for Zdenka to move her things into Tomáš's room where there was a double bed of gargantuan proportions. And thus they had their five days of almost marital cohabitation, the strange experience of making love in a bed, and of falling asleep in one another's arms and waking the next morning to find the other still there, creased and warm with sleep. Zdenka was small and fragile and she seemed even smaller and more fragile in that large bed, so light that she seemed to float above Tomáš as he lay on his back, so slender that he feared she might break apart as he lay on top of her. And yet, despite her lightness, he felt almost smothered by her presence, and longed to be back with her in the Glass Tranquillity where they could make love like casual acquaintances, without the awful ties of obligation.

'I hope you are going to marry that girl,' the professor remarked on the third day of the conference, when they were sitting in one of the lecture rooms waiting for a talk to begin. 'She seems a lovely young thing.'

Tomáš agreed that she was a lovely young thing – 'a *rusalka*,' he said, while thinking to himself, an ondine – but he didn't say anything about marriage. Marriage was the future and these five days with Zdenka – Zdenka naked at the basin in their shared bathroom, Zdenka emerging from the shower with her hair like waterweed down her back and across her face, Zdenka still wet from the shower climbing into his arms and letting herself be carried to the bed, where they made love – were the present.

When they got back from Paris Zdenka almost wept. 'We

could have stayed,' she said. 'We could have found work easily. They want doctors and physiotherapists. We could have stayed and found work and been together in freedom.'

'What has happened to your admiration of the Party?' Tomáš asked.

'I'm not thinking of the Party, I'm thinking of us.'

But the five days in Paris have become the past, and for Tomáš the past does not exist. There is only now, this pinnacle of time, the eternal present, this moment in what he calls the Glass Room, the Glass Tranquillity, with this cigarette and this view over the city.

He turns from the window. The last of the children has struggled up the stairs with the help of its mother and the place is empty but for him and Zdenka. 'What is going to happen to us now?' she asks.

'Now?'

'Yes, now.'

How can he talk about *now* when now is all that there is? You cannot talk about something except by contrast with other things. You cannot paint something unless it is different from its surroundings. The Russian painter Malevich attempted it, and what did he get? A white canvas with a white square on it. 'Now we are going to make love,' he says. 'That's what we do isn't it, when we are here? This is the perfect place to make love. It has no points of reference, no memories, no illusions. It just is.' He looks round the bare space, the chromium pillars, the white walls and cream floor, the curve of wooden panels that closes off the area they use for individual treatment, and the strange wall of patterned stone which is the only irregularity in the place. And as he looks Zdenka begins to weep.

Tomáš is confused by her weeping. He goes to comfort her but she throws him off. 'You're so cold,' she accuses him. 'In Paris you were warm and loving, but here you're so cold. And I want the warm and loving you, not this awful cold one.' And then she stops, and, having turned her head away from him, suddenly looks at him directly. 'There's another woman, isn't there? You keep me in this state of uncertainty because you've got another woman.'

Tomáš smiles. 'Don't be absurd.'

'Why is it absurd? In Paris you had only me and you were as loving as a man can be. Here you are distant and cold, so it must mean you don't have only me. There must be another woman.'

He laughs. 'That's woman's logic.' He reaches out and takes her hand and draws her to him. For a moment she is soft and supple in his arms. Then she pulls away.

'No,' she says. 'No!'

It is the first time they have ever had an argument. Tomáš doesn't wish to take part but it seems that he has no choice. The argument is about their future and when Tomáš says that there is no future Zdenka merely gets more angry. 'Of course there's a future. There's a future in which I should become a mother and you a father. There's a future in which we should get our names on the housing list and make a home. There's a future in which we grow old together. But none of that seems likely, does it? Not with you the way you are!'

Despite his protests, she continues. She has been thinking this over, ever since they got back from Paris, perhaps even before they went to Paris. Her idea is that they need a break from one another. They should be apart for a while, get things in perspective, wait and see what both of them want. Thus, soon after the delights of Paris, here in the cool light of the Glass Room, they seem to be slipping apart. It is all unbelievable to Tomáš. This is not the way he should lose Ondine, not with a banal discussion about commitments and obligations, not without that terrifying curse.

Over the days things change a little. They talk to each other on the phone, exchange words in a meeting at the hospital, and finally meet up for a drink. The present is losing the malign influence of the past and Paris is slowly becoming nothing more than a memory. They talk about it as though it is a piece of fantasy with little grounding in real life. They even recall different things, Tomáš remembering a visit to the Panthéon that Zdenka denies happened, Zdenka a market on the Île de la Cité where there was a stall selling animals, an incident which Tomáš denies. She insists. There were tropical fish, caged birds, mice, even a sleek and self-sufficient rat; but he cannot recall the place. They laugh about their different memories of these events, but for him all this is symptomatic of what he believes, that memory and imagination are the same thing. He has need to imagine the Panthéon, the temple to no gods whatsoever; Zdenka has need to recall brilliantly coloured fish swimming round and round in a tank.

History

'I've got a story to do in your part of the world,' Eve tells Tomáš one evening.

'In Židenice?' He assumes she must be referring to the area where his parents' house is, but that is such a dreary and uninteresting part of the city that he cannot imagine what the story might be.

'No, the hospital. Actually the Department of Physiotherapy.' She says it deliberately, aware of the significance of what she is saying. 'I wonder whether I will meet your dancer.'

Tomáš has told Eve all about Zdenka, everything except her name. He has told her about the dancing and about their making love there on the floor of the Glass Room, and about the trip to Paris and what has happened since. Is that a betrayal of Zdenka? But it seems to Tomáš that confession to Eve, for whom he has feelings of companionship that are quite unlike the intense feelings of a lover, is not betrayal in any real sense. His relationship with Eve has all the intimacy of that between a doctor and a patient, where anything may be said and all will be held secret.

'How will you know if you do meet her?' There are, after all, a number of young women who work in the department, five, to be exact, along with three men.

'Oh, I'll know your little dancer all right.'

Tomáš suddenly has a desire to see the two of them together, to see his Ondine and his Berta talking to one another, the one all-knowing, the other ignorant. 'Maybe I'll be there. Maybe I'll show you round. If it's about the physiotherapy department you ought to have one of the doctors on hand.'

'That's up to you. But it's not about the department as such – it's about the building.'

'The building?'

'It's a most important house in architectural terms. Didn't you know that? The Landauer House. There are people who want to restore it, turn it into some kind of museum. The State Committee for Architectural Heritage or something. Haven't you heard? Well, we're going to do a piece on it.'

'I've heard something about it, but who cares what it was in the past? Now it's a gymnasium for the physiotherapy department. That's what it's for. It's valuable as a gymnasium but it's impossible as a house and worthless as a museum. Museums are just like churches, they're memorials to something that's finished – the past or religion. Either is pure fantasy.'

'You ought to join the Party with views like that.'

'You know I couldn't join the Party. The Party believes in history.'

It seems absurd that they should argue about something so abstruse, so arcane and obscure as Party doctrine, but they do, Eve claiming that the Party believes in exactly Tomáš's kind of history, a fantasy history, a history of imagination and forgetting, and Tomáš exclaiming that she is wrong, that the Party really thinks that it is right, that history is, for the true believer, a kind of scientific laboratory in which the laws of dialectical materialism are worked out. The difference between this argument with Eve and his argument with Zdenka is that this one ends in laughter, and the two of them taking off their clothes and getting into Eve's narrow bed; whereas the argument with Zdenka remains at the very core of their separation.

Zdenka

For Zdenka the Glass Room is a place of dreams, a cool box where you can project your fantasies and sit and watch them. When she was a child her mother used to laugh at her, call her a dreamer, tell her she always had her head in the clouds and the trouble with having your head in the clouds was that you can't see where to put your feet. Later, when Zdenka became a promising dancer at the ballet school in Olomouc, her mother would say that a dancer with her head in the clouds was all right as long as she didn't fall off the stage. One day Zdenka did precisely that – she fell off the stage and broke her ankle. The break was complex and it took some months to heal, more months still to return to something like normal. But never again could she go on points. Dancing was still possible, of course, the modern dance of her heroine Isadora Duncan or Martha Graham, but her ambition, her dream of going to Prague and perhaps from there to the Soviet Union, to dance with the Bolshoi or the Kirov, was at an end. So Zdenka shrugged her shoulders (narrow, fragile, sculptured like an anatomy model) and changed the direction of her life. She abandoned the dream of dancing and took a course in physiotherapy and dreamed of helping crippled children to regain their mobility.

Dreams are like memories. Zdenka remembers Paris. She remembers walking down the Champs-Élysées and turning into the avenue Montaigne. Tomáš knew who Montaigne was – the first truly modern writer, he told Zdenka; a sceptic and a humanist – but had never heard of Isadora Duncan. Zdenka knew that Isadora Duncan was memorialised in bas-relief on the façade of the Théâtre des Champs-Élysées, but had no idea that a writer called Montaigne ever existed. So she recalls that moment for standing opposite the theatre and seeing the image of her heroine up on the façade, whereas Tomáš recalls the moment for the lecture that he delivered on Montaigne's scepticism, his doubting of history and advocacy of imagination.

Zdenka dreams of Paris. Her dreams are more than mere sightseeing. They are also dreams of an ideal world in which she and Tomáš might live in intimacy and harmony for the remainder of their lives.

'I had a wonderful time in Paris,' she tells the woman from the Committee for Architectural Heritage, who has come once again to look round the building. The last time the woman came she was unable to see the gymnasium because there was a callisthenics class going on and without a proper authorisation from the hospital authorities entry was not possible. But this time there is no class and the woman has brought with her all the authorisation that one could wish for.

'It's a wonderful city,' the woman agrees, 'especially when you are young. And in love. Were you in love?'

'I was,' Zdenka admits, 'but it didn't last.'

'Often that is the way with Paris.'

The representative from the Committee for Architectural Heritage is a fine-looking woman in her fifties. That is Zdenka's estimate. But not the kind of fifty that her mother is – a fat and shapeless fifty with slack grey hair, tired features and confusion in her eyes. This woman is slim and elegant, alive. Her face is that of a person who understands things, a face etched in experience. Zdenka feels she will understand about Tomáš.

'There was this most marvellous coincidence,' she explains to the woman as they go down the curving stairs into the Glass Room. 'My boyfriend was on the same conference as me. Can you imagine that? We had five marvellous days together.'

The woman smiles. It is a smile both sympathetic and knowing. 'But it didn't last.'

Zdenka returns the smile. It is, she knows, a smile without humour. People are practised in this expression; it is almost a national characteristic. 'No, it didn't last. He's a doctor here at the hospital, in fact. That's why we went to Paris, to the conference.

But now we've sort of drifted apart. Do you think that was a result of being together in Paris?'

Why does she ask the woman this? Why does she let these small pieces of intimate knowledge slip out? Once said, words cannot be unsaid. The woman cannot unknow these facts now – that Zdenka has broken with her boyfriend, that he is a doctor at the hospital, that they were in Paris together. If the woman cares to she is now able to identify Tomáš. If the woman tells other people, they will be able to identify him. In this world of reported truth and half-truth, of lie and rumour, Zdenka's love for Tomáš may be entered on some file, assessed by some functionary, used for or against. 'Do you know Paris well?' she asks, hoping that one banal question will distract from the revelation.

'I went there often before the war. But not since. It's not so easy these days, is it? You were very lucky.'

Zdenka pushes open the glass door and leads the way through into the gymnasium. The curtains have been pulled back and they walk across a lighted stage with the whole city as their audience. Behind her the visitor gives a small sigh, maybe a sign of longing, maybe a mere exhalation of regret. 'I'd forgotten how marvellous the place is,' she says. 'But what happened to the windows? It used to be all plate glass.'

'I've no idea. I only know it as it is. It's ideal for what we do here.' While the woman looks around Zdenka explains about the children. 'Space and light. Their lives are too often dark and closed, shut away indoors because they can't go out to play, that kind of thing. Coming here is a kind of liberation for them. And for me. You know I dance here sometimes?'

The woman walks over to the onyx wall and touches it as though caressing the face of a loved one. 'I didn't know you were a dancer.'

'I trained for years until I had an accident. I couldn't go *en pointe* any longer and that ruined it for me. But I can still do other kinds of dance. I run classes here for children as well. Two evenings a week.'

'Maybe you'll dance for me?'

Zdenka blushes. For some reason she blushes beneath the woman's gaze, as though she has just been asked to do something indecent. The woman smiles. This smile is intense, not a casual

348

thing bestowed unthinkingly, but a kind of communication, as though she is saying that Zdenka has made her smile, that Zdenka is worthy of her smile, and that it is a smile to be shared. 'This place used to be a place of music,' she says. 'Did you know that? Maybe you pick up echoes of it when you dance. Do you think that is possible, that a place can store the echoes of its past? The piano used to be here, just here.' The woman points. 'The Landauers used to hold recitals.'

'Did you know the family? What happened to them?'

The woman shrugs. 'He was a Jew.'

The word 'Jew' clouds Zdenka's mind. The Jews are like ghosts in the country, forgotten people whose shades haunt the alleyways and streets of certain towns. You think you might see one in the cramped cottages of a one-time Jewish quarter or in the shadows of an abandoned synagogue, but you never do. In Hranice there was an old Jewish cemetery which the children used to venture into, a frightening place of tombstones and ghosts, peopled only by the dead. But there were no living Jews in the town. Then, when she was seventeen, she went to Terezín with the Union of Youth. This was not long after the Communists took power, in the days when she truly believed. Her group had been camping in the hills and they went to visit the Museum of the Resistance in the small fortress outside the town of Terezín itself. Zdenka and a friend had separated from the group and walked down the long straight road that led from the fortress across the river, to the garrison town that had been, so the story went, the ghetto of the Jews. She remembers the moat, the walls, the desolate barrack blocks inside, the weeds growing up in the streets, and the old woman shouting at them from an upstairs window. Was the old woman a Jew, one of the few left behind? Was that possible? What she shouted they didn't know, but she and her friend ran all the way back to the fortress museum to rejoin the party. They talked about it on the journey back to camp. Why was the town abandoned like that? Why was it only the Resistance that was remembered in the museum of the fortress? Why was the memory of the Jews being left to die?

'Were the Landauers killed?' she asks.

'They were lucky. Lucky or clever, or whatever you want to call it. They escaped at the time of the Nazi invasion. To Switzerland . . .'

'And now?'

'I lost touch with them during the war. When I was deported . . .'

'You were *deported*?'

There is a moment of uncertainty in the woman's expression, as though she is trying to decide what to say. 'I spent three years in the camps. And when I came back . . .' She shrugs. 'How was I to get in touch again? And then the revolution came. It was a shame. The children must be about your age by now.'

Zdenka says how old she is. She feels that she needs to tell her, to give some personal information to this woman who has come into the place as a stranger but somehow – this is only her second visit – seems a friend.

'There you are. Martin would be just three years older.' The woman walks around the onyx wall, reappearing on the other side silhouetted against the light from the windows. 'I'd like to see you dance,' she says. 'In here. In the *Glasraum*.'

That's what she calls it: *der Glasraum*, in German.

Encounter

The meeting with the journalist is arranged for two days later at eleven o'clock. There will be a photographer as well. Tomáš discusses it with Zdenka on the phone. 'There is more to all this business than meets the eye,' he advises her. 'Apparently there is a move to try and take the building away from the hospital. People want the place restored, turned into a museum or something. A representative of the hospital ought to be present.'

'You mean we'd be thrown out?'

'Something like that.'

After that conversation the woman from the heritage committee does not seem quite so attractive. On the other hand the prospect of seeing Tomáš again gives her a little thrill of excitement. She is waiting, trying to choose the moment when she says to him, come back to me, come back to me on your own terms. Let us meet as we used to, after work has finished, here in the department when everyone else has left for their own houses, their own apartments, their own families and their lives. Our life can be here as you wish, in the Glass Room. *Pokoj.* Tranquillity. That is all she wants, all she will demand from him. The quiet of the Glass Room, the quietness of their making love here in the cool light of the evening.

The woman from the heritage committee arrives at the appointment before all the others, slightly ahead of time in fact. Greeting her at the front door, Zdenka addresses her as *soudružko*, comrade. Comrade Hanáková. That seems to give the correct sense of formality that she feels towards her now. But the woman just laughs. 'Oh, come on. I think we can dispense with that kind of thing. You must call me Hana. We're friends, aren't we? You are going to dance for me.'

Zdenka laughs at the idea, but it is not a dismissive laugh. Rather, it is a happy one. Despite the possibility that the building will be taken away from the department of physiotherapy the idea of dancing for this woman with her grave face and amused eyes seems to Zdenka to be a delight. She tries her name out, as though she hasn't heard it before. Hana. It seems a name of some beauty, as though beauty can reside in just two syllables that are echoes of each other almost like something in a nursery rhyme. Ha-na.

As she is hanging Hana's coat, the journalist and the photographer arrive. The photographer is a tall, casually dressed man who says little but immediately starts getting out his equipment – battered black cameras and lenses and a tripod. They are like bits of weaponry that fit together with clicks and grunts. The journalist is the one who does the talking. She shakes Hana's hand and Zdenka's hand and smiles very warmly at Zdenka and insists that they call her Eve. 'We're waiting for someone from the paediatric department of the hospital,' Zdenka says.

The journalist raises her eyebrows. 'Why is that?'

'They have overall control of this facility. We are really just an offshoot.'

The disparate group wait in the hallway of the building, in the strange aqueous light that comes through the milky panes of glass. People push past on their way from one office to another. Eve asks Hana some questions about the place, about when it was built and by whom. Zdenka glances at her watch. The photographer takes photographs of the hall, moving people aside so that he can get a clear shot. His camera stands on arthropod legs and he invites Zdenka to look through the viewfinder (he has to lower the tripod to her height). To her surprise she discovers the world in a fish bowl, the warped figures of Hana and Eve floating round one side, the curve of the milky glass wall, the staircase winding downwards like a vortex, and the front door bending open and a diminutive Tomáš entering, like a fish swimming into view. Two fishes, for there is someone else following Tomáš, a stout, balding man with a coarse, peasant face.

'Am I late? I'm very sorry,' Tomáš says. But he isn't sorry, Zdenka can see that. He is pleased that he has kept them all waiting. She watches as he shakes hands with the photographer and Hana, and greets the journalist by name. 'Hello, Eve. Fancy seeing you here.'

'You know each other?' Zdenka asks.

'Old friends,' says Tomáš.

Zdenka notices that the old friends exchange amused glances. And she can see – *sense*, not see – something else: a small pulse that passes between the two old friends like the small shock of electricity you get in summer when you touch the handle of a car. A pulse of energy. Zdenka senses it but doesn't quite understand it. 'Old friends,' he repeats, and Zdenka wonders where the emphasis lies – on *old* or on *friends*?

Then the bald man introduces himself. He addresses them all as *soudruzi*, comrades. He is, he tells them, chairman of the District Committee with responsibility to the Party for the Blackfield area. Hana, it seems, already knows him. 'Comrade Laník,' she says as they shake hands. 'How you have come up in the world.'

'That's the whole point of the revolution, isn't it?' he replies. 'The proletariat is in power now.'

The tour of the house takes an hour. It is led not by Zdenka but by Hana with occasional interruptions by the chairman of the District Committee. This is architecture not physiotherapy, art not science. And she appears to know everything about the place, from the details of the architect himself to the birthdays of the children of the owners. The man called Laník knows other things. He knows the date of construction and the materials used. And what happened to it after the family left, during the war. Together these two recount the history, the story, the past that leads to this present of six people walking round the space, looking at perspectives and vistas, at details and delights. The journalist scribbles away in shorthand, turning over pages of a ring-bound notebook. Comrade Laník insists that Eve explain to her readers how he defended the house against counter-attack by the forces of bourgeois Fascism. Tomáš watches and smiles distantly, as though he understands a deeper truth than a mere recounting of the past. And the shutter of the photographer's camera makes that repeated mechanical sound, that unlocking and locking of the doors of light to send momentary images from the present into the light trap of the past.

When everything is over there is uncertainty over matters of departure and farewell. And then the following things happen: Laník says he has an important meeting to attend and must bid the comrades farewell; the photographer shoulders his bag of gear and says he has to get the films to the lab; the journalist gives Tomáš a kiss on the cheek and follows the photographer out; and Hana says goodbye and tells Zdenka that she will be in touch. Tomáš and Zdenka are left together in the physiotherapy building, which Zdenka has now come to think of as the Landauer House.

They talk. She wants to know things about the journalist – how they met, how long they have known each other, how well they know each other – but she daren't ask. There's a feeling that knowledge is a dangerous matter, that illusions may be nurtured in ignorance, that Eve Whatever-her-name may be an intruder in the mythic world that she and Tomáš have created down here in the Glass Room, the world of Ondine and Palemon, the world of love detached for ever from the incessant pressures of the past and the future. That was the trouble with those days in Paris, that they took the two of them into the world of contingency and consequence, a world where decisions must be made. Better by far to exist in this limbo.

'Do you want to come round after work?' she asks. There are people moving around upstairs. One of her colleagues looks in and says, 'Is it all over? Can ordinary human beings get back to work?'

'Is that what you want?' Tomáš asks, touching her cheek with his fingers as though to assure himself of the fragility of her pale skin. He knows that beneath this integument there is muscle and connective tissue and blood and bone, the architecture of a complex machine that is her face. He has explained all this to her, and of course she knows it too. She studied the musculature of the human body, both for her dancing and then for her physiotherapy training. But all she feels is the surface, the touch of his fingers. And all he feels is the surface of her cheek, soft, sleek interface between the world outside and the world within.

'Of course it is,' she says.

Architectural Treasure
is Hospital Annexe

No one can have any doubt that our city, renowned for its man-
ufacturing, is also a treasure house of architecture. Have we not
been fortunate to have one of Europe's principal architects as city
architect ever since the heady days of liberation? So it is no surprise to come across examples of design that are worthy of
inclusion in any glossy tome dedicated to the buildings of the century. How is it then, that one such treasure is doing service at the
moment as a children's gymnasium? There is nothing more important to the future of our city, our country and the cause of
socialism itself than a healthy and well-looked-after younger generation and your correspondent would be the last person in the
world to begrudge sick children the best of environments in which
to pursue the treatments necessary for their cure. However,
whether such care needs to take place in an architectural treasure
is a matter for debate.

The place in question – this architectural treasure – is the
Landauer House in the Blackfield district of town. Perhaps you
know the place? It's a pleasant residential area full of bourgeois
villas (now, fortunately, occupied on a more rational basis than
they were during the pre-Socialist years) overlooking Lužánky
Park and the whole of the city centre. Your correspondent went
round it with a member of the State Committee for Architectural
Heritage, the group appointed by the city council to look into the
whole question of how we treat the past. This committee member
filled me in about the history of the house. 'It was built by the

prominent capitalist family, the Landauers,' she told me. 'In the late nineteen-twenties they obtained the services of the renowned architect Rainer Abt to design what turned out to be the last of Abt's European work, before he fled to the United States in 1938. In architectural circles the Landauer House is generally considered his masterpiece.'

While the upstairs rooms – bedrooms and bathrooms – are pleasant enough, it is the living room that strikes you. Our photographer was over the moon about the place, hurrying us this way and that to get the perspective right. He kept extolling the merits of the light that floods in from the south-facing windows. 'Light and space,' he said, 'that is everything you need.' And light and space you certainly have. Can you picture a room of two hundred and thirty square metres for a family of four? But can you also imagine such a room having two entire walls of glass, and with a view right across the city to the Špilas? Apparently the furniture, specially designed for the house (those capitalists certainly spent their money!) has all disappeared, although there are some specimens in the Moravian Museum. But the structure of the building, the striking chrome pillars that support it, the partition wall made of pure onyx slabs that divided the sitting area from the so-called library, the spare and functional flooring of cream linoleum, is in more or less original condition. Only the windows have been changed, the original plate glass, destroyed by a bomb blast during the war, replaced by small panes. In the old days two of the window frames could be lowered, at the touch of a button, into the basement so that you could almost step out into the garden. Although the single panes have now been replaced by more practical windows, I was told that the lowering mechanism is still in working order.

That the place has survived in such fine form we owe to the former caretaker, Josef Laník, who is now on the local District Committee. He recalls the days of the Landauers well enough – a life of indecent luxury, he says – and the dreadful days of the war when he had to maintain the building as best he could while the bombs fell around it, and then the time of liberation when he and his sister defended the building against the Nazis, before finally handing it over, safe and sound, to the fraternal Soviet forces. And now he is hoping to see the building open to the public so that

356

ordinary people can enjoy what was once the privilege of the very few.

There are some strange things in this city of ours. We possess a dragon that is in fact a dried, stuffed crocodile. We have a twisted pinnacle on the portal of the Old Town Hall that tells of an architect's anger with the city fathers, and a stone manikin on the church of Saint James that marks some medieval argument between the city and the church authorities by baring its buttocks towards the cathedral. And we have a house that is one of the gems of functionalist architecture – but we don't take any notice of it.

Confession

'Can we meet somewhere?' the caller asks. The voice is familiar, but Zdenka can't place it. 'For a coffee perhaps. Are you free sometime tomorrow morning? Do you know the Zemanova Kavárna?'

'Yes, but who is this talking?'

There is laughter on the other end of the line. 'I'm so sorry. I should have said. It's Comrade Hanáková.'

Zdenka feels a small, shameful snatch of excitement. She regretted Hana's swift departure that time when the journalist came to see over the department. She wanted to talk with her, tell her things, tell her that this doctor who followed her tour of the house is actually her lover, the one who went to Paris with her, the one for whom she dances. And now she can.

So the next morning she asks one of her colleagues to substitute for her and changes quickly out of her uniform. 'I'll be back in half an hour,' she says. Is that what it takes? Half an hour seems a generic figure, as you might say 'for a few minutes'.

The meeting with Hana in the café is like a meeting of old friends. There is even an exchange of kisses, cheek to cheek, as though they are sisters. That is how Zdenka feels about this woman. A friend, a sister, but with something more exciting than that in the background because after all you know your sister (she has to imagine that because she is an only child) and you know your friends. But this woman who works for the heritage committee is entirely unknown.

'How are things with your boyfriend?' Hana asks.

'Do you know . . . ?' Zdenka often starts conversations like that. It annoys Tomáš. 'You say it when you know that the other person doesn't know,' he complains, 'so why say it?' But still she keeps the habit, just trying to keep it under control so that it doesn't sound silly. 'Do you know what . . . ?'

Hana laughs and catches her hand across the table. 'You're so funny. How can I know until you tell me?'

Zdenka blushes. 'We're back together again.'

'That's good news.'

'Do you realise that you've met him?'

'I think I do, yes.'

'You guessed?'

'I could tell by the way you kept looking at him.'

Now it is Zdenka's turn to laugh. She is so happy that Hana has met Tomáš, so happy that she knows about him. 'Was it that obvious? What do you think of him? He's handsome, isn't he? A bit of a cynic, but very loving.'

'He's a good-looking man. Do you meet there, in the Glass Room?'

'Yes, we do. Sometimes we get away to his family's *chata*, but during the week, that's where we see each other.'

The woman smiles. It is a wry smile, creased with age and experience. 'The Glass Room appeals to men like him. They find it rational. Cool, balanced, modern. But don't be fooled.'

What does she mean? She looks round the café, at the people coming and going, at the waiter coming over to them, wiping his hands on his apron. 'It was here,' she tells Zdenka, 'that I met the man who almost destroyed me.'

'*Destroyed* you?'

'He was sitting at this very table. Isn't that strange?' And she tells Zdenka how splendid he looked in his uniform as he rose from his chair to offer her the only spare seat in the whole café. 'Really a very lovely young man. A perfect Aryan.'

'He was a Nazi?' Zdenka speaks in a whisper, as though that is the greatest crime, fraternising with the enemy, the very people whom she has been brought up to loathe.

'Who knows what he was? He was a scientist, and a musician. It seems a strange combination, doesn't it? He was working at the Landauer House. It was some kind of laboratory then, a biometric laboratory. We made love there just like you and Tomáš. That is what you do, isn't it?' Her eyes ambush Zdenka, bringing a rush of blood to the girl's cheeks. 'Of course it is. Don't be fooled by the Glass Room. It is only as rational as the people who inhabit it.'

'This man. Were you in love with him?'

Hana's expression is bleak, almost as though she is ashamed of what she has to say. 'I did it because I wanted to help my husband.'

'Your *husband*?' Zdenka now pictures a man at home, where before she imagined that Hana was on her own, a self-sufficient single woman. Is there a family? Are there perhaps children, grandchildren even? How old is she? Fifty? Sixty? She realises how little she knows of this woman whose beauty seems scarred by memory.

'My husband was a Jew. I don't know what I thought this man might be able to do, but I was desperate, Zdenka. Do you know what it is to be desperate?'

Of course she doesn't. She knows what it is to be sad and miserable, but those emotions are almost enjoyable. They throw moments of happiness and laughter into a sharper relief. When Tomáš is content, then it is all the better for knowing how unhappy he can be.

'Your husband,' she asks, 'what happened to him?'

'I don't really know.' Suddenly Hana's face seems ugly, the features clenched as though against a cold wind. 'They came to our house. I don't know why. Perhaps my German told them to, perhaps not. I don't know. I don't even know what happened to him, either. But the Gestapo came to our house during the night – they always came in the night – and took us both away. That was the last I ever saw of him. I discovered after the war that they sent him to Theresienstadt.'

'I went there once with the Union of Youth,' Zdenka said. 'The place was like a graveyard.'

'He was there for a year or so and then in January 1943 he was on one of the transports to Auschwitz. That's all I know. Poor Oskar. That was his name. Oskar. He was much older than me. Good Lord' – she laughs, but without humour – 'if he had survived he would be over eighty by now. He was older than me and

I betrayed him many times, but he was the only man I ever loved. Does that sound very dramatic? But from where I stand now it seems to be true.' Now she is holding Zdenka's hand across the table, and there is a stillness between them as they look at each other.

'And what happened to you?' Zdenka asks.

The woman lets slip her hand and looks away, at the café with its grimy walls and tawdry fittings. 'God, how this place has run down since the old days. It looks like a workers' canteen. I suppose that's appropriate, isn't it? A works canteen in the workers' paradise. Now that we are all equal who needs a stylish café? That's the trouble with equality: it's the equality of the lowest common denominator.'

'You don't want to tell me?'

'Oh, I'll tell you, if that's what you want. I ended up in Germany, at Ravensbrück. Do you know about Ravensbrück? It was the only concentration camp for women. Somewhere north of Berlin. Why did I survive? Luck of course. And love. Does that sound incredible? I found love in Ravensbrück. There *was* love in Ravensbrück, among all the fear and the squalor.' She smiles, a sudden and illuminating smile that pushes the memories aside. 'Will you dance for me?' she asks. 'Will you dance for me in the Glass Room and remind me what beauty can be? Will you do that?' There is a surprising earnestness in her asking, almost as though she were pleading.

'Of course,' Zdenka replies. She reaches across the table and takes Hana's hand back. 'Of course I will.'

Zdenka's feelings for Tomáš are confused. He wants to return to how they were when she was his water nymph, his Ondine dancing for him in the cool spaces of the Glass Room. But surely to return to that is to return to the past. So she is in two minds that afternoon when she meets him in the Glass Room as arranged.

'I had coffee with that woman from the heritage committee today,' she tells him. Golden sunlight slants across the roofs of the city and through the windows, lighting up the onyx wall in a strange and fiery glow like the smouldering of embers.

'Why? What on earth did you want to do that for? They're planning to take over this place and turn it into a museum, I told you that. Why do you want to encourage her?' And then, suspiciously, 'Are you sure about her? What did she ask you? Are you sure she is not an informer?'

The whole country is penetrated by informers and agents of the secret police. One becomes the other, the agent recruiting an informer through threats or blackmail, the informers recruiting others, gossip becoming intelligence, a casual comment – 'What times we live in!'; 'Whatever next?'; 'Who'd have thought things could come to this?' – becoming a subject for delation. Is Comrade Hanáková someone like this? You can never tell. The expert informer, or worse, the agent provocateur, is well drilled in making self-deprecatory statements in order to lure the unwary into a trap. Is Hana Hanáková such a person?

'She was going to show me the photographs that they took during the visit to the gymnasium, but she'd forgotten to bring them. She talked about her husband most of the time.

'She's got a husband? Remarkable.'

'What do you mean by that?'

'I would have thought she'd scare men off.'

'Her husband is dead. He was a Jew and he died in the camps. She was in the camps as well. In Ravensbrück.'

'Does that make her trustworthy? Anyway, you don't need to get the photographs from her. I've got a set from Eve. I'll bring them over.'

Eve. Is mention of Eve a deliberate provocation? 'How well do you know Eve?' she asks him. 'You seem very friendly.'

'Are you jealous?'

'Do I have reason to be?'

They stand looking at each other. The light from the windows shines directly in Zdenka's eyes so that Tomáš is little more than a silhouette, but she can read his expression clearly enough. She doesn't need to see his features. It's the cast of his face, the way he holds himself, the small motions of his head and hands. 'We were engaged to be married once,' he admits.

'Engaged?' It seems incredible. Tomáš, the man who refuses to plan for the future, engaged to a woman!

'I broke it off, but it was mutual, really.'

'When was this?'

'Years ago.'

'And now?'

He is silent. For a second, a mere fraction of the eternal present that Tomáš inhabits, he is silent. And by that minuscule pause Zdenka knows. 'Oh, it's all over, if that's what you mean. We bump into one another occasionally, that's all.'

But it is not all. She dare not mention it, but Zdenka has understood. Eve and Tomáš sleep together.

That evening, in the Glass Room, with the curtains drawn and the lights casting pools of pale gold on the floor, Zdenka dances for Hana Hanáková. It is a slow and sorrowful dance, not to the music of Ravel but to the music of Janáček, the most sorrowful piano music that Zdenka knows, written when the composer was mourning his beloved daughter, Olga. She improvises this dance of death there in front of the onyx wall, the mournful notes of the piano sounding out of her gramophone and echoing within the soundbox of the room like the sound of tears echoing in a still, dark tank. It is her great performance, the one she never achieved on the stage in Prague or Leningrad or Moscow, wherever she might have danced had circumstances not decreed that she should fall one day and break her ankle. She dances it in memory of the Landauer family who lived here; and she dances it in memory of Hana Hanáková's husband who died in Auschwitz; and she dances it in memory of her own love of Tomáš which is now in the past, a memory that will be treasured and regretted in equal measure.

Hana watches her with an expression of rapture, and at the end, when the dreadful arpeggios that signify the crying of the barn owl have died away to silence, she doesn't applaud. Possibly she is still because applause is a meretricious gesture, a public gesture to show others what you feel, whereas what she feels is for herself alone. Zdenka runs over to her and kneels down, and takes her hands as though to comfort her.

There is a moment when they stay like that, as still as stones, the girl kneeling at the feet of the woman. And then Hana breaks the stillness. 'Look what I have brought you,' she says, turning to the briefcase that she has put on the floor. 'Those photographs I promised. And I brought one of my own,' Hana adds. 'It's almost the only thing that survived from the pre-war days. I thought it might interest you.'

The photograph shows a thoughtful man and a smiling woman with a baby in her arms. Between the two adults is a little girl. They are standing in a place that Zdenka recognises instantly, the terrace of the upper floor of this very building, just above their heads. Beside them is the curved bench and behind them the sand-pit. The man is wearing a formal suit and the woman's dress is rather old-fashioned, something from a previous generation, the skirt cut narrow, the shoulders padded. The whole photo has an indistinct quality to it, like an incomplete memory. There is something about the cast of the sunlight, as though it comes from the present to illuminate this small moment of the past.

'These are the Landauers. Viktor and Liesel, with Martin and Ottilie. Ottilie was my goddaughter, although poor Viktor didn't approve of Liesel's choice. I think I agreed with him. Fancy making someone like me a godmother!'

The man appears to be looking at a point somewhere to the left of the camera, but the woman is watching the photographer intently. That's the impression the photograph gives: she is not looking at the camera lens, but directly at the photographer. 'We were so happy,' Hana says. 'So very, very happy.'

By contrast the photographs taken in the house just a few days ago are bright and glossy, professionally considered, but they don't have the import of the older one, the weight of time. Hana takes them from their envelope and the two women glance through them. There is a view of the building from the garden, and some shots of the interior, the gym just as it is now with its exercise mats laid out in a row in front of the onyx wall like a row of graves in a cemetery. There are fisheye views of the entrance hall, some with their own figures swimming in the bowl of the lens. And there is a group photograph taken in the Glass Room, just there by one of the chromium-clad pillars, Hana and Zdenka on one side and Tomáš and Eve on the other, the stout chairman of the District Committee detached from the group like an uninvited guest.

Tomáš and Eve are holding hands.

It isn't an obvious thing. They are standing close to one another, Eve with her notebook held up to her chest in her left hand and the other hand down by her side. Tomáš is on her right, with his right hand up on the chromium pillar as though for

364

support and the other hand, his left hand, down by his side, out of sight of the couple on the other side of the narrow pillar, out of sight of everything except the all-seeing eye of the camera. He is grasping Eve's right hand. More than that, their fingers are intertwined. No casual gesture that but a thing that requires practice, knowledge, intimacy.

Zdenka is shocked. Hadn't she expected something like this? But it is seeing the proof that is so upsetting. This is neither memory nor imagination: it is just the plain evidence of the camera, unwavering in its observation. Here is proof of Tomáš's betrayal.

'I didn't know how to tell you,' Hana says, putting her arm around Zdenka's narrow shoulders. 'I didn't want to hurt you. But I didn't want him to continue to deceive you.'

Zdenka allows herself to be comforted for a while. Then she excuses herself and goes to the bathroom to wash and change. The face that looks back at her in the mirror is no longer that of a sophisticated adult who has been to the West, to Paris, to an international medical conference: it is the bruised, pale, washed-out face of a young girl. 'What will Hana think of you?' she asks her reflection.

When she returns to the gym she feels the need to apologise. 'For burdening you with my unhappiness,' she explains.

Hana smiles, and takes her hand and holds it tight. 'But I don't mind that. I'd rather you burdened me with your happiness, but if it has to be your unhappiness then that's all right by me. And maybe, who knows, I can do something about it?' She lets Zdenka's hand go. There is something deliberate about that movement, a sense of determined separation. Zdenka watches her cross the room to the onyx wall. She stands beside it, leaning against it as though for support. 'Can I tell you something? I'm not sure that this is the moment, but then I'm not sure when the moment may be. Maybe there is no best moment for something like this.'

'Something like what?' What can Hana intend by this sudden change of mood? They have been close together, united by the dance, and then by Zdenka's misery and Hana's comfort, and now quite unexpectedly they are apart and Hana is speaking in this rather formal tone, as though about to explain something difficult. Perhaps it is something to do with the gymnasium itself, that now has to be thought of as the Landauer House. Perhaps she is going to explain what Tomáš claimed, that the Committee for Architectural Heritage or whatever it is called wants to throw the physiotherapy department out of the house and turn the building into a museum.

'The fact is that over the last few weeks, meeting you in the house, talking to you, chatting over things like old friends almost – don't you feel that? don't you feel some kind of sympathy?' Hana gives a little laugh, something wry and bitter. 'Well, the fact is that I have fallen in love with you. I might never have said this at all, but now I feel that I must. Maybe it repels you, to have another woman say this. Especially a woman who is almost twice your age and old enough to be your mother. But there you are.' She shrugs, as though the little speech is of no consequence, a mere trifle, something Zdenka can take notice of or not as she pleases. 'I thought I ought to make myself clear in case there are any misunderstandings. I'm in love with you.' She opens her hands. It is a gesture of helplessness as much as revelation, the gesture of one who says, look, I have nothing more than this. 'That's all there is to it.'

The confession comes as a shock. It doesn't repel Zdenka, but it is certainly a shock. She is not a complete stranger to the attentions of other women. There was Isadora Duncan's example, she knows that. And at ballet school a teacher who had once been a prima ballerina of the Kirov paid a great deal of attention to her, sometimes caressing her improperly when adjusting the position of her legs at the barre, occasionally snatching a kiss from her when they were alone together. 'You are so lovely,' she whispered once in her heavy Russian accent, kissing her very gently on the mouth. But then there was a problem with another of the girls and the teacher disappeared, leaving only rumour in her wake and a thin deposit of guilt in Zdenka's mind.

'I'm sorry,' Hana says. 'I should have kept quiet.'

'No. No, please.' By her reply Zdenka somehow turns the negative into an affirmative. 'I can't just respond like that. You've surprised me. I can't just say this or that.'

'It doesn't repel you, does it? The idea of affection between two women.'

'No, it doesn't. Not repel.' She looks round the room as though for a way out and sees only Hana smiling at her. 'I find it ... strange. I think you're very beautiful. I said that before and I meant it. I think if you were younger you would frighten me.'

The older woman laughs. 'My darling Zdenička, I would never frighten you. It is *you* who frightens *me*. Anyway, let's just leave it, shall we? You know how I feel and I'm pleased for that. Let's just leave it there and we'll go and have something to eat, and then I'll take you back to the hostel and you can think about what I have said. We're not like men. It is perfectly possible for us to remain friends without being lovers. How often that has happened between women? I will leave it all to you.'

Zdenka spends the next few days in a state of heightened nervousness, going about her work in a haze of confusion and bewilderment. The children are her only distraction. She urges them on in their efforts, cajoles the ones who are reluctant, tries to restrain those who are in danger of overdoing their efforts, encourages the weak and praises the strong. When Tomáš rings she talks to him in neutral tones, so much so that he asks whether everything is all right, whether she is feeling unwell. She is fine, she assures him and tries to bring the conversation to a rapid close, in case his presence on the other end of the line should somehow upset the disturbing choice she has been presented with. She doesn't understand how to act. This is not the story of Ondine. In Ondine there is merely the nymph's love of Palemon and his betrayal of her. There is nothing else.

After work she has one of her dancing classes, a procession of little girls in tight, pink leotards who primp and prance and try to do what they cannot truly do yet, which is to appear fluid and feminine. She shows them, demonstrates *plié* and *port de bras*, feeling her own body as something that is almost foreign, as though she has discovered herself in someone else's limbs and torso, someone strange who yet has all the attributes she thinks of as her own. The mothers who collect the girls at the end of the lesson seem to be over-protective and demanding, asking about their daughters' progress, insisting on their talents and possibilities. 'Is she ready for Prague?' one of the mothers, the wife of a Party official, asks. The question implies that one day the girl will be ready: it is merely a matter of spotting the moment. Whereas the fact is that the girl will never be ready, her talent is limited, she stands out only among amateurs. Zdenka does not want to have to argue with the woman, however tactfully and pleasantly; all she wants is to be alone. 'We will see,' she says. 'We will bide our time. The worst thing you can do with a ballerina is to push her beyond her natural development.'

When finally everyone has gone, Zdenka stands for a long while on the stage of the Glass Room looking out through the windows, across the sloping garden, through the trees at the distant view of roofs. It is as though she has an audience out there, rows and rows of watchers, every one of them Zdenka herself. She turns away from the audience and crouches at the gramophone. The needle drops, with a hiss, onto the narrow band of silence at the edge of the disc before making a small, precise click and sliding into the groove. The liquid notes of 'Ondine' flood out through the Glass Room. Zdenka stands up and faces the windows and begins to dance, slowly, fluidly, not for any audience but for herself alone.

Comfort

'May I come round and see you?' Hana asks on the phone. She has rung the direct line into the gymnasium, to the battered, old-fashioned receiver that sits on the desk and is answered by anyone who happens to be passing. 'Physiotherapy,' they say. 'If you want to make an appointment you'll have to ring the main switchboard.'

'Is that Zdenka?'

'Yes. Yes, it's Zdenka.'

'May I come round and see you?' Her voice is hesitant, as though she is fearful of Zdenka refusing.

'Yes.'

'Are you alone?'

'The others are just going.'

'I'll be there in half an hour. Will that be all right?'

'Yes, that'll be fine.'

She replaces the receiver with care. One of her colleagues looks round the door and says goodbye. 'You got one of your classes this evening?'

'No, no I haven't.'

'Then I'd push off home if I were you.'

But you're not me, she thinks. No one is me. Except me. Everyone else leads a balanced, calculated life. She crosses to the windows. How strange the Glass Room seems. The walls are as insubstantial as her own presence. Reflections glitter. Light refracts. She tiptoes across the gleaming, milky floor as though walking lightly on water, careful not to break the surface and plunge down into the depths. Ondine, she thinks, breathing deeply to try to inhale the calm that is all around her.

When she comes Hana looks anxious and slightly confused, like someone who has just woken from a deep sleep and is not quite certain of where she is. They greet each other cautiously, neither of them alluding to what has gone before. Zdenka goes into the kitchen to make coffee, the *turecká*, Turkish coffee, that Hana likes. 'How are you?' she asks as she brings the coffee out. There is something about the enquiry that makes it sound like what you might say to someone who has recently been bereaved.

Hana is standing at the window looking at the view. It is always the view that draws the eye. 'I'm fine.' Then she adds, 'Look, there's something I wanted to tell you. I think I should have said this the last time. So that you know everything about me.'

Zdenka is about to speak, but Hana holds up her hand. She attempts a smile. 'Please. I want you to know everything before you say anything.'

Zdenka places the glasses of coffee on the table. The coffee grains are settling in the bottom of the thick dark liquid. 'All right, tell me.'

Hana lifts the glass to her lips and blows softly across the surface of the coffee. She sips, cautiously in case the liquid is too hot. Then she puts the glass down with exaggerated care. 'You see, I've never told anyone. Never.'

Is the Glass Room a place for secrets? Surely it is a place of openness and transparency, a place where no one can tell lies.

'I had a baby. In the camp, I mean. In Ravensbrück.'

Zdenka gasps. She has been expecting other things, the careful broaching of the subject of their last conversation, the question of Hana's love, with all the incongruities and difficulties that it implies; and instead there is this: I had a baby in the camp.

'A *baby*?'

'I've never told anyone before.'

'You gave *birth* in the concentration camp?'

'That's what I said.' Her features have that rigidity, the expression of a mourner at a graveside. She looks away through the window at the view. There is silence. Zdenka cannot, dare not ask anything more. Hana's presence, her very existence, seems to hang on a thread. 'I wanted you to know, that's all,' she says, as though

370

somehow the knowledge is a gift, a small, very fragile but very precious gift.

'Who was the baby's father?'

'It was the German I told you about. The German scientist.' She looks at Zdenka and smiles. It is a curious smile, without humour, infested with sorrow. 'I always thought I was barren. I would have loved a child, but it never happened with my husband, nor with any others that I went with. I suppose that's shocking enough, isn't it? That I tried with other men. And then this German . . . He didn't want to have anything to do with it, of course he didn't. But I wanted the baby.'

This confession hits Zdenka with an almost physical force, like a blow across the face. She feels the sting of tears. 'Haničko,' she says. Just that, the diminutive of Hana's name. Nothing more because she can think of nothing more. There are no words of comfort.

'And then they arrested me and took me off to hell and I wanted the baby even more. Can you believe that? I went to somewhere in Austria first, somewhere near Linz, and then they put a whole lot of us on a train – cattle trucks, just thrown in like animals – and we went right across Germany and ended up somewhere to the north of Berlin. Of course we didn't know that then. It was just a wilderness. Barbed wire and rows of huts. The women in my hut looked after me. The place was chaos and things like that happened, women looking after you, women giving birth. All sorts of things happened.'

Zdenka is silent, almost without breath. Breathing seems difficult, as though something is constricting her throat. Eventually she dares to speak. 'Was it a girl or a boy?'

'A little girl. Just a little girl. She had dark hair, I remember. And a wrinkled face like an old woman's. And she cried, a short, sharp cry as though she was gasping for air. Perhaps she was, I don't know. I even gave her a name. I called her Světla. Light in the darkness. I loved her. There I was in the middle of hell and I had found love.'

'And what happened to her?'

'They put her to my breast for a while. She tried to feed, but of course I didn't have milk. Nothing. And then they took her away.' She looks at Zdenka and shrugs. 'I never saw her again. That's what they did then. Later on they had a maternity hut and women were allowed to keep their babies for as long as they could. As long as they lasted. But when I had Světla that is what they did. They just took the babies away.' Hana seems to gasp for air. It is as though the Glass Room has suddenly become airless. 'I used to imagine that somehow she would survive and we would be reunited when it was all over. If I had died, then my side of that fantasy would not have been fulfilled, so that became a reason to survive. I suppose you could say that Světla saved my life.' She begins to weep. There is no drama, no convulsion, just the slow seepage of tears. 'I'm sorry,' she says. 'I have never told anybody any of this, do you realise that? Never. By knowing this you know all about me. There's nothing else.'

Against this story the myth of Ondine is nothing. Against this, Tomáš's denial of history is a mere fancy. History is here and now, in the beautiful and austere face of Hana Hanáková. There in the Glass Room of the Landauer House, feeling as helpless as a person at the scene of an accident who doesn't know how to staunch the bleeding, Zdenka goes round the table and puts her arms around the older woman and tries to comfort her. And all around them is the past, frozen into a construct of glass and concrete and chrome, the Glass Room with its onyx wall and its partitions of tropical hardwood and the milky petals of its ceiling lights, a space, a *Raum* so modern when Rainer von Abt designed it, yet now, as Hana Hanáková sits and weeps, so imbued with the past.

5

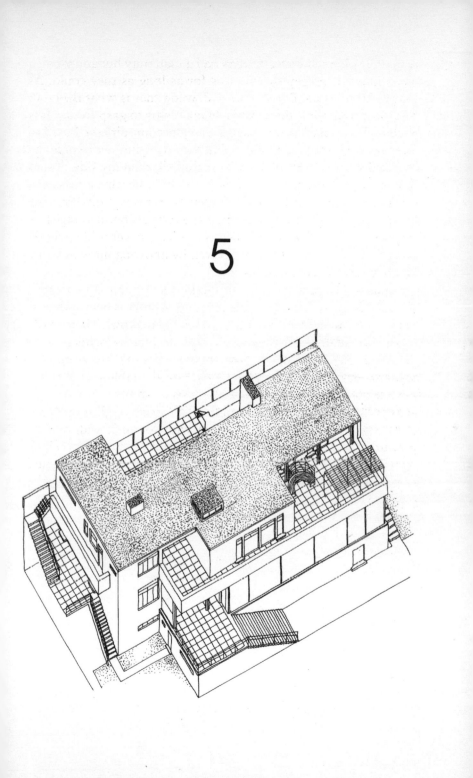

Contact

Veselý had driven from the city that morning and had lunch at a diner in Falmouth. They'd followed him of course. They were driving a two-tone Oldsmobile and he kept them in his rear-view mirror easily enough all the way through New Haven and Providence and across the bridge at Bourne. When he went into the diner they even followed him in and sat down just three tables away, two fresh-faced, crew-cut exemplars of the American way of life, the kind that would have been in the army if they hadn't been in this line of work.

He had been warned clearly enough. 'Make it easy for them,' the security officer had said. 'Drive slowly and steadily and don't make any hasty turns. You make it difficult for them and they'll make it difficult for you.'

When the menu came he ordered baked scrod, and then went to phone the embassy. He was under instructions to report in at regular intervals. They wanted to know that everything was all right, that no political incident had occurred, no one had kidnapped him and that he had not decided to defect. That was the irony of the matter: they were as much checking on your own loyalty as your safety.

As he got up from the table one of the men followed him. Perhaps they thought he was going to leave by the back door. Should he should acknowledge the man's presence? Should he say hi and wish him good day or something? But in the event he just dialled the number and stood there holding the receiver to his ear as the man went past to the men's room.

'Falmouth,' he said when the duty clerk answered. 'At a

diner . . . No, I don't know the address. Does it matter? Betty's, that's what it's called. Yes, Betty's.'

Then he cut the connection and dialled the place he was going, the woman he had already spoken to, just to confirm his appointment for the afternoon. She hadn't forgotten. No, of course it was all right. She would be waiting for him. She sounded wary on the phone, suspicious of this man from the Embassy. But then, who wouldn't be?

The man came out of the men's room and went back to his table just as Veselý hung up the receiver so by the time he got back to his own place both of his followers had resumed their meal and their subdued conversation and their undisguised examination of the prettier of the two waitresses. They didn't look at him and didn't even bother to move when he paid the check and got up to go; yet the Oldsmobile was behind him again when he drew out of the parking lot.

From Falmouth he followed the coast road. It was a fine, sunny day and the sea glittered, creaming along the beach to the left. He was in good time, so where the road ran along a spit of land between the ocean and a brackish inland lagoon he pulled the car over to have a look. There were beach houses among the dunes. Gulls screamed overhead. Sailboats tacked back and forth between the shore and the island that lay offshore. The Oldsmobile waited in the background while he stood there savouring the breeze and the taste of salt on his lips. They were probably wondering what the hell he was up to. Searching for submarines, maybe. But all he was doing was looking at the ocean, because he had never seen it before.

At Wood's Hole he stopped at a gas station to ask for directions. The pump attendant scratched his head. 'The Landor place, you say? That'll be Gardiner Road, I guess.' The Beatles blared from a transistor radio in the shack at the back of the forecourt. 'Lady Madonna'. They had been playing it in Prague when Veselý had left only two weeks ago. The pump attendant gave directions and then looked at Veselý sideways. 'Where you from, then?'

'Czechoslovakia.'

The man nodded. 'That'll be communist,' he said, as though sharing a piece of exclusive information.

'More or less.'

'Can't say I approve of them Commies. But now they say things are different, at least in your neck of the woods.'

'For the moment,' Vesely said. 'We're keeping our fingers crossed.'

'Them Russians. That's what you want to watch.'

Wanna watch. Vesely agreed. We wanna watch them Russians.

It wasn't difficult to find the house. It was numbered plainly enough and there was even the name on a board by the mailbox: Mahren House. They'd left the umlaut off which was typical enough of the whole country really – anything to make things easy. He turned in to the driveway and pulled up in front of the door. The house was one of those clapboard buildings that abound in that part of the world, an expensive place with gardens all round it and two cars in the carport and boat on a trailer parked alongside. He noticed a man standing at a downstairs window watching as he climbed out of the car, but when he rang the bell the door was opened by a woman. She was far too young to be the one he was going to visit. She was blonde, and dressed younger than she looked: jeans and a kind of kaftan top, with her feet in sandals. You could imagine her listening to Dylan and The Byrds and arguing about Vietnam. Or strumming a guitar and playing 'We Shall Overcome'. Or sailing. You could imagine her out to sea with the salt wind in her hair. A little boy, equally blond, stood watching from the back of the hall. 'Yes?' the woman asked.

'I've come from the Embassy. I rang earlier to confirm. To see Mrs Landor.'

She flashed a nervous smile, just a flicker of welcome. 'I'm her daughter. You'd best come through.'

The house was all wood inside, wooden floor, wooden walls, wooden ceiling. Like a glorified *chata*, he thought. 'Maminko,' the woman called as she showed him into the living room, 'it's the man from the Embassy.'

The living room spanned the whole depth of the house. It was a cool, expansive place with modern furniture. The paintings on the walls were abstracts with a vaguely nautical feel to them, as though the strokes of paint were sails and hulls, the blocks of blue and white were sky and clouds. A picture window showed the lawn at the back and, beyond some bushes, an azure smear of sea. The breath of air conditioning was like a sea breeze.

There were two other people in the room, a woman sitting in an armchair beside the unlit fire and a young man standing by the window that overlooked the front drive. The woman was in her sixties, Veselý guessed. Her hair was pulled back to show fine, strong features. There was the shadow of her daughter there in the shape of her face. Her grip was firm as they shook hands but her look was wayward and uncertain, as though Veselý was not the only person she was expecting and she was trying to see if there was anyone else coming through the door behind him.

'Please sit down, Mr Veselý,' she said. She spoke in Czech but with a heavy German intonation, an amalgam of sound that came out of the past, from a time before the revolution and the war. 'It's most unusual to have a visit from the Embassy.'

The young man – no older than Veselý himself – turned from the window. 'There's an automobile out there with two men in it.' He spoke in English. 'They're watching the house from across the road. Is that anything to do with you?'

'They follow us wherever we go.'

'Who do?'

'The FBI. Domestic Security Division.'

'You mean those guys are on *our* side?'

Veselý shrugged. The man seemed angry about something, but what was there to be angry about? The meeting had been arranged in advance and Mrs Landor had seemed happy to go through with it. It was hardly Veselý's fault that the American authorities tailed him. 'I don't see it as being a matter of sides.'

'*You* may not. There are plenty of people here who do.'

'Martin, please!' The older woman's voice brought silence. 'My son has just driven down from Boston, Mr Veselý. He is upset because he has had to take a day off from work to be here. Under such trying circumstances I hope you live up to your name.'

Veselý smiled at the joke. 'I'll see what I can do.'

'Can we speak English, please?' the young man said.

'Of course we can speak English, if Mr Jolly is happy with that. But I have so little opportunity to speak Czech these days it seems a shame. Now, may we get you a cup of tea or something? And you can explain what this is all about.'

The daughter went to make the tea. Veselý sat in one of the armchairs with his briefcase propped on his knees. It was only then he noticed the white cane propped against Mrs Landor's chair, and understood the reason for her vague and uncertain look. She was blind. Even now she was trying to sense exactly which chair he had sat in, her head moving so that she might pick up the faintest sound from him. Echo-location, he thought. Like a bat. 'It's about the house,' he said, and her eyes centred on him.

'I know it's about the house. You told me that in your letter.'

'*Our* house,' the son said. 'Sequestrated, first by one illegal government and then by another. And don't tell me about the Beneš decrees because I don't believe they'd have force of law in any civilised country. Anyways, even in Czechoslovak law the decrees only apply to those Germans deemed to have been Nazi sympathisers. They could hardly be applied retroactively to people who were driven into exile by the Nazi invasion.'

Mrs Landor smiled. 'Martin is a lawyer.'

'I'm afraid that I can't offer any view about the legality of the situation,' Veselý said. 'All I know is that the house is there in Město and the city authorities feel that it should not be used for its current purpose . . .'

'And exactly what is that?' Her English was marked by German intonation just like her Czech, the precise sounds tripping off her tongue like the steps of a dance.

'Apparently it has been used by the children's hospital as a gymnasium. Physiotherapy.'

'How strange.'

'And now they want to do it justice and open it to the public. A museum, they want it to become a museum. I'm afraid I have not seen the place, but they say it's an architectural masterpiece. We contacted the architect—'

'You've spoken to Rainer von Abt?'

'The cultural attaché has. It seems von Abt likes the idea. He calls it his finest piece of domestic architecture . . .'

'I'm surprised he didn't tell me about this.'

'I believe it was through him that we managed to contact you. It wasn't easy to find out where you were. I understand there was a name change . . .'

She nodded. 'We weren't trying to hide. Or at least I don't think we were trying to hide. My husband changed the name to Landor for business purposes. Landauer seemed difficult and the Americans like things to be straightforward.' She smiled in Veselý's direction, a smile of complicity. 'So tell me why you have been tracking us down.'

'The authorities of Město wish to invite you to be witness to this handover. All expenses would be paid by the city, of course. I have a letter here from the Ambassador conveying such an invitation.' Veselý removed the letter from his briefcase and held it out uncertainly, wondering who might take it from him.

'Maybe we should wait for Ottilie.'

But Martin Landor took the proffered envelope. There was a pause while he examined the words carefully, as though searching for weaknesses. When he looked up he had the look of a lawyer delivering a judgement. 'If you were to accept this invitation, Mother, it would amount to a de facto recognition of the legal ownership of the property by the city.'

Mrs Landor smiled. 'But, de facto, the city does own the house, Martin. We haven't lived in the place since you were a little boy. Thirty years ago. How can we go on pretending that we still have rights over it?'

At that moment, the daughter came in with a tray of tea things, porcelain cups, little pots with Chinese decorations. 'Rights over the house?' she asked. 'Is that what this is all about?'

'They want Mother to go and visit,' Landor said.

The little boy was offering Veselý *bábovka* cake. 'Mommy and me made it specially for you,' he explained. His mother had paused, a teapot in her hand. '*Visit*? Return home for the first time? How amazing!'

'I've told her not to accept. They're just looking for recognition of their ownership.'

'There is just one thing I'd like to add,' Veselý put in. He was trying to discern the currents underlying the smooth, affluent surface of this group. Where, he wondered, was the original head of the family? What had happened that had brought the son to that position? 'Our country has changed in recent months. You know that, the whole world knows that. This invitation is part of that change. Maybe you should consider that. We want to return to normal relationships with all our neighbours. This visit is part of that opening to the West. We want to talk about the past, admit the errors of the past. Socialism with a human face, as they say.'

Landor turned on him. 'So you're not only trying to confirm the confiscation of the house. You are also trying to use my mother in a political game.'

'The political game, as you call it, is not a game to the people of Czechoslovakia. It is a matter of life and death. By travelling to the country your mother may be helping us.'

It was the inclusive pronoun that did it. *Us*. Martin Landor made some kind of noise that may have signified grudging agreement. 'Quite so,' said his mother firmly.

'And there's also this,' Veselý added, reaching into his briefcase once more. 'Another letter, I believe from someone on the architecture committee of Město. It's marked "personal".'

He held the envelope out. This time the daughter took it. 'Shall I open it, Mother?' she asked, but she had already done that: Veselý could see a scrawl of handwriting. Ottilie frowned, turning the pages over to glance at the back. 'Good grief!' She looked up in astonishment. 'It's from Auntie Hana.'

There was a silence in the room. Mrs Landor moved her head as though she was trying to see, as though she was trying to peer through fog. 'Hana? Hana Hanáková? I thought she was dead. I thought Hana was dead.'

Ottilie looked down at the letter. '*Moc pro mne znamenáš*, she writes. You mean a lot to me. Is that correct? *Líbám tě*, I kiss you, *Hana*. How extraordinary. I think I even recognise her handwriting. I remember those letters you used to get in Switzerland . . .'

Her mother held out her hand. 'Let me have it.'

'Don't you want me to read it for you?'

'Let me have it,' the older woman demanded. She took the letter and held it for a moment, and then put the page down on her knee and ran her fingers over the spider scrawl of writing, almost as though she were sensing something through contact. Veselý had heard of people in the Soviet Union who could read through their fingertips, read newspaper stories and such like. For an absurd moment he wondered whether this was one of those cases.

'Can it really be Hana?'

'That's what it seems. Here, let me read it to you.'

But Mrs Landor seemed reluctant to surrender the letter. 'I think we'd better be left alone. This is a private matter.'

Her son looked bemused. 'Alone?'

'I don't want it read out in front of everyone. I want to be alone.'

'You sound like Greta Garbo, Mother. Stop being dramatic.'

'Do what Maminka says,' the daughter snapped. 'Show Mr Veselý round the house or something. And take Charlie with you.'

So the two men and the little boy left the room and stood awkwardly in the hallway while the women dealt with the letter. Outside the sitting room Landor seemed willing to put the legal mask aside for a moment, like an attorney chatting with an opponent outside the courtroom. He asked about the situation, about what was happening in Prague and the rest of the country, about the threats and the possibilities. 'The Soviets won't allow things to go on like this, will they?'

Veselý shrugged. 'Secretary Dubček is no fool. It's not going to be a repeat of Hungary.'

'So what will it be? A surrender like 1939?'

'We hope it won't come to that.'

The man seemed to consider. 'Strange, isn't it, what can happen to people? Here I am, an all-American guy, and yet I was born there, spent my first few years there. But now the whole Czechoslovak thing just seems like a sort of dream, a fantasy world that happened to another person. Hell, I was younger than Charlie when we left.'

And then they were called back in, like children being summoned back to the company of adults. The daughter was sitting on the sofa, sitting forward towards her mother with the letter in her hand. Mrs Landor was sitting in her chair and staring into the distance. 'We always thought she was dead,' she said to no one in particular. 'We heard that she'd been arrested and deported. That was in 1942, when we were in Cuba. And then . . .' Her eyes tried to find Veselý. 'You know what it was like immediately after the war, Mr Veselý? Maybe you don't. Maybe you are too young. Anyway there was great confusion, the Germans being expelled – the *odsun* they call it, don't they? – and displaced people trying to get home and you couldn't get any information. My own family had left Moravia anyway, and my husband's were all killed.

382

They were Jews, you see, Mr Veselý. They died in the camps – Auschwitz, Sobibor, Treblinka. And then the Iron Curtain came down and it was as though the whole country had vanished. We couldn't hope to find out anything more. And now she's alive.'

There was a silence. Veselý watched the Landors trying to come to terms with this piece of their past. During the war his own family had done what any ordinary family did. They'd got by. They'd made do. His father had worked in a factory and his mother had been a nurse and they'd got by. But for these people it had been different. However privileged they might have been, their whole world had been torn up and scattered to the winds.

'It won't be easy for me to travel,' Mrs Landor said eventually.

Martin seemed amazed. 'You're not seriously suggesting—'

'Certainly I am suggesting.'

'Don't be ridiculous, Mother. Quite aside from your own difficulties, you'd be travelling to a country that is in the middle of political turmoil.'

She looked in her son's direction. 'My dear Martin, I've known political turmoil that you can barely imagine. And I know what your father would have wanted . . .'

'You can hardly drag Pop into the argument . . .'

'And Ottilie would travel with me.'

Ottilie was bright-eyed with the possibilities. 'I'd love to see the country again. And Auntie Hana. She was a real character from what I remember.' She appealed to Veselý as though he might adjudicate on the matter. 'My God, I have memories, Mr Veselý, but they're childhood memories. Everything's the wrong size, you know what I mean? In my memory everything is large, the house . . . the house is huge. Have you seen it?'

'I'm afraid not.'

'Acres and acres of space, that's how I recall it. It'd be fascinating to see it all again.'

'Under the circumstances, I'm sure that you would be included in the invitation,' Veselý said. 'But of course we'd have to wait for confirmation by the city authorities.'

The son came away from the window where he had been checking on the Oldsmobile again. 'As your lawyer I cannot recommend this course of action,' he said.

Mrs Landor smiled. She was smiling into the space between

Veselý and her son, so that it was unclear where the expression was directed. 'But Martin, you are *not* my lawyer. Mr Feinstein is my lawyer, you know that. And I expect him to take instructions from me, not the other way round.' And then her eyes seemed to focus on Veselý, and she was still smiling. 'We'll come if you can arrange it. My daughter and I will come.'

Letter

'Look,' Hana says, holding out sheets of typed paper. She has come breathless into the Glass Room during one of the ballet classes. There are girls (and a single androgynous boy) standing around the space in various balletic postures, like so many Degas dancers.

'Five minutes' rest,' Zdenka calls and goes across – she moves in bright quick skips, like a dancer – to the older woman. 'What is it, Haničko? What is it? You look shocked.'

'It's what you see. Read it.'

Zdenka glances down at the typewritten page and shrugs. 'It's in German. I can't read German. I can barely say *auf Wiedersehn* . . .'

Hana takes the letter back and looks at it thoughtfully, as though maybe its content will change if examined hard enough. 'It's from Liesel Landauer, only she doesn't call herself Landauer any more. Apparently it was too difficult for the Americans. They've changed it to Landor. Elizabeth Landor.'

The dancers watch without much interest, occasionally flexing a leg, sometimes rising into an arabesque or dropping into a *plié*, like clockwork toys that are running down.

'She's written to you after all this time? You said . . .'

'I know what I said, but we've been trying to find them through official channels. Apparently the Embassy succeeded, and now there's this. It's addressed to me personally. I'll read it for you—'

'Darling, the class—'

Hana is suddenly angry. 'For God's sake, get them to do their exercises or something. Surely they can keep themselves amused?'

385

Of course they can. Of course. Zdenka has not seen Hana like this, with anger beneath the pacific and thoughtful exterior. So she gives instructions to her pupils – practise this, work on that – and then moves with Hana to the other side of the onyx wall. Hana is agitated, her face pale and her hand, the hand that holds the letter, shaking slightly. She holds the pages out to show Zdenka, as though that alone will justify her interruption of the class. But of course it doesn't. Zdenka cannot read the German, so she cannot see the mistypings, the uncorrected errors, the neighbouring letter substitutions, the occasional place where, for a phrase or two, every letter has been transposed to the row above or the row below on the keyboard, or shifted left or right, making the sense unintelligible.

'Liesel has gone blind.'

There is a moment of stasis. The word *slepý* sounds through the brilliance of the Glass Room, the place where light is everything, where reflection and refraction are paramount. There is a chrome pillar near them. Their reflections are thrown off the metal surface, elongated by the curvature.

'*Blind?*'

'Here.' Hana points to the page, to the words *Ich bin blind geworden.* '*Blind, slepý.*' She reads on, translating as she goes:

Is that a shock to you? Of course it will be. It seems so strange and rather frightening. I have spent years going back and forth to hospitals and clinics but they don't really seem to understand, and some of the specialists here in Boston are meant to be the best in the world! They use long words that seem to mean they don't know anything. 'Idiopathic', that's one of them. The blindness just seems a random thing, but in truth I suppose it is no more random than anything else in life. Anyway, Ottilie is very good with me and comes rushing to help when I need.

And then Hana looks away, towards the glass of the conservatory where ficus and cycads stand solemnly against the light just as they used to do in Liesel's time, and tears come to her eyes. It is quite unexpected, even to Hana herself, this weeping. She stands there in the shadow of the onyx wall with tears welling up in her eyes while Zdenka looks on helplessly. 'I loved her, you know that?' she tells Zdenka. 'I loved her like I love myself. It was as though – ridiculous because we were so different – as though we were twins. And friends. And lovers. That was always a shock to her because she was a mother and because she loved Viktor as well. Do you mind my telling you this?'

Zdenka shakes her head. Love seems a relative quality, not a unitary thing that can exist independent of an object. Love *for*, love *of*, never just love. There are different grades of love, different shades of love, different scents and tastes of love. It is not like happiness or misery, qualities that seem dull and limited. Love is limitless, she feels. You can love one person one way and another person another way and your store of love, all the different loves, is never diminished. And she loves Hana. She loves her as a daughter loves a mother, as a pupil loves a teacher, as friends love and lovers love, all these things all the time. 'I don't mind,' she says. 'I don't mind if you don't mind.'

Hana returns to the letter, reading it awkwardly, turning it from German into Czech as she does so:

I'm writing this without Ottilie's help so that I can say things that I maybe wouldn't otherwise. I hope I haven't made a mess of things and you can read it all right.

Hana looks up. 'I knew her here, in this room. Better than anywhere, I knew her here.'

Viktor died in 1958 in a boating accident. I'm sorry, I shouldn't tell you something like that so casually, but how else? Maybe you already know. Maybe the embassy have told you. You know how he took to sailing when we were in Switzerland? When we came here he took up the sport again, but this time on the ocean of course, and that was how he died, when the boat he was in capsized. Now I am alone, except for Ottilie and her husband, and Martin of course, who is a lawyer and lives in Boston. I am, I must tell you, an American citizen now, and so was Viktor. And the children, of course. We did that in 1948. You can imagine why. And that's when we changed the name to Landor. It

seemed easier like that, to spell it as the Americans pro-
nounce it. Viktor started up a business – Landor Marine it
was called – here in Falmouth, building boats, just small
things – cabin cruisers, speed boats – and that is where I still
live, with Ottilie, who is an angel. She has a little boy, so I
am a grandmother. Charlie was born after the accident so
Viktor never knew him which is a shame. He would have
been so proud. He would also have been proud of Martin
who is a successful lawyer working for a Boston law firm.
That's what you come to treasure.

Hana stops. 'There's more, lots more. Maybe you'd better deal
with your pupils. Maybe it'd be better if I didn't read it to you.'
'That's all right,' Zdenka says. 'That's all right.'
But what is all right isn't clear. Is the past all right, is the fact of
lost and wasted years all right? She turns to the class and starts to
put them through their exercises. Hana finds a seat and reads
again what she has already read.

It is not easy for me to talk about Viktor to you. In a way I
always loved him, but he was dishonest with me just as I
was dishonest, I suppose, with him. Anyway, he had his life
and I had mine. There was even a time when I had a
milenec.[1] You would have been proud of me! He was called
Piet and was of Dutch origin and worked for Viktor's company and was much younger than me and we were very
happy in a child-like kind of way. I don't know what he saw
in a woman of my age (this was in the early 50s and he was
more than ten years younger than me!). He used to call me
his 'Czech mate'.[2] You understand the pun? That came to an
end at about the time of Viktor's accident. But I never knew
a love like yours, Haničko, never knew one so intense and so
deep. There, I have said it. Anyway now I am here with
Ottilie and her husband who works at the marine biology
place and looks at sea urchins all day. They are blind too, I
suppose. I have written enough, perhaps too much. I will

[1] In Czech in the original. *Milenec*: lover, boyfriend.
[2] In English in the original.

388

take up the invitation to visit but you can imagine how difficult it will be for me to travel. And what about the political situation? But how much I would give to be in the house again! I am pleased, I suppose, that it should be kept as a museum of some kind although I don't really like that word. Museums are where you keep works of art, but the house is a work of art in itself. A memorial perhaps – to Rainer and Viktor, and, in a small part, the 'me' that was!

Please do write and tell me everything. Your loving,
Liesel.

Return

Someone is coming towards her. She can sense the form, perceive the nucleus of shadow against the light. Somehow she knows. What is it? A sense of motion, that particular movement, the sway of her hips as she walks? Perhaps even the perception of her scent. Or the sound of her breathing. She says the name before anyone speaks, says it as a statement more than a question.

'Hana.'

'Liesi! God, you recognised me. How on earth did you do that?'

She feels arms around her, a smooth cheek against hers. Both sensations are familiar. They don't have to be dragged up from the depths of memory: they are already there, buoyant at the surface. Tears? Perhaps there are tears. 'You don't forget things. You store them up.'

'And is this . . . ?'

She turns to her left where she knows Ottilie will be. 'Ottilie.'

Hana makes a noise like a child, some kind of cry of joy. Liesel puts out a hand to touch them as they embrace. 'Let me look at you,' Hana is saying. 'Let me look at you.' And Liesel can imagine it: Hana holding Ottilie at arm's length, as though to create lines of perspective and place the younger woman in the context of a past that seems so distant. Thirty years, and war, makes it seem a century. We were all so happy then, she thinks. And suddenly she can see. As though the curtains of time have been drawn aside and everything is clear again. She can see Martin and Ottilie playing on the terrace outside the windows, and Viktor sitting in the library pondering something in the newspaper, and Hana, vibrant with her presence and her promise, standing beside her as they look out over the garden. And a small bright figure appearing at the bottom of the garden and walking up the path towards the house, hand in hand with a little girl. Katalin, with Marika.

'What do you think about her?' asks Hana.

'Katalin? I like her.'

'I'd be careful if I were you.'

'I think she's wonderful. I don't know what I'd do without her.'

More people, a dozen people or more are circling round them to shake her hand. She can sense them, but she cannot see them. She can see light and shadow, space and substance. 'Don't be silly, Maminko,' Ottilie is saying. 'You'd do perfectly well without me. You know you would.' There are more hands to be shaken. Someone is talking, about her, about the house. 'A treasure that belongs to the city, and the country, and the whole world. This symbol of peace.'

A round of applause is directed at her, as though she has done something remarkable. 'Comrade Landauerová,' says one. There's something familiar about the voice. 'Don't you remember me?'

She struggles with the memory, the coarse accent, the undercurrent of sarcastic laughter.

'Comrade Laník,' the voice says. 'Josef Laník.'

'Good gracious, Laník. How are you?' And she realises, with a small prick of guilt, that she never knew his first name. 'What are you doing? What a surprise.'

He talks, at her, not with her. About his trials and tribulations. About the way he looked after the building, about the dangers and the fighting. About the bomb, about the glorious liberation by the fraternal forces of the Soviet Union. Does he mean then or now?

'We must catch up,' she assures him. 'We must have a good talk.'

People are crowding round her. She feels trapped, claustrophobic. She has never felt this in the Glass Room before: the oppressive crush of people. 'Let's get some fresh air,' she whispers to Hana. One of the group – their host, the chief of the urban planning department – has begun to give a speech about the house and its place in the canon of European architecture. Hana leads her towards the terrace.

'I never expected Laník,' Liesel says. 'He always gave me the creeps. I think he used to spy on me.'

'That's no surprise. He's a Party official now. Good Soldier Švejk promoted to captain. That's the nightmare really: the whole damn country has been ruled by people like him, a whole army of Švejks. And just when we seem to be getting something different, the fraternal Soviet Army returns to liberate us.'

'What will happen now?'

She feels Hana's shrug. '*Normalizace*, they call it. Normalisation. The Švejks will come back, I suppose. If they ever really went.'

They've reached the door to the terrace. She can feel the cool air on her face and the daylight. Behind them the man is still talking. '*Tento klenot domácí architektury*,' he is saying. A jewel of modern domestic architecture.

'Are we being rude? Should we stay and listen?'

'Let them be. They enjoy the sound of their own voices. Liesi, there's someone I especially want you to meet.'

She senses a small shadow standing in front of her and when she reaches out a slender hand is slipped into hers. 'Zdenka,' a voice says, and then adds something rapid in Czech in which Liesel catches the words 'honour' and 'delight'. 'Hana has told me so much about you.'

How much? she wonders. The woman is small and light. Liesel senses that. And beautiful. How can you sense beauty? Does beauty have a smell? Is Hana's scent, the smell of grass and vanilla, also the scent of beauty?

'Zdenka is part of the staff of the clinic,' Hana says.

'We work with polio victims,' the other voice explains. 'That is what the gym is for.'

'The gym?'

'This room. The Glass Room.'

Someone else approaches and introduces himself as a doctor, representing the hospital. Tomáš, he says, shaking her out-stretched hand. She finds his grip firm and uncompromising. Not unlike Viktor's. 'It's very courageous of you to make the journey over here. Especially in the light of what has happened.' He means the Russians. He means the tanks in the street and the heavy hand of the Soviet politicians.

'I couldn't have done it without my daughter.'

'She couldn't have done anything without you.'

That makes her laugh. He is an attractive person, this Doctor Tomáš. They stand outside on the terrace – mercifully it has stopped raining – while the speeches go on inside and Tomáš talks about the clinic and his hopes for the future. And the future of the country. 'It is still hopeful, isn't it?' Liesel asks. She's doing exactly what she was told not to do – talking about the political situation. But she senses that she can trust this man. That's one of the things that blindness has done, taught her to listen to voices, to trust and not to trust. 'Socialism with a human face. Is that all over?'

Tomáš laughs at her words, but she can hear shadows in his laughter. Viktor's laugh, she thinks. 'Do you know about encephalitis lethargica?' he asks. 'I'm sorry, of course you don't know about it. Why should you? It's a rare disease, a kind of sleeping-sickness with no known cause. You get occasional cases everywhere but there was a particular outbreak in the nineteen-twenties in America. Since then the sufferers have been in a state of suspended animation. Asleep, if you like. There is no treatment and no cure. That is how our country has been for the last two decades. Asleep.'

'And now? Surely it has woken up.'

Again that laugh, coming out of the darkness. 'Recently they discovered a new drug. It's called L-Dopa. They tried this new drug on the people with encephalitis lethargica and, lo and behold, the patients woke up. They'd been asleep for forty years and they woke up! Can you imagine the shock, to go to sleep when you are fifteen, say, and wake up over forty years old? Where has your life gone?'

'Is this true?'

'Of course it's true. Just last year. It sounds wonderful, doesn't it? A miracle cure. Of course the patients are a bit behind the times and have a lot of catching up to do. But at least they've rejoined the world. The only trouble with L-Dopa is that the effect of the drug wears off after a while. They tried increasing the dose but it was no good. Slowly, with the doctors looking on helplessly, the patients slipped back into their sleep. Just like this country. That's exactly what is happening here. In six months' time do you think you will find me here? Of course not. I'll be sweeping the streets or something. This country is falling back into a coma; God alone knows whether it will ever wake up again.'

'What a strange young man,' Liesel says when he has gone.

'How do you know he's young?'

'You can tell by the tone of voice. And the anger. Only the young are angry.'

'So you're not angry, Liesi?'

'Me?' She smiles, facing in the direction of the garden. 'No, not at all. I'm happy.'

'So am I.' Hana takes her arm and leads her down the steps to the lawn. The sound of conversation, the architects and the museum people, the experts and the journalists and the politicians, is behind them.

'Is it Zdenka?' Liesel asks.

'Zdenka, yes. How on earth did you know?'

Liesel smiles. 'Is she very beautiful?'

'Yes.'

'I thought so. And you're happy?'

'I haven't been as happy for . . .' Hana pauses. 'Since you were here.'

'That's a long time ago.' Tentatively they cross the lawn. 'The silver birch?' she asks, straining to hear it, the sea-sound of the breeze in its leaves.

'Destroyed in the war. Laník's bomb. Can you imagine, it missed the house by so little? They've planted another one. The idea is to return the garden and the house to exactly what it was.'

'It can never be that.'

'Of course not. But they want to recover the furniture, as many original pieces as possible. And use reproductions to fill the gaps.'

'Maybe they'll have waxworks of us to occupy it.'

Hana laughs. 'What would we be doing, I wonder?' They reach the bottom of the garden, and pause, facing up towards the house.

'I wish I could see it,' Liesel says. 'It hasn't changed, has it?'

'Everything changes. Even buildings.'

Ottilie is on the terrace, calling them to come back. They want to take some photographs. The two women begin to make their way back up the slope towards the house. 'And what about the Cuckoo?' Hana asks. 'You didn't say in your letter. What about her?'

'Katalin?' Liesel remembers the little group as it was in those distant months before the betrayal of Munich but after other kinds of betrayal: she and Viktor, Ottilie and Martin, Katalin and Marika. 'Isn't it strange how people come into your life for a while and then vanish?'

'She vanished?'

'She was going to come with us to Cuba, she and her daughter. Do you remember her daughter? But they stayed behind. When we left France they stayed behind.' She turns to Hana and feels that she can see her, there in the mists of memory. 'It was better that way. Things work out for the best in the end, don't they?'

'Do they?' Hana asks.

1990

The house exists, fixed in time and space like a fossil. Repair work is done, badly. Some of the original furniture is collected from the Moravian Museum and returned to its approximate place in the building. The bathroom fitments are updated, and ruined; but the window panes of the Glass Room are removed and plate glass restored so that the space is finally returned to its full lucid splendour. People visit, small, uninterested groups from the fraternal soviet states – trade union groups and visiting dignitaries mainly – and later, occasional visitors from the outside world, adventurous tourists with a vague interest in architecture or architecture students with a compelling concern over the position of Rainer von Abt in the history of the modernist movement. Somewhere in all this, on a cold, wet day in March shortly after the fall of the Iron Curtain, comes Marie Delmas. She is a small, nondescript woman, unnoticed by any of her fellow passengers on the train that brought her from Paris to Prague, or onwards from Prague to Město. For most of her adult life she has lived and worked as concierge in an apartment block in Paris, her world limited to the streets of her *quartier* in the twentieth, the church and the market and the park, and the cemetery where every Sunday she visits, amongst the crowded tombs of the celebrated, the grave of her husband. She has been drawn to this foreign adventure by one thing only, a simple coincidence, that one day in the public library on the rue Sorbier she leafed through a book on modern architecture and found herself looking at a photograph of her memory.

La Villa Landauer, the caption said, *élévation sud*.

She sat at the library desk, shocked, remembering that view as one remembers a scene from a childhood dream, something with little context and no meaning, a place of memory and confusion and contentment, and seeing it now in a glossy print, a hard, fast thing – an object. For Madame Delmas has a secret, known only to herself. She has a childhood that goes back beyond the Sisters by whom she was brought up; it is another life, peopled by strange, half-apprehended figures and informed by a different language, some of which she still remembers. Her vocabulary may be limited, her syntax childish and undeveloped, but she speaks German. So when she arrives at Město railway station it is German she uses to ask someone where she can find a hotel for the night and in German that she asks for directions as she walks through the streets of the Old Town.

Město is only just emerging from the twilight of the Soviet era. It is shabby and run down, and cheap; even with her meagre savings, Marie Delmas can afford the Hotel U Jakuba, the James Hotel, which is the best the place has to offer; and the presence of a church nearby gives her some comfort. At home the Church is her prop and staff, her comfort when she feels alone, which is most of the time, because Madame Delmas has nothing and has had nothing. Few friends and no family, except for the husband whom she married when she was thirty-five and who died when she was forty-five, leaving her childless and penniless and with no more security than the job of concierge that gives her a roof over her head and a modest salary in her pocket. So she visits this church in the city of Město to recite a decade of the rosary and ask for blessing on her adventure, and to say a prayer for her husband and another prayer for the person she has prayed for every day of her life – her mother. Then she makes her way to the bus-stop in Malinovsky Square to catch the 77 bus that the receptionist at the hotel has told her will stop near the Villa Landauer.

The bus takes her to Drobného, a grand street, almost a boulevard, with two carriageways divided by a strip of muddy grass. It runs alongside a park and she is reminded of the park in her quarter back home, where she walks often and sits sometimes to feed the sparrows. No sparrows today in the cold of March in Město. The grass looks bruised after the onslaught of winter and there are still patches of snow on the ground. At the focus of the paths is a deserted bandstand, like an ornate cage for exotic birds; but the birds have long ago flown away and the season is not yet ready for their return.

Madame Delmas stands on the pavement looking round. No memory stirs. Occasional cars pass by, and grimy buses with their destination plates announcing unpronounceable areas in the northern suburbs of the city. Was she ever here? Is this whole adventure futile? On the other side of the boulevard there is a shallow crescent set back from the road. A few cars are parked there – Trabants, Wartburgs, the oft-repeated jokes of the Soviet era. Fine terrace houses loom over these vehicles like indignant observers from a more affluent past. They resemble some of the better buildings in her own *arrondissement* in Paris, like the one she herself runs and which she has left in the care of some temporary concierge with a distinctly Algerian cast to his face. But she didn't cross half of Europe by train in order to be reminded of home. She came to reclaim a small fraction of her past. Behind the buildings is a hillside and to the left of the crescent there is a break in the terrace where a street of steps climbs the slope. The houses on either side are broken and grimy, like toys long abandoned in an attic. Schodová. That, the map in the guide book suggests, is where she must go.

Workmen smoke and watch as Marie Delmas climbs the steps. At the top she consults the map in the guide book again, and turns right onto Černopolní, a quiet road running across the hillside. There are suburban villas, the houses of the bourgeoisie that prospered in the brief flowering of the First Republic, before disaster struck. Some of them have the date of construction on their façades: 1923, 1927, 1931. Madame Delmas has read the history. She knows the dates and public events; now, as she walks along the pavement, she waits to see if personal and private history will ambush her. Which it does, but quietly and modestly, for the building that appears on her right is smaller than in memory, reduced almost to the nondescript: a square garage whose doors (shut) come right up to the pavement, then a low fence with a gate and, beyond the fence, a wide esplanade of paving stones that glistens in the wet and gives the impression of a shallow pool. The building itself, as low-slung and anonymous as a sports pavilion, is reflected in the water as though it is standing on an inverted, blurred watercolour image of what is painted above it in hard-edged acrylic. And she knows that this is it. Warped, distorted, refracted by the prism of recollection, this is the place that lives in her memory. She was here.

She stands there in the drizzle wondering how to get in. The flat roof of the building forms a kind of porch between the main house and the annexe on the right and there are people moving around there, out of the rain, as though waiting for something to happen or someone to come.

Madame Delmas tries the gate and finds it locked. The figures under cover look her way. There is a conversation going on between two members of the group, looking her way and then going back to talking. Some kind of argument. She tries the gate again and searches for a bell push or something. She almost expects a button with a name plate alongside it. *Landauer*. But finding nothing she shakes the gate like a prisoner trying the bars of her cage.

'Look, can you just wait there a moment?' one of the figures calls. A lady. The voice is American, that strident, imperious tone that she hears at home in the cemetery mainly, looking for the tombs of the famous. 'You do speak English, don't you?'

No, she doesn't speak English. Marie Delmas replies in French, and then, sensing incomprehension, repeats it in German. 'I thought the house was open to the public on Wednesdays,' she says, feeling foolish admitting it, as though she should have known better.

The reply comes back, unexpectedly matching her German: 'We have a private visit, but I'll see if you can join us. Just wait there a moment and I'll see what I can do.' The lady turns back to the figure beside her, a short fat man whom Madame Delmas recognises now as one of her kind, a member of the international freemasonry of caretakers and janitors. The two argue for a while and then the man comes over, scowling and muttering something in Czech, to unlock the gate and allow this interloper in.

'You see, I've booked a private viewing,' the *Américaine* explains as Madame Delmas joins her in the shelter of the roof. 'Of course that's fine by this fellow – he's got his orders about that. But in his world if you have a private viewing you don't just bring people in off the street. So there's a problem which is no problem really, but there you are.' The woman is expensive in her dress and her manner, a sharp confection of dyed blonde hair and tailored jacket, but incongruously wearing sneakers below her trousers. Her face is lined, the skin burnished by sun and the quick polish of cosmetic surgery. There is someone else with her, a young man in his thirties, hovering in the background with that embarrassed look of someone who suspects that he is being talked about but cannot understand what is being said. 'This is my son. We flew into Vienna yesterday and drove up this morning. We're waiting for someone else but it looks like he's been delayed.'

Marie Delmas tries to register what the woman is saying. But she's thinking, imagining, looking around her at the forecourt of the house that doesn't look like a house at all, dredging up the past from that section of memory that seems to belong to another person, a person who was smaller than she is, so that now everything seems shrunken, as though it's a model of what it once was, this stretch of pavement, that view between the two parts of the building – a blur of winter trees, rooftops, church spires piercing the cloud, the distant view of a fortress – and the curve of milky glass that hides the front door.

'I'm sorry, I didn't quite understand . . .'

'I'm afraid my German's a bit rusty. Don't find much use for it back home. But you're in now, which is what matters.'

There's another woman, a guide presumably, standing at the front door to the house. 'Let's get a move on, Milada,' the *Américaine* says to her. 'We can't wait any longer, and for Christ's sake, he knows his way here.'

Madame Delmas looks around trying to remember, trying to capture a glimpse out of the corner of the eye of memory. 'I must thank you very much . . .'

'Oh, don't mention it. We visitors need all the help we can get in this place.'

Milada opens the door and leads the way in. They go through into the hallway and stand there bathed in the pale, amniotic light that comes through the panes of milk-white glass. Light without dimension, light that bears you up and floats you like a sea creature drifting with the tide. Marie remembers, but what she remembers is mood and moment, the subtle flexing of memory, not this literal place that Milada is describing in uncertain English

400

out of which Marie can only pick occasional words, gleaming nuggets of comprehension: *Family. Nineteen and twenty-nine. Nineteen and thirty-eight.* Milada opens familiar doors to display unfamiliar spaces, empty of reference, empty of anything. *Rooms. Landauer. Lady. Bathroom.*

The bathroom is tall and white-tiled, lit from skylights, like a sluice room in a hospital ward. Marie remembers it. She remembers sound booming in the pipes and the scalding water and the steam rising. She remembers being there in the hot water and a young boy laughing at her.

They move down the corridor, which is narrow and awkward. The American woman is talking to her son in English, pointing things out and shaking her head in disapproval. In one of the rooms she says, in German, 'Look at the state of the shutters. It's such a shame.' And Marie agrees, it is a shame. Who maintains the place now? Who owns it? Why doesn't the caretaker see to things like this? The bedroom seems small and box-like, with rudimentary furnishings: a bedframe, wall shelving that might have been bought in a discount store and assembled by the handy-man of the house.

'I was here once,' she says.

'This isn't your first visit?'

'No, I . . .'

'Doors,' Milada says, pointing to the ceiling. 'Terrace . . . children.' Words as disjointed as memories. There is something of the seaside about the terrace – weather-beaten concrete, a pergola made of rusted piping, a plank abandoned in the wet. Ghostly children flit uncertainly across the space, like leaves blown by the wind, one of them Marie herself.

'What happened to them?' she asks the guide, hoping that she will understand German. 'What happened to the family?'

'Please, no questions. We now descend to the main living room.'

The American woman gives a look of resignation. 'I'll tell you later,' she says, and they follow the guide back to the hall, to the stairs that lead down to the lower floor. Marie remembers. She remembers running and laughing, with Ottilie following her, chasing her, swinging on the rail halfway down, secure in the knowledge that her father is not in the house to stop them. Marie counts the steps as they descend – twelve steps down, then a turn at the landing and a further nine steps down to the lower floor. Milada opens the door and steps forward. 'You come this way,' she commands, and they go after her through the door into space.

Marie breathes in sharply, as though startled, as though struggling for breath. She has never remembered it like this. The floor – ivory linoleum – runs away from her feet like a surface of still water mirroring the glass wall beyond it. Chromium pillars stand in the water, their convex surfaces throwing reflections round the place. She can almost hear the lap of liquid as she stands there hesitating to cross, even though Milada is doing just that, walking across the surface as though it were nothing more than linoleum. 'Here we find ourselves in the living room of the house,' she says. 'Upstairs there is the sleeping, down here there is the living.'

She stands in silhouette against the light from the windows. Through the plate glass beyond her you can see the slope of the garden, and beyond that across the roofs of the city. There is the spire of the cathedral in the distance and the castle hill hunched against the clouds, capped by the grim helmet of its fortress. Marie remembers the name. The Špilas. In the Špilas there are prisoners, bad people kept in chains.

Are they Jews?

Not Jews. Jews are good. Tatínek is a Jew.

'Here,' Milada says, 'is celebrated onyx wall. Here family sat.'

And her own mother as well: Marie can see her mother, the figure that haunts her, the presence that resembles her so that she, Marie, is a partial reflection of what her mother might have been, but only the plainness of her, not the beauty, not the lights and darks. And not the eyes. Marie remembers her eyes, the light blue of the sky as it appears now over the castle hill in a break in the cloud.

The American woman is saying something complicated to her son, something that involves frowning and shaking of the head and pointing at this and that. 'Do you see what I mean?' she asks, and the young man does see because he nods his head and says, 'Sure, Mom.'

And Marie tiptoes across the floor and looks round the celebrated onyx wall in case her mother might still be sitting there, like a patient in a doctor's waiting room, the anteroom to oblivion. But nothing remains except the chair she might have sat in, a low-slung crossed cantilever of aluminium with leather squab cushions. And the memory.

'Onyx wall is made to the architect's choice, of one piece of onyx from mountains of Atlas. Observe patterns.'

She does as she is told, observes the patterns, sinuous veins that snake across the stone. The colours are pale gold and amber, streaked with tears. Almost the only colour in the whole space, which otherwise is white and ivory and mirrored chrome and transparent glass. 'What happened to the family?' she repeats. 'Landauer. What happened?'

'Family left in 1938,' Milada says impatiently. 'The house is possession of the city. Museum. Now it is museum.'

But it isn't a museum. It is vibrant and alive, a chord struck on the piano that stands there in the shadows behind the onyx wall, a complex chord that shimmers and reverberates, gaining volume with the passing of time, echoing as a piano echoes to the noise of children and the crying of adults.

Marie has to put out a hand to steady herself. Then she sits, suddenly, on one of the chairs.

'Please, it is forbidden to sit!'

'What's wrong?' asks the American woman coming over. 'Are you all right?'

She shakes her head. Her mother is there, inside her head. Perhaps she's trying to shake her out. 'I was here,' she says, brushing tears from her eyes. 'My mother and I, we were here.'

'When?' asks the *Américaine*. 'When were you here?'

'Please,' the guide says. 'Not to sit in chair.'

'Oh, let her be.' The *Américaine* crouches down, her hand on Marie's shoulder. 'Aren't you feeling well? You just rest a bit and don't take any notice of her. Maybe we can get you a glass of water.'

'I'm all right. Really.' She tries to get up, then sits back down. 'I used to live here,' she says to this American woman who seems sympathetic, who will perhaps listen to this tale of loss and forgetting. 'Many years ago, with my mother. That's why. The memories.'

'You used to *live* here?'

'Before the war. Just a short time. My mother was a nanny. The children, there were the children.'

'Ottilie and Martin.'

Marie looks up in surprise. 'That's right. How do you know that? Ottilie and Martin.'

The American woman's expression is cut through with confusion. 'Marika?' she asks. 'Are you *Marika*?'

'How do you know Marika?'

The American woman is on her knees now, holding Marie's hands. 'I'm Ottilie,' she says, an absurd idea because Ottilie is a child, a mere twelve years old, trapped irrevocably in distant memory. But this woman with the weather-beaten face and polished skin and dyed hair is claiming this identity, laughing and crying at the same time while the other two watch, Milada no longer complaining about the chair being sat on, the young man looking bewildered.

'For God's sake, I'm Ottilie.'

And all around them is the Glass Room, a place of balance and reason, an ageless place held in a rectilinear frame that handles light like a substance and volume like a tangible material and denies the very existence of time.

Afterword

The title of this book, *The Glass Room*, needs some explanation. It is, as is clear, a translation of the original German – *Der Glasraum*. *Raum* is, of course, 'room'. Yet this is not the 'room' of English, the *Zimmer* of our holidays, with double bed, wardrobe and writing desk beneath a print of some precipitous Alpine valley. Within the confines of the Germanic 'room' there is room for so much more: *Raum* is an expansive word. It is spacious, vague, precise, conceptual, literal, all those things. From the capacity of the coffee cup in one's hand, to the room one is sitting in to sip from it, to the district of the city in which the café itself stands, to the very void above our heads, outer space, *der Weltraum*. There is room to move in *Raum*.

So: *The Glass Space*, perhaps; or *The Glass Volume*; or *The Glass Zone*. Whichever way you please. Poetry is what is lost in translation, as Robert Frost so memorably said. So we do our best with this sorry and thankless task, aware that we will be condemned for trying and condemned for not trying. Take it as you please: the Glass Room; *der Glasraum*.